EVERDEEN BOYS
BOOK I

Kindred Rivals

JORDAN
LEE

SPARA
SOLACE

Content Warning

This is a spicy book, so you can expect to see some explicit, consensual sex scenes between our guys, including spanking. There is some sensitive subject matter, such as feelings of rejection, shame, and loss, parental issues, harassment, and mild alcohol use.

such lonely darlings
crack the spine, crease the pages
fly to Everdeen

CALDOR COMMONWEALTH

Port Winchester

CITY
TOWN
ROAD
RIVER
LAKE

Honeycrest Hills

Bluegill Bay

Rosewick

Everdeen

Baronstone

LEON COMMONWEALTH

AURELIAN MOUNTAINS

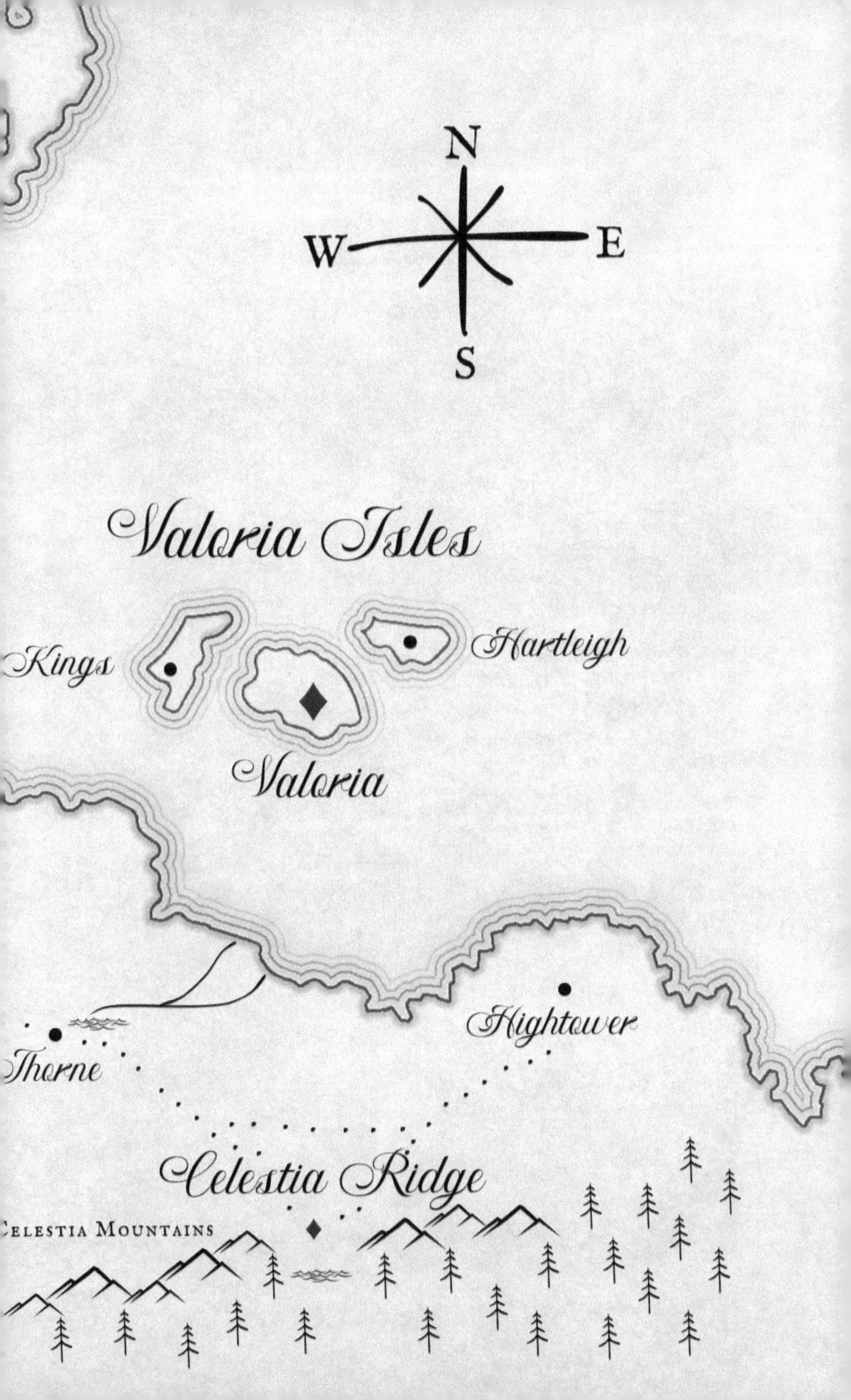

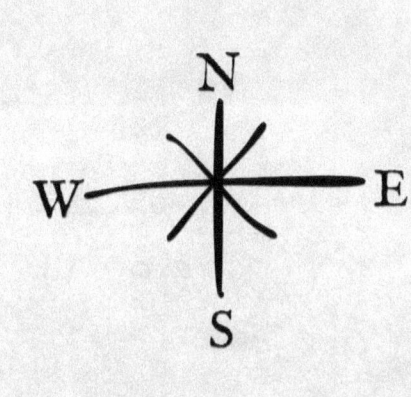

N
W
E
S
Valoria Isles
Kings
Hartleigh
Valoria
Hightower
Thorne
Celestia Ridge
Celestia Mountains

 *When life gets you down, go buy a tea set...*

1

Ambrose

"Shit!"

As soon as the curse escaped my lips, Emiline winced and asked, "Are you alright?"

"I'm fine," I muttered as I looked at my throbbing thumb. My sister had been droning on about a man eyeing her at yesterday's social, and when she'd mentioned *who*, it took me by such surprise that I'd hit myself with my hammer.

Narrowing my eyes through my dusty glasses, I stood from the ground and glanced away from the chair I was attempting to build. We were outside the old red barn, and a breeze tickled my cheek, blowing off sawdust.

"Jonathan Wilkes? Honestly, Em, you've never even mentioned that scoundrel before."

She only smirked from atop my work table and crossed her arms, her back straightening in that prissy way that showed it didn't matter what I thought about whom she liked. Her lively, warm, brown eyes and auburn curls matched mine. She was older than me by only a few minutes, as she liked to tease. At twenty-five, Emiline had a better head on her shoulders than myself for sure, having a job she loved and turning the heads of every man who walked past her.

She was allowed to do such things without reprimand from our father, so perhaps I was jealous of her freedom.

Even so, I didn't like her eyeing Jonathan Wilkes. He ran with a few other socialites I didn't care for, real miscreants of Everdeen. They often hung around the distillery along the river, acting like tough know-it-alls. They weren't a good crowd.

I bent again and slammed the hammer onto the nail to finish my chair, only for the leg to crack right down the grain.

"Oh, fuck it," I snapped, setting the chair upright. It wobbled horribly. "Wonderful. Guess we have firewood for tonight."

I rubbed the back of my sweaty neck and felt a sharp stab of pain from my sore thumb.

"Alright, show me your hand," Emiline commanded.

I held it out while she slipped off the table with a thump of sensible boots against the packed dirt. Her blue, layered skirts swished as she joined me. A moment later, my hand was in hers, feeling wonderfully warm in ways that made me miss our mother.

Emiline turned my red thumb about. "I'd say you're a true woodworker. Mr. McHugh would be proud of you. You've learned so much working with him, bruises and splinters included."

I gave her a tight smile as I pulled my hand away. "Yes, well, it isn't McHugh I'm trying to impress."

She frowned, knowing well who I meant.

"Father hasn't set foot in this barn in years," I went on. "It would be nice if he at least acknowledged something I've made." I crossed my arms as I looked inside the barn packed with handcrafted rocking chairs and stools. There was also a dining set I finished staining last month, collecting sawdust. My best work.

"If only you could open a shop to properly display your lovely furniture." Emiline sighed from beside me. "That would be sure to catch Father's eye in your interests. And then you'd be able to turn a profit from your skills."

Yes, if only. Such wishful thinking. Father would never recognize my talent, and he would never allow me to leave the bank.

I inhaled the damp air to cool the flush from my cheeks and smelled fresh rain. A glance at the sky confirmed dark clouds looming on the horizon. A gathering storm. Good, our fields needed a solid soaking.

It was quiet out here in the beautiful countryside. Far off in the field stood the enormous live oak known as the Everdeen Oak, the marker for Everdeen's founding over three hundred years ago. Past it, a wide line of trees bordered the river flowing through town. My eyes swept across the horizon, following along until they landed on the faint buildings of Everdeen. The town was far enough that we couldn't hear the constant bustle, nor see the traffic of horses, carriages, and the rare car, yet close enough to enjoy my walk to work at Somerset and Sons Bank.

When I wasn't at the bank working, I was here in the barn making furniture. I sometimes even slept in the hayloft, where I kept extra clothes, blankets, food, and books. It was a home away from home.

That made me sound like such a recluse. Maybe I did hide away in the past year. The more I thought about my father's plans for my life, the more sullen I'd become. One day, I'd be managing the bank, raising a family, and running this entire estate on my own. It was all so daunting.

Better to focus on Emiline's poor choice of suitors.

"So, Jonathan..." I started, eyeing Emiline closer. "I suppose you like him."

Her lips twitched. "No, you don't have to worry. I know all about Mr. Wilkes, and he isn't my type. I just wanted to stir you up. If he winks at me again, I'll throw him a nasty look."

"Good. Maybe pull up your middle finger too."

She smacked my shoulder in play. "You must really hate him."

"And his friends," I muttered. Emiline knew more about me than anyone, but she didn't know of my past fling with Jonathan's slimeball friend, Damien Cooligan. "Help me get the work table in before it rains?"

Nodding, Emiline stepped up to the table, and we both hefted it inside the door. Then I wiped the sweat from my brow.

Emiline's boots crunched over old hay as she stood beside me. "And what about you?" She nudged my arm with her elbow. "Is

Father still trying to set you up with a potential bride?" When I nodded, avoiding her gaze, she went on, "Hm, well, perhaps your sister can help you find one? I heard recently that Catherine Wilkes is hoping to wed soon."

"Really? Jonathan's sister?" I shook my head.

"She's the complete opposite of her brother. She even knits mittens for the children at the—"

Before she could finish her sentence, I threw her a sour expression, and she let out a laugh. I knew Emiline suggested Catherine to tease me. "Could you see me with such a pious woman?"

"Well, she *is* nice," Emiline added.

Nice? "I don't want nice."

"I figured. Then tell your dear sister what you *do* want."

"I..." I wanted to tell her that I yearned for a man who made me laugh until I cried and set my heart racing faster than a river in spring, but instead I mumbled the one thing my father had been suggesting to me all week, "I'm thinking about courting Annabelle Winters."

"Anna?" Her eyebrows raised. "She's... a good choice. She certainly has a lot of assets, and she's looking to settle down with someone too."

Her quick acceptance made me doubt her motives. I rubbed my bruised thumb to avoid her growing excitement. I didn't feel excited. I actually felt a bit sick. "Yes, the Winters' land abuts ours, and Annabelle owns it all, so if I marry her, we'll be the largest landowners in town."

"Father would love that." Emiline nodded at the plan, then cocked her head at me. "Although, you do have a choice. You don't have to marry a woman."

I closed my eyes, not wanting to broach this subject, yet here we were. "You know how Father is."

"You mean old-fashioned when it comes to our family blood-line? Yes, I do know..."

"It's more than that, Em... A Somerset son has carried on our family line for nearly three hundred years. If I break that cycle, he'll disown me."

"You don't know that."

I eyed her sharply. "I *do* know."

"Fine." Emiline sighed. "But is this what *you* want, Amby? To follow our family's *legacy*, as Father calls it? To continue an outlandish superstition?"

She had a point. But my Father never failed to mention how special we Somersets were. Lords and ladies were a thing of the past, and yet our father thought we were royal. No one had the gall to tell him he was delusional.

We were nothing special. We weren't blessed. Father happened to inherit wealth, and then he invested that wealth, became a businessman, and basked in the glory. Just like each man before him in our long line of ancestors, dating all the way back to when they arrived in Everdeen with the founding mother.

Still, I could never tell my father all that. I couldn't bear his disapproval and rejection. My throat tightened as I forced out an answer to Emiline's question, "Yes, this is what I want."

Emiline smiled with sympathy. "Alright... Are you going to start wooing Anna at her picnic?"

I hesitated as I reflected on how reserved and independent Annabelle was at social events. Even growing up in school together, we never went past small talk. The idea of entering a courtship with her, the idea of kissing her, made me grimace.

To calm my nerves, I glanced up at the hayloft. Memories flashed through me of when this barn was only an empty place to meet with the boy I'd tried to push to the back of my mind. He'd been so devoted to me, it was hard to let go of him. Humorous, daring, charming. Every time I looked at that loft, a pang passed through me.

But Zeth Washer moved away years ago. There wasn't room for such memories to resurface with the talk of courting. My duties and responsibilities to my family line were more important than my own desires. For the millionth time in my life, I pushed the memories of Zeth away and resolved to never think about him again.

"Yes," I finally said, my shoulders slumping with an enormous weight. "I will start wooing Annabelle at the picnic."

Emiline regarded me with a bittersweet expression, which meant she didn't believe me at all. She always watched out for my happiness, but I had buried it a long time ago.

Thunder rumbled from outside, causing a stool nearby to vibrate, and Emiline and I both flinched. When the rain began, I rushed over to the open barn doors to watch with her. The wind whipped at our clothes, sending crisp, chilly air around us. Sighing, my twin looped her arm through mine and laid her head against my shoulder.

I breathed in the laden air as we both marveled at the beauty of the long grains and grasses swaying and swishing under the gloomy sky. Rain was so calming, and my heart skipped a beat with excitement at what was approaching.

I loved a good storm.

2

Zeth

"Chin up, back straight, hands relaxed," I reminded Millie over the slow clop of our rented horses as we rode into Everdeen. My back burned from the long journey, yet I still managed to ease my shoulders and raise my head, because we had a plan. It didn't matter how many barns we slept in to get here from the City; we would succeed.

However, my sister lost her patience two towns back and slumped into her saddle in rude reply to me. Her split skirt was designed for riding with modesty, but even that was hitched up until Millie's hem lay above her laced boots, looking all willy-nilly and un-lady-like, damn her.

I frowned at her something fierce.

When she rolled her brown eyes like a child, I looped my reins into one gloved fist and pinched the long bridge of my nose with the other to keep from swearing, just like stopping a sneeze. It only worked half the time. Luckily, this time it worked.

That didn't stop me from hissing, "You're the one who came up with this con, so what happened to being a prim miss while I act the rich gent?"

"Well, I'm pooped," she huffed from under her white bonnet. It was tied beneath her chin and charmingly plump cheeks, all flushed in a pretty way. Her glare wasn't prim at all. "And annoyed with you. You and your pompous advice."

"Mils—"

"Where's my brother? The fun one. I want him back, so please remove that branch from up your ass."

"Up my—" *Inhale. I love my sister, I do.* "Mildred Louise Washer, that's hardly appropriate."

Her nose squished, and she muttered, "To hell with propriety."

A deep laugh rose up my chest, and I let it out with a shake of my head. Twenty years with a younger sister felt like a curse some days, while the rest were a delight. I adored her, even if she did rile me up more than average lately.

She was right to think me stodgy. Life gave me no choice. We never had it easy, being on the edge of poverty, and now with Mum gone, too much depended on me. I was doing a crummy job of providing for the last of my family. We barely owned more than the clothes on our backs.

A willful sister only made it harder. I needed to get that through her bonnet-covered head. "God help me, Mils. Behave for once, eh?"

When she leaned sideways to argue, I shot her my sternest man-of-the-house look. I was good at those, always had been, and Millie demurred with a drop of angry eyes. She even straightened into an almost-proper posture in the saddle. Her lacy, white blouse and brown duster fit her curves well. She appeared snitty but proper as we rode along Main Street.

"Thank you," I rewarded her. Good behavior deserved rewards, and a lady should be complimented, even if said lady preferred to be treated like a man. She hated feminine compliments. That's when the devil took me, "You know Mils, you look quite beautiful today."

As expected, Millie's head popped right up with a glare that promised damnation, and I was most certainly going to hell for enjoying her heated defiance. I chuckled with delight while my shoulders eased into the familiar companionship.

Was it wrong to tease my sister? Probably.

Did I enjoy teasing her? Yes, yes I did.

Grinning, I brushed some trail dirt from my dark blue pants. Our new ensembles came from selling our small apartment in the City. The tailored clothes were expensive and necessary to the con, but that didn't change how powerful the fancy duds made me feel, as if I deserved to wear them. I loved my jacket especially and planned on buying another like it as soon as I married well.

I needed to marry someone like the owner of the carriage that approached us. Motor cars were the new toys of the rich, yet the glittering display of this carriage's black paneling and iron trim still demanded respect. Millie and I moved our horses into a single file to make room. Other riders did the same, and the carriage passed with an awe-inspiring spectacle. My, how the rich grew richer while I was away.

Even the old town was bigger and nicer. It was no capital city, like the one we'd left, but judging by the new estates we'd passed entering town, and the bustling inner streets, Everdeen had expanded to at least 15,000 townsfolk. And from the looks of it, a variety of people of different cultures and nationalities were working and living here, sharing in Everdeen's health and prosperity. It was nice to see my hometown succeeding and her people happy. Hopefully, I could say the same about myself and Millie soon.

We continued clopping along Main Street. Next to me, Millie pulled a folded page of newspaper out of her coat to look over the sketch of the woman featured there. She had done that a lot since she saved the article gossiping about Annabelle Winters' ungodly wealth and recent visit to the City. We'd gone to school with the elite woman, and reading about her travels since her family all passed sparked Millie's idea to return to Everdeen—find Anna, con her, court her, and settle into a secure life. I didn't need to stare at a sketch to memorize that plan. I remembered Anna's prim-miss appearance well enough.

More interesting was the cute bakery cafe up ahead. It used to be a simple bread shop. Now, it had fancy iron tables painted white set up outside like many of the City's eateries. Folks dressed as well as us basked in the sunshine and sipped from dainty tea sets. The scents of baking delights we couldn't afford smelled heavenly.

I savored the aroma with a deep breath and recognized the tall silhouette of the baker standing in the shop's open doorway. His hair had grayed on the sides, yet his eyes still danced with joy as he clapped his flour-covered hands to clean them. He once knew me as the neighborhood kid who used to drool on his display windows before buying the oldest loaves.

I lifted my new cap to him, as if I wasn't returning to Everdeen with a bag full of lies. First impressions, and all that. Thankfully, the baker nodded back at me nicely. I don't think he recognized me now. He even motioned for us to visit his shop.

My stomach rumbled in agreement, but I ignored it to ride on. I ignored Millie's stomach rumble too as I turned to her. "After our plan succeeds, we can visit the bakery every day for the rest of our blessed lives."

Millie glared at me with petulance. "This town looks so different from what I remember. Pray tell, good sir, how much farther? 'Cause I need to piss."

Dear heavens. A glance around confirmed no one heard her, and I ran my tongue over my teeth to stop a choice swear word or ten. *Respectable.* I was respectable.

I raised a hand to physically push up the edge of my lips until Millie took the hint and mimicked my tepid smile. Only then did I answer her, "The Laundry isn't far. A block. Perhaps two."

"I miss her." Millie's admission came out of nowhere. Grief was proving to be like that. Her simple words hit me hard and brought on a new set of tears.

I nodded and added softly, "As do I."

Too fresh, Mum's passing. I pushed the melancholy back. Now wasn't the time, yet that didn't stop a shadow from settling over us both. A real shadow. Above the rooftops, heavy clouds rolled in quickly.

"Just great," I grumbled at the darkening sky. I hated rain. And I didn't want to get my new suit wet. At least the old place was near.

Mum's will was read last month, and my inheritance stirred up our plan from there. Patting my jacket lapel, I heard the rattle of paper and felt the iron key over my heart. I'd rather have Mum back.

"There it is," Millie exclaimed softly, and my eyes flew to the next business in the long row. This one had two large windows downstairs and the name WASHER painted boldly in black across the front. Our name was the only nice thing about the worn-down facade. Above that, two smaller windows on the second floor had creaking shutters, and the entry door's red paint was chipping off, exposing old layers of blue, yellow, and green. Even the display window curtains hung half off their hooks. Not that it mattered, because the glass was too layered with dust to see anything inside.

That didn't stop me from seeing the past. Memaw's grey head bent over her sewing in the display window, her glasses shining in the sunlight every afternoon when I came home from school. Beyond that, Uncle at the long counter taking payments. I used to join him there to recount money and balance the books while his strong hand patted my shoulder. And behind that, the backroom where Mum pumped water into a massive copper tub, scrubbing laundry before draping it on rope lines to drip dry. I used to run through those wet rows chasing Millie. Her high peals of laughter still echoed in my ears, along with Mum's reprimands.

Then there were the memories of Amby. Of his big brown eyes glazing over from my explanation of quadratic equations, and his warm shoulder against mine as we spent hours on the front stoop just talking, as best friends do...

I slowed my horse to a stop at the empty step, marveling at how much I'd forgotten in the nine-plus years since leaving. So many good memories... all of them twisting painfully inside my gut. Thankfully, we already planned on selling the laundry.

"Let's go." I raised a leg and nearly fell to the ground as I slipped gracelessly off the large horse, groaning as my stiff body objected. I was no stranger to physical labor but I rarely rode a horse.

There was a post ring at the walk, so I tied my reins and helped Millie do the same before pulling our belongings from the horses. It wasn't much, two blanket rolls and a carpet bag for us both. I set those in front of Millie so I could remove the saddle and tack from my borrowed horse. "We'll find the livery stable later. For now, let's take our belongings inside and assess the situation."

"Assess the sit—"

"Get your ass inside before it rains, eh? And let's look at this dump," I rephrased. "Better?"

"Much. There's my brother." Millie chuckled with sparkling approval as she tucked a blanket under each of her arms. Before I could help, she also squatted to pick up one bag in each hand, and then stood to her feet well balanced. "Alright, lead the way."

A proper lady wouldn't carry the bags, yet Millie seemed happy to help, and it saved me a trip, so I shrugged. That left me with only the saddle, so I hefted it onto my shoulder and stretched my stiff knees to lead us to the alley where a side door waited.

Thick ivy had taken over the laundry's alley wall since we left, but I still found the family entrance easy enough. It was just as dark and damp here as I recalled. It even smelled like lye soap. Or maybe my imagination was playing tricks on me as I shifted the saddle to reach for the key in my jacket and jiggled it into the keyhole.

The door unlocked softly. When I tried to open it, though, the wood refused to move. I tried again and felt Millie watching me like I didn't know how doors worked. After a third push with no success, I explained, "I think it warped from the dampness."

"Well, that's great," Millie mumbled. She wedged herself in front of me to stand sideways against the door with all we owned in the world still tucked under her arms. She appeared quite determined as she glanced up to say, "On three."

I gripped the cool handle and turned it. Ready, I called out, "One, two, three."

Millie slammed her shoulder into the door while I pushed. The wood rattled. Her weight in addition to our belongings, and my clumsy effort, made the old door move with a scrape and squeal. Suddenly, the support was gone, and we both stumbled into the dim building.

The door banged against the wall, causing dust to puff around us. A blanket rolled into the cloudy room.

"Graceful," I chuckled, straightening myself before dropping the saddle and trailing straps on the floor. I removed my cap and waved it to clear the air around us before hanging it on a peg by the door. Millie did the same with her stuff.

With her bonnet removed, Millie's brown curls popped free, all this way and that like a dandelion. Her current hairstyle was the longest I'd seen on her since she was a teen, with her curls falling to her cheeks. I didn't doubt she would cut the lovely ringlets soon, so I stole my chance to ruffle them now.

She slapped me away with a warning glare that made it clear she was no longer a child. I conceded with a doubtful look, then we both squinted into the low light.

The washroom was large and empty. The laundry lines were gone, and the brass basin sat dry. Everything looked...

"Smaller than I remember," Millie finished for me. She walked forward and leaned over the stone well, proving how tall she stood now.

"Makes sense. You were only eleven when we moved."

"And you, sixteen, but still a pipsqueak."

"Gee, thanks," I grumbled as I joined her in the old washroom. The back windows were filthy, and I was certain the walls were inching closer. I'd never possess the expenses to make this place like new again. "The quicker we—"

Just then, thunder rolled, and I turned back for the door to find it even darker outside. "I need to get the other saddle before it gets soaked." Heading out, I warned, "Don't fall in the well, 'cause I won't save you."

"As if I need saving."

Her laughter followed me down the alley as I returned to the horses and undid the buckles on Millie's saddle. Seconds later, a drop of rain hit my cheek. Then another. The fat drops sped up, and I cursed until the leather slipped free from the horse's back. Racing inside, I barely got a boot in before the storm hit with pelting rain. A swift twist of my knee swung the door closed against the wind, and I had to lean back against the wood with a grunt of effort to shut it tight. That door needed fixing, quick. Thankfully, repair projects didn't scare me, even if I didn't know a damn thing about fixing a door.

I set the tack next to our bags with a sigh and removed my gloves to brush off the rain from my jacket while wandering around the long counter to inspect the empty storefront. It was dark, dusty, and dingy, with cobwebs in the corners. The whole place needed a good cleaning. We were the first to enter since Uncle died four years ago.

When I returned to the washroom, Millie was gone. Maybe she fell into the well after all. Surely I would have heard. I walked over to the walled basin and glanced into the watery pit, calling into it, "Mils?"

"Up here," she returned. From upstairs, and not in the well. Relief washed through me, followed by concern, because her reply struck me as overly sentimental.

A staircase ran along the side wall from the door, so I took it two steps at a time. Thunder rumbled through the wall, and I shivered at the top where Millie crouched in the open doorway. I instantly worried about her until I saw where she was staring, at the door jamb of our old living space.

The familiar notches and pencil marks she found had me aching in denial. I didn't want to see the proof we'd resided here. I wasn't the boy I used to be. I had left this all behind. That didn't stop Millie from standing slowly and touching a few marks as she rose, including one for our dad when he was a teen. So many times I stood here staring at those signs that proved he once grew up in the laundry too. He also left it behind, when I was only fucking five. Good riddance.

Millie stopped at a mark around the height of my chest in a neatly penciled script that spelled her name. She glanced at me with her eyebrows gathered in confusion.

"Do you remember?" I asked. "That was the day we moved."

"I do... I just can't believe I was so tall at eleven." Her face softened while she moved her hand to trace her name at a lower spot. "You wrote these. You always took care of me, didn't you?"

"I did." And I always would, because she was like a daughter to me.

Mum stayed when Dad left, and she loved us. She was illiterate and busy working with her in-laws at their laundry, making what little they could. That left the job of overseeing Millie to me at an early age, though I never minded. We ate little, slept in the same bed, and helped around the laundry. Most days were spent at the local schoolhouse. And although the rich kids weren't nice to us, I made friends with Amby, the banker's heir, and life became better for everyone.

Amby really was the best part of school. Well, him and numbers, but numbers made sense to me. Numbers behave and follow rules. Memories do not behave. I understood that as I found Amby's taller mark on the door frame above Millie's. I still remembered him standing there, biting his lip to keep from laughing at me for needing to tiptoe to mark his height.

Millie touched the cursive name and whispered, "Visit him."

"No, he's married, I'm sure," I reminded her for the tenth time since we decided to return to Everdeen. Amby didn't want me. He refused my marriage proposal without debate so he could find a wife and have children. I was just a boyhood romance, a fond dalliance. He didn't shed a single tear over me. It was hard enough leaving him the first time, so I certainly didn't want to stir up those old feelings by visiting him now.

I cleared my throat and inspected my dusty riding boots. "Enough of that. Let's finish the assessment."

She eyed me with disappointment. "Are you still set on selling?"

"Yes." I didn't know how else to emphasize the necessity of funds to her sentimental brain, so I repeated myself, "Yes."

"But look at this mark. This one here," Millie pleaded from the door frame.

Sighing, I glanced back to see what other memories she felt compelled to drag up. She was pointing at my name with a twitch to her lips that spelled trouble. "We're five years apart. So why was your mark when we left not much higher than mine? You were really short for a teen."

"So what? I'm tall now. Over six feet tall, thank you very much. No need to dwell on the past."

Millie snorted. "Shall we mark your great height now? Celebrate the grand achievement."

"Enough," I groaned heavily, trying to play along, but my heart wasn't in it.

I left her to march around the small room and inspected the four-poster bed where we would need to sleep wedged together, as we always did. The dipping mattress smelled of old hay, but a few tugs to one of the bedposts proved the wood frame was steady. Well crafted. The floral scroll work was indicative of the Leon Commonwealth, just south of the forests beyond Everdeen. If I remember right, the antique bed came with Memaw when she married. Was she Leoneas? If so, it explained our darker hair and light olive skin. How odd that we never knew Memaw's origins. It made me feel guilty, evaluating her bed to sell once we were done here. It would fetch a good amount of cals. We could add it to the sale of the laundry for my dowry to Anna.

Beside the bed sat a dresser Mum used for her clothes. I doubted anything remained. Still, I opened a few drawers to check. Each one stuck, because of course nothing would be easy. I set my feet and pulled until a heavy tug did the trick. Each drawer squealed open, all empty. Thankfully, no nasty bugs either.

We didn't need the dresser, so it could be sold immediately. That was a month's worth of food. Mum would understand.

Just then, rain pattered against the shutters with a gust of wind that sounded like it blew into the upper floor. A storm was certainly here. Thankfully, the glass and walls appeared solid against the rain, as was the ceiling. The apartment was deserted, yet nothing seemed too far gone. Nothing a good cleaning couldn't fix.

I strolled past Millie to peep into the only other doorway upstairs and braced myself to see our old bedroom and kitchen. A flash of lightning drew my gaze to the shattered hole in the window. Thunder boomed through it. At least the narrow alley walls blocked the rain from entering, leaving the floorboards dry. However, the cupboards hung precariously off their hinges, their doors all opened. One cabinet looked ready to fall off the wall, while another one held twigs and leaves. When I walked over to inspect it, I realized the twigs were part of a larger pile of leaves. A nest? I shivered and ignored it.

The rest of the room was stripped bare except for an old iron oven. Gone were our bed and baskets. Gone was the desk with the built-in chair I had stolen from school on a dare. There weren't any marks on the walls from our wrestling fights, and I didn't even sense the hunger or frustrations that had plagued me in childhood. No proof remained that we grew up here. Everything was... empty.

The only thing on the floor was a pile of plaster. Plaster that came from... I didn't want to look up, but I did... yes, the ceiling. From a large crack. It ran across half the room. And if the nasty stain was any indication, water was leaking in.

My shoulders tightened, and I ran a hand through my hair to slow my disappointment. Maybe it wasn't so bad.

Debris crunched under my boots as I tried to find a hole opening directly to the rainy sky. I didn't see any holes. Only the crack. How do you fix a ceiling? How much does that cost? Was one dresser with stuck drawers enough to hire a roofer? Then there was the broken window, the warped door, and the paint-chipped door out front that also needed repairing to make this place presentable again. So much for food. Fuck, I was hungry.

Thunder clapped louder this time, and I closed my eyes against the tumble in my head. Emotions rushed out anyway—despair, guilt, regret, frustration, resentment, fear—heaven help me. It all lodged in my throat, choking me. Most of all, anger. What did I do wrong? How was *this* my life? Why was a run-down building my inheritance?

I knew I should be grateful to have this, but I didn't want a failed laundry. I wanted my family back. I wanted a thriving business, a big house and a comfortable life that came with a promising future. I wanted to receive social invitations to picnics in the post-mail, my own pew at the chapel, and a wife on my arm who made people jealous. Fancy clothes. Boring hobbies. Maybe a rocking chair where I can sit and grow old. And a cat for my lap. Not an alley cat, but one from a store with fluffy soft fur and a pretty pink ribbon around its neck.

A tender hand rubbed my arm, and Millie's skirts rustled before she spoke. "It'll be fine. I'll assist in cleaning our place up."

Our place?

I wanted to curse at the reminder of what we owned. Instead, I clenched my jaw fiercely to hold everything in. A few ragged breaths through my nose later, I managed to pop open a single eye without crying, so I squinted at Millie with a tub full of doubt.

"You consoling me?" I huffed. "What's this? Are you actually acting like a lady now?"

"Perhaps."

That had my other eye popping open, and I scowled at her. "Perhaps? Mils, you hate cleaning, and washing, and cooking, and anything of that sort. You complained endlessly about it in the City."

"True... but I still did it. Keeping house was better than sitting around bored while you and Mum worked, and I'll do the same here," she declared with a determined nod that bounced her curls. Then she observed the crack. "And that damage isn't so bad. A little elbow grease is all we need. Where there's a Washer, there's a way, isn't that right?"

"That's what Mum always said," I sighed heavily in agreement before pulling her in tight to kiss her cheek. She was as warm and squishy as always, and her strong arms felt wonderful as she squeezed the tension out of my chest. Maybe she squeezed a little too tight, but that made it feel like perhaps everything would be alright.

We had a plan, and most importantly, we had each other. Plus, Millie certainly had the gumption to make our dreams come true.

She preened. "Just you wait and see, we'll make this place into a home again, and I'll be the perfect lady. A right proper miss."

Fate chose that moment to send a fat drop of water to plop right onto Millie's cute nose from the crack in the ceiling. She blinked and sputtered, then my newly reformed sister exclaimed more vehemently than any well-seasoned sailor, "Well, shit."

3

Ambrose

Annabelle's picnic started at noon, and like every picnic I'd attended since I was fifteen, it was very boring. I found it harder to be cordial with people I didn't like with each year that passed. However, when I spotted Benjamin Dawson openly kissing Richard Smith nearby in Annabelle's garden, I couldn't help but smile.

I liked them, at least. They'd been seen together for a while, and with Richard being outside of Benjamin's elite circle, they were the talk of the town. It was refreshing to see two people of different social statuses come together. A couple sharing a public courting kiss at a social event was akin to proposing marriage.

Several people clapped for them, while a few others turned up their noses and continued eating from their fancy picnic blankets. My youngest sister, Hattie, put a hand to her chest, touched by Benjamin and Richard's kiss before the two men nodded at everyone and walked off to the garden.

Sighing, I went back to eating with Hattie, wishing I could share such a kiss with someone I loved and adored. A man who could come in and sweep me off my feet, a man who would take care of me and show me how much I meant to him...

"Ew! Amby, get this thing off me!" Hattie squealed as she drew up her hands, garnering attention from several people sitting around us.

I set aside my plate of partially eaten strawberry shortcake and narrowed my eyes at the culprit of her whining. A large June beetle crawled along the bottom of her yellow dress. I moved over and plucked the green little guy off, and she smoothed out her hem.

I let the bug crawl over my hand, admiring how its color gleamed in the sunlight, but Hattie wasn't having it.

"Amby, I swear, get rid of it before it lands on my food!" She swatted at my hand with hers, and the beetle flew out to land on someone's plate nearby. A woman shrieked and threw it down, and my lips twitched in amusement.

I grabbed Hattie's gloved hand and got to my feet as Catherine Wilkes glanced around to search for who could have tossed the bug her way. When her sharp gaze narrowed on me, I pulled Hattie away from our blanket. We both stumbled off through the picnic on the lawn and further from the house, our hands over our mouths to stifle our laughter.

"Goodness, Catherine is not going to like you after that!" Hattie exclaimed.

"I'm rather fine with that, actually." I ticked off another potential bride that Emiline and I had talked about before.

Hattie looped her arm around mine as we made our way to Annabelle's backyard garden. My sister's golden ringlets flowed over one shoulder, and her dazzling blue eyes gleamed in the sunlight. Having been out of school for a few months, my baby sister had her mind set on a higher education at the nursing institute for girls come autumn.

I couldn't believe how fast she'd grown. Only ten years ago, she'd been running around carefree with me through the fields. Those were good memories. Vibrant, spirited, fun...

"It's a beautiful garden." Hattie cupped an orange hibiscus in her palm. "Anna has kept it up since her parents passed."

I eyed the maintained gravel paths and organized beds of daffodils and tulips. The yellows and purples popped out at us, and Hattie bent to pluck one. The garden was so properly trimmed, the bushes immaculate and the flowers perfectly aligned. There was too much order, as far as I was concerned. It was much different from our small flower garden at home, where moss grew between the walkway bricks, various plants grew out of worn pots, and ivy climbed the trellis.

I liked our unruly garden much better.

We continued along the paths so Hattie could point out the different species of roses. Once done, I planted my hands in my pockets as we strolled out of the garden and past the blankets to the terrace along the back of the house.

Our father stood there in conversation with one of his wealthy colleagues, Edward Cooligan. I drew in a deep breath as we approached his tall, lanky frame. Edward had a particular disdain for me. The Cooligans were a family who believed strongly in arranged marriages, and his son Damien was already betrothed to someone else. So when Edward found Damien and I getting handsy in the back room of his tobacco shop five years ago, he tore into me. I'd given him sass, and he'd thrown me out of his shop.

Thankfully, I no longer cared, as Damien turned out to be as rotten as a spoiled egg.

As we reached my father, I straightened my back and adjusted my glasses. Necessary, with how piss-poor my eyesight was at seeing things from a distance.

"Ah, there you two are." Father nodded at us, then gestured to Edward. "I was telling Mr. Cooligan how you will be stepping up at the bank soon to take on the family business one day, Ambrose."

My stomach dropped at the mention of the bank. I tried to put a warm welcome on my face anyway as I regarded my father. He was every bit the poised, respectable man required by Everdeen's elite society, always dressed for the occasion, standing tall and slim. His brown hair was parted and combed over in a fashionable, tame style —a sharp contrast from my unruly curls—and his thin mustache coiled outward, twitching as he inclined his head to hear my reply.

"Father and I have talked over plans," I finally said, trying my best to appear the gentleman I didn't want to be. "I just hope I can conduct business as well as he has with the bank. He's so prominent around here, I'd hate to ruin his reputation by stepping up too early."

Hattie's cough hid her sideways stare at me, but there was no backtracking. What I said already hit Edward's ears, and now he was sporting a curious expression. He could easily see I didn't care one whit about the bank.

"Ambrose often underestimates himself," Father clarified to Edward. "My son's humbleness is one of the things I love most about him. It'll make him an excellent leader of Somerset and Sons one day."

"Thank you, Father," I replied carefully, wondering where such compliments spawned from.

Father nodded. "And when you court Miss Winters, you'll prove to the town that a family man is hiding in there, ready to fulfill his destiny as a Somerset."

My expression faltered. I wasn't very good at hiding my distaste, and Hattie's look of pity over her flower confirmed that I wasn't masking my feelings very well either.

Edward's eyes darted from me to my father. "Do you seriously think your boy can win one of the wealthiest women in Everdeen? She's become more popular since returning from the City with the newest car design. Half the town wants to court her."

"Only half?" Father blustered, raising an eyebrow.

Edward quipped back with a humorous, "The other half is female!"

"I've heard quite a few women share their interest in Annabelle as well," I said. It did make sense, as she was smart, and beautiful, and had a huge tract of land.

"Mm, afraid you'll lose to better options?" Edward Cooligan cooed mockingly, and I'd never disliked the cocky man more.

My father seemed to take his words as jest, and chuckled. "There's no competition to my boy, is there, Ambrose? You're going to get the girl." He placed a firm hand on my shoulder and squeezed. I knew that grip of his. Father expected me to start pursuing her today, and so far all I'd done was wander around with Hattie.

Shit, it was hot. I loosened my tight collar and searched for an escape. That's when the shadowed porch and open door of Annabelle's house called to me. "Yes... I think I'll step inside for a moment and search for her now."

"That's my boy. Real go-getter." Father clapped my back as I took a step. His affectionate push threw me off balance, and I tripped over my own feet before catching myself to practically run away toward the house.

It felt wonderful to escape. The house was cool as I stepped into the open hallway and pulled off my cap. As soon as the door closed, I leaned against it and sighed heavily. It was quiet in here, the air smelling of baked apples. The kitchen must be near. I walked away from the delightful aroma and headed for the front of the house in search of a parlor where I might reasonably hide for the next few minutes... or perhaps a lifetime. Oh, how I hated these social events. They were a reminder of how my father expected me to fit in among the other gentlemen and talk about boring things, such as banks, and to marry within my status.

I'd much rather be throwing June beetles around instead. Or having an adventure through the woods.

I was surprised the hallway was so long as I passed closed door after closed door. Curious, I opened one of them to find a storage closet filled with various tea sets before shutting it back. The next door was a smaller room that held a desk and several polished book-cases. This wasn't the parlor, so I shut it and moved on.

My, this house was enormous, much more so than our little country manor a few miles down the road. Frustrated, I rounded a corner, only to find another hallway. Even more surprising, a well-dressed man stood halfway along the corridor at a hall table. His cap was tucked under his elbow as he held up a large vase in both hands, inspecting the intricate, blue designs closely.

Stopping quietly, I squinted at his back, admiring his slim physique, broad shoulders, and dark hair. How lovely. When a sense of familiarity washed over me, I drew closer. In fact, as the man shifted to the side, I blinked in surprise.

I *did* know him. One look upon his face made all the memories of our past rush back, and the next words out of my mouth were, "Zeth? Zeth Washer, is that you?"

The man jumped and glanced at me guiltily as the fat bottom of the vase slipped from his hand. Then he swiftly tightened his grip on the mouth of the vase to set it on the little hall table with barely a sound.

Once it sat there, he turned as if I didn't just catch him in the act and walked toward me with grace. Or perhaps it was stealth, because I couldn't hear his steps over my pounding heart. It *was* Zeth, my best *friend*. My first *love*.

"Well, well," Zeth said, a tight smile tugging at the corners of his handsome lips, and suddenly I remembered those lips on me in the hayloft of the barn. "If it isn't the esteemed Ambrose Somerset. Fancy seeing you here."

"Oh." Seeing him again after nine years sent me into a whirlwind of emotions, and hearing my formal name on his tongue slowed my mind to a standstill. "Well... I do live here."

He narrowed his eyes at me as the smile slowly fell from his face, and I wondered why.

But did it matter? Zeth was really standing before me. He was back in Everdeen, looking incredibly grown and dapper with styled, brown locks and dressed in a nicely-tailored blue suit. He looked like the most appetizing thing I'd ever seen in my entire life. Better than strawberry shortcake with a large dollop of whipped cream.

My mouth watered... because I liked whipped cream, of course.

He stopped close to me, smelling strangely familiar, like a mix of hay with lye soap, and... When in God's name did he grow to be taller than me?

"Goodness." I stuck my hands in my pockets. "It's been so long since I last saw you. What, a decade at least?"

"Nine years, two months, and six days. I see the banker's boy hasn't gotten better at numbers yet," Zeth teased a little cruelly as his brown eyes raked me up and down. "Or maybe you never cared enough to keep count of the days since our parting."

My mouth fell open, and then I snapped it closed. I wasn't sure what to say to his precise calculations—had he missed me, or was he just being an ass? Perhaps I didn't count each day, but I felt them in my heart as they passed. He had no right to say I didn't care about him. After *nine years, two months, and six days* apart, this is what he had to say to me upon our reunion?

I stood straighter to try and match his height, though there was no way I could reach it now. "I'm very good with numbers, thank you. And I didn't have a reason to count days, since our parting was mutual." I'd counted by years only, not days. He didn't need to know that.

A delightfully thick eyebrow quirked up. "Was it mutual?"

I hesitated for a moment before saying, "It was."

"Of course," Zeth scoffed with a shake of his head. "It must be nice to always be right."

Was he being bitter over our past? I thought we parted on good terms. Then again, our breakup was mostly my fault. Zeth once promised to stay true to me, that he'd come back for me after he left Everdeen, but I refused his proposal because I needed to produce an heir for the Somerset bloodline. He knew that. Didn't he? Perhaps... I'd read him wrong so long ago.

We stared at each other for a moment. I itched to mend his bitter feelings. Hoping to ease the air between us, I shook off his response. "Well, it must be nice being really tall now." I tilted my head and gave him a playful grin. "I could get used to looking up at you."

I certainly sounded stupid, but it was worth the embarrassment when Zeth's old humor broke through with an amused snort. When his shoulders finally eased into a friendly pose, even better. And when Zeth ran a hand through his gorgeous hair to mess up the silky locks and sighed "Damn, I've missed you, Rosie" *that* was the best.

My soul glowed hearing my *old* nickname that only he could call me. His words sent me spinning again, and I beamed at him. Oh, how I'd missed him too. How he always had my back, how he made me laugh when I was down, how he kissed me...

The light suddenly dimmed from my spirit as it occurred to me that I wasn't sixteen anymore, and neither was Zeth. We were both twenty-five now, and here he stood before me once again, a heartbreak I never thought I'd heal from. Somehow, I'd stitched the wound and kept moving with a deep scar. Seeing Zeth again was like poking at that scar. The pang of suffering was a good reminder that I wasn't in this house to flirt with my old boyfriend, no matter how much we missed each other. I needed to set a boundary between us now; I needed to focus on my family's needs.

Clearing my throat, I finally corrected, "It's Ambrose."

When Zeth's dark eyes shifted back to his previous caustic demeanor, I immediately regretted those words. He nodded slowly before glancing away. "Oh. Well, *Ambrose*, tell your missus hello from me, and compliment her fine taste in both men and Chince vases."

My mouth fell open, his words making me feel oddly giddy at the compliment. "What? No... Annabelle isn't my missus, but that is her vase."

"When you said you lived here, I assumed you married little Miss Annabelle who used to clap dirty erasers on your back to clean them. Why else would you be roaming around her dim hallways?"

"I should be asking you the same. Why are you in here picking up vases instead of outside at the picnic?"

Those alluring eyebrows shot up, and Zeth took a step closer. "Hm, are you calling me a thief? Do you remember me so poorly?"

"I didn't say that. Don't put words in my mouth."

The strained smile Zeth gave me in reply reminded me of how he used to get angry at me in the past. He would clam up and walk away rather than talk about whatever issue we had, so I half expected him to do the same now.

"So, then I take it Miss Winters is unattached?" he asked instead.

"What do you mean *unattached*? I'm sure Annabelle's very attached to her vase."

Zeth's lips twitched. "Then she won't be offended when I add my admiration, now will she?"

I narrowed my gaze. Zeth always had a way of saying things that made me think twice. It was the mischief in his heavy voice. He was up to something. But when the troublemaker closed the gap between us with a gleam in his eyes, all rational thought abandoned me as I stared at him. And I noticed from this close that Zeth's eyes weren't just brown. There were specks of gold around the edges that created a mesmerizing amber I'd somehow forgotten, or made myself forget.

Zeth crowded toward me, and I retreated a step until my back hit the wall. He came in close, his breath tickling my face as he purred, "So, Ambrose, did you ever marry anyone?"

Before I could sputter a reply, Zeth's hand was in my hair, stroking through the curls and smoothing them out. I held still. Why was he touching me? And why did I want it so much? That simple brush against my scalp lit my whole body on fire.

His touch was so gentle, it was killing me. I wanted to feel more, wanted his strong grip pushing me, pulling me. I'd always wanted him to explore our sexual limits. He never understood the hints I threw at him when we were younger, and I was too afraid to ask. Now, his dominance over me was clear. Who was this new Zeth Washer making me swoon?

No. *No.* These thoughts were temptations, and that was the last thing I needed. "I'm not married," I finally answered. "Not yet."

"Not yet?" Zeth's sharp gaze dropped to my mouth. "Hm, I can't decide whether I should be flattered or insulted by your failure to commit since we parted, so maybe a kiss will settle it."

Zeth's meaning blurred as he gripped the hair on the back of my head to hold me still. A delightful tingle shot down my neck, and I might have made a small noise in my throat. His claim was strong, yet gentle. It was perfect. *He* was perfect.

It was even better when his firm body molded into me in all the right places. My heart thrummed like a hummingbird's wings as I searched Zeth's face, seeing that slight bump in his nose and how full his dark lashes were. And that sweet scent coming from his neck... Curses, why did laundry soap smell so good? Nothing harsh like perfume, but something that mixed well with his skin and had me roused.

I drowned in his intense gaze while his attractive lips parted to ask, "If I dared you to court me now, would you finally say yes?"

I blinked at him. *Court Zeth?*

"I... I..." I couldn't. My father would forbid me. And yet, as I slid my hand along Zeth's solid chest to push him back, I froze. The way he overshadowed me was titillating. The way his thick eyebrows lowered over those stormy, daring eyes made me forget where I was.

He had me under some kind of spell I couldn't escape. As his lips moved closer, I raised my chin, my mouth parting to accept his kiss, oh so willing to let him have his way...

But he didn't kiss me. Instead, he tilted his head to brush his cheek against mine, and disappointment flooded me. He inhaled deeply against my neck, his breath blowing over the top of my collar, hot and sensual.

"Is this how you felt when you rejected me?" Zeth whispered, his voice below my ear. "Having all the power in our relationship... must have been fucking satisfying."

When Zeth leaned back, my face grew hot in humiliation at being tricked by him. I didn't feel as if I had any power when we were younger. Before I could argue, Zeth stepped away to straighten his jacket lapels with the oddest expression, as if we were in the middle of a casual conversation over tea; calm and clear-headed, which was *not* how I felt at all. He had me feeling flustered and hurt, embarrassed and...

Huffing, I brushed past him, making him stagger slightly but he grabbed my arm.

"Wait..." Zeth sighed heavily. He let me go, and I stood still next to him, choking down my sentiments as I waited for what he had to say.

"Maybe I'm being unfair. I didn't return to town for this."

"For what, to trick me? To rub it in my face how much I hurt you?" I snapped, and Zeth's expression turned to stone. No, he didn't return to town for me. He was at Annabelle's picnic. And why? I suddenly didn't want to know why. The why bothered me.

But it didn't matter. I wasn't here for Zeth either, or his bitter touches. I was here to court a woman. Not a man. Men couldn't have children, and those little spawn were very important for my father's legacy.

"I'm trying to find Miss Winters," I blurted out, before I got too worked up over this man. "Have you seen her?"

Zeth's face dented in slight annoyance. "Of course you're chasing the richest woman in town. Good luck with that." He bent gracefully to retrieve his cap from the floor and slapped it against his thigh before tugging it on. The smile he gave me didn't reach his golden eyes. I'd never seen him sound so insincere as he said, "I guess I'll be seeing you around, Ambrose. May the best man win."

I regarded him sharply, trying to figure out what he meant by that. When he stepped away from me, it felt like losing him again, this time as a friend. My whole body shook in silent fury. Part of me wanted to pull him back and tell him I was sorry for how things ended between us before, but the other wanted to smack him upside the head for how he'd treated me.

Thankfully, he left before I could do either.

4

Zeth

"Fucking hell," I swore as soon as I got out of earshot.

When Amby entered the hall looking just as adorable as I remembered, my dormant desires overtook me. Those cute, wire-rimmed glasses didn't hide the confused glances that always made me kiss him, and those wayward, auburn curls still begged to be tugged and cherished... *Shit*.

I instantly longed to find the old Amby in there. The one who turned our after-school tussles into holding hands. The one whose subtle touches told me he enjoyed my affections. The Amby who boldly dared me to kiss him when we were fifteen. *That* was the Amby I once loved with my whole being. But I was a scrappy kid with dreams in my pocket while Amby sat at the top of society. I never deserved him. I did everything I could to not lose him. Yet, I lost him anyway.

Now, here we were as strangers standing almost eye to eye. *Ambrose* drew a line in the sand between us with no concern for me or my feelings today, just like he did before I left town. Always so spoiled. So callous. He ended our relationship because his rich dad was more important than anything between us. His precious Somerset legacy meant more than our bond. I was the only one who cared, despite what he said otherwise. He'd used me for fun... The selfish prick.

That's why I tricked him with that pretend kiss. He'd long since crushed my heart and tossed it out like trash, so I showed him how heartless I could be. But when I pushed Amby against the wall to toy with him, I didn't expect his needy response to weaken me. Gaining some slight control over Amby was a new experience, one that made my blood race. Suddenly, I wanted him more than ever. The worst part was that those eyes of his were *begging* me to take what I wanted. The way he looked ready to kiss me...

"Damnation." Swearing didn't help. Not at all.

I needed to cool off. I couldn't believe I was thinking such things.

Reaching the front entrance hall, I opened the screen door and crumpled sideways against the frame, holding the door wide to encourage the shadowed porch breeze to blow its cool air upon my face. I needed to collect myself before meeting with Millie. My darling little sister would never understand this frustration, and she certainly wasn't about to grant me a drop of pity for fraying at the edges if she guessed at my lustful desires. Millie never so much as batted an eyelash at a man. She seemed immune to sexual temptation. Maybe it was because she was a few years younger than me. That was bound to change. If only I were so similarly inclined, it would make our mission that much easier.

My whole reason for returning to Everdeen was to marry for money. Now that little idiot was going to get in my way. It was bad enough to be in the same town, but to be pushed together constantly... What a torturous way to spend my time. Just one exposure to Amby made me forget my whole plan and crave his playful and daring affection like a man starved. And I knew how it felt to starve.

I would just have to make sure I didn't give him a damn inch. If Amby wanted to marry Anna, he would have to fight for the prize, because I couldn't change course. She was the only socialite in Everdeen without parents to dissuade her from marrying me. Amby, on the other hand, possessed all the wealth and status to marry anyone he wished. I sure as hell wasn't going to bow down to him. Never again.

"Such a brat," I vented into the breeze.

Was that me? Sounding so angry? I learned how to crumple my desires and emotions like paper long ago. There was no point in getting carried away or wishing for something that couldn't be. I knew my place. I knew my path. I wanted this house, and this land, and that damn vase Amby thought I was stealing.

Glancing around the porch, I found it blissfully empty. The picnic sprawled behind the house and, if the light laughter was any indication, still went on its merry way. The town's rich folk all lounged on blankets without a single care for how the food arrived in their pampered hands, or how a man like me saw a vase as two months' worth of comfortable sleep.

I wasn't a damn thief. How dare he? He didn't know what I...

Enough.

Focus on the picnic, let *Ambrose* go. Anger wasn't the answer. I needed a level head to win myself a fortune. The cards were stacked against me, but I was smart and amiable. And I had Millie. Well, not at this moment. Where was she?

A rustle came from my left. Like a summoned ghost, Millie's smiling face rounded the corner of the house and approached quickly. The way her yellow blouse caught the sun like a beacon, and how her huge steps made the split of her skirt swing open, had me all tense again. Damn, what were people going to think of her? I told her not to wear riding attire to a picnic. We'd spent good money on a pretty dress for this sort of social, but no, she refused to dirty the white lace. It didn't matter to her that all the other ladies were wearing white lace.

As Millie leaped up onto the porch, I muttered, "Speaking of brats."

"What's that?" Millie raised her brow.

Stepping out, I shut the screen door with an example of how to stay quiet. Then I met her halfway across the porch and greeted her politely with, "I *said*, 'I'm so happy to have you by my side.'"

"Instead of being your enemy," Millie elaborated with a breathless laugh. She wasn't wrong. "But you didn't say that, did you? No matter. I forgive your thankless tongue."

"So kind."

My sarcasm was palpable.

Millie eyed me with a squint. "What's wrong with you?"

I shrugged. She didn't want to hear it. Besides, her dainty straw hat with a yellow ribbon that cost more than my shoes was tilted to the left, so I straightened it. Instantly, one curl popped free. I huffed at it and tucked it back under the hat. "It's 'bout time you finished scouting. I was starting to think you might actually need a search party. So, did you find a good spot to fall?"

She nodded enthusiastically, causing the curl to pop out yet again. "There's a hidden pond just through the trees behind the garden. Shall I show you?"

"A pond? I never knew about that."

She gasped. "You mean there's something my dear brother doesn't know?"

I squinted beyond her to the treeline behind Anna's house. I wasn't in the mood for her right now. "Better still your sass, young lady. We're about to go into the woods. You don't want the Field Witch to eat you while we're in there."

Millie tsked. "Threatening me with a ghoul who eats naughty children won't work anymore. Have you not noticed these?" She pushed out her ample bosom to make her point.

I half chuckled and half groaned at her, "Manners, Mils." She only rolled her eyes at me like I was someone's grandpa. Why was I blessed with such a charming sister? "Alright, thank you for finding the hidden pond. Will you kindly show me?"

"Aye, this way." Millie jumped off the porch with both feet. Then she slipped around the side of the house. At least she avoided the picnicking visitors by fleeing along a far trail through the garden.

I followed at a moderate pace until she disappeared into the trees. Fearing I may lose her completely, I lengthened my stride and enjoyed the tug and pull of solid exercise. It felt good. Moving. Taking in the fresh air. Accomplishing something. Even if it was only making my way into a clump of trees and finding Millie moving between them.

She was acting like a child leading me in a game of hide and seek. It felt like old times. I hunched over and hastened my steps, careful of the roots and branches, to catch up to her. Then I tagged her shoulder. When she spun to smack me, I sprang away with a laugh.

Millie had stopped walking, but no matter, I still tagged her.

She rolled her eyes at me again and flung her arm out, pointing. I followed her yellow sleeve to see we stood at the edge of a pond. No, it was a small lake. The water was calm and clear with a deep drop not far from the shore. A faint tangy scent in the air hinted at a salt and mineral lake. Those were rare and valuable for healing properties and natural resources, but horrid for staining clothes. My gaze swept around the hidden swimming hole, taking in the surrounding lush bushes and trees. It was all rather beautiful.

A red bird on the far side of the lake splashed in the shallow edge. The pretty thing stopped to stare at me with annoyance before fluttering into a nearby tree. We never saw such sites in the City. Just puddles. And rats.

"Isn't it lovely?" Millie breathed in awe.

"This... could be ours." If I married Annabelle Winters. I could see myself sneaking here after a satisfying day of work and stripping down to my skivvies to jump in the cool water. Splashing around like that bird. It would feel heavenly.

My mind betrayed me by imagining Amby jumping in right behind. He would complain about the water being cold, so I would move closer to warm him with a hug, and he would splash me in the face, I was certain. Stupidly, that sounded wonderful. Even better, once I dunked him under. He would pop back up, and then Amby would say *"I dare you to kiss me"* just as he did that first time in the barn.

"This is perfect," Millie rudely interrupted my fantasy.

Here I was thinking about Amby again, but now it was with visions of us together instead of my angry reflections from earlier. I couldn't get him out of my mind since seeing him again, and that fucking bothered me. I couldn't court Amby, and I didn't return to court him either. I had returned to Everdeen to make Millie happy and safe, to provide for her like an older brother should. Nothing about this included my pleasure. It wasn't about me at all. It was time to put our plan into action.

Millie would hide here while I begged for Anna's help in finding my poor, lost sister. People love to offer assistance if it makes them feel good. I'd lay it on thick too, my worry and helplessness, so when we did find Millie on the ground by the lake pretending to have twisted her ankle, Anna's sympathy and attention would make wooing her from there quite easy. Ambrose would lose this war.

"Was your mission successful?" Millie asked.

Nodding, I rattled off what I discovered in the house, "Miss Winters is unmarried, and still very wealthy, if the expensive decorations and elite company are any indication."

Millie tilted her hat to give me a glance. Perhaps my words had been too sharp. Or disgruntled. I certainly was disgruntled, but she let it go with wise grace. "Then, everything's working out well. Shall we start?"

Her lips tilted up in pure mischief. Such a sinful child. I didn't know where she learned that. Not from me.

Or, maybe it was. The mix of emotions stirring within me felt mischievous as I straightened the hair at the sides of my cap. Playing Anna false was wrong, I knew that, but being good had gotten me nowhere. We needed to even out the scales, and who better to cause mischief than the Washer siblings? Ambrose Somerset be damned.

Resolute, I turned to Millie with a smile that most likely matched hers. "Aye. It's time to win a wife."

5

Ambrose

After lingering in Annabelle's house to recompose myself, I stumbled out onto the front porch to find only empty carriages and cars in the gravel circle with a small group of drivers chatting nearby. I made sure no one else was about before making my way down the porch steps and along the path that wound around the house. As soon as I heard the commotion from the picnic, my steps slowed, and I felt my composure breaking again.

I was shocked to see Zeth out of the blue. I'd just been thinking about him in the barn, but he was the last person I'd expected to see anywhere in Everdeen, and at Annabelle's picnic, of all places. How long had he been back in town? Since when did Zeth attend elite parties?

I thought back to how close he'd come to me, how he'd caressed my hair. And curses, I still *smelled* that lye soap as if he were here now. He'd teased me about courting, even tried to kiss me, only for it to be a cruel trick.

After all this time, Zeth was bitter over how we broke up—God, what a fool I was! Although, his words about me having power in our past relationship made my blood simmer. I could only assume he meant it was because I had wealth. If he had a problem with me before, why did he bother proposing when we were younger?

What a jackass.

I had to find Annabelle and speak with her. I was here to woo her into courting, after all, and I needed something—anything—to distract me from thinking about that tall, handsome rogue. *Dear God, did I call him a tall, handsome rogue?* I needed to get myself together.

As I came into the backyard, I saw a few of Annabelle's maids already gathering picnic baskets and blankets. Small groups of people conversed on the terrace, so I passed them and made a line straight for Annabelle.

She stood in the middle of a few admirers. Her blonde hair was pinned into a loose bun with golden strands falling around her slim face, and her blue eyes shone like diamonds. Even her cheeks flushed like pink roses. She was slender, poised, standing with the grace of a princess... And I was but one of many who wished to know her better.

I looked around at my competition. Most of them were around the same height as me. One man was balding, while another was sweating profusely. A short, black-haired woman drowning in emeralds fanned herself. I was certain I could do better than any of them here.

That is, until I opened my mouth. I knew I would lose my words as soon as I tried to talk to her. I had already prepared myself for this exact scenario this morning, but Zeth had ruined it all. I couldn't think now, not after he'd shown his face and gotten me so worked up. Even so, I had to try.

I shoved Zeth out of my mind and inched closer to Annabelle as a man left her circle. To my dismay, every time I tried to cut in and speak with her, someone else would step in and do it before me. After a minute, I tried again, putting up my finger and opening my mouth to break in.

But a young man asked, "Miss Winters, do tell me more about the car you purchased while in Port Winchester. I'm thinking of buying one myself."

"You look so dashing driving it," the black-haired woman added with a coy smile.

Annabelle granted them equal attention, and I sighed, ready to give up and leave. I searched for a way out when I saw my father nodding at me in the distance. I couldn't disappoint him. Straightening, I cleared my throat and stepped in front of Earl Langley, a man a few years older than myself. He grunted as I knocked him back and took his place to stand in front of Annabelle.

"Oh, Ambrose!" she started. "How lovely to see you. I saw Hattie earlier. She's looking for you."

That wasn't at all what I was expecting her to say. Was she already trying to get rid of me? At least I could tell Father she pointed me away to find my sister. But no... that was an excuse.

Instead, I raised my chin, trying to appear at least a little taller than her, even though we were nearly the same height. "That's actually what I'm here about." I stared at her for a moment, my lips glued together as I forgot everything I planned to say.

"Um..." My mind went blank. The other two men beside me muttered something to each other, and my face went hot under Annabelle's waiting gaze. Finally, I blurted out, "Hattie and I were talking about going to the river to fish. Well, she doesn't like to fish, but I enjoy it. She mostly reads while I do it. Fish, that is. I was wondering if you'd like to join me instead tomorrow."

The others standing behind me snorted with amusement. They were right to tease; I had just asked the dumbest question imaginable. Annabelle was so elegant. What was I thinking?

"That's Ambrose for you, moving on to his next conquest. We know how this will end," Earl murmured to someone behind me. I stood tall and straightened my jacket, not caring what they thought.

"Join you fishing?" Annabelle's question didn't sound prim. In fact, her eyes brightened in excitement. "Well, I haven't gone this year yet. That sounds fun!"

I let out a breath of relief, hopeful my father would be proud of me for this. "So, tomorrow... Should I come and fetch you, or would you like to walk?" I gritted my teeth. *Fetch* her? "What I mean is, I can bring a carriage, or we could walk or ride."

"Walking sounds fine, Ambrose. We can fish at my lake and not have to walk far." She squeezed my arm, sounding kind and appreciative like she did back in our school days, and I ignited with pride.

But then her eyes drifted to the side as the other men wandered away. I followed her gaze to a familiar, devilishly handsome face coming right for her. As soon as I saw Zeth, my body went hot. What was he up to now?

"Anna," Zeth exclaimed softly, sounding a bit winded and rather relieved as he reached us both. He spared me no glance as he took one of Annabelle's palms as if pleading. "I hope you'll forgive me."

"Oh, Zeth Washer, is that you? It's been ages. Why do you need my forgiveness?"

"For our last day together." The huskiness of his voice hinted at a thousand shared intimacies that should have been mine. Zeth had always hated Annabelle for being the teacher's pet. What was he on about?

Annabelle must have felt the same as me because she appeared confused.

Zeth let go of her with a remorseful pout to his lean face. "That frog that leaped out of your school bag during geometry, that was me."

"You were the frog?" Annabelle asked, the corners of her eyes crinkling with playful surprise.

Zeth played along by making a ribbit sound, and when Annabelle laughed, I wrinkled my nose to stifle my smile. Damn me for wanting to laugh at him too. I should be wanting to slap him instead. It was outrageous of Zeth to flirt with Annabelle as if he hadn't had his hands on me just ten minutes ago.

I inspected him sharply for faults, my eyes straying down the front of his sleek blue jacket. It seemed his new height also came with a hint of strength beneath his clothes. His build was wider than I remembered and his attire nicer than the chapel donations he wore in his youth. Did he come into wealth?

When Zeth found me staring, I hoped he saw my scowl directed at him. He was ruining my moment with Annabelle so he could move in on her. His games made my veins surge with fire.

Zeth's gaze flitted between me and her. "I'm sorry. Am I interrupting something?"

I raised my chin. "Actually, yes, I—"

"That's nice," Zeth cut me off with a wave of his hand, the bastard. Then he turned to Annabelle with puppy dog eyes. "What's important is that I needed to find you, and... May I still call you Anna?"

When I inhaled sharply, Annabelle glanced strangely at me before nodding primly at Zeth. "Of course."

"Isn't that Washer?" a man muttered behind me as he passed us. Another guy answered him with a rude jab. Recognition was hitting them all, and from their tone, they weren't happy to see the Washers' son included at the picnic.

The lively glow in Zeth's eyes faded. Maybe he'd heard the rising gossip, but he seemed indifferent as he rose to his full height. "Anna, I sincerely beg your assistance. My sister attended your precious picnic with me and has gone completely missing."

"Millie's here too?" Annabelle asked.

"Yes, kind of you to remember her." Zeth glanced around, his forehead creased. "I've searched everywhere and simply can't locate her. Perhaps you know of a place where my little sister may be hiding?"

I narrowed my eyes at Zeth's polished words, as if he'd rehearsed his own lines. "You didn't seem concerned about her earlier."

"I didn't know she was missing," he explained with a quick glare at me before facing Annabelle again.

She tugged her hand free from Zeth's to place it against her chin, thinking. "I have many trails behind the house that wind throughout the woods. If she wandered that way, no doubt she found the gazebo or the lake. Shall we go look?"

"Of course." Zeth beamed as he held out his arm, and Annabelle hesitated before she took it.

When they moved away from me and headed for the garden, I followed right behind and blurted out, "I'll go too!"

Zeth glanced over his shoulder. "There's no need to accompany us, Mr. Somerset."

"Well, if your sister is truly missing, as you say, don't you think we should gather a party to find her?" I put out my hands to emphasize the supposed seriousness of the situation.

"Good idea, Ambrose," Annabelle agreed. "We should all search."

Zeth nodded before he glared back at me with sheer annoyance. He gestured to the tree line with long and graceful fingers. "Well then, Mr. Somerset, why don't you take the lead? We'll follow behind."

I frowned, turning my face before I could huff steam out of my nose in front of him. I'd asked him to call me Ambrose, not *Mr. Somerset*. If he called me that one more time... Growling low, I guided the way through an arched trellis covered with lovely pink roses. Surrounding us was the garden, where a few people chatted in the flower rows, and before us were the woods.

Behind me on the path, Zeth spoke smoothly to Annabelle. His words weren't clear, something about our old teacher. I slowed my steps to listen as Annabelle giggled. I made a sour face they couldn't see, rolling my eyes. Zeth had never liked Annabelle, the liar. Yet here he was flirting with her.

Sighing, I glanced over to find Hattie standing near a butterfly bush with a man leaning close to her in conversation.

It was none other than Damien Cooligan. He was gawking at my little sister's bosom, the devil. Unfortunately, I knew too well about his antics. A couple of experiences with him led me to conclude he was nothing short of scum. I wanted my sister away from him.

When I halted, Zeth feigned concern at Annabelle. "It appears our chaperone is needed elsewhere. Pity."

"Just one moment," I assured him while I pushed my glasses higher onto my nose. There was no way I would leave Zeth alone with Annabelle, but I wasn't about to leave my baby sister with Damien either. "Perhaps Hattie has seen Millie. I'll go get her."

In my rush, I tripped over a stepping stone. I quickly righted myself and hurried on, hoping no one witnessed the fumble.

"Oh, Damien," Hattie giggled and smacked his arm lightly.

"You'd best stop with the jokes, you're making my brother march over here."

Damien turned and raised an eyebrow. His gaudy red-and-gold-striped jacket was so atrocious, it blinded me. Even so, it was hard for anyone not to notice his tall stature and light hair that fell past his shoulders in a long braid, or the way his green eyes wandered along my body before meeting my face with a smug smile. It was a shame his good looks were sullied by his ego. He often got what he wanted through manipulation, and I'd seen him roughhouse several people for speaking ill of him or his equally awful friends. God be damned if I let this awful man take advantage of my youngest sister.

"Amby." Damien nodded. "Haven't you had enough of interrupting everyone's conversations today?"

"No, actually, I was hoping to interrupt one more." I looked from his smirking lips to Hattie's curious stare. "We're going for a walk in the woods to find Zeth Washer's sister. Care to join us?"

"Zeth's here? Where?" She peered around me to wave at Zeth, and I instantly regretted saying his name at all.

Damien's gaze narrowed. "You mean that little hooligan you used to run around with? The washer boy?"

"That's the one."

"Oh, well I was about to go for a walk with Hattie myself." He looped an arm around her back.

"No, you weren't." I captured her hand and pulled her away from Damien.

"Mm, he sounds jealous," Damien told Hattie, his eyes still on me, watching. "Maybe your brother can go with us? I'm sure he can find a long branch or a hard twig to whittle, since he likes handling wood so much in his barn."

I shot him an icy glare before moving away and leading Hattie along with me, and Damien chuckled crudely from behind as we left. What a cad.

Shaking my head, I led the way with her to where I left Annabelle and Zeth, who were far ahead now.

"Amby, why did you do that?" Hattie whined.

"You shouldn't hang around Damien," I shot out, quickening my pace from the garden path and into the woods. "He's a rake."

"I know that. I would have slipped away if he made me uncomfortable. I'm a big girl. Don't you know I can handle myself?"

When I glanced at her, she regarded me in that delicate, poised way that told me she indeed had a better head on her shoulders than I did at her age. Who was I to tell her what to do?

I nodded thoughtfully. "I know, you're much smarter than your big brother."

Hattie hooked her arm through mine with a laugh. "Thank you, Amby. Now, what's all this about Zeth being back and searching for his sister? I was just a kid when I last saw him. Do you remember the rope swing he made me? I was so mad when Father took it down."

I remembered. Zeth used to pull her back on the swing and run with her, ducking right under her flying skirts to swing her high, and Hattie squealed to high heaven with joy. The splintered seat and old rope had creaked something fierce, so Father dismantled it after Zeth left. "It wasn't safe."

"Pish posh. Maybe Zeth can make me a new one."

"He's not here to make swings."

"Then why is he here?"

"Well..."

When I glanced up, I finally saw Zeth and Annabelle walking ahead, too close together for my liking. I stared daggers at his lean back, wondering why he was interested in her. That frog wasn't the worst thing he did to Annabelle. He once put a dead mouse in her cup of hot chocolate during the winter festival. She'd hollered so much, she'd cried. I don't think she knew Zeth was the culprit. Well, really both of us... I had dared him to do it, after all.

Perhaps Annabelle was being a good hostess and letting Zeth apologize for the past, or she was being polite to Zeth because he asked for help. Or perhaps she was returning Zeth's advances...

That idea made me walk faster.

"Come on," I told Hattie. "Let's catch up. If you see Millie, let me know."

"Right!" Hattie nodded and searched. Her efforts sent her blonde ringlets fluttering with each swing of her head. Then she halted, making me stumble, and pointed. "Oh, look there, Amby!"

I followed Hattie's finger to a deer next to a tree in the distance. The animal stared at me briefly before startling. Zeth and Annabelle turned around right as it leapt away, and they joined us.

"That deer reminds me of Ambrose," Zeth commented to Annabelle on his arm. "Cute and skittish."

Hattie giggled loudly at the insult—such a wonderful sister—while Annabelle puckered her lips politely. A glimmer of humor shone in her eyes.

My neck flushed as I racked my brain for a retort. Nothing witty came to mind, so I continued walking. When something yellow caught my eye, I peered around a tree to see someone wedged between the bushes ahead.

"Is someone there?" I asked, and they all turned along with me.

"Fuck, Mils," Zeth muttered rudely. He sprang into action, trudging through a mud puddle and abandoning Annabelle on the path with Hattie and me.

Just when I felt victorious about that, Zeth pulled a young woman from the bushes, and Annabelle gasped and strode over to help.

When Hattie started forward too, I grabbed her arm to stop her. "Wait."

Something wasn't right. Surely, this was some ploy on his part, and I wanted to see it play out as Zeth intended. Millie certainly groaned dramatically as Zeth steadied her. She even hissed as she limped from the bushes.

"What did you do?" Zeth reprimanded his sister with concern. He plucked a few twigs from the tangled curls under her straw hat. "You were supposed to—"

"Did you see the deer?" Millie interrupted. She waited for a nod from Zeth before fawning on, "It was so cute, I had to follow it. There weren't any deer in the City." She tossed a hand up to her brow, knocking her hat even more askew. "And then I slipped here, foolish me."

Seeing Millie again reminded me of the pest who wouldn't leave Zeth and me alone. Always dirty and rambunctious, wanting to be one of the boys. Now, here stood a grown young woman. Why was she wandering off into the woods and falling into bushes?

Was this some kind of game to get Annabelle's attention? With that acting, it probably was. The Washer siblings were working together to fool them all. Those rascals were always devious. The jig was up.

Huffing, I marched over to them, but the sight of Zeth on his knees stopped me. His fancy trousers were caked in mud, and he genuinely appeared worried as he unlaced Millie's boot. When Zeth managed to pull it off, Millie gasped. The tight boot had left red marks in her skin. Her ankle was definitely swollen. She tried to step a socked toe on some solid dirt and winced hard.

Millie swayed, and Annabelle rushed over to offer her arm, uncaring that she had to step a boot into the wet, slippery ground herself. The mud squished loud enough to hear, but Annabelle kept her graceful posture and managed to protect her white hem like a true elite lady. Millie took Annabelle's arm and stared up at her with a blink of dark brown eyes.

"Here, I can help too!" Hattie passed me so suddenly that she knocked me backward into Zeth, who was still kneeling in the mud. I almost fell right over him, until his strong hands grabbed me to keep me upright. Once I was steady, I pushed him away and glowered.

Zeth got to his feet with a crooked smile on his lips. What was the devil smiling at? His mood shifts were exasperating.

"Oh, dear," Hattie giggled and raised a hand to her lips as she pointed to my backside. "You, uh..."

I twisted and glanced at my trousers to see that a muddy handprint had claimed my ass... The rest of the group all snorted in amusement. When Zeth chuckled too, I glared at him for getting me dirty. Instead of seeing humor in his amber eyes, they filled with a possessive gaze.

Heat roared through my body, and goosebumps made me shiver delightfully. I cursed myself for wanting his touch again.

Zeth stepped closer, wiping his hands down his thighs to clean them, looking as flushed as I felt. "Shall I help you clean that off?" he asked with a hint of huskiness that didn't belong at picnics.

"You've done enough." I sneered and stepped back to give myself some distance. I tried to wipe the mud off myself, only to get it on my hand. Then I gave a defeated sigh.

The girls were already trying to get back to the path with one of Millie's arms slung around Annabelle's shoulders.

Feeling useless, I asked, "Shall I fetch a cart?"

"We'll be fine, Ambrose, thank you," Annabelle reassured me. When we reached the path, she paused to readjust her hold on Millie's curvy hip.

Annabelle swung her head around to find my sister reaching the lane with Millie's mud-soaked boot held out wide in her pinched fingers. "Hattie, will you kindly skip ahead to alert my staff that Miss Washer needs a room for the night while she heals? And call for Doctor Light, he's here at the picnic. We'll need his services to make sure nothing is broken. Mr. Washer, you're welcome to stay as well. To care for your sister, of course."

"Too kind," Zeth replied so close to me, I jumped. "Far too kind, Miss Winters. I wouldn't want to be an inconvenience, and the gossip—no, we can return to town—"

"Nonsense, you're staying. Now run along, Hattie, if you please. We'll be right behind you."

Annabelle's command of the situation had the girls moving swiftly. Hattie first, then Millie and Annabelle, while Zeth and I were left to watch in amazement.

What just happened? Millie and Zeth were sleeping in Annabelle's house tonight?

Maybe Zeth and his sister didn't plan her injury, but the cramping in my gut told me something smelled foul about absolutely everything today. Poking around Annabelle's house and inspecting her things, worming his way into her good graces, and devising a way to stay with her overnight.

As Zeth turned to follow the girls, I grabbed his arm and pulled him around to face me. "What is this all about, Zeth?"

"To what are you referring, Mr. Somerset?" Zeth smirked. When I gaped at him, he shrugged me off and began walking.

I followed him, his long legs giving no respite, and I had to skip a bit to keep up. "This." I gestured back with both hands to where he'd pulled Millie from the bushes before I jerked my arm out at the girls ahead. "*That*... When have you *ever* liked Annabelle Winters?"

"My past feelings have nothing to do with my intended future, Mr. Somerset."

"Are you planning to marry her for her wealth?"

Zeth's gaze shot to mine in disbelief, then he shook his head. I knew that appalled face of his anywhere. He didn't like what I said. I wasn't surprised when he offered no reply. No clarification, no denial. This was just like him, shutting me out and not talking.

I grit my teeth, refusing to let him push me aside this time without an answer. "I'll take your damning silence as a yes."

"Take my silence any damn way you want, Mr. Somerset."

"Stop calling me that!" Something in me was breaking, and I couldn't quite pin down what it was. I think Zeth heard it too, as he eyed me. After a long pause, he laughed.

"Look, Rosie," he smoothly quipped my pet name, and my eyes flew to his. "My plans—"

I tripped over a root and landed on my knees in the dirt with a grunt. I ignored the pain in my knees and stared at the ground, wondering why I was so flustered and confused over Zeth, why my emotions were swirling so fast. When his shadow fell over me, I peered up at him in humiliation.

I thought Zeth was going to offer me a hand up. Instead, he crossed his arms and stared down with pity, and perhaps with a hint of concern. Huffing, I got to my feet again and brushed off my trousers. Once I straightened, he walked on.

As I matched his steps, he continued in a clipped tone, "My plans are none of your business. You made that clear long ago. So why do you care if Anna welcomes me warmly back into her life?"

"Because this isn't you."

"What bullshit," Zeth sneered. "What isn't me? Dressing well? Being witty? Men can change, you realize, and I worked hard to improve my station. Maybe I'm even proper enough to marry, eh? You should let Anna decide that for herself."

"That wasn't what I meant!" I opened my mouth to say more, then snapped it closed and clenched my jaw. Would he even believe me if I explained? This smooth-talking Zeth before me was so different from the one I'd grown up with. It felt like he was pretending to be someone he wasn't. There was no way to say that without insulting him, so I hung my head in shame and stared at my shoes as they moved.

"For fuck's sake, Amby, enough with the pouting. I'll confess, I returned to court Anna, but I didn't plan on moving into the Winters estate tonight. Millie injured her ankle, and Anna has a mind of her own. Is that what you want me to say?"

"Well, it's an answer, at least." I adjusted my jacket. He'd finally given me the truth, but I wasn't going to let it end here. I wasn't going to let *Zeth* have *Annabelle*. "You won't stop my own efforts to court her."

"What do you want? More wealth? Societal acceptance? You don't even like women," Zeth huffed, glaring sideways at me. "You're just chasing Anna to appease your dad, like the good little rich boy you are. You're a grown man now. Isn't your act getting old?"

My fists curled, my face going hot as my steps slowed. Zeth shook his head and kept walking. He had no idea how *angry* his caustic words made me. I stared at his back, my eyes burning into him as a surge of adrenaline came over me. Unable to think of a reply, I did the only thing that felt right and rushed up to smack the back of his head, making his cap fly off. Zeth flinched and turned to me, looking furious.

I couldn't help it. It was a fucking childish thing to do, but he'd pissed me off. My blood was boiling, and I retreated right into old habits we'd done when we were kids who got into heated arguments like this one. I stood there with my arms by my sides, drawing in several shaky, rapid breaths as I stared at him, silently daring him to do something back.

Zeth kept his dark gaze on me as he bent to retrieve his cap.

When he straightened, his arm flew out to smack me in the chest with the soft material, making me flinch. His firm voice hit me harder, "Don't you dare start something with me."

I raised my chin and straightened. "I'm not afraid of you."

His thick eyebrows raised. Zeth somehow appeared calm as he returned his cap to his head and stepped close. It was oddly gratifying seeing how composed he could be, even after I'd pushed his buttons. He stared at me as if he wouldn't take any of my shit. But he was still giving me the attention I wanted, and that alone made my anger melt into something else, a tension that felt like someone stretching a rubber band between their fingers and waiting for it to spring loose.

Zeth leaned forward, and I flinched as he came close to my ear and whispered, "I'm not afraid of you either, so leave me the fuck alone."

When Zeth pulled away, my shoulders fell. I watched him leave the trail to walk into the open toward Annabelle's house. By now, the girls were already there. Something sharp pierced my heart, a fresh barb sinking in. Zeth had never told me to leave him alone before, at least not like *that*. I knew all of Zeth's emotions like the back of my hand. However, I admit I didn't know this new one; a colder side of him who talked to me as if we didn't have a past together.

It put a knot in my stomach. I couldn't figure him out, and his hurtful words got to me. I had to swallow them down and not think about them. I had plans of my own, after all, and I couldn't let him get in the way of them.

Zeth Washer told me to leave him alone, but he wouldn't be seeing the last of me anytime soon.

6

Zeth

Standing in Anna's parlor, I drew back the window's burgundy curtains to spy on Amby outside. He was holding the fancy Somerset carriage door open, and I wished the gravel drive would open up to swallow him whole. He had such nerve butting his freckled nose into my marriage plans, insinuating I had nefarious plans for Anna. He was right, but fuck him for assuming the worst of me. I wasn't a thief. I had morals. I was hard-working and studied culture. If only I had returned last year. Then, I could have shown him a successful version of myself who wasn't hiding failure.

Amby's dad joined him outside the carriage. The man still had the same big mustache, fancy duds, and snobby, thin posture as he entered his gleaming black vehicle with black iron trim. It surprised me that he hadn't purchased a motor vehicle yet. Then again, Mr. Somerset was an old-fashioned sort of man.

Amby's sister, Hattie, piled in after that. I always liked her, and was glad to see how prim and pretty she'd grown to be.

But not prettier than Amby, damn him. The man was gorgeous, with breath-stealing brown eyes behind gold glasses. I could see them glimmering from where he sulked in the drive. I had told Amby to leave me alone because I found everything about him irresistible. I couldn't stop staring. And that kissable mouth yapping away at me—so annoying. I wanted to kiss this grown and persistent version of Ambrose Somerset into submission. The pull was magnetic.

Outside, Amby's pert lips twisted, and his auburn curly head tilted toward me, staring at my window like he felt the pull too.

"Mr. Washer?" Anna asked from the parlor entrance behind me. I flinched with guilt and rubbed a hand over my face to refocus on my responsibilities, then I turned from the window to welcome my future wife.

But it wasn't Anna greeting me, it was a maid in the doorway with Doc Light. His ear-length, frizzled, gray hair looked the same as I remembered, and he nodded with the same condescending air. "Hard to believe how tall you've grown, young man."

Why did everyone have to point out my new height? I sighed, "Thank you?"

He chuckled and walked around the matching settees to join me by the single window. I let the heavy curtain swing back into place and motioned him to the snack tray Anna's servant brought in earlier. The assortment of cheese was probably leftover from the picnic. I rarely saw such a spread.

The doctor seemed appreciative too, even though he'd attended the event. He gathered pieces of cheese onto a napkin from the half-empty tray. I must have eaten most of it without even noticing. Whenever there's food, I tend to take it. Doc turned with his cheese pile to admire a painting of ducks, so I slipped the rest of the crackers into my pocket for Millie before stuffing a few sausage slices into my mouth.

That's when Anna entered the room. I felt like an orphan at the chapel's charity lunch with my greedy mouthful, so I chewed quickly and swallowed before Anna caught on to my poor eating habits. Luckily, she didn't notice, or she was too polite. She claimed the edge of one settee with grace while motioning for Doc Light to sit opposite her.

Anna ignored me, or she let me choose a seat, so I stayed by the side table with the food tray. Plus, seeing the Doc again made me weary, so distance seemed better. He'd been the one to patch me up many times over my wild youth, and Mum never had enough money to pay him. Most times, he made me feel inadequate. Once or twice, he helped for free before shooing me off with a candy sucker.

"How's that shoulder of yours?" Doc Light asked with a nice enough smile. I had my mouth full again, with cheese this time, so I shrugged that shoulder. Turning away, I parted the curtain slightly for a peek. Amby's carriage was leaving. Good riddance.

Doc turned to Anna, "Can you believe Mr. Washer here severely injured himself trying to steal a chicken from poor Fanny Denver? He probably wanted one for dinner, but slipped off the roof of her chicken coop instead, falling directly onto a broken fence post. The thin pole completely impaled his shoulder. Nasty business."

"He didn't!" Anna exclaimed from behind her hand. I couldn't tell if she was mortified by my childish behavior or sickened by the gory story. Either way, stealing and falling was not the impression I wanted to make today. It was bad enough to be covered in mud from creating such an imposition.

Yet the man went on, "It was the young Somerset boy who bravely dragged Washer to me. Mr. Washer was blubbering like a baby and bleeding all over my exam room. It took me hours to extricate the post, cleanse the wound, and stitch him properly. Fine work, on my part. Saved his arm and his life."

Anna's brow creased at the blubbering baby part, but she politely refrained from commenting. That didn't stop my ears from burning with embarrassment. What was the Doc doing? Trying to ruin my play for Anna's hand?

I went back to stuffing a sausage into my mouth and muttered around it. "Left a scar, but I healed." I swallowed and pointed out the important bit everyone ignored, "And please note Ambrose Somerset's presence in your delightful story. He wasn't innocent. He was my accomplice. He egged me on."

"Egged?" Anna snorted with delight at my play on words, missing my point.

Did no one listen? "He dared me to do it."

"Ah, yes, you and Somerset were the Daring Duo." Doc laughed and shook his head. "Got you both into plenty of scrapes as boys."

"I remember." Annabelle chuckled, as if she knew something I didn't. "Why did Ambrose dare you?"

I opened my mouth to answer her, then snapped it shut. I didn't remember why, only that Amby dared me to climb the chicken coop, so I did. Amby dared me to do a lot of stuff back then, including jerking him off in his barn. "Well, a fence post sticking out of my shoulder kinda erases the point of the adventure, but Ambrose isn't as innocent as he seems. And I don't steal chickens."

That sounded childish. I heard it, clear as day. I avoided Anna's intent gaze and focused on the troublesome doctor. "Now tell me of my sister, is she faring better? No battle wounds?"

"None at all, though the darling did twist her ankle," Doc Light sympathized, as he should for my dear sister. "So I gave her a dose of laudanum to ease the pain tonight, and another dose for the morning. She needs to keep her ankle elevated and rest it until she can walk again. I'll write up the invoice tomorrow."

My head spun with the cost calculations. If I sold the dresser in Mum's room, that would pay his bill, but then how would we buy food? Or fix the roof? Or continue this con?

That's when Anna chimed in, "I appreciate you staying to see her, Doctor. Please send the invoice to my clerk. It's only right that I cover your cost since she fell on my property."

That's right, everyone knew the Washer kids were too poor to pay the doctor. How damn polite of Anna to cover my embarrassment, though she didn't need to make Millie and I sound like an expenditure. Did my con fail already?

I nodded to them both with an expression that stretched tight. "Excuse me. I think I'll check on my sister."

I didn't wait for dismissals or replies. I stormed out of the room and took the stairs three at a time, needing to escape their disdain before I became sick. They didn't want me here, the washer boy.

Anna no doubt saw through my facade. Just as I gained an inch, I lost a mile.

The upstairs hall was even longer than the hall downstairs, and this one confounded me with doors that went on forever. Thankfully, I followed Anna's maid earlier to see where she stashed Millie —the Lilac Room—so I slipped through the door and closed it behind me. I leaned back against it, holding the handle tight. I shut my eyes to block out the world. My breath raced and my head hurt.

"Zeth, you alright?" Millie asked.

"Of course," I lied, popping open my eyes to make sure she looked well. She did, thank God. "Just worried about you."

"The doctor says I'll live." She struggled up from under the blankets. Her loose curls were a riot around her head, and her plump cheeks were a healthy pink.

I let go of the door handle to stroll over to her side and took her hand in mine. It was cool to the touch, so I buffed her fingers to warm them. "I just made a fool of myself downstairs. Our plan might be out the window."

Millie yawned adorably, and her lashes fluttered against the laudanum taking effect. "I doubt anyone could dislike you. You're probably jumping to conclusions. I'm sure our plan is fine. Anna likes us. She wouldn't let us stay otherwise." She gave me a lazy grin. "Don't think the worst of things."

I didn't want to talk about this. It was best to brush what happened in the parlor under the rug. Clearing my throat, I nodded at her. "You in any pain?"

"A bit."

The door of the Lilac Room opened, and Anna's blonde head popped in. She found me frowning over Millie's hand.

"Do you need anything?" she asked sweetly.

"I'm feeling a little cold," Millie answered. "Perhaps another blanket?"

"Of course. Anything."

And Miss Annabelle Winters went off to fetch my sister a blanket. The woman had something like twelve servants, yet she was serving Millie like royalty.

"Mils, what spell did you cast on her?"

"The Washer charm," she giggled and snuggled further into the two blankets she already had on top of her. A second later, Anna scurried back in and flipped a third blanket out and over the pile.

Tucking three layers of fluffy blankets around Millie seemed excessive, but our host did it with care, as if these two were old friends. Anna was five years older than my sister. Surely they hadn't played together in school. Besides, Anna was always helping with grading papers while Millie plotted elaborate excuses for losing hers.

Now, Millie complained about the cold with a hand to her forehead like a fair maiden who wouldn't shut up after being rescued, and Anna... she played along. She tested Millie's forehead with the back of her hand. And when Millie asked for a fourth blanket, Anna agreed, but she failed to hide a silly grin behind the wisps of her golden hair.

As soon as our amused host left in a flurry of skirts to scrounge up yet another unnecessary blanket, I shook my head at my sister. "Did you injure your head in the fall? Anna knows you're being a fool."

"And strangely, she likes it!" Millie blathered with excitement. She tugged the blankets to her chin, and then she frowned. "Perhaps she's lonely here, all by herself in a big house. Maybe she doesn't feel useful."

"Unlikely," I scoffed. "She has the running of this entire estate to keep her busy, and a battalion of servants to keep her company. I saw seven downstairs when they bussed you in, maybe another two maids upstairs, two hands in the stable, and one gardener on the grounds. So, not lonely. There must be a reason she's tolerating your 'poor me' act."

Millie pouted. "It's not an act. I really hurt my ankle."

"Aye, Doc Light confirmed it." I leaned over to kiss her cheek. That smoothed out her annoyed look, making me feel a little better. I didn't mean to release my anger on her.

Millie waved me off, and the masculine plaid on her nightshirt caught my eye. It probably belonged to Anna's deceased dad, and hopefully no one would explain that to Millie. She believed in ghosts. She claimed to see them many times growing up. I didn't want anything to ruin her happy mood as she settled.

Burying my hands in my jacket pockets, I found one full of crackers, so I set those on the side table for Millie to eat if she became hungry.

"I love you, grumpy bear," she assured me.

"Grumpy bear?" I asked in offense. We hadn't used nicknames at bedtime in years. Hearing the wrong one now made my stomach tighten. "What happened to Clever Cat?"

Millie blinked like she forgot I was there and scrunched her face. "You never talk. Ever. So now you're not clever."

"Well, I guess I still love you too, Sassy Cat," I grumbled back. What did she mean, I never talk? I talk all the time.

The tincture must be easing Millie's mouth as well as her pain. I needed to watch her closely until sleep took her.

A dark green chair at Millie's bedside beckoned me, so I sat down. It was so plush I nearly moaned. I scooted my tired ass deeper and crossed my long legs to acquaint myself with my new favorite chair.

"Alright," I rested my elbow on the chair arm and raised a finger in the air to catch Millie's glazed eye. "So... one night of rest in that bed, doctor's orders. Then we have to go back to the laundry."

"Do we?" Millie moaned at the same time Anna asked, "Do you?"

I flinched and spun in the chair at Anna's return. She was standing in the doorway with a new blanket, this one knitted from red and green wool. How long was she standing there? Guilt flooded my cheeks as I quickly reviewed the past few minutes. Anna might have heard us talking about her, though she didn't seem angry. Just the opposite, she appeared pleased.

Anna even offered, "You can stay longer. I am enjoying Millie's 'poor me' act."

I groaned. "You heard that?"

"It's fine." Her kind, blue eyes reflected like a clear summer's day. She was nice enough looking... kind, polite, and intelligent to boot, but there was nothing that made my heart flutter.

I rubbed the velvet arm of the chair—so damn soft—and swore to use it as my own when I moved in. It was one of the benefits of marrying Anna. But... I liked the chair more than her. Was that horrid to think?

Instead of answering that tasteless question to myself, I glanced up. Anna was still by the door with a blanket in her arms. Her tilted head and evaluating stare made me feel like a frog again, only this time I didn't ribbit to entertain Anna. It felt like my attractions were spread out with pins for her to dissect. And she found nothing there.

Flustered to be so obvious, I sat up and brushed dried mud from my thigh. And when that fell from my pants to dirty the carpet, I cringed. "Excuse me, ladies, I should seek out my own bedroom. We don't want rumors, now do we?"

"What sort of rumors?" Millie hiccupped, and my head rotated to glare at her for being crude.

Anna chuckled like a bell and moved in to cover Millie with the knitted eyesore. Clearly she was getting to the bottom of her blanket reserve. "It's foolish to worry about what people think of you, Zeth. Let them talk. Be yourself."

I swallowed, uncertain if she was referring to my lack of interest in her or the doctor's rude teasing downstairs about my past. Or maybe she was simply spouting off platitudes.

Anna moved her blonde head to catch my troubled gaze with confidence. "Do what you want, but tonight I aim to smother you both with kindness, as a welcome back gift. I'm truly glad you came home."

Home. She meant it. Even though I was a horrid kid to her, Anna sounded excited to have me and Millie back in town. She welcomed us into her home with open arms.

I mentally chewed on that as Anna went about pouring tea that I didn't notice steeping in the corner. Cups filled with polite splashes that Anna must have practiced as a child, and then she strolled over to hand me a delicate cup and saucer decorated with lilacs, clearly designed to match the room. I sipped without tasting

JORDAN LEE & SPARA SOLACE

because the concepts of kindness, and a real home, felt foreign. I didn't expect either.

I once called the old laundry home, but that place was nothing more than an empty shell without furniture or family. This chair felt better than anywhere I ever lived, with its plush seat and soft velvet arms that hugged me close. Something this nice remained forever out of reach. Maybe I didn't deserve a home, though I wanted it desperately. I wanted this house. I wanted Anna's kindness.

Anna was sitting on the edge of the bed now, petting a few of Millie's brown curls as my sister drank from her cup. I was grateful for Anna's assistance, making sure Millie didn't spill her tea. Anna had spunk and compassion. She said she didn't care about rumors, and I admired that, but she probably had enough money to pave a way through all the troubles. She was lucky.

A soft voice cleared their throat, and a maid appeared in the doorway. When Anna straightened on the bed and nodded, the maid spoke to her, "The Ivory Room is ready, ma'am."

"Thank you so much, Betty. Mr. Washer will sleep there tonight, close to his sister, in case he's needed. It's been a long day already, so I'll have supper brought to your room if that's alright, unless you require anything else?"

I didn't know who Anna was asking until the maid turned to me with a patient prompt. I turned to Anna, "Oh, no, thank you."

Lumbering up from my favorite chair, I set the teacup and saucer on the side table before giving Millie one last peck. Her tired eyes were closing. Anna was right, this was my cue to leave the ladies for the evening.

Thankfully, Anna was already removing a few of the unnecessary blankets. My needy sister certainly ate up that attention. Maybe Millie was the lonely one, and Anna happened to notice. It would do Millie good to make some friends.

I stepped through the doorway to join the maid in the hall, granting Betty what little charm I had left in me tonight. "Thank you. I'm sure I can find the Ivory Room myself. Am I correct to guess that it might be the one painted ivory?"

The maid twitched her lips and nodded. She seemed to like me well enough. I had a way with women if I tried. Betty bowed low, as if I actually were a gentleman, and walked along the hall to head downstairs. Her steps slowed halfway down. She was checking to see if I left her mistress safe.

And I intended to do just that. But then Anna slipped out of the door and closed it behind her with a soft clink before motioning for me to follow her away from the stairs.

My heart kicked up a few paces at Anna's boldness while she led me into the room right next to my sister's. With the curtains closed, it was dim. Anna shut the door behind us and made her way to a little table to turn on a lamp. The room suddenly glowed softly, and the white walls appeared warm and inviting.

It was a little surprising for Anna to test our compatibility so quickly. She didn't strike me as overly interested prior to this moment, yet here she was luring me into a bedroom and sending me excited glances as she approached with a spring in her step across the lush carpet.

"Miss Winters," I said, since formality seemed appropriate as I adjusted my collar. Damn, it felt tight. "I should tell you that I wish to court you officially with hopes of an arranged marriage between us in the future."

If that didn't spell out my lack of attraction to her, I didn't know what would, besides a simple *fuck off*.

Thankfully, she nodded sweetly. She even paused briefly in her pursuit of me. Then all too quickly, the mischievousness was back in her expression. This wasn't the Anna I remembered who scolded me with soft shushes for talking behind our teacher's back. This Anna appeared playful as she continued moving closer with a bouncy stroll until she stood right in front of me with an expectant glance.

Well... how hard could it be to kiss a woman? I planned on marrying, after all, so I needed to do more than press my lips to hers if we wanted to have children. And she probably wanted children. I should just kiss her now and get that over. It would make our public courting kiss easier. But why did she have to look so sweet, like my little sister?

I couldn't help it, trepidation overtook me. I leaned my head away from her. I didn't like how Anna's blue eyes twinkled at me, or how her head tilted in observation. I wanted to beg the woman to stop when she tiptoed higher to whisper as devilishly as Millie, "Do you want to go fishing tomorrow?"

7

Ambrose

The picnic tables were laden with food. *Too* much food. Food that didn't make sense in the slightest. Everdeen may have been full of wealthy country folk, but seeing snails and—ew, was that eel? It wasn't food that people in Everdeen ate. Yet here it all was for the taking, along with every familiar face I didn't want to talk to. My father talked business without taking a breath, while Marigold held a snake beside him.

Why was my oldest sister holding a snake? She let it slither around her arm and neck, the dark scales brushing against her blonde hair. When Emiline and Hattie made their way to her, I tried to shout. Nothing escaped my mouth. Then someone stood in front of me, a shadow swallowing me whole. I glanced over to see a dashing smile and golden amber eyes fixed on me. When Zeth moved forward, my troubles melted away. He drew close to me and swept his knuckles against my cheek. Then he kissed me. Something stirred deep in my chest for this man. A man I had known my whole life, my best friend, my—

A knock sounded on the door, ripping me from my dream, and my eyes shot open to find the dimly lit ceiling above me. My clothes were damp, and sweat beaded on my head. My, these blankets were *hot*. Upon throwing them off, I peered down at the bulge in my trousers. Sighing, I sat up with a groan, trying my best to ignore the fact that such a thing had arisen from dreaming about *Zeth*. The room was cast in shadow, and a quick glance at the window told me it was late evening.

"Amby, are you alright?" came Emiline's voice from the other side of the door.

I pulled the linens back over my lap before saying, "Yes. You can come in."

The door opened gently, and Emiline peeked inside before stepping fully in. She held a lamp and set it on the end table before sitting beside me on the bed. I could feel her staring at me, but I didn't meet her gaze. Not yet.

"Well?" she asked.

"Well, what?"

"You missed supper, and you took a nap. Either the picnic really did a number on you, or you're bothered by something."

My twin never missed a beat with me. She knew my moods like the back of her hand. "The picnic was full of the usual noise and crowd. You know how both give me a headache. I needed to sleep it off."

"That's not the whole truth."

She was prodding me to talk, but I just wanted to forget all about today, so I only stared ahead.

"Amby..." Emiline took my hand. "Please talk to me. I know when you're bothered. Don't make me pry it out of you like I have to with Father."

Her words got to me. I know she didn't mean to insult our father, though it was true the man never shed a tear or shared his troubles. He listened, and that was about it. Emiline was the only one who could get through to him, and still only *sometimes*. He was the shining example of what a man should be, what *I* should be—resilient and unbothered.

The mounting pressures of finding a wife and taking on the banking business always formed such a tight knot in my stomach, making it harder to let out how I truly felt about it all. I did need to let it out.

"Em..." I finally met her gaze to see her auburn braid shining in the dim light, and her face creased in concern. No, I didn't want to talk about Father right now, so I closed my mouth instead.

Emiline's thumb gently rubbed the back of my hand. "Hattie told me Zeth is back in town. And that Millie twisted her ankle in the woods."

I blinked at her, coming out of my straying thoughts. "Well, it didn't take Hattie long to give away the events of the entire day over supper." I couldn't ignore the talk about Zeth even if I tried. My sister knew I had loved him, that I had spent so long being heartsick over losing him. I rubbed my face with my hand and finally said, "He's here to court Annabelle."

"What?" Emiline drew back, so startled she gave a laugh. "Zeth Washer would *never* court someone like Anna."

"I know!" I shot to my feet, no longer able to hold it in, and began pacing the floor. "She's not his type, for one. Second, why would he come back here after nine years and show his face unannounced at the picnic? Third..." I huffed out and stopped as it struck me. Despite our parting, I thought we'd remained friends. At one time, we'd matched together like apples and caramel, like cheese and wine. We were the Daring Duo, a pair who always got into shenanigans. But Zeth didn't want to be near me now.

After that near-kiss he tricked me with, the only thing I could think about were his last words for me to leave him alone. Those words shouldn't have cut me so deep, yet here I was, thinking deeply about them anyway. No wonder I felt so affected. I was still tied to him by a thread, even if it was thin. Zeth's cruel words to me were born out of bitterness for how I had ended things between us nearly a decade ago. He'd even counted the exact days we'd been apart.

He must really hate me...

"Amby?" Emiline leaned forward on the bed.

I frowned, then heaved a hot breath as I pulled open my dresser drawer to get a new shirt. "I'm fine."

But I wasn't. I wasn't fine, and Emiline knew it. Rather than push the subject, she got to her feet.

"Get dressed and come downstairs. I have supper saved for you. Then maybe we can sit on the deck and have lemonade?"

I nodded, and she squeezed my arm with affection before leaving.

I changed my shirt and glanced around my room. It wasn't as big as the rooms I'd stolen a peek of in Annabelle's house yesterday, but our historic country home was cozy and warm. It had been a family estate for two hundred and fifty years. My father adored Everdeen's history, so much that he invested in the local museum. He did his best to preserve our home too. While a few things had been updated to make life easier for us, especially in the kitchen, he made sure certain pieces of furniture and outdated equipment were well-maintained. We didn't even have electricity, though he was looking into acquiring it.

Ivory wallpaper with burgundy flowers covered the walls of my room, and the wooden floors shone from recent waxing. My dresser was made of fine oak stained in cherry, and the mirror and wash basin matched. It was all so orderly and precise. So very... *Father*.

The green-cushioned window seat, however, was the one thing I loved about this room. I stared at it now, remembering how Zeth used to climb up to my window and sneak inside while the rest of the house slept. For years, it was a way for us to continue our shenanigans. We'd often play tricks on Hattie while she slept before sneaking out to the river till midnight. The year before Zeth left, it had been his way to climb in and meet me in my bed. His scent had stained the sheets for a long time. Even after he'd left, it had taken several washes to remove it.

For months after Zeth had gone, I peered out my window hoping he would return, only for disappointment to smother me every night. Until finally I slept on my left side so I couldn't see the window anymore. The disappointment was easier to deal with that way.

I moved to the door and made my way into the hall. My head was such a mess; I was being pressured to court a woman who was also being pursued by my past lover. I shook my head at the absurdity of the whole situation as I rumbled down the stairs, taking the steps at a hurried pace as always. When I stepped through the foyer and into the parlor, I was surprised to see my eldest sister sitting with my father, a teacup in her hand.

Marigold turned to me with poise. Not a blonde hair was out of place in her neatly styled bun, and judging by her smart dress, she'd come straight from the bank. At thirty, she was already married, and lived close to the bank so she could be there quickly if need be. She was poised and intelligent, much like Annabelle, but her face always held a permanent stone-like expression. Marigold never cared for me, so I never cared for her. We mostly stayed out of each other's way unless forced to converse, like now.

"Ambrose." She dipped her head toward me.

"Marigold." I looked from her to Father, who was still wearing his attire from the picnic. From the tired expression on his face, he no doubt had some sort of lecture he was about to deliver.

Their silence meant they'd been conversing about me before I arrived. That was fine. I would make my way to the kitchen and let them continue their gossip. "Well, I'm going to get a quick bite to eat."

As I started forward, Father's firm voice stopped me in my tracks, "Aren't you going to ask how your sister is doing?"

I clenched my fists before forcing a smile on my face and turning around. "You look well, Marigold," I told her.

Her lips tightened as she eyed me from head to toe. "I wish I could say the same of you."

And there it was. Only one minute in the same room with her and already she was being a thorn in my side. "It was a long day."

"*Very* long," Father piped up. His blue, round eyes found mine. "But I had household duties to attend to once we arrived home, while you stalked off to your room."

"My head was aching, I had to sleep it off."

"Pah," Father waved his hand and raised his pipe to smoke. "When you own this estate, you'll have no time for such things."

I didn't want to engage further in this conversation. Doing so would keep me in the room longer than I wanted to, and my father was determined to deliver a lecture, so I waited.

"Jack and Marigold have turned Somerset and Sons into an increasingly prosperous venture, returning greater dividends each year. One day you'll take the reins at the bank, and you'll need their support. Which reminds me." He puffed generously on his pipe. "I have a position I'd like you to take soon. It'll help prepare you. And of course, Miss Winters' involvement would be especially beneficial in growing our branch numbers."

"You're wanting to expand?" I asked in surprise. Was the Bank really doing so well that my father could afford to establish another branch elsewhere?

"Where have you been in the past year or two, Ambrose?" came Marigold's snide, poised voice, sounding much like the snake she held in my dream. "Certainly not thinking about the family business. Your head is always in the clouds."

I shifted from one leg to the other and cast her a bitter look. It was better than pulling up my middle finger at her. Ignoring the talk about the bank, I glanced at my father and said, "I'm not the only one trying to court Annabelle. You saw everyone around her today. I'm one of many who wish to court her. And Zeth Washer is one of them—"

"Zeth?" Father's brow furrowed in confusion. "Hattie told us she'd seen him at the picnic, but I didn't know he was pursuing Miss Winters. That certainly..."

"Makes things *very* interesting." The annoyed expression that crossed Marigold's features didn't surprise me. She never liked Zeth, and had endlessly lectured me about how rotten a scoundrel he was, and how he would drag me down with him. The joke was on her. I ended up a failure on my own. And Zeth? He wasn't rotten, or a scoundrel, although he acted a bit like the latter earlier...

When my father heaved a long sigh, blowing out smoke with it, I raised my hands.

"But don't worry," I continued. "I'll be taking tomorrow off work so Annabelle and I can spend the day together."

"Oh?" Marigold perked up, as did my father.

"Yes... We'll be taking a stroll to the lake." I paused for a moment before I finished with, "To fish."

Marigold's eyes widened. She sometimes went fishing with her husband, Jack, so I wasn't sure why she was so surprised. "Annabelle Winters doesn't seem the type to do that sort of thing."

"Well, she told me she hasn't been in a while and agreed, so she must enjoy it." I snipped, and when I crossed my arms, my sister smirked.

My father placed his pipe between his lips and grunted his agreement with her, eyeing me as if he was trying to decide whether to laugh or applaud me. Then he muttered, "Bring her flowers."

"You don't want him to overdo it," Marigold intervened. She was right about that, at least. "But I do suggest a gift for her. Women expect gifts."

I nodded, knowing well from our school days that a gift wouldn't flatter Annabelle. She didn't strike me as a material person, though she certainly had a lot of tea sets in that closet... What Marigold should have said was, only women like *her* expect gifts. My sister was vain like that.

"Right, you know, I'll ask Emiline what she thinks right now." I clasped my hands together and turned to make my way into the kitchen.

"Oh, Ambrose," called Marigold's overly confident voice. Freezing, I rolled my eyes before turning to meet her smug expression and waited for her to continue. "Do be sure to wear something less... drab." When she tilted her head, I shot her a sour glare before finally turning and leaving the parlor for the kitchen, where Emiline was shuffling around.

Our maids and cook had already been sent off for the night, so my twin held out a plate of leftover pork chops and vegetables for me.

"Thank you," I told her. Leaning my elbow on the counter, I slowly took a bite of potato. Eager to talk about something other than myself, I asked, "How are you doing at the shop? Arthur give you any raises for all the extra time you've been spending there lately?"

Her lips tugged up at any mention of the tailor shop. She'd been working there for nearly a year, and she loved it. "I'm doing well. Arthur wants to use one of my designs for a dress to present at the showcase in a few months. *The Belle* will be coming here from Port Winchester to make selections for their weekly fashion journal. Ever since Anna went to the City in one of the shop's dresses, we've gotten an influx of attention."

"Em, that's amazing." If anything could brighten my day, it was this. Seeing my sister beaming with pride warmed my soul. "I'm happy for you." I hugged her, and she laughed.

"You can hug Arthur too. I wouldn't be able to have this opportunity without him." The way her cheeks flushed pink had me wondering if she liked Arthur. I knew he'd had eyes for her since he was ten, but I never told her. My dear friend made me swear an oath of silence.

"You'll get your big break too, Amby," Emiline reassured me, and I wondered if she'd taken my sudden silence as a reflection of self-pity. She moved around the counter to grab some cups from the cabinet. "I know you want more than a job at the bank. I feel like one day you'll find it, perhaps sooner than you think."

I shook my head, hoping she didn't mean a life with Annabelle. "I don't want to talk about me."

"No? Perhaps someone else then..." Emiline stood straighter as she set the cups on the counter, brown eyes glimmering in the lamplight. "You seemed rather upset telling me about Zeth earlier. So... what will you do when you come face to face with him again?"

I focused on the glass of the back doors. I didn't want to think about what I'd do, but Zeth's face swept through my mind regardless. All his callous words from earlier washed through me, and this time they reignited my anger. That *almost-kiss* he fooled me with pissed me off the most.

Jerk.

I shoved a piece of broccoli in my mouth, not at all wanting this food but forcing it down anyway.

"It doesn't matter if I see him again," I finally muttered. "*Thieves* and bankers don't mix."

"Oh, Amby," she hummed as she took a jug of lemonade from the counter and poured it into the cups for us. "You're not a banker. And Zeth isn't a thief, no matter what the townsfolk have said about the Washers before. Join me outside when you're ready." She grabbed her cup and made her way out of the kitchen and to the front door.

I only lingered for a moment, taking one last bite of food before picking up my cup and following her. As I came into the foyer, I halted when I caught voices from the front porch. A glance through the slightly open front door revealed my father with his arm around Emiline's shoulders. Father and Em always talked about their day. That was their *thing*. It was clear in the way he held her close that he was proud of her place at the tailor shop. He was proud of Marigold as well, enamored with her mind for business, and bragged about her to his clients and anyone else who would listen. With Hattie, he doted on her acceptance into the nursing institute and spoiled her any chance he got since she was the last child.

And me?

There was nothing special between Father and me. I was his beneficiary because I was a man, and I had downright disappointed him by getting into more trouble than I was worth growing up. His lectures had always been about the school fights I'd gotten into, or the pranks I'd pulled with Zeth and Arthur. He never cared to hear me explain that I never backed down from a fight at school if someone threatened one of my friends, or that I was just a kid having fun. And later on, when I got older, he even knew I preferred men over women and allowed me to rendezvous with a few of them. But at the end of the day, he expected me to marry a woman.

My father had no qualms with same-gender marriages; they'd been accepted for centuries. However, in his own household, the Somerset ancestry was important. His father had passed the house to him, and his father before him, and so on and on, over hundreds of years. They all believed that if our paternal bloodline was broken, it would destroy our family's fortune.

Who was I to ruin centuries of Somerset tradition?

So... I needed to prove myself to my father, to myself. I had to win Annabelle. If Zeth wanted to play games, I'd partake, but I couldn't let him get in the way of carrying on the Somerset legacy.

I couldn't let my father down.

8

Zeth

Waking up in Anna's enormous house was a dream come true. Never had I slept in a bed so comfy. Lazily, I stretched my bare body against the clean sheets—so crisp—and rolled over to face the pretty papered wall of ivory with pearl embellishments. The thick ivory curtains glowed beautifully with the growing spark of a new morning.

The thick blanket felt safe, no wonder Millie wanted so many, but I tossed mine off with a big flourish to slide my legs over the side of the bed. The air was warm. A servant must have stoked the fire before I woke to make sure I was comfortable. I wiggled my bare toes in luxury. How splendid. And even better, my clothes were folded in a stack by the fireplace. Even from the bed, they looked as crisp as the sheets. Hand laundered early this morning by someone besides me.

I could get used to this.

I slipped off the bed and padded my way to the fireplace. Plush carpet squished under my bare heels, followed by smooth hardwood that transitioned to heated tile before the hearth. My clothes sat on a side table. I admired a stiff pleat in my collar with a finger, and lifted the jacket to see if the mud was cleansed from my new pants, and it was. I couldn't help but scoop up the whole pile and hug it close, like a fool.

I buried my nose deep into the cotton to smell how clean it was. Not plain old lye. No, nothing so simple at the Winters estate. My clothes smelled wonderfully like orange essence mixed with starch. Actually, they smelled like money.

Oh yes, I could get very used to this life.

Miss Annabelle Winters—the teacher's pet, always prim and proper with her nose in the air—had welcomed me, the town washer's son, to sleep in her house. She nodded with acceptance to my plans of courting. And I still couldn't believe she wanted to go fishing with me today. She seemed so excited about it as she invited me. She'd practically giggled.

Not wanting to be late, I dressed quickly and visited Millie's room next to mine. She was lying peacefully like a doll in that manly nightshirt. The side table next to her held a glass of water but no more medicine, so she was going to be sleeping for a while. I backed out softly and closed her door to avoid disturbing her recovery.

Someone else helped my baby sister. I pondered that for a moment in the quiet upstairs hall. I wasn't jealous, no. Perhaps a bit relieved? It was a refreshing change, that was for certain. Not a single day passed without feeling the weight of being an older brother and Millie's sole guardian.

Did the rich understand how good they had it? Servants, separate rooms, and lazy mornings? Fishing on a workday for the simple pleasure of sport. No responsibilities. No worries.

Feeling lighter, I bounced my way down the stairs with both hands in my jacket pockets and a whistle on my lips. The jaunty tune wasn't appropriate for mixed company, but the servant standing in the front hall where I landed was a nice-looking chap around my age, and most likely enjoyed a bawdy song when off duty.

He shot me a narrowed gaze from under his dirty blond hair. Then he stiffened his back and uttered, "Good morning, sir."

Okay, maybe he didn't enjoy fun at all, but at least he greeted me.

"Fine morning," I replied with sunshine in my voice. "Has the mistress awoken? We have a date."

The man's mouth twitched, but his face remained impartial. He didn't even look at me. He faced the parlor I used yesterday with Doc Light and waved to that door. "Miss Winters asks that you stay there."

"Of course. Thank you." My murmur might have sounded a bit grumpy. I was just waking, that's all. Nothing to do with how the servant made it sound like I belonged outdoors.

He led me over, so I obeyed and entered, watching the man curiously as he shut me inside, alone. No matter. I didn't care what a servant thought of my visit. Anna wanted to go fishing with me. If all went well, maybe I could give her a courting kiss and propose as early as next week. By summer, that man would work for me.

Straightening my tie and vest, I glanced around at the matching burgundy settees with nice paintings of scenery behind them. A few tables and shelves were cluttered with clocks and useless figurines. I picked up the closest, a shepherdess with sheep, and tipped it over to examine the mark. Huttington, mid-century. Worth a pretty cal. But not my style. Neither were the statues of foppish men in heels nor the various dogs. If Anna wasn't attached to them, maybe I could convince her to sell the knick-knacks. I could auction them off and invest in land.

A soft knock sounded on the door. Anna. She didn't make me wait long.

I quickly repositioned the shepherdess on the side table, making sure she sat just so, and turned to the entrance. Today was the day to woo myself into this home permanently. I put on my most charming and beguiling smile.

The doors opened by the same chap, only this time he sent me a not-so-impartial smirk. Behind him strolled in Amby. My former friend and lover. I asked him to leave me be, yet here he was visiting Anna the very next day. His message was clear that we were enemies, but part of me didn't want to hear it.

That's why my stomach tightened as I drank in his full head of auburn curls, all wind-tossed. His lean chest and stomach showed

73

that he ate well but still stayed active. His deceptively casual jacket and slacks in dark gray with a green, pin-striped vest all looked plain while vomiting wealth. It was in the details. The ebony buttons. The flattering alterations.

I bit back my anger while Amby's lively brown eyes glanced around the parlor for Anna before landing upon me in the middle. That's when his pale face scrunched behind those damn adorable glasses.

Amby nodded at the steward with a "Thank you" and the man shut the doors, closing us together.

My smile soured. "What are you doing here?"

Amby flinched at my harsh tone before glancing away. His lips narrowed, showing some fire still in his spirit, and his jawline appeared a bit pointed at the sides. Strong-willed. Tempting to grab. Was he smooth-shaven or rough from a night's growth? Fuck, why was I even thinking about him? I needed to prove myself to Anna and the town. Whether Amby shaved or not didn't matter one whit.

That strong jaw turned back to face me and broke the silence, "I see Annabelle didn't let the dog out this morning."

A dog? Is that what they all thought of me? "You better watch it, I bite." I snapped, furious.

"Oh, I'm terrified," Amby waved his hands in mock fear.

I growled right back, "You should be."

Pinching my nose allowed me to avoid looking at Amby, but I heard his tsk of annoyance. He flipped my morning into the rubbish, the spoiled brat. He didn't even cushion his words. He was the one who shouldn't be here, who shouldn't be calling me a dog.

I nodded. And nodded. My anxious thoughts all these years were true; he never loved me. He was never a friend. My chest felt a little odd. Funny, I didn't notice how the burgundy color of the settees matched my bleeding heart. And the carved legs, ending in lion's paws with sharp claws—those matched the ones Amby hid in his soft touch all those years.

The settee was over a century old, expensive, and far more valuable than me. I wasn't born with wealth, and that's all that matters to the rich, like Amby. They didn't do manual labor.

They didn't apprentice in the City as I did, working long hours for years to improve my station. Wasn't I better for that? I wasn't a dog. I belonged here, not outside. I learned the manners of a proper gentleman, and could act like a gentleman, even if Amby couldn't.

I nodded again and motioned to the damn settee with the grace of a king. "Have a seat. I'll order tea and biscuits."

There was a bell on the table, so I rang it sharply, and a moment later the chap at the door entered. I stated my order for refreshments. He had the good training to bow quickly before speeding off to the kitchens, though the quick pace might have been due to my imperious glare.

Amby watched the door close and made a sound I used to hear his father make after something impressed him. I ticked that as a win.

"So kind of you to visit. Did you have a nice ride over?" I drawled, sitting with a false calm that hopefully hid my unease. I claimed the spot Anna sat in yesterday and crossed my legs with lazy grace. Leaning back, I looped an arm over the back of the three-person chair while I motioned for Amby to take a seat in the chair facing me.

Amby stubbornly stood firm and tucked his hands into the pockets of his trousers. "What are you doing, Mr. Washer?"

"Isn't it obvious? Making myself at home."

Amby glanced around the room. "But this isn't your home. I wonder if I should let Annabelle know what you're doing. Of how *conniving* you're being."

"That's rather rude. Millie sprained her ankle and Anna invited us to stay." I raked my eyes over him, from his polished shoes to that annoyed twist of lips. "I assure you, the only con here is you, pretending to like women enough to marry one."

I thoroughly enjoyed how Amby's mouth opened and closed as if he had a retort but didn't know how to get it out. His face went red as a tomato too, and my lips tilted with glee at getting the upper hand.

When his awkward arms couldn't decide between crossing or

staying at the sides of his body, pointing that out to him seemed like a fun thing to do. "Stop fidgeting and sit. Tea should arrive soon."

Amby swiftly crossed his arms and stood still in defiance. Maybe he didn't like being told what to do like a dog either. It was difficult to keep the smug feeling from my face, but I managed as I thumbed a crease in my pants.

Amby couldn't come up with something to say back. His face flushed, and that exquisite jaw tightened. Good, he was flustered. He made his way over to one of the end tables beside the settee to fiddle with the shepherdess figurine, poking at it nervously.

Then the figurine fell on the table with a jarring rattle that made us both jump. A second later, the thing's head rolled right off the side and fell onto the carpet in sweet retribution. Oh, Amby was such a troublemaker.

"Shit," he cursed, right as the door opened, and I never saw him move quicker than he did as he picked up the proof of his crime. He stuffed the figurine head into his pocket like a guilty little boy, and I snorted softly at witnessing the poor shepherdess' murder.

"Tea, sirs," a soft voice chimed in. The maid from last night stood in the doorway with a tray and full service. Finally, someone who liked me.

"Ah, Betty, do set it here," I instructed, and waved her to the coffee table at my legs. Amby's gaze shot to me. My familiarity with Anna's household clearly got under his collar. After Betty set the tray down, I nodded her out and sat forward to open a little lid over the sugar. "Still two lumps?"

Amby scowled as he pulled the figurine head from his pocket and tried to place it back on the body. "I'll wait until the lady of the house is here. We have a date."

His stubbornness made my blood boil, so I inhaled the first twenty replies that all started with *fuck you*. Then I used the small tongs that sat on the tray to pinch two cubes and plunk them into the far cup before pouring tea over them. He liked his tea fucking sweet.

In my own empty cup, I splashed the tea in less gently. I liked it bitter. I wanted to taste something other than water.

Dainty biscuits sat on the tray, so I slipped two of those into my jacket pocket to give to Millie later before stuffing another into my mouth. Chewing, I leaned back with my little saucer and cup. They didn't chatter with my frustration, and for that I was grateful. I took a moment to appreciate the red roses on them, matching the settees.

Did Anna have a tea set for every room? She had at least fifteen rooms, not counting service quarters. Did she have a room just for storing all the sets? Did the tea set storage room have a matching tea set too? In case you wanted to drink tea while admiring your tea sets in the damn tea set storage room.

The wealthy were absolutely ridiculous.

And Amby hovering without joining me for breakfast was really pissing me off.

My fingers tightened around the cup as I washed down the food with tea and tried to pay attention to the taste. Not Amby. Not his wayward curls. Not his angry glances.

"So, a date?" I shrugged and grabbed another biscuit. "Funny, I have one as well. Maybe you're here on the wrong day? No matter, you might as well enjoy the tea while you can because you'll hardly appear proper once Anna sees how you beheaded her poor statue. It's forty years old from two regions away. I bet Anna's mother bought it. Pity."

"Oh." Amby nodded. "So, did you and *Annabelle* have a conversation about this particular statue last night? Or are you just making things up as you go?"

"Clever analysis, but no. I studied antiques. Take this—" I was glad my voice sounded calm as I held up my cup and quickly glanced at the maker's mark. A bear with seven stars. "This is a Blesswood from their Eaton factory before it burned down in seventy two. A kiln malfunction. You would think that tragedy raises the value. However, the market is only moderate right now. I'd estimate fetching twenty, maybe more, for a full set of Blesswood, if you gather the right buyers to auction."

It felt good to be talking business again. The rattle of numbers and facts that could be categorized and noted. It eased my frustrations while I filled with pride. I wanted to demonstrate my learning to the very man who thought I was nothing but a thief and a dog. Maybe if Amby understood how hard I worked while away from him, how I funneled my anger and frustrations into learning a prosperous trade... then he would see me differently.

And by the surprised expression on Amby's face, he did appear astonished with my training. "Hm," he started, "Does all your knowledge make it easier to pawn your loot?"

"Fuck you."

The curse flew out quickly, and everything in me deflated. I didn't regret the sound of my bitter anger, not for one second. Amby deserved to feel how deep his snotty insults cut. They cut to the bone.

But he didn't stop. He walked closer to stand over me as he taunted, "Did I strike a nerve? Perhaps, you would rather I just... *leave* you *the fuck* alone."

Before I knew what was what, the tea was gone, set aside, and I was standing in Amby's face. How dare he tease me with my heartfelt request. I glared down at him, happy for the new height between us as he stepped back. But there wasn't a single speck of remorse in Amby's brown expression. Of course not.

Chuckling low, I leaned closer. Amby's legs backed against the end table, making him stagger, yet his burning eyes dared me to proceed. His will to fight sent awareness along my spine. I shook it off because Anna's parlor wasn't the place for a sparring match. Though, that fuming face had me wanting his wonderful ass under my hand. I could grab those wonderful, prominent hips of his to spin him around, and then pull him down over my lap...

Oh, that was damn tempting. My right hand flexed before I curled it tight. No... I could use words. And a commanding voice, "I think you're better than this disrespectful behaviour, aren't you, Rosie?"

Fuck, I missed my name for him on my lips, and judging by the way his cheeks tinted pinker, he did too.

"Why are you cornering me like this, Mr. Washer?" Amby let out a snarky laugh and looked away. "Maybe you should just... back off?" He pushed against my chest with his fist.

I captured his hand and stood my ground. His wide eyes snapped back to me as he tried to pull away, but I unbent his fingers with another purpose, to rescue the little porcelain statue's head. His hand felt warm in mine, and the calluses on his fingers surprised me, not to mention Amby's collection of healing cuts. Even his thumb was bruised. A stupid urge rose in me to ask what caused them, and to take that thumb into my mouth.

No, I didn't need to be thinking like this. Instead, I folded the tempting thumb back in and closed his empty hand, meeting his gaze again. His chin was raised, that defiance still there. I shouldn't like willfulness so much. *Fuck me.* "So... Here's how this proceeds. I'll stop swearing at you, and you'll leave nicely."

Amby snatched his hand free and sneered, "I'm not going anywhere. I'm here to take Annabelle fishing, not indulge in your little ego boost."

"Fishing?" I snorted. It took a lot to ignore the rest of Amby's words. "Anna very intentionally invited me to go fishing with her today. While in my bedroom last night, I might add."

It was low, but the barb hit. Amby's brow gathered, and he stuttered, "W-what? No... *I* specifically asked her yesterday during the picnic."

I didn't know what was going on, but Amby went to grab the porcelain head from my hand, so I jerked my arm away. He stepped forward to wrestle it back, so I flung my fist high to keep it from him. My four-point-five inches on him meant he couldn't reach it without jumping or climbing me, and I dared him to do that with a challenging stare.

It was childish, I know. We used to play like this in our youth, only Amby had the advantage before, and having it now felt far too deliciously thrilling to stop.

"Zeth!" Amby huffed. "Just give me the damn head." He jumped up to grab the piece.

I held it higher with a laugh, nudging him back. When he grabbed my arm, trying to pull it down, I dug my free hand into his curls to hold him still.

Amby gasped, a sharp intake that had me tugging his head

closer by his hair until his lips touched my ear. I wanted to hear him whimper, to make him beg for mercy. Instead, he let out a few soft breaths and gripped my jacket in his hands, as if he wanted more. I felt his anger shift to need...

And fuck me for needing him too. This rough play came out of nowhere, yet it felt so right between us. When Amby used to ask for *more* when we played around, maybe this was what his hints meant. He wanted to be roughed around and shown how much I needed him, how much I wanted him, instead of passively obeying his commands. Because he was certainly enjoying my fist in his hair, making him whimper.

"Such a hungry boy." I tilted closer to purr into his ear, hearing my own voice coming out harsh and approving. "You don't want me to play nice, do you?"

Amby clenched his jaw against mine for a rough second before he asked, "I don't deserve nice, do I?"

"No." I fisted my hand tighter, keeping him in my arms as I considered how much pain hid behind his words. Maybe I wasn't the only one hurting with memories and regrets. I'd probably never know, but I knew I wanted what I could take of him in this lonely moment. His curls were so soft and slick in my fingers, his body hot against mine, his breath desperate in my ear. I tugged him even closer and rubbed my unshaved cheek against his.

That sharp jaw of his felt incredibly smooth, and for a moment, he gripped me tighter.

"Zeth..." Amby exhaled, his fingers uncurling in my jacket. He placed his palms against my chest and pushed slightly. "Let me go."

When my hand released his hair, he shoved me away with enough force to make me stagger back. Like the dog he thought I was, the bastard.

A door opened a second later, and a polite voice asked, "Am I interrupting?"

Both of us froze with guilt before spinning to where Anna stood in a pretty blue dress that no doubt cost a month of my former salary.

Amby was quick. He smoothed out his hair with a chagrined

expression. "Annabelle, you look beautiful this morning." Then he stepped forward and nodded at her. "Zeth and I were just discussing pottery. Who knew he was so good with history?"

"Because I'm an auctioneer and appraiser," I clarified with some spite. *Not a thief.*

Amby turned and regarded me with a mixture of surprise and doubt. Of course he thought I was lying. That's what crooks did, lied and stole.

He wasn't completely wrong to doubt me, because I was lying slightly. I lost my job. I was fibbing by omission, and felt bad about it, but Amby wasn't innocent either.

"Ambrose broke your figurine." I pointed a thumb at him before clasping my hands behind my back to hide the head.

Caught, Amby stiffened. He stared at Anna and her eyes widened, a teacher-marm expression that had Amby clearing his throat before swiftly saying, "My sincerest apologies, Annabelle. I-I can reimburse you for it, or perhaps we can go to town so you can pick something else out to replace it?"

Weaseling another date out of his error? Tossing around his money. Perfect play.

Anna was smart. Did she not see through Amby's insincerity?

Her smoothing brow said she didn't. Typical. Being a cute, rich boy had always excused Amby's misconduct while I received the blame. I was named the troublemaker. Pinching the bridge of my nose didn't suppress my scornful, "Spoiled brat."

Amby flinched and glared at me, hearing the slip. It didn't bring me any joy... because I was better than this. Why was this brat dragging out my worst? Fighting, flirting, and cursing.

"Oh, Ambrose, don't worry about that old thing." Anna waved it off with amused warmth, shining from him to me, and back. "Home is where the heart is, after all, not in material possessions. That's what my mother always told me."

I scoffed at the weak sentiment. Her mum was a fool to recite such flowery nonsense. But then, matching tea sets granted her the luxury of platitudes, didn't it? Anna owned enough *material possessions* to comfortably believe that possessions don't matter. Anna probably owned a pillow with her mum's nonsense embroidered right into it.

My fist clenched.

Well, I could burn the embroidered pillow once we married, but first I had to add my apology to Amby's stack. "I'm sorry too, Anna, for my rudeness. I don't know what got into me."

I refrained from shooting an accusing glare at Amby, just barely. That's what the old me would do, to make sure Mrs. Marsh struck both our hands with a ruler for being rambunctious boys in the classroom.

But I was a grown man now, for fuck's sake. I moved through the parlor with only Anna in my sight. Her lovely braids circled her head like a golden halo, and her delicate eyebrows rose higher with each claiming step I took until I joined her by the doorframe. She didn't look awed by my magnificence as she tilted her head at me, but she did appear slightly interested. It was a start. It was something.

I offered her my arm in gratitude. "Shall we go fishing now? You said you know of a secret spot on your property?"

"Yes, where Annabelle and I were going to fish," Amby had the nerve to say while fixing me with his hard eyes. He approached Anna and offered his arm as well. His posh clothes were nicer than mine. He didn't need to do much to show me up. Even his offer to Anna sounded smooth, "Shall we?"

And she laid her delicate hand on Amby's arm. She fucking took his arm. They made a dashing pair while I was left lowering my offer. That was my lot, my place. I didn't need them to point it out, especially when Amby's sassy grin said he won that round. That grin only grew as he led Anna out to the hall, where we stopped for our caps. When we reached the door, Anna asked me to grab the fishing gear like their servant.

Amby was beaming.

Oh... I knew how to wipe that smirk off his handsome face.

But I waited. It took devious patience while Anna led us toward the lake that Millie and I discovered yesterday. I let Anna and Amby walk together along a trail leading to the woods. I strolled behind them with the fishing poles over my shoulder and the basket containing the bait and extra hooks swinging lazily in my hand. My only goal was to appear like the perfect picture of an entitled man.

I waited while a chill breeze made Anna shiver, and Amby offered his jacket to her. That was fine, the whole chivalrous jacket thing was passe. I ignored the fuss she made. And I ignored Amby's shirtsleeves, with that fine white material that exposed some definition in his arms, as if the man labored in some way, or how his green pinstripe vest was tailored nicely to a trim waist and round ass. I didn't focus on that at all. Instead, I thought about all the ways I might mess with him once we started fishing. Ways I could steal Anna's attention.

I even waited while we peacefully made our way through the woods, so that Amby's guard could lower. When Anna laughed politely at his conversation, Amby—*Ambrose*—looked over at me with snarky pleasure for entertaining her in front of me.

That was my signal. I came up beside him and leaned toward him with an innocent blink of my lashes, and asked in my most curious voice about the one thing Ambrose hated the most, "Mr. Somerset, why don't you tell us about your business? Are you managing the bank yet?"

9

Ambrose

My body went rigid at Zeth's question. To say I was unprepared was an understatement. I was *never* prepared to talk about *Father's* banking business. I hated banking, and that hadn't changed since we were kids, so why was Zeth torturing me with it now? No doubt to thumb a sore spot.

I had done well so far in keeping myself poised in front of Annabelle, so I paused briefly to think of a reply before answering, "I'm working my way up to managing the bank. In fact, I'll begin training soon. It's quite a lot to learn as I climb the ladder, but I'm enjoying it."

"Oh, really?" Zeth tilted his head. "Which part do you like?"

"Ah... granting loans," I hedged. He didn't need to know that delivering mail was what I liked most.

"Delightful," Zeth hummed, sounding for all the world like he caught me lying. My body flushed despite the chilly breeze.

We needed to drop this subject, fast. I locked eyes with Zeth's golden hues, quickly darting them toward Annabelle and back. My warning had to be clear that talking about the bank made me nervous. But Zeth smirked, as if he had more up his sleeve.

"We should visit the bank this week, Anna, to witness Ambrose hard at work," Zeth continued. "His bookish nose buried deep in paperwork. Could be entertaining."

My, he was persistent in humiliating me. "Loans are hardly entertaining," I corrected. Did he think I looked bookish because of my glasses? I pushed them up my nose, hating how right he might be.

"I never thought you'd work in the bank," Zeth pressed on, undeterred. "You never had an interest in it when we were younger. In fact, I remember when you wanted to throw eggs..." Zeth paused for a moment before he shook his head. Maybe he was reliving the pain of falling from the chicken coop and injuring his shoulder. It still pained me as well, and I winced just thinking about it. I never meant for him to get so hurt from a *dare*. But Zeth didn't seem bothered now as he dug up our past. "Aye, why don't *you* tell Anna about your plan to egg your father's establishment on the day of the Founders Day festival?"

"Oh, Ambrose, you wouldn't! Is that why you dared Zeth to climb the chicken coop?"

"Zeth told you about that?"

Amusement glimmered on Annabelle's face as she nodded. I didn't want her to think I wished harm to my father's business like a naughty child. It didn't matter that we were children. It was supposed to be a secret. All our adventures were a secret between me and Zeth. And he'd betrayed our trust.

My nose twitched, and I shot him a spiteful stare. When Zeth flashed a devilish grin, I decided to turn the tables. "Enough about me, Mr. Washer. I imagine auctioneering has some excitement. Where do you work?"

Zeth delayed a moment, glancing forward, no doubt to come up with his next lie. "Ah, looks like we arrived."

Is he serious?

I fumed inwardly but let his diversion go since we indeed had reached the lake. The path opened up to a large body of clear, greenish-blue water. The sun peeked over the surrounding tree tops, the rays of light creating a lovely morning haze.

Annabelle nudged me over to a log that was strategically placed by the water. Zeth followed and set the basket down, his lean body moving gracefully. I thought tall men were supposed to be awkward in their limbs. Damn myself for admiring how he'd grown in all the right places.

When he straightened and held a fishing pole out to me, I eyed him with distrust. With how childish he'd acted with the broken statue head, he was bound to throw the pole in the grass or accidentally break it. To my surprise, he handed it over.

Good. Hopefully, this was the start of him toning down his backhanded comments and jokes. If he did, I'd offer him the same grace.

"You get the shortest pole, pipsqueak," Zeth teased with a playful wink.

And there it was. I should have known he wasn't done with the insults. I snatched up the pole, especially annoyed by that outrageous wink. Zeth's words and actions held some warmth, as if he liked me a little shorter than him. I had to admit, I liked it too.

No, *no*, I didn't like it. I didn't like how tall he was, or his stupid wink.

Zeth turned and sat on the far edge of the log while Annabelle joined him. Reluctantly, I followed, sandwiching her in.

Annabelle didn't need any fishing lessons from me or Zeth, and I was happy to see how she took control when I offered to help bait her hook, as I used to bait Zeth's. He hated bugs and anything that crawled. Annabelle, however, dug into the small container of worms I'd brought as if unbothered.

Zeth sat there eyeing the bucket of dirty worms with distaste. Or eyeing me with distaste. That part wasn't clear.

"Come on, you two, let's relax and have some fun," Annabelle told us.

"Hmm," Zeth agreed to having fun without agreeing. He squinted in the mid-morning light as he touched different parts of his pole. "I haven't fished much, and I'm a bit of a City boy now." He glanced at Annabelle. "Would you mind showing me how it's done?"

My eyes narrowed as I baited my own hook and ignored his fat lies. Fishing when we were boys had been one of our favorite pastimes. This was also how Zeth fed his family during most of the summer. We often spent our afternoons catching enough for all the Washers to eat.

As I watched him eye the pole while Annabelle instructed him on where to hold it and how to reel, I wondered if he *had* come into some money. Maybe Zeth really hadn't fished in years. Perhaps he was only worming his way into Annabelle's affections by trying to be charming, in an aggressive way. Or maybe he wanted Annabelle to grip his pole.

"Yes, you've got it now. You're a quick learner," Annabelle assured him.

When she turned to me, I felt stupidly tempted to forget how to fish too. Instead, I stood to toss the line out with a skilled snap. After the bobber hit the water, I settled on the log again with a rather dull sigh.

Annabelle straightened. "I'm sure Ambrose wouldn't mind giving you a few tips as well."

"Oh, for the love of—he doesn't need..." I immediately stopped myself. Just being in this man's presence made it so easy to fall into the lax man I was around Emiline or Hattie. I couldn't let Annabelle hear how improper I really was when no one was looking. Clearing my throat, I asked, "So, Mr. Washer, how long are you staying in Everdeen? Don't you have to get back to your job in Port Winchester?"

He flinched from my reminder that he still owed us an answer. It felt like there was more to the whole appraiser thing, so it was better to make Zeth ruin his own chances with Annabelle. Besides, I was curious if he planned on staying in Everdeen.

"I'm between jobs," Zeth smoothly quipped a non answer. The way his shoulders tensed was a sure sign he was fibbing. "We moved from the City because Mum just passed."

"Oh," Annabelle replied softly, reaching her free hand out to pat Zeth's shoulder.

My mouth fell open. The news pained me. I knew how much Zeth loved his mother. I recalled eating dinner at the Washer's shop every now and then growing up. I didn't realize until later that she had spared her own plate to give to me, something that made me full of remorse.

And now she was gone...

I swallowed hard and watched my line in the water. After a moment, my eyes drifted over at Zeth again, that barb in my heart digging deeper. I wanted to give him a hug right then to comfort him. Instead, I opened my mouth to tell him how sorry I was for his loss.

"I'm—"

"My condolences," Annabelle cut me off and leaned into him. "I understand how hard loss can be. Both my parents are gone too."

The way Zeth blinked back tears had me feeling bad for being so frustrated with him, which only made me angry at myself. When Zeth sniffed and leaned behind Annabelle's back to raise a challenging eyebrow at me, I met his gaze with confusion. Was he using his dead mother to gain Annabelle's sympathy? If so, he really was a dog.

He even made a show of clearing his throat before going on, "We returned half a week ago with plans to sell the laundry. There's a lot to repair, but I hope to stay in Everdeen once I'm done settling Mum's estate. I wish to start a family here." He paused to dab at a tear. "If all goes to plan, I'll open my own auction house."

"That's a fine idea," Annabelle agreed, receptive to Zeth's suggestions.

I gripped my fishing pole so hard I thought it might snap. The feeling of wanting to hug him and console him, but also wanting to slap him, confused me more than anything.

When Annabelle's line tugged tight, she pulled it up and began reeling it in. That's when Zeth—the bastard—had the gall to *smile* around her at me so wickedly that I felt I might combust right on the spot.

Breathing in deep, I collected myself. I could fight fire with fire. I had prospects, a large estate, a family name steeped in Everdeen's history, while Zeth had half-truths and handsome grins. I couldn't let him win. "Well, I suppose there's decent money to be had in the laundry if you sell it." I watched as Annabelle reeled in a fish, and for some reason, the idea of Zeth selling the laundry pained me. "Do let me know if you need a loan for a new home, Mr. Washer."

"Oh, how marvelous of you to offer, Ambrose!" Annabelle leaned back as she pulled the line, struggling a bit to reel the fish in.

"I, um, I *also* am thinking of starting a family in the near future, and hope to court someone soon," I added spur of the moment, wishing that hadn't sounded so stupid. But I'd opened my mouth, might as well finish this. "Perhaps a *strong* woman. Smart, sophisticated, one who's independent and can handle her own—"

"Got it!" Annabelle exclaimed and rushed to her feet as the fish popped out of the water. A rainbow trout flapped around on her line, and I sympathized with the dangling creature. I dropped my gaze to my shoes, wondering if she'd even heard me. My tongue went drier than a desert might feel in summer, yet Annabelle said nothing.

"Quite the proposal, Mr. Somerset," Zeth teased softly beside me.

I shot him an angry reprimand.

He shifted his fishing pole from one hand to the other, his eyes on the lake. "That was so romantic, my heart is practically melting. If you're handing out lazy proposals, why not toss one at me? Oh, that's right, because you don't think I'm good enough for you."

I let out a breath, baffled, and even Annabelle glanced over at us with curiosity as she wiggled the fish from her hook.

Zeth's gaze rose to her too, and the man actually looked embarrassed for a moment before he corrected himself with a bored shrug. "Not good enough to be your friend, that is."

It was too late. His cover-up didn't hide what he really meant. My jaw fell open again. I was starting to feel like the poor fish gasping in Anna's fingers. This whole time, Zeth thought I saw him as not good enough for me? I had *loved* him, and judging by my emotional chaos since seeing him again, I was almost certain I'd never gotten over him.

Anger coiled in my stomach at the unfairness of his accusation. I stood to my feet, eyes fixed on his fake smile. I wanted to punch him.

"They say old friends can make the best partners," Annabelle suddenly chimed in to sweetly advise before tossing her fish back in the water.

What in the world did she mean by that? I'd certainly never heard that saying before.

Zeth sighed deeply and set his pole down before standing to face me too. I couldn't believe how hard his eyes glittered as he watched me fume, even though he spoke to her, "Be careful, Anna, old friends know exactly how to hurt you the most."

"What are you going on about? You think I wasn't hurt when you left Everdeen?" I snapped back, too furious to ignore him anymore.

Zeth's gaze narrowed at me. "Oh, I'm sure you cried onto your quiche the first morning, and then quickly forgot about me before lunch."

I tossed my pole to the ground and stepped forward, forcing him to retreat a squishy step into the waterlogged mud on the shore of the lake. That made Zeth squint with distaste, and before I knew it, I raised my arms and planted both my palms on his chest to push him forcefully into the water.

Zeth fell backward, but his hand curled in my vest and jerked me forward with him. Suddenly I was falling too. My feet hit the slick mud first, and I only managed a few steps before I stumbled right into the water on top of Zeth. We were a tangle of limbs, both struggling for purchase. The water was still shallow enough here that I could sit up, but Zeth pushed me right back down.

I hissed, and as he tried to stand I grabbed his leg and tripped him face-first into the lake. He sank into the mud and then rose sputtering like some sort of sea monster.

"Ambrose, you little shit!" Zeth growled with a shake of his hands to fling the glop at me. It splattered against my glasses, and they drooped down my nose.

Zeth huffed for a moment before he leaned forward swiftly. I flinched, ready to start throwing punches if I had to, but he only reached for my glasses and gently removed them, so I faltered. When he threw me a handsome, blurry smile, I wondered if we were about to shake hands and call a truce. Instead, his fist curled in my shirt, and the mud slipped out from under me. I tried to clutch Zeth's shirt to hang onto him as the world spun. I only managed a yelp as Zeth threw me into the deeper water.

A shock of ice bolted through me. I swam up until I broke free with a big inhale. I wiped my eyes and found Zeth before me, his back turned as he tried to escape the scene. Growling, I lunged toward him and grabbed his waist to pull him under, and we both plunged this time.

Hands pushed me down hard, and water rushed up my nose until I choked. And then the hands pulled me free from the water. I coughed and gagged as my feet miraculously found the bottom of the lake, and I scrambled to shallow water. I wiped the hair from my eyes to see Zeth storming up the shore.

Annabelle watched us emerge from the water with her hands over her mouth. Zeth reached her first, a soggy mess, and handed her something. He glared back at me before kneeling to grab his cap and pack up the fishing gear. Even from here, I could see the roughness of Zeth's movements and the stiffness of his back as his jacket clung to his broad, muddy shoulders. My legs felt shaky, but I managed to plough my way to the shore to join them at the log.

I found my cap in the mud and grimaced as I picked it up. Annabelle met me with a sympathetic gaze as she held my glasses out to me.

I took them and blew the water off before sliding them over my ears. They were bent, as Annabelle didn't look quite right through the splotchy glass.

Wincing, I took them back off and pocketed them inside my soaked vest. They would have to be fixed later. I watched as Zeth dug into his jacket pocket and pulled something out with a light growl.

When he shook the pocket contents off, soggy biscuit chunks fell to the ground. I squinted at them in confusion, recalling the times he'd pocketed food to take home to Millie when he was younger... and poor. Was he taking food from Annabelle's because he needed it?

My stomach tightened with worry.

"Can you see alright, Ambrose?" Annabelle touched my arm.

A cool breeze blew through my soaked clothes, and I spoke through chattering teeth, "I'm fine. My glasses may be broken, though."

"Damn it all," Zeth growled, stepping his long legs over the log to reach me. "I didn't break your glasses. Do you think I'm a complete ass?"

"I didn't say you broke them," I sassed. "Only bent them."

He grabbed me by my shirt collar to pull me up to see him eye to eye. I grabbed his arms to steady myself and raised my chin to challenge that determined low brow on his furious face. I wouldn't back down from a fight.

"Go ahead, hit me," I seethed, my voice full of fire. "I told you I'm not afraid of you."

Something in his dark eyes faltered, a slight dent that told me he wouldn't lay a hand on me. He let me go, and my heels hit the solid ground again. Then he grabbed the fishing gear and stomped past Annabelle and me, apparently done with us.

Annabelle rushed behind Zeth, calling out to him, "You can both change into dry clothes at the house!"

Puffing out my cheeks, I trudged after them both. After pushing Zeth in the lake, I felt somewhat bad, but his drenched suit made my lips twitch, because honestly, he'd deserved a dunking for insulting me. In the distance, Annabelle and Zeth became blurry. It was easy to keep track of her blue dress, though my fast pace had me tripping over every tree root in the way to catch up to them.

"Are you alright without your glasses, Ambrose?" Annabelle asked. "I can help lead you back if not."

"Oh, nonsense, I'm not that blind." As soon as the words left my mouth, my foot hit a root, and I stumbled right to my knees like the awkward idiot I was.

"Oh, Amby!" Annabelle cried so loudly, the birds flocked from the trees above. At least she was concerned enough to use my nickname. It honestly made me feel bad for how much I was pretending to want her as a wife.

Heavy footsteps squelched toward me seconds later, and I found Zeth's muddy shoes in my path. I glanced up to see him standing before me, still looking furious, but he offered a hand to help me.

I didn't feel like pressing him further, so I took his hand and stood with pride, despite the fact that my clothes were heavy with water. My thin shirt clung like a second skin, and my shoes were squishy. My hair must be a frazzled mess too.

"Thanks," I muttered.

Zeth answered with a stiff arm offered out, as any fine gentleman might. I stared at him in a battle of wills, noticing how strands of his dark hair hung around the sides of his forehead.

Annabelle walked by with a chuckle that said we were being idiots and continued along the path. She knew how close we'd been growing up, but she didn't know we'd been lovers for a whole year before we parted. She seemed amused by our childish spats. "I'll meet you two at the house. Take your time."

Zeth looked like he was going to stand there offering to help until moss grew on his feet. Rather than continue our stubbornness, I grabbed his wet jacket sleeve with my other hand, so it wasn't so intimate.

He started forward with one arm balancing the poles and basket, and the other arm balancing me. I trusted him to lead me for some reason. His soft grunts told me when to lift my feet over roots, and I wanted to tease him for the silent treatment. I let him seethe instead, and opted to squint at the scenery as we walked.

When a breeze blew our way, I shivered and inadvertently coiled against him. Kicking myself for my actions, I drew away slightly, wishing for my jacket that still warmed Annabelle. When I glanced at Zeth, my heart stilled. He stared intently at me, as if trying to figure me out. What did he see? Why was he looking at me?

It didn't matter. I turned to face ahead again, feeling somewhat vulnerable now.

Zeth stopped and set the basket aside while I took the moment to rub my arms through the wet sleeves. He shuffled around me, and then something heavy plopped onto my shoulders. His jacket. He had given me his *jacket*. Yes, it was waterlogged, muddy even, but he'd put it on me regardless to ward off the chill. And God, how *good* it smelled, even being wet; like Zeth himself, a mixture of soap and skin that was *him*. My teeth clenched as I pulled it tighter around me by the lapels and continued on at his side until we reached the end of the path.

Annabelle's estate loomed in front of us. Zeth dropped off the fishing gear at the back door before we rushed inside. By now, I had shrugged off Zeth's jacket and hung it on a peg, along with my cap, and made my way over to Annabelle.

"I apologize for dripping all over your floor," I said.

"Don't make a fuss, Amby. You and Zeth should get into some dry clothes. Zeth, you know where the Ivory Room is. Please lead Amby there, and I'll have Betty sort through and deliver some of my father's clothes to the room."

Zeth's jaw tightened. I wondered if he didn't like being ordered by our hostess. If he actually *wanted* to wed Annabelle, he would have to get used to a strong woman telling him what to do.

When he turned for the stairs, I followed. We made our way along the upstairs hall until we reached a door. Zeth opened it to step inside, and when I followed him in, I realized why it was called the Ivory Room as the walls blurred white.

Well, I couldn't blame Zeth for wanting something like this. That's what he was after, wasn't he? Annabelle's riches? This house? The vase...

I unknotted my tie and began to undo my vest. Around the fourth button, I froze, realizing we were no longer young men used to walking naked around each other, but grown men who hadn't seen each other in nine years. It felt so natural to strip in front of Zeth, and that fact alone made my cheeks heat.

Perhaps Zeth thought the same because his tie, vest, and shirt all sat half off his right shoulder, and his arms were frozen too. A mark on him caught my attention, so I shuffled forward to see better, hands still stuck on my own buttons. His back was to me. I knew he heard my shoes squeak, but he remained rooted to the carpet as I leaned in.

His sleek muscle was marred with a jagged scar on his upper shoulder, midway between neck and joint. That was the exit wound from the fence post, and it wasn't pretty. From the exit, a long, smooth scar ran up and over the top of his shoulder to connect with the matching wound that I knew marred his chest.

I winced as I envisioned the fence post impaling him there, recalling how scared I'd been that he might die that day. I had cried for hours as I waited for Doc Light to help him.

I lost Zeth anyway. My time with him had happened, and now it was gone. He wasn't back in Everdeen for me. He was here for Annabelle. And I had ruined his morning plan to woo her into courting. But dammit, *I* was trying to woo her too. Still, that *one* thing he'd said that pushed me over the edge tugged at my mind, and I had to ask.

"Do you really think it only took me one morning to get over you?"

Zeth's head tilted, then he inhaled sharply. His shoulder blades tightened. He didn't answer. I shook my head, frustrated. When something thumped against the chamber pot, I looked over to see Zeth's crumpled shirt there.

I turned, ready to lay into him about how clothes should go into the linen basket, but when my eyes landed on his bare back, my breath hitched. Good God above, his arms and shoulders were wonderfully muscular. The very sight of him made my blood rush so hot through my body that I was sure Zeth could feel the warmth radiating from me. I tilted my head to get a better view of those muscles in his back, all the way to his waist.

I had to stop myself from groaning.

I bit my lip and turned away, annoyed with myself for getting stirred by him. His silence was even more irritating. I suppose he was going to continue acting like a child. Looking around, I found the linen basket near the window and pranced over to drop my vest there instead.

"Well, at least I'm a gentleman and don't throw things where they don't belong." I pulled my shirt out from my trousers and started to unbutton it. "I also answer when someone is trying to talk to me."

Zeth's arms paused for a moment before he slipped his thumbs under his waistband and pushed his clinging trousers down, exposing an exquisite ass. My eyes widened as I stared. It was round in all the right ways, with little dimples in each cheek. I fondly remember pushing my thumbs into each dimple and teasing him. Such a thought had fire filling my face again as Zeth kicked his socks and trousers off and bent over to gather the mess. And that round ass filled my vision again. When he stood, I roved over the front of his lean body, recalling the feel of every curve and bump on him. Those curves were more defined now, and that chest of his had much more hair. God, how I wanted to explore him.

Oh shit.

I turned around as I pulled my shirt off, trying my best to ward away past feelings that were rousing all parts of me. No, no, this wasn't good.

I cleared my throat. "Would you mind changing somewhere else?"

Zeth huffed softly. When his trousers hit the linen basket right next to me with a loud slap, I jumped and spun around to see him glaring at me. There was a different heat there, something that made it clear Zeth wasn't going to leave. Instead, he started across the room toward me.

I raised my chin again, trying hard not to lower my gaze as I took a step back, but he stopped within arm's length of me. "Are you going to speak to me now... or are you going to continue the childish antics?"

"Do I look like a child?" Zeth growled softly, and no, he didn't appear childish at all. His strong presence was so overwhelming that I didn't hear his next words as he closed the space between us. His fingers curled into my waistband, and he tugged me forward so hard I stumbled into him.

I grunted, my hand grabbing his arm for stability. Then I did something I shouldn't have. I locked eyes with him, staring daggers at him as I pushed my other hand slightly against his bare chest, surprised by the springy feel of hair there, but I wasn't ready to move away.

His sharp knuckles felt good against my stomach as he held me close.

"Are you still a child?" he challenged in a hushed whisper.

Goosebumps rose along my skin. "No. You're the one who tricked me yesterday with that would-be kiss. Such a hit below the belt."

"I couldn't stop myself from touching you, and that made me angry at myself and you," he admitted while his gaze dropped to where my hand lingered in the hair over his heart. Zeth's rough hands dug deeper into my waistband, making me gasp. His eyes sparked as they watched my reaction. "Just like how we can't stop touching now."

I stared at him for a long moment, ready to give him that kiss anyway. So much that I even leaned into him. Zeth seemed willing and ready to kiss me back. But I let out an exasperated sigh. Nothing good could come from kissing while naked in Annabelle's *house,* of all places. Especially with how tense Zeth still felt. I needed to know what he was thinking.

"Are you going to talk to me now, then?" I asked. "Since you enjoy touching me so much."

Zeth laughed. "You want to chat? About what? About how you broke my heart? So... how long did you mourn me then? A week? A month?"

"A few *years.*" I exhaled and focused on his perfect golden-brown eyes. My stomach fluttered from the way Zeth regarded me as if he was willing to listen further, but was unsure what to expect. "I finally had to accept that you weren't coming back. My heart broke too." I felt the beats beneath my palm pick up.

One of Zeth's hands rose to cup my chin, and he nudged me up to meet his gaze again, where I found him staring at me with something between disbelief and awe. His brow knitted tightly. "If you were so heartbroken, why did you tell me to forget you? To not write? To let you marry? That made me think you didn't care. That you never cared about me."

My stomach knotted, making me feel sick. I could have told him I tried to write to him, but my letters were always returned. Either he'd returned them, or I'd gotten the wrong address. Judging by what he'd said, it was the latter. "My father..." I started, afraid of how to tell him how much my father badgered me about marrying. "He expects me to marry and carry on the Somerset name... I don't have a choice."

"Don't toss the same shit in my face, Amby." Zeth pulled his hand from my chin, and I instantly missed it. "You refused my suit because I was the poorest kid in town daring one of the richest boys to marry me. And I don't even blame you for choosing money over me, but I wish you had fought to be with me. Just say the truth, you used me. I was never important to you."

"No." I shook my head frantically. "No. Zeth, that isn't true..." I wasn't sure how to put my thoughts into words. They were all in a jumble. "I was afraid... I was stupid. A coward." I *wanted* to talk to him, but nothing I was saying was coming out right.

Zeth cut his gaze away from me as he spat out, "You're afraid to lose your wealth and position. I understand perfectly, but do you want children? Do you honestly want to marry Anna?"

Fear gripped me as my father's words rang in my head, about our ancestry, our deep familial roots. My body trembled as I closed my eyes and nodded. "Yes... I do."

"Huh, you're still a poor liar, Amby."

Zeth's quick fingers appeared at the buttons of my trousers, slipping them free within seconds. My eyes popped open, and I tried to push his hands away, but Zeth was too strong and nimble, and with a *whoosh* he pulled my trousers straight down until they tangled at my knees. I let out a breath of shock.

"Sit," Zeth commanded sharply. I didn't know where that deep, manly voice emerged from. I tripped back rather than sat on my own, not even knowing a chair was behind me until my ass hit it hard with a slap I felt in my balls, and Zeth purred, "Good boy."

I blinked at him as heat rose in my face. No one had ever uttered such a thing to me. It had me swooning, and my whole body simmered with a strange fire. This was a new side of Zeth I'd never seen before.

His movements slowed as he bent on one knee to pull each of my wet shoes off before setting them neatly at my side. He lifted my legs up next to pull off my trousers, and I didn't even care to argue.

Next went my socks in a delicious roll of wet wool that exposed my feet and the bumps the fabric made in my skin, but Zeth rubbed those out with a strong thumb stroke that had me nearly groaning. Maybe Zeth disliked me, but the way he was taking care of me right now told me otherwise. He was hurt, angry, and taking it all out on me. And I deserved it.

Zeth was right, I was a poor liar, because the truth was I loved everything he was doing to me now, while hating the fact I was pursuing my father's plans.

My body responded as Zeth tossed my soggy clothes into the basket. I covered myself quickly with my hands while he moved away to rummage through the clothes basket. Then something touched my ears and nose. My glasses.

They still had a splotch of dried mud in one corner, but I could see through them now. Zeth had straightened them, not perfect, but enough. It was a caring thing to do. My chest struggled to move as I blinked up at him like a lost puppy.

The firm curves of his shoulders and neck were brilliantly outlined in the hazy light from the windows. This close, I could see the goosebumps rising on his skin. All of it snatched my breath away, especially when he'd commanded me to sit. *Good boy.* Those two simple words made me feel... desired. I wanted to hear him say it again.

I was suddenly all too aware of the distraction between my legs. Zeth also seemed aware, as his eyes drifted down to see how badly I was covering my excitement.

"Good luck with that marriage, Ambrose," Zeth huffed at me and turned away.

Confusion swept over me. Was he going to act as though he also didn't get aroused from undressing me? Another ruse, cleverly played out, the devil. Even so, I watched those beautiful ass dimples stomp over to the bed. Zeth swiped a blanket from the top. He tossed the heavy thing to me, and I barely had time to wrap my whole body in it before footsteps echoed outside in the hall.

Zeth stripped off a sheet to wrap around his waist like a skirt just as someone rapped against the door. Guilt hit me as Annabelle's maid entered and curtsied with a pile of clothes. She set them against the wall and slipped right back out.

Without a word, Zeth moved to pick up the clothes and sorted them out on the bed. Not once did he look at me. We were back to the silent treatment. He had tricked me again, into responding to him physically to prove that I was still interested in him. In men.

He remained calm as he chose a pair of trousers, while my head was spinning. Zeth's presence made me so flustered. He was the first person in years to see right through my facade. He knew I didn't want to marry a woman. He knew I didn't want to be a banker. He also knew how to make my body *sing*. I wanted him to touch me more, and then just as powerfully, I knew this had to stop. As he'd rudely pointed out, I had too much to lose.

I huffed, "The next time we meet, you'll do well to keep your hands off me."

"Then stop looking at me with those doe eyes," Zeth muttered. "It's almost like you want to distract me, but it won't work again."

My lips twitched, as it made sense now. I was a *distraction* to his goal to marry Annabelle. Or perhaps, a temptation. Well, Zeth did say may the best man *win*.

Standing up, I let the blanket fall from my frame and walked casually to the pile of clean clothes in front of him. Hoping to give him an eyeful, I bent and picked up a shirt. I would become the perfect distraction. Let's see who won this game.

10

Zeth

"Ow! Zeth, are you trying to sprain my ankle again?"

"Of course not," I grumbled at Millie, half listening to her complaints while helping her dress the next morning. Trying to get her injured foot into an everyday skirt should have been child's play, but here we were in Mum's old bedroom with Millie balancing on one foot while I squatted to hold the skirt low enough for her to step in.

It didn't help that I was distracted. Ever since seeing Amby's round ass strutting in front of me yesterday in the Ivory Room, with those perfect hips, I couldn't think straight. And his blissed out expression after I called him a good boy... Fuck, he got me heated. I never realized how thrilling it might feel to take control over him and also take care of him. I longed to wrap Amby in a warm towel to dry his wayward curls while also wanting to spank his ass for being such a brat.

Millie's fingers dug into my shoulders like an eagle's claws to draw me back to the task, damn her. I grunted and nudged her injured foot into the circle and hefted the skirt's waistband over her thighs. Although we bought the skirt last month, the waistband strained at her hips, and I needed to tug and wiggle the fabric up to her waist. Millie snorted softly at my efforts.

I was glad my actions didn't offend her. I stood and stepped around to her back, tucking in her shirt as I went. Then I pulled the waist strings tight, looped two rabbit ears, and tied the knot snug. It felt good to succeed at something so domestic and nurturing, to feel needed.

"You could have just tossed the skirts over my head, you know. It's easier," Millie teased, unappreciative. All domestic bliss went out the window.

"How the fuck would I know that? I don't have hips," I snapped. Huffing my way around her again, I ignored her and straightened her blouse tucks. Millie was trying to annoy me on purpose because she was my little sister who showed love through making my life a living hell.

Once I reached her front, I eyed her fiercely. "I've not dressed you in skirts since you were six. Why didn't you tell me earlier?"

Her brown eyes sparkled with mischief as she answered, "It was fun to watch you struggle."

"Gee, thanks."

"You've been in such a grumpy mood since the picnic, I thought you could use a distraction. Tell me again what happened yesterday while I was passed out."

"Nothing. We went fishing. Me, Anna, and Amby. Anna caught a fish."

The crease in her forehead told me she knew that wasn't the whole truth. "Then why were you wearing those frumpy old clothes when you helped me home? And why did Anna's servant deliver your laundered suit to our door at first light this morning?"

I opened my lips to tell her... what? That I baited Amby to get angry, and when he did, he pushed me into the lake? Heck, I went too far. Amby wasn't the one who deserved a soaking. And here was Millie, pressing me to succeed with Anna, while I was stripping wet socks off my old lover and drooling with visions of sucking his big toes. He had the handsomest toes, knobbly with traces of red hair.

And I still couldn't believe that Amby told me he'd been heart-broken and mourned my loss for years. *Years.* I thought he didn't care. I thought my love was one-sided. So I returned to Everdeen with bitterness and acted like an ass. Amby was right to reply with rudeness. I deserved it.

"Zeth?"

Millie. I closed my eyes from her inquisitive gaze and inhaled deeply. Old hay from Mum's mattress and the faint smell of wet plaster hit my nose, good reminders of our situation. We needed to get out of the laundry, so I needed to marry. And there was the problem. That was the only way to put a roof over our heads that didn't leak, and food in our mouths.

Resigned to my tasks, I fetched the rickety chair I'd found downstairs and positioned it by the bed. I tapped it as a sign that my sister should sit already. She huffed over, careful of her injury, and plopped down.

I rewarded her with an answer. "I fell into the lake. Alright? Please let it go."

"You fell—"

My stern look thankfully cut off her teasing.

"That's right," I continued. "So yesterday was a disaster. Even Anna's staff couldn't clean out the mineral stains from my clothes. Now we need a new suit and a new way to woo Anna, and we don't have money for either."

Millie fidgeted her toes on the warped floorboards as she started plotting a new devious plan out loud about going horseback riding, because rich people love horses. That reminded me of her sprained ankle, which was touching the floor as she sat on the chair. Doc Light had told her to keep it elevated.

I decided to fix that by grabbing both edges of the chair from the back. I hefted it up with her still in it, and she squealed. She held onto the seat, half-grabbing my hands, but it was quick work to spin her toward the bed and set her down. I fluffed some blankets and carefully lifted her leg to settle the bruised ankle on them.

"How are you so strong?" Millie exclaimed with wide eyes.

I sat slowly on the bed, facing her with a shrug. "From moving furniture for the past nine years. It didn't get into the auction house by itself, now did it? But I'll need help moving the dresser downstairs so I can display it in the window to sell, and you're in no shape to assist."

"Mum's dresser?"

I didn't like the sound of disappointment in her voice, so I ignored it. "Aye. Needs to be sold. We won't eat otherwise. And I want food in my belly again."

"I guess," she pouted with her cute cheeks. "Seems a shame. Maybe Amby can help?"

Help put food in my belly? I imagined Amby holding a cracker with cream cheese and popping it into my mouth, his thumb entering too as I licked the cream free. I cleared my throat and tried to remember what Millie asked of me. She suggested that Amby help... "Help with what exactly?"

"Moving the dresser, of course. What were you thinking?"

"Oh, yes, well, what were you saying about horses?" I circled back a few topics to distract us both. My fixation on Amby was consuming me.

It was *Anna* I should be fixating over. Anna on a horse. Pretty, with her teacher's expression... and that did nothing for me. Amby wasn't the only one lying about his attractions. Still, I had to press on. I leaned back on my arms and looked at Millie. Her button nose rose with excitement, so I gave in, "So where should I take Anna for this horse ride?"

"Around her expansive land holdings, obviously. Admire them. Let her see you as a possible lord for her land."

I sat up to boop her nose. "You sound ridiculous."

Millie eyed me seriously. "I'll go in case you need a witness. You know... for a courting kiss. Once you see how well she sits on her horse, you might be tempted to be ungentlemanly."

"Ah yes, excellent idea for you to attend," I agreed while rubbing my neck. I doubted I would be tempted to do anything, but I should make our courtship official. The sooner the better, for our plan.

"With such a strong will, Anna's bound to be a fine rider. You'll be distracted by her bun, wanting to unravel her hair and see how her lovely blonde locks fall on her lily white shoulders..." She sighed. "You won't be able to resist her enticing lips."

Millie's talk was meant to get me going, but my interests sat on one man's shoulders my whole life, unfortunately. He would be the one to tempt me into kissing him under a tree. Heck, Amby would probably dare me, like the first time he dared me to kiss him.

I nodded agreement to her silly talk about Anna, and Millie's face brightened with flushed enthusiasm for her plan.

Riding with Millie and Anna wouldn't be too bad, once Millie's leg was better. And escorting Anna around was a good idea because Amby wouldn't be there. We just needed to keep our rented horses to a trot. Unlike Anna, I wasn't a fine rider. I didn't want to fall in front of my future spouse.

Feeling a bit doomed to do just that and embarrass myself like yesterday, I stood with a foreboding heave off the mattress. "I'm going to clean the windows now to display the dresser. We need the money, especially if we're paying for horses again. You gonna be good here?"

"Of course. You see this wonderful view, don't you?" She motioned across the bed to the dusty window. It was about the only thing she could look at from her angle. "What more can I ask for?"

"Shush, Sassy Cat." I chuckled and left her for the first floor, taking the stairs two at a time to feel the rush. I sorta liked cleaning and was in the mood for manual labor, to sweat things out. I needed to cleanse myself of these lingering desires for a certain redhead.

Grabbing a bucket and a cloth I borrowed from the neighboring store, I pumped some cold water from the well and went up front to remove the curtains. I set them aside in big piles to launder later and rolled up my old shirt sleeves. Then I got to work scrubbing the big shop windows from the outside.

The first wash mostly moved around the layered dirt in heavy streaks. Soap would have helped, but we were out. By the second wash, my shirt was damp in the front, but the glass was finally clean. I moved inside and repeated the process.

Now, if only Amby could be wiped from my mind so easily. I even thought I saw him strolling along Main Street. The man there had a carrier bag strap across his chest, hands tucked into his pants pockets to keep them still, and his capped head hung low. It could be him. Or it was any number of young men in this town. I shook my head at getting so bothered.

The cleaning didn't help as much as I hoped, as working alone only made me think about Amby more.

Sunshine caught a streak in a high corner, so I dipped my rag in the bucket, squeezed brownish water out, and tiptoed to get the spot. When long drips slid down the glass, I followed them with the rag until I focused out the window again to see the loveliest auburn curls peeking out from the front of a gray cap.

My heart lurched in my throat. It really was Amby. Under the brim and gold-rimmed glasses, sharp brown eyes met mine through the window, and my breath caught at how gorgeous he looked today. Nothing different, but different all the same. Maybe it was the way his appreciative gaze roamed my body and raised arm while I remained in the window.

I peeked at myself to see what he saw. Water running along my bare arm and clinging shirt. Old clothes for cleaning. Damn, I was a mess. Backing up, I tossed the rag and wiped my hands on my backside, then ran them through my hair, hating how shaky I felt after just one glance.

Another glance proved he was still there. Even worse, he started for the door.

My pulse raced. What did Amby want? To talk? To reminisce? To threaten me away from his future wife? Ugh, none of it mattered. Talking was a pointless activity. We both had goals to marry the same woman, and I was determined to win, despite how horribly I flirted with Amby while we changed yesterday.

Hiding was also pointless. He already saw me, yet nothing could convince my feet to move forward on the dingy old floorboards while he knocked. I stood quite frozen. Amby squinted at me through the entry's side window with confusion.

There was no help for it, Amby wanted to visit, for whatever reason. I made my way to the door—damn myself for pitying a rich boy—and opened it.

Amby's hand was up midair, ready to knock again. He lowered it, his gaze landing on me, and I hoped he didn't see a complete mess. Or how lost for words he made me. His lips twitched, but he remained stout. When our eyes locked, he blinked, waiting for a sign to speak.

I nodded in greeting, and his words rushed out, "Afternoon. I was delivering statements when I found this one." He cleared his throat and shuffled through his bag before pulling up an envelope with our old City address and Mum's name, Nora Washer. Her name was crossed out and written over with mine and the laundry's address. A hand stamp showed the letter had traveled there and back again, probably after we left. I accepted the thing and rubbed the print before turning it over to open.

Inside, a statement dated last month listed the laundry's yearly property tax, a hefty amount. I never thought about it, but I guess it made sense that Mum paid the taxes each year after Uncle and Memaw passed. She was the last adult Washer. Now it was up to me, but how could I possibly pay?

I couldn't. So what did that mean? Steep interest rates? Stopping me from selling my property? Losing the laundry completely? I folded the letter and slipped it back into the envelope, pretending I never saw the damn thing. "Thank you, is that all?"

"Um..." Amby pulled on the strap of his bag. "How is Millie doing? I wanted to check on her."

"She's surviving," I answered with a scowl. "Do you make personal calls with all your deliveries?"

"No, only yours." He gave a tight smile.

It was kind of him to ask after Millie. It was also annoyingly cute how he stood on my stoop and kept clutching his bag strap. He looked like a puppy.

Despite my better judgment, I stepped back against the door to hold it open and waved him in with grandeur. "Please forgive my poor manners for not offering refreshments, but my matching tea sets and silver services are still boxed up," I teased, praying he would take my joke as the truth. "And I hear there's a statue murderer on the loose, so those are safely hidden too."

He gave an adorable little laugh as he stepped inside and glanced around the empty laundry.

I disliked how he must be seeing spiderwebs in the corners while his own house was a spotless museum. Amby lived in a mansion, while I used to sleep in the kitchen above us. There was nothing to be done about his witnessing my poverty in plain sight. I should make this short.

"It's kind of you to visit Millie, but she's upstairs in the bedroom. It's not proper—"

"Is that Amby?" Millie's booming voice interrupted me, and I rolled my eyes. From the heavens came a scuffle of steps that shouldn't be happening at all. Millie was making her way to the staircase which she yelled down from a moment later. "I heard someone knocking."

"What part of 'keep your leg raised' do you not understand?" I boomed back at her, not caring that Amby flinched next to me, or that I was acting like riff-raff. "Now get your ass back in that chair."

Millie gasped dramatically. "Zeth, such language! I thought you were a dandy gentleman."

Oh, she was lucky to have a floor between us. I wanted to toss her into a corner until dinner.

Amby didn't help my embarrassment. He crossed his arms and said, "I prefer it when you're not a gentleman."

Then he winked at me.

That racy wink gave me goosebumps, and I shivered at his suggestive words. There was no denying the attraction that still lingered between us.

What was he doing? Why was he flirting with me? Maybe he enjoyed the way I undressed him yesterday and couldn't forget that spark either. Maybe he wanted a brief fling with me before one of us committed to courting.

What a thought. I rubbed the goosebumps off my arm and scowled. I wanted to flirt back, but that was the old me resurfacing, the kid who wanted Amby's attention from across a classroom. The kid who did anything Amby asked, be it jumping into a freezing lake or doing his math homework when the lessons got too tough for him.

"Well?" Millie yelled again with a whine in her tone. "Why so quiet? Are you two smooching or something? I'm bored and dying here, so come up already."

Amby laughed and pushed up his glasses. Before I could explain my sister's lack of decorum to Amby, he hung his cap and dropped his bag on the floor before moving from my side.

He strolled right to the bottom of the stairs, making himself at home. I followed to deposit the tax letter on the counter and joined him in the dim light of the dusty backroom. He held onto the rail to call up the stairwell, "Hello, Millie, dearest. I wanted to see how you were doing."

She stood at the top and shrugged. "I'm stuck with my brother, so... it's going as well as can be expected."

"Poor thing. Has he been neglecting you to clean?" Amby turned and nudged me playfully. I deepened my scowl, not liking this turn of events at all. Amby shouldn't be here, yelling like part of the family. He turned back to Millie. "Is there anything I can do for you?"

Amby was out of line, but Millie lit up. I could see it from here. She gushed, "You can help Zeth carry the dresser downstairs. He's far too weak to lift the little thing all by his lonesome. Watching you both struggle with it will be fine entertainment for me."

"She's calling you weak too," I pointed out to Amby in a whisper in case he didn't speak the spoiled-brat-sister language.

He caught my eye with a nod before answering, "Lifting furniture is one of my daily pastimes. I think I can handle it."

"Excellent! Come on up."

He lifts furniture daily?

I pondered that as Millie moved away from the stairs. I didn't want him to linger, plus, he was dressed real nice in a suit with crisp, ironed pants. Carrying an old dresser was bound to ruin his fancy duds.

He started up, but I caught his arm to stop him. "This will get you dirty. You don't have to do it."

109

Amby regarded me with a raised eyebrow. "I'm not worried about clothes, Zeth."

Of course not, he had the money to replace anything he damaged. I felt all the more embarrassed by my shabby attire, so I certainly didn't want him to see our sparse bedroom. My only option now was to nod my head sideways and grant Amby permission upstairs.

Amby squinted at me for a brief moment while I feared he might be reading me like a book, but he only took a readying breath and proceeded up the steps.

I followed behind him and couldn't help but notice how nicely those fancy pants fit Amby's tight little tush. When we were teens, we never went beyond using our mouths or hands in the front, but I'd heard what sex between men could entail, and exploring Amby's ass held a lot of appeal. His pink nipples and narrow chest were tempting enough, not to mention how that trail of dark red hair at his navel had haunted me all night long, so maybe it was better not to stare at his ass.

When we reached the top, Amby stopped at the doorway notches, because of course he would, and rubbed his bruised thumb against my written name with a grin that brought back my annoyance.

I slapped his hand away, and he grunted with surprise.

"I was *short*, everyone knows. Move on." My grumble had enough drama to make Millie proud. It also had Amby chuckling, so I nudged him into the room with two hands to his back. And I might have noticed how firm he was.

"I always liked this room," Amby said, looking around. "Your mother kept it decorated so warm and cozy. She was the kindest woman I've ever known. I'm truly sorry to hear of her passing."

His eyes lingered on me briefly before darting to Millie.

I blinked and nodded, at a fucking loss for words. I didn't know why it meant so much that Amby praised Mum. I cleared my throat and pinched my nose to the bone. Thankfully, that kept the tears back.

Needing something to say that wasn't about my dead mum, I

pointed into the room. "The dresser's, um, over there. Let's get it into the shop window already."

No one remarked upon my gruff voice as I walked over to it and patted the top, but I could feel their concern, so I got to work removing the top drawer to make the dresser lighter.

Obviously, I tried to avoid Amby's gaze, and that made the walls feel like they closed in on me a bit. What was he thinking? And why did I fucking care? Before he visited, I didn't care if my shirt was worn through or that I couldn't serve tea. But now, I hated feeling so exposed as a failure. And when the very first drawer got stuck, I hated that too, because I couldn't do anything. Amby watched a fool losing control.

I tugged harder, refusing to give up, and the top drawer squealed of warped wood against wood before giving in. I managed to stop myself from flinging the damn thing out and set it on the floor with a sniff. When I went for the two middle drawers, they moved with difficulty, but didn't make me look like an idiot.

"I've got this last one," Amby said, rushing over. He pulled off his jacket and handed it to Millie before squatting at my side. I stepped aside to watch him from above as he tried to pull the bottom drawer free. As if finally on my side, the dresser didn't let go at all.

Amby was slim in good places but I saw his bare arms yesterday, and he'd grown some nice definition. He wasn't weak. I held the dresser top while Amby pulled until his face went red as he tried to maneuver it out. Maybe he was playing around, or he really was having as much trouble as I did. Either way, I felt better.

When it finally budged free, Amby flew back on his ass with the drawer hitting his face. He blinked his large brown eyes in a bit of a daze, and I feared he might have hurt himself, so I quickly bent to a knee at his side. I inspected his face for injury while Amby dropped his gaze, and I found myself staring at the light dusting of freckles over the bridge of his nose... a nose that I was clearly viewing without gold frames.

"Fuck," I exclaimed, looking around him, "Where'd your glasses go?"

"Here," Millie chuckled. She nudged them with her foot, and I quickly rescued the fragile frames before she stomped on them. There was no knowing with my dearest sister.

I made sure the glasses weren't damaged before carefully setting them over those wonderful freckles I used to kiss.

"Thank you," Amby said softly.

I moved back to help him to his feet. Once standing, we stayed hand in hand for a moment, both of us frozen as we stared at each other. His palm was warm against mine, and I realized how good my fingers looked wrapped around his smaller ones.

When I glanced over at Millie, I found her blinking at us, her face a mixture of baffled and amused.

Amby withdrew his hand quickly. "Um, do you want to carry the dresser first, then come back up for the drawers?"

"Yes," I agreed.

"Alright."

I nodded. Short, and to the point. That's how we should interact. No need to get all bothered when all we were doing was moving furniture together. I waved Amby over to the far side and positioned myself closer to the stairs. Crouching, I placed my hand into an empty drawer space. Amby moved to the other side, and I watched his form closely to make sure he didn't hurt his back. But his position was good, like he also knew what he was doing. I was impressed.

Amby caught my gaze around the dresser to ask, "Do you want to go first, or carry it from the top?"

Going first would place most of the load on me, and that's what I wanted, so I offered, "I'll be bottom."

Amby's eyes widened, and then he blinked. I hadn't meant for my words to sound so... sexual. But I rendered Amby speechless, and I treasured how his face went red as a tomato before he quickly disappeared behind the end of the dresser.

"Ready when you are," I heard him say.

I swallowed and ducked behind the dresser too, feeling far too much heat in my face for a simple day of moving furniture. I huffed to clear my head and found my words again.

"Ready," I said, and damn my voice for dropping a few pitches. It sounded like I invited him to do something else. Thankfully, Amby ignored me and the dresser moved. I quickly grabbed on and lifted too until we had it in the air. "You good?"

"Yes, are you?" Amby tried to keep his voice steady through his little grunt. It was kinda adorable.

I led the way to the stairs, shuffling slowly. Amby followed along, looking a bit flushed and pinched, yet his grip appeared secure and his back straight, so I picked up my pace, and we reached the hall without issue.

The first step was always a challenge. I was about to say that when Amby gave me a nod to point out my position, and I believed his earlier bragging without a doubt. Why did he have experience moving furniture?

Maybe my face asked my question, because Amby tossed me a told-you-so look. I stuck out my tongue playfully at him and found the first step with my shoe's tip before stepping down.

I continued faster as my confidence in us rose. This wouldn't be so hard after all. Halfway down, Amby called from over the dresser top, "Still alright?"

"Yes, you're doing well. I'm impressed." The praise was warranted. He deserved it, and the words felt good for me too.

"Giving compliments now? You're full of—" He grunted as he stepped down, "surprises."

"I'm being serious. You're good at this." I don't know why it felt like Amby needed to hear that. When he didn't reply, I focused on the next step, then two, before saying what he really needed from me, "Thank you for your help."

"I'm happy to help. You should come to my house sometime, and I'll show you what I've been up to."

"Is that flirtation? I'm being serious."

"So am I. I have a few things I could give you for the laundry."

The dresser slipped free from my left hand and crashed right into the wall with a loud bang. It slammed into my shoulder with a solid thump that stole my breath and pushed me back, forcing my shoe to slip right off the step. The sickening release felt like falling from a tree. Without a doubt, I was about to bite the dust.

Then my shoe hit the tiled floor.

I didn't die. Opening my eyes, the lower floor came into view.

"Fuck," I muttered with relief, and rested my head against the angled dresser. Prayers would have been better than swearing, I guess, but I'm not a praying sort.

"Zeth, move!"

"Don't think I can. I'm trying not to piss myself, thank you very much."

Amby suddenly grunted, and the dresser shifted closer to me. When my shoes slid back against the tile, Amby motioned his curly head toward the floor where the dresser was still suspended a few inches from my feet.

"You make an excellent bookend," his voice strained, "but I'm the one holding this thing up. I'm about to drop it on you."

"Oh." I swiftly pulled the dresser backward so we cleared the last few steps with a speed that might as well have been falling. When Amby joined me at the bottom, relief washed through me just as Millie tried to descend the steps with a desperate grip to the railing. The fear I had felt was all over her face.

"We're alright," I called up to assure her. I spread my arms out to show her I still had my limbs. "Go sit. We're fine."

She sent me a disbelieving look, but did as I said.

When I glanced toward Amby, he was heading for the front of the shop. The floorboards creaked beneath his shiny black shoes, stirring up dust from his steps. He stopped before the large windows, and the sunlight beamed down on him, making his auburn curls appear redder.

Curious, I walked over to see him holding his right hand at an angle in the light and pinching the base of his fingers.

My fears hitched as my gaze roamed over him. "What's wrong?"

"You maimed me." Amby didn't meet my gaze, as if mad at me for putting him into such harm today. But I knew that pout of his. He wanted my attention. I leaned over and grabbed his hand with a huff. And although his fingers were red and abused for sure, a close examination didn't find any permanent damage.

He was throwing bait to me on purpose, and like an idiot I was taking it. Even if he was joking, if Amby said he was hurt, I wanted to help.

Millie always needed a distraction when in pain, so I ran a thumb into Amby's shirt sleeve and rubbed his wrist with strong strokes. His smooth skin distracted me. Then I asked what I always asked Millie, "Is something broken? Can you wiggle your toes?"

Amby released a rough breath and eyed me sharply with disbelief. The distraction worked.

Sunlight shifted through the window, making Amby's glasses sparkle. The delicate frame was still slightly bent from the fight in the lake. Or maybe the dresser drawer had dented them once more. Either way, the two glass ovals weren't parallel. They sat roughly five degrees off from each other.

I wanted to fix them again, but Amby's sulky mouth moved, so I shifted my focus to listen, but no words came out. There was a smartass comment shuffling around in there somewhere, and the returning sass had me suppressing a grin. This was the Amby I remembered. Not the shy thing he presented to Anna.

I deserved his teasing right now. I wanted it. Maybe the dresser hurting him was my fault. My hand had slipped after he offered me castoffs from his house.

"I got a splinter." Amby pouted playfully as he held up his hand.

"Where?"

He blinked and pointed to the lower joint of his middle finger. "Here."

I took his right hand gently in mine and grimaced as I finally saw a dark splinter wedged into his skin. Damn, that really did look like it hurt. I was a cad. I needed to fix this, better than I did with his glasses. I smoothed my thumb over his palm, surprised and also glad he let me. This close, I could see more scratches and nicks in his skin. What had caused them?

"You going to take it out for me?" he asked softly. "Or just stare at it?"

I met his eyes, and my heart skipped a beat. I was enjoying holding his hand again, to be honest. His fingers were long and slender, and also calloused. I wondered what they'd feel like on me...

Clearing my throat, I raised his hand to my open mouth so I could suck the splinter out. I licked his soft flesh once to wet it and firmed my lips to apply pressure when Amby jerked his hand away so quickly, he seemed to disappear.

"What are you doing?" he laughed nervously. "I don't want your mouth..." and his flustered expression contradicted every damn thing he was about to say. He'd taken a step back, but he sure as hell wanted my mouth on him. He wanted me sucking, just not there. Not right now. His eyebrows drew together, as if he might finish that statement, but he deflated and continued, "That's not how to remove a splinter. I've tried it before, and it hurts. We need tweezers, or a needle."

I adjusted my pants with a smile and shake of my head. "I don't have those."

He didn't like that answer. "Epsom salt?"

I didn't even know what that was. Who had fancy salt? "No."

"Then white vinegar sometimes does the trick, mixed with water." This time, he looked hopeful, like everyone should have vinegar. And maybe they should, if they cooked. Or cleaned. We used to have a big jar.

This was getting embarrassing. I rubbed the back of my neck and glanced toward the laundry room with its pump and well. "I have water."

When he didn't reply, I felt myself sweating over how pathetic I sounded in an empty laundry that was my only asset. The stark-white envelope I left on the counter only made it worse, threatening to take the laundry away from me. Ambrose Somerset won. He exposed my con. I was gold-digging, and now my chances of a comfortable life, my chances of owning epsom salt, whatever-the-fuck-that-was, were over. He messed it all up by making me care about his stupid hand. I lost my future over a splinter. Pinching my nose wouldn't change a damn thing, but I tried.

"Just water?" he asked, almost sounding concerned.

I spun on Amby so fast he flinched. And that made me laugh like the madman I repressed during his whole visit. With the laughter came spite, "That's all I have, alright? Water. So go ahead, go tell Anna how poor I am. Tell her how you brilliantly tricked me by coming here and revealing my con with your pouty lips that tugged on my sympathy. Your romantic words yesterday about mourning me. Who's the fucking liar here? So you win Anna. And don't bother inviting me to your wedding, 'cause I don't have anything nice to wear."

"Zeth…" he sighed, his face falling. "I would never spy on you."

I scoffed. "That's the whole reason you're here right now, to expose me, to distract me! And to deliver this—" I grabbed the letter, crumpled it into a ball, and lobbed it at his head. It flew so far off target that Amby didn't even need to duck. "You're trying to seize my inheritance too, aren't you? Well, your strategy played out perfectly."

Amby shook his head. "Why would I steal your inheritance from you? You're talking out of your ass."

"Get out." I couldn't stand the sight of him. It was foolish to let him into my residence and into my trust. Once again, my hopes got dashed, and there was nothing I could do about it. Amby was just the latest person to betray me. My stomach twisted, and I stormed to the front door to rip it open. The glass rattled as I turned on Amby, "Get the fuck out of my life."

My rage echoed in the empty space, and Amby's brow gathered. But he pulled up his mailbag and walked out the door. He put his hand on his head before stopping, realizing he didn't have his cap. Or his jacket. Amby turned slightly, as if he might come back to retrieve them, but when he saw my displeased face, he quickly turned back on his heel and left.

11

Ambrose

Keep your head up, Amby.

I repeated the phrase to myself as I finished lunch with Annabelle at one of Everdeen's finest eating houses. My mood was rather sour after the exchange between Zeth and me yesterday at the laundry, and it had been hard to focus on talking, especially with how many people stopped by our table for a quick chat with Annabelle. Her popularity as the wealthiest woman in Everdeen had me a little baffled. Didn't they know it was rude to chatter on while someone held company? Perhaps manners were fading away.

After lunch, we made our way to a boutique that sold figurines and other accessories, as well as a few clothes. I hoped to buy Annabelle another statue to replace the one I broke in the parlor. While she searched for one, I browsed other areas of the store until she came up to me.

"Isn't this a lovely bracelet, Amby?"

I glanced over to see colorful leather bands woven like a braid with three beads in the middle. Two were white, and the other was real silver. "It's very pretty. Would you like that too?"

"Actually, I was thinking of getting it for Millie. As a get-well gift."

"For... Millie? Oh, of course." I put out my hand to buy it, but she held onto it.

"I'll pay for this myself, Amby."

"Very well. Did you find another statue?" I glanced around at the porcelain dolls—which I found unsettling—and statues of various people in romantic poses. Hopefully, Annabelle didn't pick out the most expensive one. It would be difficult to explain the purchase to my father.

"I think I'll only get the bracelet. Don't you worry about the statue."

"But I owe it to you. Especially after how foolish I acted for pushing Zeth in the lake the other day. I ruined our time together. I want to make it up to you."

Annabelle smiled as if she held some joke I didn't know about. "I don't think you realize how much fun I had that day. And Zeth and Millie brought life back into my big, empty house. I... Well, I enjoyed it."

"Oh." She had enjoyed it, and yet I had been flirting in her upstairs room with the other man trying to win her hand. What a jackass I was.

"You're such a good friend, Amby." She beamed at me before she turned toward the counter.

I was a good *friend*? Did she just...

"Wait," I started, and Annabelle turned back with wide eyes. I rubbed my thumb, needing a clear explanation. "If you see me as a friend, then whatever we're doing now..."

"You're a wonderful man..."

That was as clear as mud. "But?"

Annabelle faltered. "But there's no spark between us. You know, that spark when you meet someone, and you know they're the one? I'm certain I feel it with someone else."

Did she mean... Zeth? It was hard to imagine them together, but Annabelle seemed to know what she wanted, and it wasn't me. Maybe Zeth already caught her fancy and lit her spark. Now they would marry, and have kids, and stroll into every event as a happy couple...

Why did thinking that make me so... jealous? My heart trembled so much, my hands began to shake.

"Amby?" Her face creased in concern.

I managed a weak laugh. "You're right. I'm sorry, I understand."

"You're going to make someone very happy one day. I would love to remain your friend, if that's alright." Her gesture of friendship was nothing but pure grace, particularly in the face of my awful, deceitful intentions. Annabelle was an incredibly kind, clever, and fun person. She deserved the best.

I gave her a friendly nod. "Of course, we shall remain friends." Even so, worry gnawed already at my bones about what my father would say. Another rejection from a potential bride. I would have to face that later.

"Did you see the rings, Amby? They're gaining popularity among men," she suggested before making her way to the clerk.

Straightening, I searched through the jewelry in various baskets. A few rings with small, colored stones embedded in the metal caught my eye. Beside the basket was a placard explaining that the colors changed from blue to purple to red and even black, depending on how one was feeling. People used them to stay calm and collected.

My shaking thankfully subsided as I picked up one of the rings and tried it on. The colors seemed to swirl as the ring turned an amber color. I read over the placard to find what that meant: Nervous, mixed sentiments.

"Hm." I turned it around on my finger and rubbed my thumb along the silver designs of the band. What a unique ring. A handsome ring. The place where the stone lay was wide and flat, setting it apart from the others. It also appeared well made. For some reason, it reminded me of Zeth. Would the stone shift to black if he put it on? He certainly needed to cool his temper.

God, even a piece of jewelry was reminding me of Zeth.

I thought back to yesterday at the laundry. When I delivered the letter to him, and he mentioned he only had water, I was concerned for his well-being. But now I could see how my actions could have come off wrong. I *did* flirt with him to distract him away from

Annabelle, after all, but it'd also come so naturally to me. Everything came naturally to me with Zeth.

His words to get the fuck out of his life had hit me hard. But Zeth had recently lost his mother. Not even two months ago. It had to be difficult to lose your mother *and* have to pack up and leave to sell his inheritance. I knew the feeling of losing a mother, and knew Zeth was in pain. Maybe that's why he lashed out. Part of me wanted to comfort him, even if he was cruel. Perhaps I could make it up to him.

Taking off the ring, I made my way to the counter to pay for it.

"Oh, you found something?" Annabelle asked.

I held it out in my palm. "I did. Nothing fancy."

"An aura ring. I do love those. They make great gifts for friends. And you know, bonds formed through friendship can never be broken." She winked before she whisked away.

What was she on about? A good friend? Yes, but she spoke in riddles, and I hated those. Was she talking about me and her, or someone else?

After we paid for our things, we left and walked along the shops outside. I was surprised by Annabelle's quick pace and had to focus on keeping up with her swishing skirts.

"Would you like to head to the bookshop?" she asked. "I'd like to get a new collection of poems since the poetry salon is coming up soon. Do you have a poem you're going to recite?"

"Oh... I'm not sure yet. My mother had several books. I sometimes read from one of them."

"I remember your mother fondly. She's so missed."

My spirit glowed hearing that. "Thank you. My mother loved reciting poetry at the meetups. It's why my father still attends them. Going to the bookstore sounds lovely. I think I may find something too."

Annabelle suddenly walked faster.

I was so wrapped up in following her that I ran right into someone else. The impact knocked my cap back, and I let out a breath as several cans of beans fell onto the sidewalk.

I immediately bent to pick them up. "My apologies—" My

voice trailed off when I saw Zeth squatting beside me, hurriedly scooping the cans into his arms.

I picked up the last one, hesitating as I stared at him. Zeth snatched it from my hand with a glare and stood. Gritting my teeth, I rose as well. Of course, he was still angry with me. He'd accused me of spying to tell Annabelle he had nothing but water, and now here I was with her the very next day. This wasn't good.

"Zeth!" Annabelle exclaimed. "So good to see you."

Zeth stood tall in his blue suit, but a few water stains marred the fabric. He shifted his armful of cans in front of him awkwardly, nodding to us both. "Miss Winters. Mr. Somerset."

Oh, how I fucking hated him calling me that. He had to know it by the way my face soured. From how Annabelle hesitated, the sudden formalities threw her off too.

For a moment, we all stood awkwardly, until Zeth said, "Pleasant weather, isn't it?"

I peered up to see white clouds spanning over the sky. Was he trying to make the space between us less tense?

"Spring is so unpredictable," Annabelle replied politely and glanced at me, expectant.

I straightened, already hating this small talk. "Um, yes. The air is damp. I think it may rain later." What an idiotic thing to say.

"Don't worry, Amby, there's sunshine behind every storm cloud."

Annabelle's positive outlook on life was far too chirpy in the given moment. Even Zeth rolled his eyes.

"Well... I actually don't mind a good storm," I clarified. "Too much sun really is flustering. I'm not sure why everyone hates the rain so much."

"Only you would describe sunshine as flustering," Zeth said with a snarky bite. "Did you not appreciate that lovely quote?"

"Of course I did. And I do... like sunshine. Just not all the time. Surely you have a quote about rain?"

Zeth's brow lowered at me as he snipped out, "Rain, rain go away, come again another day. Little Ambrose wants to play."

I cocked my head at him. "Cute. Still being childish, I see."

"Me, childish?" He laughed. "Did you come to that conclusion before or after you pushed me into the lake?"

My eye twitched as I glared at him. His challenging stare kept us both rooted firmly to the sidewalk, neither of us willing to move.

"Oh! There's Margaret." Annabelle suddenly waved across the street to someone I recognized from Chapel. "I've been meaning to ask about her daughter. One moment, you two."

She bolted across the street without a care, leaving us blinking after her. I swallowed hard as my gaze shifted back to Zeth. We seemed destined to keep running into each other, even if it was to throw insults around. But my, how wonderful he looked with his dark brown hair combed back and those amber eyes shining in the sunlight. Yes, that was indeed a plus to the sunny weather.

When he turned to face me, I looked away to glance at the shop window of the barber. The shop's wooden sign was wonderfully crafted. I was sure I could make such signs myself. As I pondered it, my hand slipped into the pocket of my trousers, and I felt the ring I'd bought. It was supposed to be an apology gift, but Zeth had me riled now.

"Congratulations," he said, his voice cocky.

"I'm sorry?" I glanced at him again, clenching the ring in my fist.

Zeth's face dented slightly. "On your success with Miss Winters. I'm sure you two will be very happy together."

"Oh... Well, see, Annabelle and I are—"

"Tell me, you wouldn't happen to have any rich friends looking to marry? Perhaps one who wouldn't mind a thief and poor commoner for a husband? I need someone who doesn't have a precious legacy to uphold."

His words hit me like knives, cutting me deep, and I had to turn away to keep from breaking. He probably wouldn't believe me if I told him Annabelle and I were only friends now. And I didn't want to tell him, because a selfish part of me would rather Zeth hate me than see him with Annabelle. I didn't want him to be with her. He didn't need to know she still fancied him, that she felt a... spark. I wouldn't be the one to make that union happen.

Letting the ring fall back in my pocket, I raised my chin and said, "Well, I may certainly know of someone, but you told me to get out of your life, Mr. Washer, so I can't help you." I tipped my cap at him. "Good day."

Walking past him hurt more than his insults to me. When had I ever turned my back on Zeth like this? None that I could think of, and it pained me so much. I had to keep it together.

When I met up with Annabelle again, she peered around me. "Where is Zeth going? I was hoping to invite him along to the bookstore with us."

"Oh, he had to get home," I said, sure he wouldn't want to join us while carrying those cans around. But good thing, as he would just continue to berate me the entire time.

Annabelle frowned briefly, but then she quickly perked up. "I'll be visiting him and Millie soon anyway. Shall we continue on?"

I nodded, feeling despondent after running into Zeth. My mind worked over our meeting. I would eventually have to tell him Annabelle and I weren't courting. Perhaps in the meantime, I could introduce Annabelle to other men. That would keep her away from Zeth since she seemed adamant about seeing him.

When we arrived at the bookshop, my steps slowed. Damien Cooligan and his friends loitered outside around the doorstep. I groaned inwardly. Ezekiel Phillips gave a suggestive whistle as we walked up to the door, and I stopped and turned to him with a sharp eye.

"Hey, Amby, don't look at me like that, I wasn't whistling at you," Ezekiel said.

I made a face at him for treating a lady so poorly. "Maybe you should keep your eyes down instead."

"I'm torn. Really." Ezekiel put a hand over his heart. The other guys all laughed and shook their heads.

"It's quite alright, Amby," Annabelle said with a measured glance around the gathering before addressing Ezekiel. "Misbehaving boys get their just punishments."

Her strict tone had him standing straighter, clearly impressed. I was impressed too as she opened the door of the bookshop to walk past them. I followed quickly behind, thankful to be leaving the band of troublemakers. To my dismay, Damien trailed after me.

"Miss Winters, Amby. You both look well. Out for a stroll... together?"

"A friend's day out," Annabelle corrected, and I felt my face flush. Did she have to say that in front of him?

"Oh, really?" Damien flipped his blond braid over his shoulder. He only paid attention to me when he saw me getting cozy with someone else. "Well, maybe I can help one of you find some books."

Since when did Damien like books? He didn't even pay attention during the poetry meets. He was only there to socialize and act as if he owned the town.

"Thank you, but I do need to find the powder room first," Annabelle said. "I'll be right back, Amby."

I put up my hand, my mouth opening to beg her not to leave me alone with Damien, but she whisked away. I was already in a foul mood from seeing Zeth. I didn't need a shopping trip with Damien right now.

"Hm," he hummed. "Maybe I can help you find something you might like in the back aisle?"

Sighing, I put my hands on my hips and shrugged. "Sure. I need a book. About... whales."

Damien raised a trim eyebrow. "Whales?"

"Yes. Whales. They live in the sea. They eat... algae or something. Go find me that."

"That's oddly specific."

I put out my hand and gestured at the bookshelves. "You said you could assist."

"That's not what I was offering, but come on then."

He huffed, and I didn't actually think Damien would take me to the right spot at all. In fact, I expected him to do exactly as he insinuated and corner me in a back aisle—I wasn't afraid to use my fists on him—but as he browsed through the shelves, I absentmindedly followed along with him, letting him look like a fool as he came to a section with books about gardening.

"I recall seeing something like that the other day," he told me.

"Sure." I turned my head to see the bookstore owner, Ollie Axford, coming out of the back room. He nodded his head at me, and I greeted him back. A few others sat in chairs in corners, reading quietly. Nathaniel Rios was among them with a thick book about Everdeen's history. I never took the man for being a reader, as he was so absorbed in the distillery and spent his time throwing lavish parties, but I suppose I shouldn't judge a book by its cover. We stopped right in front of where Nathaniel sat.

"Ah, here we go." Damien pointed with pleasure to a shelf where, indeed, there was one book labeled *Whales*.

My eyes widened as I pulled the leather book out, then I glanced over my shoulder. Where was Annabelle? Surely she was finished in the powder room by now.

"So," Damien started chirpily, "What do I get for assisting you?"

"Nothing. But I am impressed you could navigate your way through a bookshop. It must have been hard for you."

Nathaniel snorted from behind us, and Damien scowled at his friend before asking me, "You think I don't read?"

"I really don't care what you do in your spare time."

"Oh, you found a book, Amby," came Annabelle's voice from behind. I looked over to see her smiling at me. "Ready to help me find one too?"

Nodding, I stepped away with my book and from Damien without a farewell. Seeing Annabelle brought my spirits back up. At least... until I thought about Zeth. Because the truth was, nothing good could come of us being friends if she was still interested in Zeth. He made me feel like a gathering storm on the horizon, and it was only a matter of time before the clouds broke.

12

Zeth

"Thank you for looking," I said politely to the third person this morning who declined to buy Mum's dresser. This woman had actually turned her nose up at it. That made being nice a challenge, but Mum would be proud of me as I waved the woman goodbye without hitting the rude bitch with the door on the way out.

Once she was gone, Millie entered the room from the stairwell and limped past the counter to join me on the dim sales floor. Her gaze flew to the sale sign and then to me. "No luck?"

I sighed. "None. We have a grand total of nine 'no thank yous' since it got moved downstairs."

That was two days ago since I kicked Amby out for flirting the truth out of me. One day since I ran into him with Anna. I still couldn't believe he won. He made me so furious, the selfish brat. Inconsiderate rapscallion. Greedy rich boy. Uncaring snot. Rubbing my nose, I tamped down twenty-two additional phrases that occurred to me for former friends and lovers who tricked you and stole your only chance for security.

Millie, on the other hand, hummed a little ditty as she opened the door and held it, waiting.

I followed and locked it behind us. I was glad to find the day sunny and the sidewalk bustling. "Well, if nothing else, it's encouraging how much business this location gets. That's a good selling point for the laundry. The new owner can have a successful little business here. So... on to shopping for clothes?"

She held her arm out to me, like she wished to escort me, so I huffed and accepted her gentlemanly offer. "Aye, lead the way."

What she really needed was my support to walk straight. Her ankle was still healing. I wouldn't have suggested the outing, but my best suit went for a swim in a lake, so I needed something that wasn't stained. Millie suggested the tailor shop mentioned in her news clipping about Anna. Without money, that was today's challenge.

"Do you really think they'll give us credit?" Millie asked.

I stood straighter and glanced ahead. "I can only hope. How else will I look good for Anna?"

I didn't have the heart to tell Millie that Amby ruined our con. Or how *I* ruined our con. There was nothing to be done about it now. I had to start searching for a new target, a new man or woman to dupe into marrying me and taking us into their home. And I needed to appear rich enough to marry.

"I'll shop for new clothes too," Millie added. "Perhaps some pants this time."

I had enough to deal with already, so I glared at her with my we-talked-about-this face. "You still have the white lace dress."

"That's a picnic dress," she whined.

"Which you refused to wear to the picnic, so you can still use it."

Millie pouted over the dress.

When we passed a few town citizens, I tipped my cap to them all, and Millie politely nodded. Everyone seemed nice, and even curious, but went about their busy way.

Once we reached the shop, Millie opened the door with a playful taunt while I walked in with a swagger that said I didn't care that my wallet was empty. What I expected to find inside was the tailor, along with lots of fabric and readily available suits and dresses. And if I was lucky, a new elite to become my spouse.

What I didn't expect to find was Amby sitting in a blue-cushioned chair with his legs crossed and a book balanced in one of his hands. He acted like he owned the place. I wouldn't be surprised if his bank did own the property.

His sister Hattie was there too, modeling a dress in front of a mirror, and Amby's twin, Emiline, bent beside her with a measuring tape in her hand.

Three Somerset siblings all turned to stare at me. Amby was the most surprised I'd seen him since coming to Everdeen. What, did he think I didn't go shopping?

I finished strolling in and ignored Amby, speaking to Hattie instead, "What a nice surprise meeting you here, Hattie darling. And in such a lovely ensemble. That rose quartz color suits you. And Emiline, it's wonderful to see you again." I turned back and motioned to my sister, who was doing her best to mimic my stroll. I only hoped I looked so debonair. "You remember Millie, I'm sure."

Emiline relaxed and got quickly to her feet. Her face brightened as she stepped forward and grabbed my hand. She always seemed to be the most welcoming one of the bunch, and it was clear on her friendly face that she at least wanted me here.

"It's so good to see you, Zeth, and Millie." She nodded at us. The auburn curls that escaped her braid annoyed me. I didn't like how similar they were to a certain brother. "What can I do for you today?"

I couldn't help but seek out those matching curls a few feet away, and found Amby scowling at me from behind his book. I inhaled and met Emiline's waiting gaze, which still appeared so inviting.

"Someone stained my suit, so I find myself in need of a new one. I was hoping that I might..." Feeling the silence of the room, I leaned in closer to Emiline and whispered, "Could I commission a suit on loan? Something nice, but not too nice. My funds... are tied up with investments."

The embarrassment that blew through my cheeks almost made me turn around and leave. I didn't want the rest of the Somersets to know our circumstances, if Amby didn't tell them already. No one needed to witness my failures written in red ink, filling my ledger columns.

"Oh, of course," Emiline whispered back with a dash of mischief that reminded me of Amby. She wanted to help me? I never felt so grateful. "Just give me a moment." When she whisked away, I tried not to take it personally. It wasn't her fault that slipping into a rear door meant abandoning me to a room full of people trying to translate what just happened.

So, I ignored them. I offered my arm to Millie, so she wouldn't limp, and led her over to some fabrics in a back corner. As soon as we got there, I lifted a corner of velvet from a tall bolt and showed it to her, while also listening for voices.

Emiline was indeed in a second room asking someone for permission. She spoke so softly, I didn't catch everything, but I heard enough to feel like a beggar. My arm tightened against Millie's, ready to flee. However, she caught my eye and sent me a I'll-beat-them-up-for-you look. Bless my crazy sister.

"How is your foot, Millie?" Hattie asked as she continued to admire her dress in the mirror. "It was quite a nasty fall the other day at the picnic."

"It's healing nicely, thank you. So kind of you to ask," Millie replied so politely over her shoulder, I checked to make sure she hadn't been replaced.

And then I heard—we all heard—the answer to Emiline's question in a voice so masculine and deep that the answer nearly broke down the door, "Certainly, we can help poor Zeth!" *Poor Zeth?* Now I definitely wanted to leave. "He can pay us back in trade, or—"

"Hattie!" my sister suddenly yelled so loud I flinched away from her. "Zeth wasn't lying about that color. It's charming on you."

"Thank you!" Hattie yelled back. One would think the girls stood miles apart instead of standing a few feet away.

Amby smiled from behind his book. Was he enjoying my humiliation?

I fumed at him as Hattie yelled between us, "I chose pink

because it means affection and kindness, like one of the ribbons at the Founders Day Festival coming up in a few weeks!"

She was so loud, I could no longer hear the man's voice through the door. The girls were saving me from complete humiliation, bless them. Thankfully, this drama didn't last long because the door opened and a towering, beefy fellow with broad shoulders, chestnut brown hair, and bushy beard entered the sales floor. He found me instantly with kind green eyes and clamped my shoulder as if we were best friends.

Actually... we had been friends. Good friends.

I let go of Millie to slap the tailor's solid shoulder. "Arthur Honeycutt? Is that you, old rascal? You're a giant. Now I know how everyone feels seeing me again. What are they feeding you?"

"Brussels sprouts." Arthur's laugh reached into his eyes, bringing back so many memories of playground tussles and king of the hill games. He was a year older than us, but never used age to his advantage. He was always the loudest out of Amby and me, and always the biggest. Now, he was practically a bear. "Zeth Washer, it's been too long. How are you?"

I pretended to punch his shoulder before I answered, "I've been well enough, but you're thriving, clearly." My arm gesture swept out to include the shop and Emiline, whom Arthur used to pine after as kids. Then I poked his belly. "Maybe too well."

Arthur proudly patted his belly while Emiline teased him, "That's what you get for letting my brother hook you on beer and games at the pub every Friday."

Were they married? I didn't see a ring, but the way she gazed at her boss made it clear the two had become close.

"What can I say?" Amby added, coming up beside her and speaking for the first time since I'd arrived. "I'm a master at *tempting* people. You could even call me a conman." He eyed me before straightening his jacket with a snide expression.

I huffed at him. He wanted to rub his deception in my face, and bring up mine? In front of our families. That was bold.

"Well, even so, I'm grateful our card games led Em to take this job," Arthur said.

I was surprised a Somerset was working outside the bank. "Why are you working here?"

My question was rude, yet Emiline confidently planted her hands on her hips. "Fashion is my expertise. Don't we all have that one thing we're really good at? To do what I love for a living is a dream."

How nice to afford dreams. My scoff was light enough to be ignored, but I didn't miss how Amby looked down, hands in his pockets. Maybe he was also annoyed by her lucky naivete.

"Perhaps I can gather you new clients at the institute, Em," Hattie replied from nearby. "I'm sure there will be lavish dances and gatherings at school."

Amby gave a tight smile, but he also made a visible eye roll as he turned. I only had one sister to annoy me, so I almost felt sorry for Amby's role with three spoiled ones. Almost. He deserved some torture for his privileges.

Arthur touched Emiline's elbow gently. "Go ahead and find Zeth a suit." He nodded at me. "Let's get beers sometime soon and catch up."

"You'll drink me under the table, but I'm in," I agreed, forgiving the earlier embarrassment since he honestly sounded happy to see me again. Arthur granted me mercy, even if he did yell it from the rooftops. Such kindness was rare. Maybe I did have a friend in Everdeen. A friend who wasn't trying to destroy me.

Arthur turned to go back to the room he'd come out of before, while Emiline began pulling a couple of suits off the racks already in the store.

"Em, what about my dress?" Hattie pouted.

"That one's just fine," Emiline said firmly. "I have your adjustments to get it fitted. Now go on to the back and change."

"Oh, alright." Hattie tsked and held up her skirts as she headed for one of two curtained alcoves.

Emiline led me to the other room with an armful of clothes. She held the curtain open and motioned for me to enter. When we slipped in, I instantly liked the cozy little space. She waved to a plush stool and I sat. I watched as she hung up three suit jackets and explained a few things about each that didn't matter to me. All I wanted to know was the price. She never mentioned that, like a skillful salesperson who knows how to gain my interest first. Or maybe cost wasn't something she thought about.

When she left, I picked the jacket that looked the least expensive. Its dark-brown color paired well with my other clothes, so I could get by with the same old shoes and cap. I slipped it on and glanced in the little dressing mirror, but that barely showed my whole chest. After a moment of indecision and trying to see myself, I gave up and slipped out of the room's curtain.

Amby stared right at me from the chair. He was more relaxed, with one elbow on the arm of the chair and the other holding his book in his lap.

I, on the other hand, might have frozen halfway through the curtained door... or maybe I looked charming. I hoped for charming as I swallowed and sent a dashing grin to him. Then I sent a grin around the rest of the room. Millie was roaming the jacket rack, and Hattie was already standing dressed by the counter.

I moved to stand where Hattie had stood on a raised dais, a central spot for the shop with wide mirrors. The chairs all around me made a viewing station. I ignored the audience as I evaluated myself in the mirror, pleased at how well this jacket hung on my shoulders. Extending my arms, I liked how long the sleeves were, needing no alterations. That would also save me money.

"Oh, this one is nice," Emiline commented. "It fits perfectly, too."

"It's a little washed out," Amby said dryly. When my eyes locked on him in the mirror, he was still reading his book. "It's not a very rich color."

Not very rich? As in poor? Oh, he was most certainly out to anger me.

Stepping off the dais, I made my way to the dressing room. I flicked the curtain back and tugged off the first jacket, tossing it over the stool. The next jacket had velvet lapels in a deep burgundy that appeared far more expensive. Let's see what Amby had to say about this one.

I stepped out again and went right to the mirrors, not glancing at Amby at all. Yes, this jacket was even better. "Well, Mils, what do you think?"

When she didn't reply, I looked around, finding everyone gone but Amby. "Millie?"

"I found something to try on," she called from the second room.

"That one's too tight," Amby said from behind. I turned to see his nose still buried in his stupid book. "Looks like you've been saving it from your childhood wardrobe."

I pinched my nose, successfully stopping a *fuck you* before asking, "Are you just going to sit there criticizing?"

Amby shrugged and slouched in his chair, hiking his ankle up over his other leg. "I'm only pointing out the obvious." He still wasn't looking at me, and something in his voice dripped with ridicule. "Then again, you seem to have bad luck with getting suits dirty. You should consider that while searching for the next person to con into marriage. Will they have a lake?"

Something coiled in my chest as I narrowed my eyes at him from the dais. "If you're tossing out insults, at least have the courage to say them to my face."

"Did you know pods of orca are led by a female? Interesting." Amby tilted his head at his book and turned the page.

I stepped off the dais and forced my lungs to inhale as I slowly approached him, until my thighs hit his crossed knee. Then I snatched his book straight out of his lap and turned it to see the title, *Whales*.

What the fuck?

I tossed the book to the floor, watching Amby turn to glance at it in surprise as if he couldn't believe what I had done. Leaning over, I grabbed both arms of his chair, trapping him under me as I stared at his petulant face with the same faint freckles I wanted to kiss a few days ago. The same pouty lips, strong jaw, and pretty glasses.

Amby glanced up at me with wide, daring eyes through those lenses, and my breath caught again. Why couldn't I resist him? He was nothing but trouble. He deserved some kind of punishment.

134

"Amby, dear," I said as smoothly as I could without closing the few inches between us to use my mouth to quiet him. "Since you're the expert on everything, including orcas, why don't you pick out the perfect suit for me? Look around. I'll wait."

Amby raised his chin and glared at me with flushed cheeks. "You going to make me do it? You'll have to lift this chair and take me over there. Like a servant carrying his prince."

"Oh, you little—"

"What do you think?" Millie called out, and I flung myself from Amby's chair. I barely had time to leap back onto the dais before the curtain to Millie's dressing room swung open and Emiline held it back.

Oblivious to my agitation, Millie exited with a big grin to show off a straight-hanging skirt with a men's black jacket on top. The lapels gaped open from her well-endowed bust in a pleated white blouse, and the jacket buttons nipped in cleverly to create a waist. The mix of men's and women's apparel was outrageously appealing. My sister never looked so beautiful.

"Damn, Mils," I swore without caring because she deserved it. "Are you trying to tip your cap for someone?"

"Maybe." Millie lifted her skirt to step onto the dais with me. I made room so she could use the full mirror, while I wondered the whole time who she meant.

"It looks amazing on you." Amby stood from his chair. He grabbed his book from the floor and dusted it off before setting it on a nearby table. "The blacks are rich and suit you well."

Amby's total flip from vexing to friendly didn't even bother me because my sister glowed like a candle from his compliment. When he stepped onto the dais, she gave him a big bear hug. Amby smiled at her the way he used to smile at me, with a dimple, and patted her shoulder gently. She was the one to let him go.

"Now, let's find your lost brother something," Amby said unexpectedly. He pursed his lips, as if deep in thought, and the playful Amby returned, promising my comeuppance.

What was he planning? To pick out the worst jacket? I glanced around and cringed at the slimy green atrocity hanging in the corner. Or even worse, that one with flower-embroidered sleeves. Only the worst sort of dandy would wear such ostentatious embroidery. Amby would just love to see me suffer in it.

Emiline helped Millie off the dais while Amby headed right for the flowery waste of cloth, of course. He touched the hanger, pausing, and a shiver passed through me.

I crossed my arms and glared at him, but he ignored me and moved to another rack. He rummaged around, no doubt searching for something even more horrendous, if such a thing existed, when Emiline joined him. Their hands bumped into each other over the same suit. Emiline stepped back with an approving nod while Amby pulled it out and faced it toward me.

The sleek black jacket appeared out of my price range with glimmering lapels and gold buttons. I barely dared touch the thing until Amby offered it to me by sliding his arm under the lower half to drape it properly, like a devoted servant. His slight bow and dropped gaze hinted at offering me more than a jacket.

"Will this do?" Amby asked, eyes on the floor.

When I didn't answer—because I wished we were alone so I could push him down on his knees—Amby raised his head to toss me a questioning eyebrow.

His dare was unspoken. I demanded he pick out a jacket, and he did. Now it was my turn to try on his choice, even if it cost more than I could afford. I couldn't back away from that raised eyebrow. I liked meeting Amby head-on in this odd game of wills we somehow entered. It wasn't about fighting over a woman or our past. It was just about us.

I slipped off the burgundy lapelled jacket and handed it to Millie. That left me on display in my bare shirt. I turned to the mirrors and motioned my arms back for Amby to slip his jacket choice onto me, daring him to dress me. When he moved to stand behind me with the jacket, I caught his gaze in the mirror and mimicked his dare right back to him.

Amby took a breath as he slipped the jacket up my arms and over my shoulders in one fluid movement, and his hands ran over the tops of my shoulders in a way that sent awareness through my entire body.

"Oh, that looks handsome!" Emiline said. I forgot Amby's sister was there. I nodded at her, thankful she turned to her brother. "Amby, why don't you help Zeth tie on the ascot? I'm going to help Millie change. I think we've found our ensembles for the day. Back to the dressing room, girls," she called, and Hattie joined her with Millie.

The curtain slid closed with a scrape of metal, and we were alone again. Amby drew close behind me until his body pressed to mine, stealing all thoughts as he whispered over my shoulder, "Swoon worthy."

"What are you doing?" I exhaled. All power shifted to Amby, and it wasn't the angry tension like before. Amby was being nice to me. I wasn't sure if I hated it or wanted more. I should hate it.

Amby moved away and cleared his throat. "Nothing. Sorry."

Before I could reply, Amby stepped off the dais, and I instantly missed him. I turned to watch him snatch something from a table and leap back up to face me.

"Do you want me to tie it, or would you rather do it?" Amby didn't meet my gaze as he held out the ascot.

That simple question felt like a million questions in one, yet I was sure Amby spoke about clothes. But I wanted to explore this... distraction, even if it forgave the man who ruined my plans. "You can tie it on me."

Amby's whole face was red now as he avoided looking at me, and I grinned. He reached up and leaned in close to wrap the ascot around my neck. I didn't care what the scrap of cloth looked like, only that Amby's soft lips were mere inches from mine.

I watched them move as Amby first bit his lip and quickly let it go.

"I'm never good at tying these things properly," he said. His dark eyes darted up at me through his glasses before dropping back down, appearing adorably nervous as his fingers worked with the fabric, caressing the flushed skin of my neck. Then Amby took a step back to observe me, putting a finger to his chin. "It all looks great on you. You need something else to complete it. I happen to have just the thing. Give me your hand."

I did so, raising my right hand between us, and Amby grabbed it lightly to flip it over while he fiddled for something in his jacket's side pocket. Something silver flashed as he slid a small ring onto my pinky.

I narrowed my eyes on him. "What's that for?"

"A ring. See how the stone is already changing colors? That's for me to know what mood you're in when I see you." He gave me a sultry stare as he twisted the ring on my finger. I huffed at him but eyed the small stone with curiosity. It was shifting, changing from a mottled green to deep purple, so dark it practically matched the silk of my jacket.

"Hm, almost black," Amby hummed as he continued to hold my hand. He smoothed his thumb over the stone, and I had to admit the jewelry was nice. What I liked even more was the way his fingers caressed mine, how low his voice sounded as he said, "I'm sure we can do something to adjust that color."

He was far too delicious to resist, so I leaned in to whisper against his ear, "Keep touching me, and I'll need you to adjust something else."

When Amby drew back, his eyes finding mine again, I thought he was going to turn me away, but he daringly yanked on my tie to draw me in close against his neck, and I groaned softly with encouragement. He tilted his head sideways, granting me a clear swatch of skin above his collar, so I brushed my lips against him and felt his shiver, a splendid reward.

"What's this?" he asked softly. "I thought you were angry at me."

"I am. I'm fucking furious," I mumbled against his pulse. I was already roused from our boldness. Glancing over his shoulder, I made sure we were alone in the shop and assured Amby, "But you're too damn enticing. So be a good boy and touch me."

The old Amby might have grabbed my ass. In fact, he'd done it many times when we were together. But this new, older Amby straightened to look at me, his cheeks pink and his eyes sparking with hunger. Maybe he saw the same thing from me, because Amby raised his hand and smoothed his thumb across my upper lip.

I chuckled against his thumb, enjoying the feel of his callouses against me, and spoke, "This isn't where I wanted you to touch me. I was thinking lower."

"That isn't very gentleman like of you."

"This is even less polite." I wrapped my mouth around his thumb and sucked, making him gasp. I wanted this since I touched Amby's hands in the parlor, and I wasn't sorry for taking the chance since he was so warm and solid, and so damn delicious.

I sucked harder and watched his eyes go wide. "You... are definitely... not a gentleman," he breathed as if he enjoyed stating that fact.

I hitched my hands into his jacket pockets to tug him against me, wanting him to feel what he was doing to me. Amby tensed, his other hand pressing slightly against my chest, but he didn't move away. That was encouraging. Our eyes locked, the stare between us magnetic, fiery. Amby gazed at me as if he wanted something else of his in my mouth.

Then my fucking stomach rumbled, protesting loudly. Apparently, my lack of food since yesterday meant Amby's thumb didn't count as sustenance.

"Hungry?" Amby asked, his brow furrowing.

I pulled back with reluctance and let his thumb pop out with a wet smack. Then I huffed low and raked a hand through my hair to hide how deeply I must be blushing. I didn't know what to say, so I answered with the truth, "Starving."

I was starving for Amby's attention. One touch, one look, one teasing dare, and I couldn't get enough of him. It was so confusing to have him back in my life again, especially when I should be hunting myself a spouse, but he was the only person who ever drew my eye. He had an energy that pulled me in and wouldn't let go. Even entering the shop, it was Amby I saw first. And heaven help me, I was starving for him.

I was also damn hungry for lunch.

Spinning my back to Amby, I tried for casualness. I made myself look at the suit he picked out for me. The ascot was eye-catching, a black and amber paisley that drew out the amber in my brown eyes, so I liked it. That was annoying. I wished I hated it.

Amby's demeanor seemed to change as he asked, "Would you... like to get something to eat? Perhaps at the cafe. We can get tea and sandwiches."

I turned to eye him with doubt as I shrugged off the jacket and handed it back to him. I loved the jacket too, but there was no way I could afford gold buttons and silk. Shedding the expensive material made me feel like I was turning back into the poor washer boy. And joining the Somersets for tea was more of a dream than reality. Amby's family had the money and time to waste a Thursday afternoon at the bakery cafe, but I had to wait until my con was complete, until I had some stranger's money to spend.

Fisting my hand, something tightened on my pinky, and I glanced down to find Amby's ring still on me. The stone was gray now, mocking me in a way, but I was reluctant to pull it off. Amby gave me a gift, even if he meant it as a joke, and I liked the damn thing.

Amby was still watching me, so I grumbled out, "No, thank you."

He made his way to the counter and picked up a basket. "Well, we do have some leftovers, which is even better. Cornbread and soup. Arthur made too much. You and Millie are welcome to take it."

I blinked at him, wanting to tell him we didn't need it, but on the other hand, realizing how much my body did need it. Millie too.

"I'll just set it here." Amby placed the basket in the chair he sat in earlier. "Feel free to take it if you want."

His kindness made my head a bit woozy, or maybe the lack of food was getting to me. I nodded at him and stepped off the dais, heading back into my dressing room to fetch my things. My heart was racing as I removed the paisley ascot and hung the silk on a hook. I forced my breath to return before pulling my stained jacket back on. Then I picked up that brown jacket from the stool, the one that would cost the least, and started to leave when the ascot Amby chose caught my eye. I took that too.

When I slid the curtain open, Hattie made me jump by being so close, leaning against the dressing room entrance. She wasn't watching me; she was simply waiting. As soon as she saw me, she said, "I'm glad you're back in Everdeen, Zeth. I always hoped you'd write to us. I sent Millie a letter not long after you both left."

"Oh? I don't recall her ever getting one. I would have remembered."

Hattie's face fell slightly. "It came back in the mail. Amby wrote letters to you too, but no matter. I'm so glad we reunited."

Before I could ask her to elaborate, she rejoined her family at the entrance and kissed Amby's cheek with a sisterly peck. He took her arm and glanced around her at me, so I strolled over to give Emiline my choices and pretended that the letters meant nothing. So what if he cared enough to write? He obviously never bothered to post them. Maybe they were angry letters.

I grabbed the basket of food from the chair and caught Amby's curious gaze but turned to my sister instead. "Mils, you ready?"

"Oh, yes. I'm leaving everything here and need to return for another fitting." She chuckled at Amby and his sisters, looking far happier than when we entered. New clothes and the company certainly brightened her disposition.

I was reluctant to admit that I enjoyed myself too, even if I didn't get what I wanted.

13

Ambrose

Sunday breakfast with my family was always the same. Father sat at the head of the table, while Emiline sat to his right and Hattie to his left. I took the chair beside my twin, and Mother's place had been at the other end of the table next to me. When Marigold still lived here, she'd filled in the seat across from me. I used to flick pieces of food at her when I was a child, only to get scolded by Father. But Mother always let me off easy, telling him I was only doing what children did best.

My eyes darted to my mother's empty chair now. How I missed her.

I didn't, however, miss Marigold. I was more than happy to see the vacant seat across from me, though if she were here, I'd be tempted to fling an orange slice at her like old times. For nostalgia's sake.

No, I didn't want to think about Marigold. Instead, I focused on Hattie yapping nearby and Father giving his "Mm-hm" responses as he ate his eggs and sausage.

"Oh, Em, I was wondering if I could wear that green dress for the Founders Day Festival after all," Hattie said.

Emiline sighed. "We settled on pink already. I'm stretched thin as it is at the shop. We still need final fittings for everyone's attire for the poetry salon in a couple weeks. You're just going to have to stick with what you chose."

"Oh, *fine.*"

"Pass the salt, dear," Father muttered.

I watched as Emiline handed Father the salt, and my mind wandered to a few days ago at the tailor shop, when Zeth's stomach had rumbled. I thought about it every day, constantly wondering if he and Millie had enough food or blankets. Probably not, if he was selling his mother's dresser. She'd had it for the entirety that she lived in the laundry. The memories of that place were tucked safely in my mind. Entering it once again had brought them all back. Maybe it was the warmth I felt there, mixed with the permanent smell of soap. But I didn't feel warm knowing Zeth and Millie had nothing to survive on.

It was hard to stay angry at Zeth for long, even if he'd assumed the wrong things about me. He seemed to forget he'd told me to stay out of his life the other day, because when we'd met in the tailor shop, he'd sucked on my thumb as if it was another part of my body. I recalled plenty of times where we'd done the same when we were younger, having made up after fighting with each other over something silly. Kissing and making up after an argument was always the best...

My stomach fluttered at the thought, and I smiled as I shifted my eggs around with my fork.

"What's so funny over there, Amby?" Emiline asked.

I met her curious eyes. "Oh, um, nothing." I quickly took a bite of eggs from my plate. I wasn't hungry, but I forced it down.

"Ambrose," Father's firm voice carried over the table. "You'll begin training for the new position at the bank in a week. Are you preparing for it?"

I stiffened, and his mustache twitched. Father wanted me to begin working my way up to owning the bank one day. I didn't want to step up at all. Perhaps I could stall...

Clearing my throat, I placed my hands in my lap and rubbed my thumb hard. "I'm not so sure... that stepping into a higher position at the bank is the right decision for me... right now."

My face burned, and I avoided meeting his gaze, as I was terrified of his expression. But I couldn't ignore the silence hanging in the air, nor the quiet clink of silverware on Hattie's plate. Each second that ticked by with no reaction from my father made the sweat build on my palms, and also had me deeply regretting what I'd said. Then he made a noise. It was that distinct grunt of disapproval.

"May I remind you, Ambrose..."

Here it comes.

"That the bank is called Somerset and Sons for a reason, and you are my only son."

I closed my eyes, hesitating before I said, "You have Marigold. She's much better at leading the business than me."

"She is not my son, though sometimes I wish she were."

Something sharp punctured my heart deeply. I winced as I opened my eyes and stared at my half-eaten eggs and sausage. "What does it matter if either of us is a man or a woman? She knows what she's doing, and I don't. You could simply change the name of the bank to suit *all* our family members."

"And undo our family's legacy?" He shook his head. "You've been very distracted lately, Ambrose. Perhaps instead of dallying around in that barn, you should be thinking more about your future." His voice was firm, and it instantly put me back in that dark place I always retreated to when I disappointed him. "It may do you good if I have that barn torn down."

"No!" I looked at him with some pathetic desperation in my voice.

"Father, you wouldn't," Emiline chimed in as my chest seized.

When he averted his gaze, so did I. Father had never said such a callous thing before. I willed myself to tell him what I really thought of his response, of the bank and his plan for me to continue the Somerset bloodline. But I couldn't. I was too terrified of what might ensue.

Father rose from the table and fixed me with his sharp eyes. "You *will* begin training at the bank. And you *will* do your best to court Miss Winters. Do you understand?"

When I took too long to answer him, he gave an angry huff and strolled out of the room. His footsteps echoed along the hall.

I blinked, stunned. I had actually...

"You made Father mad!" Hattie said, right as the front door slammed so hard, it rattled our tableware.

"He's mad at himself, he just doesn't know that yet," Emiline replied, grabbing my arm. "Are you alright, Amby? I'm glad you didn't give in to him."

The muscles in my body tensed as I let out a ragged breath. "I'm fine. I'm sorry you both had to witness that."

Emiline got up and hugged me awkwardly as I sat in the chair. My twin's warm embrace felt nice, but it couldn't chase away how much of a disappointment I was. "It's going to be alright, Amby. Father won't destroy the barn. He doesn't have it in him to do such a thing."

"Right." I pulled away to see her smiling sadly. When I looked over at Hattie, her face was creased in concern as well. "I'm fine. Really." I smiled at them both. "You two continue to... discuss your dresses for Founders Day. I'll be out for a while." I got up from my seat.

"You'll need a suit too, Amby," Hattie pointed out. "And also for the poetry salon."

"I'll let you pick one out for me."

Hattie squealed with delight. She had good taste in clothes, and Emiline made them well. Between the two of them, I didn't have to worry about the latest trending fashions. Not that I cared. I was much more comfortable in simple trousers and a shirt. Working outside with my hands, listening to the sounds of nature while I chopped and hammered and carved...

Yes, I needed to get outside.

I kissed my sisters and left the house, heading straight for the barn. It sat at the far edge of our land, so the exercise gave me time to think through the last few minutes, and days, and weeks. *Years.* Father was adamant about me settling down, making a family, and taking over the bank, but I didn't want the bank, or a wife. I only wanted to make furniture, to carve it and stain it and sell it, to make my living that way.

My father was threatening the one thing that made me happy. I had to hope Emiline was right, and he wouldn't destroy the barn that had become my safe haven.

If I had things my way, I'd have a house of my own that wasn't so grand. I'd be happy marrying someone like Zeth. Despite our backgrounds, him a poor boy and me a rich snot, we were alike in many ways. We fit together, like whipped cream and strawberries. Or perhaps coffee and cream. Did Zeth like coffee? Or strawberries?

Despite Zeth's mistrust, he seemed to care about me, and I had an urge to take care of him as well. I wanted to give him a home where he could loaf around after a hard day's work without his belly rumbling for food. We could eat supper together every night and relax in our rocking chairs on the porch to talk about our day. Just like how we used to look up through the loft door in the barn and count as many stars as we could. Back then, we'd lay for hours together, kissing, talking, sometimes dozing off until dark.

But dreaming about those things would get me nowhere. It was childish to desire such things when the reality of truth hit me right in the face. And the reality was that Zeth *needed* Annabelle. He needed some sense of belonging and security, that much was evident, and I couldn't give him any of that. He'd told me to get out of his life. I was ruining his plans.

And myself? My father was going to push me until I broke and gave in. There was no room for happiness.

Thinking about it all made me ache. Eager to shift my thoughts elsewhere, I came to the barn and opened the doors of my sanctuary. I immediately got to work on the chair with the large crack down its leg. I planned to replace the leg with another one and worked on sanding the new piece. After that, I wanted to detail the back of the chair with delicate ivy leaves. Getting the chair put together was part of the fun, but carving the designs brought me the most peace.

Maybe an hour went by in silent focus, sawdust and spiral wood shavings my only company, before I heard the clipped sounds of horse's hooves approaching. I paused and wiped my sweaty brow with the back of my arm, then stood to see who was riding. My sisters always walked to the barn, and surely my father wasn't coming over to apologize.

The noon sun was bright and warm as I made my way outside. When I squinted through the light, my stomach dropped. There, riding toward me on a horse, was the devil who'd been invading my thoughts all day. Alongside him rode Millie and Annabelle.

My body deflated. Seeing them together again was discouraging, but I wasn't all that surprised. Annabelle liked Zeth, after all.

I stepped back into the barn, hoping they hadn't seen me. But the image of Zeth's solid form moving up and down in a trot made my breath catch. How handsome he looked on a horse, wearing his new brown jacket. The color wasn't perfect, I didn't lie about that, but it really did accentuate his broad shoulders and chest. Biting my lip, I poked my head back outside, only to see them still trotting this way. My barn was their destination.

"Shit." I dusted off my sleeves and tried to straighten my hair. I was a mess, with my collar open and sweating. What would Zeth think?

As they drew closer, I listened carefully, hearing Millie talking excitedly about something. Then Zeth's voice was clear enough to catch as he teased his sister about manners. His reprimand was strict, but caring.

"Here we are," came Annabelle's voice. "Isn't it a lovely old barn?"

My whole body flushed with fire as I stood there, waiting for them to come in and see me. It would look as though I was hiding, so I had no choice but to greet them.

Clearing my throat, I stepped out and faced them, not realizing I was still holding my chisel until sunlight hit the silver. "Annabelle, Millie." I nodded at them both before my gaze darted over. "Zeth."

"Amby." When Zeth regarded me with a nod back, his golden eyes glimmered in the sunlight. Beautiful.

"Nice to see you all out on such a nice day." As soon as I said it, my lips pursed. *Nice to see you all out on such a nice day?*

Today wasn't going to end well. I knew it already.

147

Annabelle flashed a brilliant grin. "You as well. I'm taking Zeth and Millie on a tour of my estate. I hope you don't mind us cutting through your land."

My face faltered slightly. If she was showing him her estate, it meant Zeth had found out the truth. Annabelle and I weren't courting, and since they were together, he was still determined to win her hand, even after our flirting in the tailor shop.

The tool slipped from my hand and landed in the dirt with a *thump*. I quickly bent to pick it back up, hoping to recompose myself in the process. "I don't mind at all. I'm just... doing some work."

"On the barn?" Zeth asked. His horse had shied at the sound of my tool, and Zeth shifted in his saddle, looking uneasy with controlling the beast.

"No, actually just..." I ignored how much I disliked seeing him riding with Annabelle and planted my fists on my hips. "Wood. Some woodworking. You know, cutting and carving, all that."

Zeth's lips twitched—he was holding in a laugh at me, I knew— and I wanted the ground to swallow me whole. Their visit caught me off guard, and now my words were coming out as stupid as ever.

"Would you mind showing us something you're working on? I've always wanted to see." Annabelle sat tall in the saddle with her blonde hair braided over one shoulder.

"I really don't have much to show—"

Before I could finish, she slipped off the side of her horse and walked into the barn.

Zeth stood in his stirrup and swung a leg over his saddle to follow her. He looked like the best horseman in the world, until he stepped down and his other foot got hung up in the stirrup. Then his horse shimmied away from him, and Zeth hopped along with one arm holding on for dear life to the pommel.

When Millie snorted with amusement, Zeth glared over his saddle at her something fierce and tried to hush her while he hopped. Funny enough, Annabelle wasn't witnessing any of this comic farce. She was too busy looking inside the barn.

Yet the horse kept shuffling sideways, and Zeth kept stumbling on one leg, the space between him and his horse getting wider and wider.

When Zeth cursed, I rushed forward to grab the horse's reins. I ducked under his raised arm, the one holding the pommel, and wrapped my hand around his back to steady him. Once he hopped closer to me and stood upright, I used my other hand to help him remove his shoe from the stirrup so he could pretend nothing happened.

Zeth's arm clung to my sweaty neck, and for a fleeting moment we stood there still attached, staring intently. I tried to ignore his closeness until he tightened his grip to tug me in tighter, and murmured into my ear a heartfelt, "Thank you."

I let out a breathy laugh as I let him go. "Anytime."

When we pulled away, I made my way into the barn to find Annabelle admiring the chair I'd been working on.

"This is marvelous!" She smoothed her hand over the freshly-sanded surface. "Where did you get the wood?"

"Some from fallen trees... others I've bought from the mill at discount."

"Stay out here with the horses, Millie. Rest your ankle," Zeth said. He came into the barn, seemingly half listening to us as he strolled gracefully past the old stalls full of big haystacks. We had a new barn now for the horses but sometimes stocked extra hay here.

Zeth approached a piece of furniture while he fingered the buttons of his suit jacket to open it, knocking the sides back, and tucked his gloved hands into the pockets of his trousers in a dashing way I could never accomplish.

Annabelle watched him too. I didn't blame her. It was easy to see why she liked him. He was every bit a tall, handsome gentleman with manners and grace. Well built, solid and mysterious. But I enjoyed that foul-mouthed, playful, *real* side of him.

When I felt Annabelle's gaze on me, I picked up a sanding block, then put it back down, not sure what to do.

"How long have you been woodworking?" she asked.

"A few years."

Zeth moved again, and I watched him from the corner of my eye while answering Annabelle's next question about my tools. He glanced over a few nicer chairs at the back of the barn, and I desperately hoped he noticed my work, but his eyes roamed up to the high ceiling braces and the hayloft where we used to fool around.

"Did you see this chair, Zeth? Such fine work."

Out of all the pieces to point out, it had to be the chair with the broken leg. I didn't need Zeth looking at the shitty furniture I had broken, but he did just that. He walked closely around my back, lingering long enough for me to smell his musky, soapy scent before he showed up between me and Annabelle. I hoped he didn't see the cracked wood on the bottom leg as he caressed the ivy carving on top with his long, gloved fingers.

"I love the intricate designs here, Amby," Zeth said. "Reminiscent of the skilled craftsmanship that comes out of Zembia. Their furniture sells really well, always in demand. You clearly have a talent for woodworking. You're very good."

The way his voice hummed that praise melted me. I bit my lip to hide my smile so no one saw how much his words affected me. When Zeth raised his gaze, and I caught honest admiration in those sparkling depths, my stomach fluttered. Why was he suddenly being nice to me? Was it genuine, or a front for Annabelle?

"Did you recently learn?" Annabelle asked.

"I always loved whittling as a boy. When I worked with a carpenter at the local mill for a few years, I fell in love with building pieces and carving. This chair is far from perfect, though. I messed up and hammered too hard."

"I bet it's just fine," Zeth assured me with the calm confidence of this new gentleman he was playing as, the one who was trying so hard to be perfect for Annabelle.

That bothered me, so I crossed my arms and dared, "Alright. Try it, if you insist."

Zeth's eyebrow rose, and at first I didn't think he would take my dare, but then he planted his ass in the chair. As soon as he did, the broken leg snapped the rest of the way. It dumped Zeth—somewhat slowly and comically—onto the dirty barn floor.

It was far from graceful. Zeth's legs sprawled out on the floor, and he looked up at me in surprise. When I covered my mouth and cracked up, his eyes crinkled at the corners as he gave an uproarious laugh. I broke into laughter along with him, hands on my knees, and for a moment, it felt like we were kids. The Daring Duo once again.

When Annabelle's mouth tightened with parental dismay, it only made us laugh harder. She didn't understand this familiar companionship between us.

"What happened?" came Millie's voice. I tried to dry the tears from my eyes to see her in the doorway, still on her horse and staring from her saddle at us like we were madmen.

"Everything's fine," I told her, trying to recompose myself. "Just Zeth showing us how to gather wood for a fire."

"Although I don't suggest lying in the fire," Annabelle joked with a stiff voice that made Millie grin. "I suppose now Zeth will have to stay and help Amby fix the chair. It's the only decent thing to do. Millie, shall we ride ahead?"

"You're going to leave him here with me?" I asked, not entirely opposed to the idea, but I wasn't sure if I was going to end up with playful or scornful Zeth today.

"My brother could use some time away from us girls," Millie answered. "We should get moving before my ankle becomes too stiff."

"I absolutely agree." Annabelle claimed Millie's reins from the horse's front and mounted her own horse. "Zeth, join us at my stable when you're done. I'm going to show Millie my car."

"You are?" Millie gasped. "Can we go for a ride?"

Annabelle chuckled as she rode on with Millie, and for a long moment, I stood there watching them both in stunned silence. They rode as close together as they could, both of them chatting away.

Clearing my throat, I lent Zeth a hand. "You really don't have to help me fix the chair. The leg was already broken. I couldn't resist messing with you."

"Alright, in that case, I won't," Zeth teased with a wide grin as he accepted my hand and stood up next to me. For a moment, we locked gazes. My hand remained in his gloved one, my cheeks heating.

Then Zeth averted his eyes and pulled his hand out of my grasp to swipe at the back of his jacket and trousers. I frowned and watched as he perused my other pieces of furniture.

"I'm running out of room to store everything," I said. "If you see anything you'd like to take off my hands so I can fit more in here, you can have it."

"So when I thought you were offering cast-offs for the laundry, you were actually offering me your handmade furniture?"

"Oh... um, yes."

"Then I'm sorry. I was ungrateful in the face of your generosity."

I shook my head. "Please, Zeth, I didn't think anything of it."

Zeth nodded and strolled over to the table set, running a hand along the top as he passed. He stopped when he reached a porch rocker and repositioned it. "Are you starting a business with all this?"

"Well... I suppose it's a dream of mine. I thought about setting up a tent at the Founders Day Fest and selling a few pieces."

"That's an excellent idea, Amby. You should do it."

My head whirled from his compliment. Was he no longer angry at me? He was using my nickname, so perhaps not. Annabelle was gone, and yet he was still being kind. I wasn't sure why. When Zeth's eyes finally crossed the barn to find mine, they were warm, full of zeal and something hidden that made me feel good inside.

"What's stopping you?" Zeth continued. "To sell at the fest, I mean."

"Nothing." I rubbed my thumbnail. "I'm not sure I can make enough money off something like this, just me. It's exhausting work."

"And your dad doesn't approve, does he?"

That only brought back Father's words at the breakfast table, of tearing down the barn. When I looked down, Zeth clicked his tongue.

"I understand," he said. "But I think you have a promising start here... as long as they don't all break when someone sits on them?"

"Maybe you should try them all out for me to see if they hold up."

His lips tilted as he held my gaze. He removed his riding gloves from each finger with slow precision, and I caught the glimmer of silver on his right pinky. My stomach fluttered. I couldn't see the color of his ring, but I hoped it might reflect his contentment as he brushed his hand against the rocker's smooth seat with a sigh.

Zeth turned to sit and settled into the chair's embrace with his legs spread. Then he leaned back to start moving the chair, his smile growing wider with each rock. "You know, this may be my new favorite chair."

"You like it?"

"Mmm," Zeth hummed, closing his eyes and settling back even more. He looked incredibly comfortable as he murmured, "Thank you, Amby."

"For what?"

"You're a better man than me. You didn't tell her."

I blinked at him in confusion. "Tell her what?"

When the chair stopped, Zeth opened his eyes and leaned his elbows on his knees. He steepled his fingers and stared at them before taking a deep breath. "Amby, I gave you the perfect chance to tell Anna that I'm deceiving her, that I have nothing but fucking water. But you didn't. I knew it the moment she asked us to go riding today. Your... fairness was all I could think about as we rode."

I looked away, my neck flushing. "Well, perhaps not completely fair. I did try to distract you from Annabelle."

Zeth whistled. "Damn, so you *were* flirting on purpose. And making me think you both were together?"

"Guilty. I'm a naughty boy." I turned my head back and raised my eyebrow at him.

Zeth sat straighter in the chair and splayed his fingers out on his right hand before curling them into a fist. Then he gave me a lopsided grin.

"But..." I tilted my head. "I swear to you I'm not a spy. I'd never rat you out to anyone."

"No need to swear. I shouldn't have gotten so angry at you, not when I'm hiding my poverty behind a fancy facade. You have every right to think ill of me."

I laughed as if he were crazy. "No. Despite this... stupid quarrel we seem to be in, you're still my best friend."

"Your best friend?" Zeth rose and walked toward me with a scoff. "You didn't replace me?"

"Replace Zeth Washer?" I smiled crookedly at him. "Never."

"You're the only one who finds me irreplaceable, I assure you."

As much as I wanted to tease him back, I couldn't. Because the comment bothered me. It was a truth masked behind a nonchalant wave of humor. So, I couldn't help but move forward enough to rub Zeth's arm in a comforting way. "You don't realize how admirable you are, do you?"

"No, that's hardly the word I would use."

"I know. But that's the way I see you. I've always admired you growing up. The way you'd help others with school work and your family at the laundry. The way you helped me..." I trailed off. It didn't feel like the right time to mention our mothers. Instead, I said, "And now you know all about antiques. Working as an appraiser. I could never do that. You want what's best for you and Millie, and will do anything to attain it. You know what you want and are going for it. That's admirable, Zeth."

A prickle dug into my heart, and I pulled my arm away to rub my chest. If I had Zeth's determination, I would no doubt already be living on my own with my furniture business.

Next to me, Zeth shook his head, as if he didn't believe anything I said. Then he let out a heavy breath and removed his cap to toss it onto the work table. His dark hair was disheveled as he turned back to me with a playful smile. "Why are you buttering me up, Rosie? Is there something you want while we're alone in this barn?"

"There's no butter on my words. I spoke truthfully. I never meant to insult you the other day, but I did, and I'm sorry. I was concerned for you and Millie when you told me all you had was water. And also... Annabelle called me her friend the other day. She pointed out the obvious, that we have no spark." I crossed my arms and met his eyes. "You win."

The way Zeth's head tilted told me he took in my words and was struggling to understand. But his expression changed into the mischievous one I remembered from our youth. The one that told me he was about to pull some big prank.

"Zeth..." I started, eyeing him carefully as he took a step toward me. "What are you about to—"

He suddenly dipped down to sweep me off my feet and hoisted me up into his arms. I gasped, flailing my arms before grabbing onto his stout shoulders. Zeth chuckled softly and jostled me to adjust his grasp as he began walking to the back of the barn, carrying me like some maiden in distress. Goodness, he was strong.

"Since you admire me so much..." Zeth growled against my ear, "I thought you might wish to see more of me. Or am I wrong?"

My eyes widened in both excitement and anxiety at his insinuation that we should roll around in the hay. I couldn't help but tighten my hold around the back of his neck and move in close enough to press my forehead against his, making Zeth grin.

Without warning, his support under my legs disappeared. My arms clung onto his shoulders but gravity won, and my legs dropped before I fell backward. Zeth went right with me as we crashed into crisp softness. Hay exploded around me, as did his laughter.

I laughed with him, flicking a piece of straw at his face. "Ass," I teased.

"You should've seen how scared you looked," Zeth hummed with pleasure.

Smiling, Zeth sat up to straddle my lap, and I wrapped my arms around his hips, locking him against me so he couldn't move. He'd put me in this position, and I wasn't letting him go.

I stared adoringly at him as Zeth trailed his fingers along my arms, so featherlight that goosebumps rose on my bare forearms. When he reached my hands, he pulled them away from his hips, and I feared he might get up. Instead, he curled his fingers around my wrists and pushed my arms back into the hay, near my head. Leaning over me, Zeth held me down. I blinked at him, my face burning under his eyes. Eyes that sparkled like a glowing sunset as they watched me closely. Perhaps calculating.

"Zeth," I whispered.

"Yeah, Rosie?"

That name on his lips did things to me, things I shouldn't give in to, but I couldn't help my next words. "You're... incredibly handsome."

When Zeth's gaze dropped to my lips, I wanted him to kiss me so badly. If I let him, I was done for. I'd crumble and never be able to put myself back together. But temptation was hard to resist when it was staring me right in the face. Especially as he lowered onto his forearms until his solid stomach grazed against mine. I froze. Was he going to kiss me this time?

He certainly appeared to be pondering it as he raised one of his hands to trace the edge of my jaw with his fingertips. I sighed into his caress. It felt wonderful to have him so close, to feel his chest rise and fall against me, his breath so near it tickled my cheek. My heart was racing like a river in spring.

"Zeth, if you keep touching me like that... I won't be able to pull away," I told him, closing my eyelids against temptation.

"I enjoy seeing you react to me, and hearing what my touch does to you."

"Oh?" My lids parted slightly. "You like seeing me lose control?"

"Yes." Zeth ran his fingers through my hair. "I shouldn't, but I have this crazy desire to touch you, taste you, and leave my mark on your skin."

"Who said that's crazy?" I whispered. "What if I want you to do all those things to me... and more?"

His fingers tightened delightfully in my curls, until a soft groan slipped from me. Zeth answered with a devilish grin before he leaned down to graze my lips.

"That *more* has me intrigued," he whispered against me.

I inhaled sharply under his teasing mouth, sure he felt what his actions were doing to me below my belt. He hadn't kissed me in nearly ten years, and now I was absolutely ravenous for him. I let out a soft sigh as I said, "Do you know how much I want you right now?"

"Then be mine, one last time, Rosie."

One last time?

I suddenly burned up inside, both from how aroused I was, and also from anger. My hand curled in his collar, and I pushed slightly against him, ready to shove him away. But I couldn't. I didn't want him to leave me right now. I selfishly wanted him.

I'm sure he saw my conflicted expression as he stared intently at me, waiting. Zeth wanted me *one last time*. Not for love, only for pleasure and nothing else. And if I wasn't such a fool, if I hadn't let him sucker me into this position, we probably wouldn't be in this situation. Then again, I was ready and willing to do it. Because I was so desperate, because I was so... heartsick.

This was my punishment. For when I called him a thief. For when I pushed him in the lake. For when I tried to distract him away from Annabelle.

For when I broke his heart nine years ago.

Zeth deserved far better than me, as there was nothing else I could give him but my body. He would use me before he left and continued to pursue Annabelle. But at least for this moment, I could pretend he was mine again. That's all I wanted.

Nodding, I gripped his collar to pull him closer to me, letting him know I wanted him. Because I deserved every wicked thing that came my way. I deserved to be used.

Zeth's face relaxed, the corner of his lips tilting as he pressed them against mine. Instantly, a spark ignited between us as his tongue sought entrance. I let him in to tangle with me, enjoying the way he demanded a fight. Feeling Zeth's mouth again was different, new, and oh so profound. The way he devoured me made my mind swirl and my body light up into a fiery brilliance.

Caressing the sides of his face, I pulled him against me more, showing him how much I'd missed him, how much I craved his affections. And when Zeth sucked in my bottom lip, teasing me with how good his mouth would feel on other parts of my body, I exhaled and moved my hips against him.

He bit my lip with a groan before his rough mouth moved to my jaw. He claimed me there with his tongue before lowering to explore my neck with heated, stinging kisses.

I pulled at Zeth's jacket, trying to yank it off, and he sat up enough so I could help him out of the sleeves. My fingers fumbled at the buttons on his vest until Zeth grabbed my arms to hold them down by my sides. I stared at him through half-lidded eyes, panting as he leaned forward to apply more pressure to where his strong hands captured my wrists and held me under his hungry gaze.

"You look so fucking good like this, Rosie. All grown up, yet prettier than ever."

"You think I'm pretty?"

"Gorgeous," he answered easily.

I didn't know why I needed to hear it, but I did. He thought I was pretty, *gorgeous*. Oh, how those words lit me up inside. He had me trapped beneath him, but I felt so free in his grasp. Protected, as if I could just be myself. "You should tell me other sweet things while you take off my clothes."

"There's my daring boy." Zeth rose to sit over my hips again, releasing my arms from my sides. "But I'm not giving in so easily."

Instead of undressing me, Zeth unbuttoned his own vest with a tease of long fingers, circling the disc before sliding it through.

I bit my sore lip as I watched him, folding my arm under my head. While he stripped, I caught sight of the aura ring on his pinky. It was a reminder that he was mine for the moment as it shimmered purple, for passion.

Zeth shrugged off his vest with a movement that showed how well his muscles strained the thin white fabric of his shirt. When his hands moved to his shirt buttons to pop them open, my temptation to touch him grew with every exposed inch of skin, until that fabric joined his vest and jacket in the hay.

I whistled as I soaked him in, from his confident gaze to his firm arms and torso. "My, how you've changed."

Unable to stop myself, I touched his stomach, sliding my palm through the thick, soft hairs that trailed from his navel and up to his chest. A sharp contrast from the few hairs on me.

Zeth's chuckle rippled beneath my hand. "Are you appreciating how much I've grown?"

"Absolutely. Makes me want to appreciate other parts of you."

Zeth undid his trousers and pulled the waistband down until he was in full view. My brow perked high as I cherished how clearly aroused he was for me. He was allowing me to get so close. But then my gaze snapped back up to his eyes, the part of him I loved most. I saw lust there, perhaps something more. I wanted to see how deep I could fall into those dark pools.

"How can I contend with that?" I raked a hand over my hair, feeling so hot now.

"Ah, darling, there's nothing you need to do but enjoy," Zeth purred, leaning back over to capture me in another fiery kiss.

I grabbed Zeth's bare arms to kiss him back, letting his warmth surround me like a blanket. My palms smoothed over his shoulders, over his scar, and down his body. Breaking away from his lips, I hummed pleasantly as Zeth kissed along my face and to my shoulder. As he tugged my collar aside to taste my skin, I planted several wet pecks against his neck, doing the same to him as he did to me, each spot leaving a mark. I wouldn't be the only one being claimed today.

"You're talented with that mouth of yours," Zeth complimented with a low hum, and I moaned in response as I sucked his skin.

Pulling away, I asked, "Would you like to see what else I can do with it?"

"Is this the more you offered?"

"Why don't you lay back and I'll show you?" I moved onto my elbows, nudging him up, and grabbed his waist.

But Zeth's hand pressed against my chest to push me back, and I landed with a grunt. "No, from down there."

My blood rushed at that demand. I nodded quickly, my mouth twitching as Zeth removed my glasses, set them to the side, and shifted on his knees until he reached my face. When Zeth's hand planted in my hair, I gasped. He tugged it gently to pull me toward him, and I took his cock wholly right away.

"Fuck, Rosie," Zeth groaned as he tilted his head back. "I've missed you. Everything about you."

Everything? I closed my eyes against the sting of tears that formed from his beautiful words. He *missed* me. After all the cruel things he'd said to me about breaking up, about ruining things with Annabelle, he missed me.

I needed to focus on pleasuring him, nothing more. So I hummed my reply against him, delighting in the sounds he made, relishing his taste. Able to open my eyes now, I glanced up to see his face full of euphoria as he watched me.

"So beautiful," he groaned, loosening his grasp to caress my hair.

A pathetic whine escaped my throat before I could repress it. Hoping he didn't hear that, I pulled back enough to pay attention to the tip of his cock. When Zeth let out a heavy moan, it sent such a thrill through me. I was so absorbed in him now, giving him all the attention he deserved, all the attention I'd craved to give him since seeing him again.

"Rosie," Zeth panted. "I've fantasized about you taking me again, but you're far better than my dreams."

I pulled off to look up at him. When I planted a firm kiss against his hard length, keeping my eyes locked with his, his thumb tenderly circled a spot on my scalp.

Then he pulled away and let me go, and I licked my lips, barely able to take a breath before he shifted and bent to claim me in a rough kiss. His hands found their way between us and made quick work of my shirt buttons, popping them free as I adored the muscles in his arms. My fingers dipped into the curves and grooves, and Zeth's palms explored down to undo my trousers to expose me more.

Straddling my waist, Zeth captured my hands to pin them above my head like before. I was vulnerable with my shirt and trousers flung open for him to leisurely view. When he licked his lips, looking ready to devour me, I whimpered. I liked this Zeth who did what he wanted with me. I tried to pull out of his grasp enough to take his hand, but Zeth held me still. Damn him for being so rough, and damn me for liking it.

When Zeth's hips began to rock against me, pleasure took hold of me, and I bucked into him. Feeling his wet cock against mine sent waves of bliss swirling through my body. I arched my back, yearning for more of him as my skin broke out in fever.

"Fuck," I groaned.

"Mm," Zeth hummed and kissed my shoulder. "You're being such a good boy."

"Yeah?" My voice cracked. Yes, I was Zeth's good boy. At least I was that. My fists clenched. I was aching to touch him. When I tried to break free from his grasp again, he thankfully let me.

"Zeth…" *I want to be yours.* I threw my arms around his neck to pull him against me, hoping he could feel how much I wanted this. He was mine again. I wanted to tell him so badly how he made me feel, but I couldn't.

Instead, I let my head fall back into the hay, allowing Zeth to take full control as he kissed me, as his hands touched me everywhere. I held him so close, there was nothing between us but passion. This felt so good, to voice my pleasure as he moved against me, to grope every part of him I could. Until my hands tightened on him, and I let out a string of moans that told him I was close.

"Let go for me, Rosie," Zeth huffed against my cheek with a fiery breath.

Part of me didn't want to, because I knew as soon as I let myself go with him, that would be it. That would be the end of *us.* I wanted this moment to last. But that part of me was already building up, and after hearing Zeth's command, I grabbed the back of his head and pulled him to me as hot release rolled through me. I turned my face to the crook of his neck to muffle my cries of pleasure while Zeth shook above me with his own release between us.

"Amby…" Zeth kissed my ear. It was sloppy and harsh but surprisingly intimate.

My lips brushed against his neck as I panted, kissing all the places I'd bruised as I held him tighter to me. I didn't want to let him go. And Zeth stayed as still as his harsh breathing allowed above me, maybe wanting the same. My fingers caressed the back of his neck gently before I ran them through his hair, massaging his scalp.

I wanted Zeth to hold me, to talk to me about what we shared. I wanted to ask him if he also felt connected. Perhaps we could laze around like this for the rest of the afternoon, making up for lost time until the sun set. And even beyond then, every day.

"You okay?" I whispered after another minute, trailing my nails lightly along his back.

Zeth shivered against me. Then he nodded and sat on his knees to tug up his trousers. I dug in my pocket to pull out a handkerchief and held it out to him so he could clean off, but Zeth shifted to my side to take it and carefully cleaned me first. My heart sang from his care. I watched as he wiped himself then crumpled the handkerchief to tuck it into one of his pockets before buttoning his trousers. When he was done, he offered me a hand with a fleeting grin.

I took Zeth's hand and let him help me to my feet. I smiled, but quickly realized how quiet he was. How quiet we both were. Suddenly, the air felt awkward, especially when Zeth began buttoning my shirt, and not once did he meet my gaze. I wanted him to look at me, to notice me. Didn't he see me standing right in front of him, yearning for his attention?

I frowned as it hit me. This was all over now. We had our responsibilities to return to.

"It's alright," I told him, moving his hands gently out of the way so I could button the rest. Turning, I closed my trousers and bent to grab my glasses. I set them on my face with shaky fingers.

"I... should meet up with..." Zeth started.

"Right." I nodded before making my way out of the stall, feeling a little dizzy, and stood at my work bench.

Zeth came out a moment later with his clothes mostly in order. He raked a hand through his hair to scatter any hay and joined me to reclaim his cap. He tugged it on and looked outside. "Guess... I'll see you around."

Something shifted in my universe. It was as if a giant wave came crashing over me, enough to extinguish all the heat from my body.

A lump rose in my throat as I stared down at the bench. I picked up my chisel and nodded.

Anger and jealousy swelled inside me. At my father, at Zeth for leaving Everdeen in the first place and now coming back to pour salt into old wounds. For using me, though I'd let myself be used. I was pathetic. I was lost. Full of regret.

I was a piece of shit.

Despite this, I took a deep breath, eyes on my tool, and choked out, "Goodbye, Zeth."

He said nothing. I listened as he walked out. It wasn't until I heard him mount his horse and ride away that I glanced up. Tears blurred my vision as I watched him go. I scanned all the pieces of furniture I'd built, then looked over at the stall where Zeth and I had handled each other a moment ago. Proof of his kisses were marked all over me, just as he'd wanted. I could still feel his hands holding me down, the sound of his voice as he purred my name reserved for his lips only.

I pinched the corners of my eyes to stifle my tears, but they fell anyway.

Damn Zeth Washer.

No, damn *me*. I let him into my life again. As soon as he walked right back into it, it felt as if we'd never parted. I could have walked away at the picnic instead of tagging along with him and Annabelle. I could have stayed home rather than gone to her house the next day, *knowing* he'd be there. I could have delayed delivering the letter to his house and never helped with the dresser or given a damn about what kind of suit he wanted, or that he only had water. I could have told him to leave my barn. Instead, I let him stay and talk, let him sit in that chair he loved so much, and then I indulged in him. And I fucking loved it.

How dare he come back here and stir up feelings that took years to bury, only to abandon me again?

But I had never completely buried them, had I? I knew it when I dreamed about him. When I looked up at that hayloft every time I came into the barn and thought about what we used to do there. Perhaps that was why I continued to work in this barn. It always

163

brought back memories of Zeth. I had been holding onto him this whole time. His laughter, his affection, his determination. All of him.

I let out a painful whimper and sniffled. It hurt so much to be around him, to endure his touch and smile. He'd taken my heart with him to the City and held it there, and when he brought it back, he crushed it.

Clenching my fists, I eyed one of the extra chairs I'd built that appeared perfect, but the legs were loose. I stormed over to it and peered at the crafted wood, hating the way it sat there doing nothing but collecting sawdust. So perfect on the outside, but waiting to fall without the proper support.

Grabbing it, I upturned it and kicked at each flimsy leg until they all broke. Then I pulled off the back, yanking so hard I strained, red in the face, until it finally flew off, and a long nail jabbed my arm.

I stepped back, panting heavily, to look at the pile of broken wood. I closed my eyes against the sting on my arm from where the nail pierced me, feeling the blood running along to my wrist. It felt good to release all the pain I'd been holding in for years—from trying to please my father, to losing a sense of who I was, to losing Zeth once, and now losing him again... I had taken my anger out on something I had created. That's when it struck me.

I was angry at myself.

And now... I had two broken chairs.

14

Zeth

When I left Amby in the barn, I felt nothing.

Nothing, because I wrote every desire and doubt regarding my love for Amby onto imaginary paper and crumpled it up before swallowing it down. I trapped those emotions in my belly with everything else I should've felt for the past nine years. That's where unruly feelings belonged. It was better to stash them away safely. I needed room in my mind for more important responsibilities.

So, I rode back to the Winters estate on my rental horse, and once there, pulled up my collar to hide the abrasions on my neck. Anna blinked like a wise owl as she politely invited me in for tea. I declined. I wasn't thirsty. I didn't want to linger, or kiss her, or do anything with her at all.

Millie depended on me to provide. We had a plan, yet I wasn't following it. I failed to give Anna a courting kiss. I couldn't find the words. I could barely smile in her direction without seeing Amby lying in the hay, or feeling his arms wrapped around my neck as he tugged me close with some sort of desperation which echoed from my own soul. I remembered how enticingly Amby bit his lip to hide his excitement, how sweet his whimper sounded while I held him down.

So we left, and Millie filled my silence with pleasant chatter as we rode into town. She had a fun time viewing Anna's car, and cooed over the leather bracelet Anna gave her as a get well gift. I ensured she entered the laundry safely before I rode on with both of our horses to the stable. Once there, the kind handler who discounted our fee this morning also kindly helped me dismount. But I imagined Amby's support instead of this stranger's, just as he'd helped me this morning from the stirrup.

Amby...

The handler led the horses to their stalls while my chest struggled to move. I stood outside watching the sun set over the stable, casting a deep shadow over me while people rushed past on the sidewalk and street. I only noticed the blur of their motions until it became dark. Eventually, I stuffed my hands into my pockets and strolled back to the laundry as slowly as my feet would carry me.

My stomach weighed me down. There was a whole trash can inside me filled to the brim with wadded up papers. Memories and feelings, names and experiences, all spilling over. It made me choke, and my eyes stung from holding it in. I don't know how I reached the little alleyway covered in ivy before my trash can toppled over. I stumbled as the crumpled wads of my past spread open, and I barely reached the door without being sick.

My prior experiences with Amby were nothing like today, and holy shit, I never knew... I didn't know what I asked of him—of myself—when I requested one more time together. One perfect time. My Rosie...

Tears welled now as fear leaped off the stupid page in my stomach. I never felt so terrified as I did while Amby held me close to kiss the bruises he gave me, and gently asked if I was okay, because I wasn't. I wasn't okay. I was scared to lose him. And I was scared to chase him. No matter what I did, my heart was going to break all over again.

And that only shuffled my pages to anger. Feeling weak, my knees gave out, and I hit the ground, collapsing against the laundry's side door, crumpled inside and out. My head hit the warped wood, but I welcomed the sting. It was easier to deal with than the hostility that halted me for the last nine years. I carried such hate over my breakup with Amby that I closed myself off from others and blamed him for being an uncaring rich kid. I thought he got over me so easily, but he mourned our separation. He still called me his best friend before letting me use his mouth... and that only made me angrier at myself.

I was so damn selfish for misunderstanding Amby, so blinded by my bitterness that I didn't realize how angry I'd become at him, at this town—even at Anna and her embroidered pillows and tea sets. I'd acted like one of the wealthy pricks I despised. Amby deserved much more than that last time, and I hated myself for hurting him.

I tasted salty tears on my lips, but I didn't recall crying. I heard the sobs as they started, unable to hold them back. They tumbled around inside of me now, escaping, until they rattled my chest. Deep, horrid sounds that demanded a voice since I ignored them for so damn long. I welcomed them now. Purposefully letting the anguish out felt better than having no control at all.

I wrote those memories of helplessness down many times. I worked so fucking long to learn my trade, only to watch my dreams destroyed right in front of me. I was helpless to stop it. Dad leaving, Amby breaking up with me, Mum moving us, losing my job... *Fuck*, I couldn't control anything, I never could. I still felt like a little kid peering in from the outside who didn't belong with the elite kids at school.

Frustration filled my pages for all the times I couldn't steer my path, couldn't stop the rain, or avoid the sorrow that fate was determined to throw in my way.

Then there was the regret I felt over my mum. She wasn't clever or talented but she managed to put food in my mouth, clothes on my bones, and a roof over my head. She loved me with every scrap of her heart. She held me close on bad days. She made even the hardest thing seem possible. Then she got sick, and I watched in agony while she weakened, day by day, until eventually... she slipped away. There's some sort of hell in watching your loved ones suffer. Even worse, when you can't help them be comfortable or well, because you don't have the damn money required to heal them. Life shouldn't be about money. Yet, it was, and guilt ate at me from the inside. I didn't earn enough, *I* wasn't enough to make life possible for Mum when she needed me.

It was all... unfair. Devastating. Wrong. I was so useless in the fight that was always against me. Having to sell everything we owned because I was worthless, having no prospects except those of some socialite I was trying to trick into marriage, and having to listen, helpless, while Amby choked out his last goodbye.

That goodbye hurt. It tore something inside me, trying to rip another page free. But I refused to let that particular paper go. I had buried it at the bottom of my emotional pile because it was the hardest to read. It carried wonderful memories of mine and Amby's family while we lived in Everdeen. Now, only a half-a-page of happiness remained. I clung to that while the rest escaped with my cries into the dark.

* * *

Two days later, I waited outside the laundry in my old shirt, vest, and pants while Millie took her sweet time dressing. The late spring weather was shifting into a cool breeze, and I enjoyed the chill on my face. It was nice. Simple. I rooted myself to the sidewalk, closed my eyes, and listened to the hubbub of passing carriages, horses, and pedestrians. The longer I stayed in this small town, the more I liked it.

Two days since I left Amby. How did two days feel like a lifetime already? I hated how torn I felt since leaving him. But sometimes you have to tear things apart to create even better things, right? Like that crafter I met once who tore up old letters. She soaked those shreds in water and sifted them to make fresh paper for journals. After the barn, I was torn to pieces, and tears soaked my pages. Perhaps I was ready for a new existence too. One that could be written on new, prettier pages. Pages that involved tea sets and Chince vases.

Pages with Annabelle Winters. That was the plan. Millie and I charmed our way into Anna's life far quicker than I expected. She welcomed us with open arms. Now it was time to commit. Perhaps we could take a walk together through the park this week. I just needed to set aside my impossible fantasies for a future where I strolled publicly with Amby, and he chose to be with me. That was never going to happen. I needed to open my eyes to reality. Anna... and her huge estate, comfortable life, and social status could all be mine. I was a fool to hope for anything else.

Opening my eyes to the bright day, I blinked down at my pinky ring. The square stone glimmered a brighter amber color than before. It reminded me of the ascot Amby chose and tied around me. I also kept his embroidered handkerchief. Tokens to remember him. Items to sell, if needed, although the thought made me ache.

Unfortunately, sentimental items meant little when Millie and I were running out of soap and other basics. I also needed to make a payment to Arthur for our new clothes. Then, there was that overdue property tax bill. I tried to forget about it, but the impossible price weighed heavily on my shoulders. The only way to pay that off was to sell the laundry quickly. Or marry.

Millie strolled out of the laundry door and made a show of inspecting my shirt collar, tilting her head to check all angles, so I sent her a scowl. She was searching for the bruise that discolored a small patch of skin on my neck. The mark Amby gave me with his claiming kisses. Thankfully, my souvenir wasn't noticeable when I buttoned up, but she'd managed to see it after our horse riding adventure. I passed Millie to lock the door and shot her a don't-you-dare-bring-up-my-bruises-again look. She grinned with knowing mischief.

She tried to hide it under her lashes as she hopped off the one step. "So, Zeth... Do you think we'll see Amby today?"

"Sush," I snapped. Dear heaven, she was getting under my skin. Too much time spent cleaning while she chatted and pretended to help. "Where's the hat?"

"Here," she answered and raised the straw circle with a trailing yellow ribbon from behind her brown riding skirt. "You know, Amby has money. He can help us."

"Amby may never talk to me again, let alone lend me money.

Let's just say, I don't fit into his equation. So, let's sell your hat. Or did you change your mind?"

Millie waved for me to lead her. She suggested selling the fancy thing while we chewed on the last of our bread for breakfast, and I appreciated her sacrifice. Not that she ever liked the pretty hat.

It only took a few steps to reach the millinery and haberdashery next door. Our section of Main Street had a number of fashionable stores. I pushed a glass paneled door open to the sound of a small chime and Millie followed, watching the rocking bell above. Then she called out, "Hello Old Man."

"Greetings," the craftsman laughed at Millie's renewed endearment. He was a relic from our past. He looked up from his counter with bushy eyebrows and a nod.

In front of him sat three lovely hats in pink, blue, and yellow silk in sharp pleats with feathers and ribbons. Fancy things, for fancy dances. I could imagine Anna wearing all of them in rooms with matching wallpapers.

There were also some fine-looking caps and evening hats, so I walked by those and flipped a few of their tags. Oh... the prices were high, so I kept walking. "Thanks again," I said to the old man. "For letting us borrow your cleaning supplies."

"Anytime. Sure you want to sell your old business? It's been in your family for generations."

"Aye, I can mop, but I've never been good with laundering or alterations." I stuck a thumb at Millie, "And she pretends she doesn't know the definition of those words."

Millie stuck her tongue out at us both and walked to the counter with her hat. "Do you think you can sell this?"

"Where did you get it?" he asked. I bristled at his accusation. Despite my reputation, I didn't steal it. Before I could argue that, the milliner answered himself, "Port Winchester, of course. Lovely piece."

The City's name made me cringe. Then I felt bad for thinking the worst of the nice man.

He held up the hat and inspected the straw with new respect. "Fine weave. Aye, I could resell it. I'll give you two for it."

"Two?" I clipped, this time without offense. Bargaining was practically second nature after the auction house. In fact, my boss used to make us bargain for our pay rate each week. The better I haggled, the more money I got. "Do you take us for children? We paid eight a month ago."

"Paying too much was your fault, not mine."

I sniffed and held out my hand for the hat. "Fine, I'll get six elsewhere."

"You won't even get three. It's used."

"Used only once, and that doesn't matter. A hat from the City is rare. You'll double your price as soon as we leave. And we both know how ladies want pretty things for the Founders Day Festival. That's fast approaching. So, I'll sell the hat for four, final offer."

The old man chuckled and nodded at me with a glimmer in his eye. "My, how you've grown, Washer. Four it is. Cals now?"

"If you have them, Mr. Laurel. And..." I hesitated for a moment, then took the plunge, "by any chance, are you hiring?"

His brow rose and my hopes rose too. We needed more money than one hat's worth, but the old man's face fell. I knew the look he gave me all too well. Yet another rejection.

I waved my hand to tell him to forget I asked, then I leaned against the counter and planned. We needed to visit Arthur's tailor shop for Millie's fitting and to make a small payment. After that, the general store to buy whatever plain, yet filling, food we might afford on half a hat's worth of profit. Hopefully, we'd sell Mum's dresser soon.

Millie wandered off to the wall of men's hats while the milliner counted out the paper cals from his register. He closed it again with a jingle and handed me the money.

The new weight to my pants pocket felt wonderful as I turned back to Millie. She was trying on a black top hat with a low crown. The way it squished her curls out into a brown wedge looked darn cute. With her big curves and charming face, Millie was a gem. Too bad the hat cost more than her straw one, or else I'd buy it for her.

I tipped my cap at the old man and kissed Millie's cheek, wishing she hadn't needed to sacrifice so much in her short life.

Putting the top hat back on its hook felt stupidly dramatic. I set it on the wall with care, using the brim to make sure it sat straight, before offering an arm to my sister. "Come along, my dear. We have an appointment with silk and satin."

"So gallant." She batted her big brown eyes and took my arm, and we both headed out through the bell-trapped door. Not even six steps from the chime, Millie said, "Maybe you can marry Amby. He *is* a potential prospect."

"And maybe my ears will fall off, so I no longer have to hear your inane comments. One can only pray for the impossible."

"So rude," she huffed.

"What?" I put a hand to my ear, acting as if I didn't hear her.

Millie smacked my arm. "I'm being serious. It's painfully obvious you still like him."

Tsking, I tried walking a little faster, but she lengthened her stride to hold on to me, not giving up.

"Zeth, stop avoiding the topic. Something happened between you and Amby, and you should talk about it. Don't drown in your thoughts. It's making you grumpy."

I couldn't deny that. My steps slowed as I realized I was still raw from my breakdown the other night. Just the idea of talking about Amby made my stomach tense. I would rather push the thought of him down to ignore it. But Millie deserved some sort of explanation for my behavior. "Amby... has his father's legacy, and I have our survival to think about. We reunited briefly, aye, but we parted on shaky terms. Don't start making alternative plans."

Perhaps Millie didn't expect an answer from her grumpy, big brother, because her eyes went wide. She patted my shoulder sympathetically and assured me, "Don't worry. I'm sure he'll forgive you."

"What makes you think *I* did something wrong?"

"'Cause I know you," Millie answered with mirth. She was such a bratty sister. I tried to shake her off my elbow, but she clung on like she used to do when we were kids. So I jostled her around playfully until she snorted.

Millie didn't release me, but she did drop the subject, and I was grateful, because Amby's goodbye *was* my fault. We just started talking civilly when my lust took over, and then afterwards, I immediately pulled away. Maybe I lost him completely. Or maybe Millie was right and Amby would forgive me, yet again. After how poorly I'd treated him, I vowed never to be bitter again. We could try to be friends. I truly missed his friendship. I realized that in the barn, when I fell to the floor in a heap of broken chair wood and shared a damn good laugh with Amby. I never felt such camaraderie with anyone else, and probably never would. Perhaps that companionship would be enough. I should pursue a friendship with him. I did wonder how he was doing. Better than me, I hoped.

Millie must have let me ponder that, because we were inside the tailor shop before I knew it. This time it was empty, and I removed my cap and took a seat while Millie quickly scooted into the dressing room with Emiline. I closed my eyes to rest while their friendly chatter spilled around me until Millie came back out wearing her new jacket inside out. Emiline quickly put Millie on the dais and went to work pinning the men's jacket into a more feminine shape.

Their chatter was calming, so I didn't mind waiting. When they finished, Millie disappeared to change, and I stood to join Emiline at the counter, offering her the small payment. She accepted it, and I was glad she pulled out a receipt ledger to make it official. I didn't want her charity.

There was a larger ledger book on the counter with numbers nicely drawn into straight columns, so I began adding up those receipts for the week, avoiding everything else in my life. But the worries came to me anyway. Was Amby hurting as much as me? Was he worse? Maybe he didn't even care that we parted. No, I was certain he cared. And he had the added weight of telling his dad he wasn't marrying Anna. How did that go? Did Amby decide on another woman to marry? Was he visiting her right now? Despite my flailing mind, I reached a numerical total. And a decision.

"I've been meaning to ask," I said, tapping my thumb on the counter, "How is Amby?"

Emiline's hand paused, so I glanced up nervously to find her searching my face curiously. Her eyes were the same brown as

Amby's, but not as pretty. We exchanged a long stare while she measured my sincerity before she answered, "He's been unusually quiet, and working in the barn more. Why do you ask?"

"I haven't seen him, is all," I answered lamely. I hadn't known this new Amby who made furniture, but I knew that he'd always preferred company to isolation. Amby sounded depressed. Or maybe he was avoiding his house, specifically his father. That didn't make me feel any better, so I changed the subject, "Are you hiring?"

Just then, Millie stepped out of the dressing room as Arthur ducked through the front entrance. He led in a man from my past. If I failed to remember Damien Cooligan's uniquely light-blonde hair, then his disdainful glare as he caught sight of me did well to bring back all the times this shining example of Everdeen elite spit on my Chapel donation shoes. I was surprised his ego fit through the door. After him, his father entered, and I could feel the older man's scowl from across the sales floor. He was as annoyed as his son to share a shop with the Washers. These two were the pond scum of town; thriving on rich nutrients to stay slimy.

My hackles rose, but Arthur's voice boomed as he showed the Cooligans to some fashion books, a true friend. Millie walked right by them without a care, joining me at the counter.

"Did you pay?" she asked.

One of her curls was sticking out from the rest, so I straightened it. "Aye, just settling up."

Emiline ripped her receipt free from the pad and handed me the copy. "We could probably use one more person around here, for alterations."

For the second time today, hope rose within me.

"Me!" Millie exclaimed like a child claiming the last candy. "How fun! I'd love to, thank you. When can I start?"

My eyes flew to Millie to tell her *no*, but she was shooting me such a cute don't-you-dare-tell-them-I-hate-sewing look that I understood instantly, Millie needed this opportunity. I couldn't deny her the chance to try working. Memaw taught us both the basics, and if Millie worked hard, she could pay off our clothing debt. Besides, she did tend to read the fashion pages more than the news.

I turned to Emiline. "Thank you. Millie's a Washer, so she'll fit right in. You won't regret hiring her."

"I'll need to speak to Arthur, of course."

"About hiring Millie?" Arthur said from right next to me and Millie. "No need to ask, there's plenty of work to be done. She can start tomorrow." He grabbed our shoulders, squeezing us up against him on both sides. "Now, how else can I help my friends?"

* * *

Warm, smoky air hit me first, and then the raucous chaos of a packed house of drinkers. I grimaced, not in the mood for company, but made myself enter Everdeen's most popular tavern anyway. Earlier, when Arthur asked how else he could help us, I mentioned that I needed to fix my roof, and he suggested I meet his big brother over a round of drinks and darts after the shop closed. If Arthur's brother could assist me with repairing the laundry, that alone was worth a hangover and headache.

Determined, I glanced around the dimly lit room and found Arthur easily. His brown beard and lumbering height stood above the crowd. I made my way through the tables to where he was pulling darts from a cork game board. As I stepped up to Arthur, he turned and gave me a big, welcoming hug as if he hadn't just seen me earlier.

"Hey there," I chuckled, awkwardly trapped in his arms until he let me go. Once released, I patted his shoulder. "Already started on the beers without me?"

Arthur nodded. "I always get a head start. Makes this game much more rewarding."

Eyeing the darts in Arthur's beefy hand, I voiced my doubts, "Is it safe to toss those pointy metal things while intoxicated?"

"Depends on how sloshed you are." He nudged me with his elbow. "Don't worry, I assure you I'm an excellent dart thrower, even drunk."

"I'd say he's full of shit, if I didn't see him do it every week," said another man from beside him. He was older, in his thirties maybe, with a short and stocky build, brown hair, and a friendly face. He held out a weathered hand for a shake. "You must be Zeth. Welcome back to town. Name's Todd."

"Or big brother," Arthur teased, resting his elbow right on top of Todd's head. Todd tossed him off and smacked Arthur's chest to push him back. The two siblings looked like those stacking dolls, as if Todd was small enough to fit right inside Arthur. I could see the resemblance, and their affection.

It was Todd who turned to me next, "I hear you need a roofer." When I nodded, he raised his bearded chin. "Then I'm your man. I own the best roofing company in the Commonwealth. Just tell me where to go."

Offers always had a catch in the City. People had angles, which were usually sharp. But folk were different in Everdeen. At least, it felt that way among the middle class. The milliner had been quick to loan me his cleaning supplies without charge, and Arthur opened a credit so I could buy clothes. As I glanced between the brothers and their open willingness to assist, a knot in me eased until I could share, "I have a crack that needs filling."

"I bet you do," Arthur quipped ruthlessly.

His brother's eyebrows shot up. "If it's like that, I take back my offer to visit. I'm a happily married man."

My face burned so hot, I was sure they could feel it as I looked between the two of them. Then Arthur suddenly laughed and grabbed my shoulder.

"He's teasing."

"I am," Todd agreed with a cheery smile, picking up a beer mug from a stool near the dart board. "I like you. You're joining us for a game and drinks. We can discuss your crack later. Once we're sloshed."

"Only if you're buying," I answered playfully. This time, I could tell he was teasing. Big brothers weren't as bad as Millie always complained about.

"Zeth needs a partner for teams." Arthur looked around the

tavern. "We should ask Amby. He told me he wanted to be alone, but he's looking pretty glum tonight."

My breath caught, and I followed his gaze to where Amby sat on a stool, hunched over the bar. His chin was propped in his hand as he stared at nothing. His vest, shirt, and pants were too expensive for an evening of bar games.

He did look glum, and my heart went out to him. He shouldn't be drinking while in such a mood. Maybe I could cheer him up. Here was my chance to renew our friendship, to settle my unease. To make things right.

"I'll get him," Todd said before I could offer. He approached the bar and slid onto a stool next to Amby. The shorter man motioned to the bartender for a new round of drinks while he chatted with Amby, until Amby peeked over his shoulder toward the dart board, and when our gazes met, his face fell.

My stomach instantly dropped at the rejection. So much for my plan to be his friend.

Yet, Amby slid off his stool and made his way over.

"Hello," I muttered lamely once they reached me, taking the beer Todd handed out. A quick sip proved the hops were too rich for my taste.

Amby stiffened as he turned his face slowly toward me. He opened his beautiful mouth, then closed it before looking back at his drink, which he cupped with both hands like it held all the answers. I could tell his thoughts were swirling as much as mine.

"Evening," he finally muttered.

"Ah, come on, my friend." Arthur slapped Amby's back so hard that he flinched, and some of his beer spilled out from his mug. "Let's lift your spirits, huh?"

Amby wiped his hand off on the side of his pants. Then he slid it into his pocket as he nodded and took a gulp of his drink.

Not sure what to say next, I watched the brothers play their first round of darts. They joked while Amby and I sipped our drinks quietly. When I glanced sideways again, Amby cut his eyes away from me.

We were acting like strangers. Maybe Amby was shoving down

his feelings too. I didn't like seeing him so quiet, and I never wanted to talk to him more than I did now. I cleared my throat and swallowed, but what could I possibly say to bridge this divide between us? *By the way, thanks for the fuck. How's your beer?*

That might garner a precious laugh from him, but I didn't want to belittle what happened between us. Our union had been near perfect. Now, it would be buried and forgotten. We were destined to live as quiet acquaintances from here on out.

Those truths burned as I finally asked, "Were you waiting for someone?"

Amby straightened. "No... Were you?"

Who did he think I was meeting up with? Anna? I couldn't imagine her going out for a fun night around town. I couldn't imagine her getting drunk at all. She was more likely to attend tea parties than enter a pub.

"No, I'm here with Arthur. He's introducing me to his not-so-big-brother. Are you friends with him?"

Amby tipped his mug back for a swig. Then he sniffed. "Yes, we enjoy a game night here and there."

"I'm jealous," I quipped. "My social life in the City was just work and sleep."

"Hm," Amby hummed before he downed the rest of his beer.

The air around us felt uncomfortable, and I saw the rest of our lives feeling the same. It made me a little dizzy.

Or maybe that was from the alcohol. Either way, I needed to remove the tension. I needed my friend back. Amby's mood was souring too as the brothers finished their turn. Todd declared their total and handed us the darts.

Amby faced me, but he didn't look at me. "I'll play one game. Then I'm going home."

"One game's all you need to discover I can't throw worth shit."

The way Amby scrunched his face to refrain from smiling was a small step in the right direction. He turned and readied a dart by holding it parallel to the floor while his arm moved back and forth to judge the distance. I eyed his technique but got distracted by how well his tailored vest fit his solid chest and narrow waist. And those well-defined hips of his begged to be held. I could imagine myself standing behind him and grabbing them to pull against me. What a wonderful visual, so much that I forced my gaze higher to admire his open-collared shirt to calm myself down.

Seeing the faded love bites on his neck where my kisses claimed him only roused me more. He wasn't hiding those. A feeling of pride blew through me at how Amby so boldly displayed my marks. He declared himself taken. *Mine.*

Only, he wasn't mine, was he?

Amby's dart pierced the outer edge of the board, and he sighed, his speech slow as he said, "Shit."

"That's alright," I assured him, as a good teammate does. As friends do. "I'm sure you just aimed low to make me feel better."

"Oh yeah? Let's see if you can throw better than you can balance on a chicken coop."

I chuckled at his joking, but my concern for our future as friends tallied up higher as I weighed the projectile in my hand. When I tossed it, I tried to look like I played a hundred times prior, but my dart flew straight to the floor. My hopes to impress went right along with it.

Amby snorted from behind before his hand gripped my shoulder. "That was amazing, loved every moment," he said over the brothers' jeering.

"I aim to please," I bantered back, glad I'd somewhat eased the tension between us.

When Amby's eyes lit up, I drank in the sight. He was far more intoxicating than liquor, and I knew he tasted even better.

Todd broke the moment by nudging my side. "I hope your aim in bed doesn't match your skills in darts. You may end up like my brother here, with no wife or kids."

"Hey, I've got my cap set for someone, thank you," Arthur bantered back. Then he turned on me by tossing around a few one-liners about my bedroom *skills,* and Todd ruthlessly joined in.

My coworkers at the auction had told dirty jokes too, enough to give me a solid education, but I never felt welcome in their fold. Always an outsider. Yet, tonight, the brother's lighthearted ribbing had me laughing along, especially after Amby shot me a sympathetic glance. It felt good to be one of the guys.

"Ah, this brings back some memories of the three of us hanging out," Arthur said with a pat to his broad chest. "We should do this more often. The Tremendous Trio!"

Amby shook his head. "You can't... copy us." His eyes flicked to mine. When I smiled, he averted his gaze and scratched the back of his neck.

"Yeah," I agreed and stepped closer to Amby's side. "We've been the Daring Duo since the early school days. It's our thing."

Todd paused mid-aim. "Wait! You two are the Daring Duo? Do you know how many times I've heard people complain about you growing up?"

"We know," Amby and I said in unison. When we both eyed each other, something sparked between us.

"So, you two were responsible for the Thomas' shed burning down... I helped put it out. That thing almost caused a fire in the field!"

"Uh..." Amby started, then he grabbed someone's leftover mug of beer and took a big gulp to avoid answering. He looked guilty as sin as his throat bobbed from swallowing it down.

I shook my head at his antics. "Aye, I can tell you firsthand that jumping through a flaming hoop is harder than it appears. And we were justly punished for it. Right, Amby?"

Amby wiped his mouth before saying, "Right. My father didn't let me see you for a whole month."

Arthur tsked. "You two were so bad, I'm surprised the Field Witch didn't get a hold of you."

"Ain't no Field Witch." Todd shook his head as he removed the darts from the board. "I told you that's just the old hag who lives out near the river who doesn't like people."

"Oh no, the Witch is real," his brother countered. "I saw an actual monster in the field when walking home one night from the pub. She looks like a normal lady, until she unhinges her jaw wide enough to fit someone's whole head in there."

"I think you were drunk that night," Amby slurred, smirking.

"*You're* drunk right now, what do you know?" Arthur tousled Amby's hair, and Amby nudged him away with a faint smile before taking the darts from him.

The air relaxed around us, and I was grateful to my friend for stirring such memories, even if they were ones of Amby and I being troublemakers. It connected us, and that's all I wanted.

"So tell us, Zeth," Arthur piped up. "You looking to settle down?"

"Oh..." I turned to see Amby watching me curiously. My mouth went dry at the thought of mentioning Anna in front of him. "I returned to town with plans, aye. Marriage, kids, and the rest." I raked a hand through my hair to avoid seeing Amby's reaction to my words. "I wouldn't mind children someday. They're pretty great to have around. Snotty, but fun."

Amby stepped up beside me, his jaw clenching. "Right, Zeth here has decided to court Annabelle Winters." He threw his next dart so aggressively that it splintered the wall.

"Goodness, that's quite the endeavor," Arthur said with something like bemused disbelief.

Todd nodded. "Yeah, best of luck to you."

"With charm, who needs luck?" I assured Arthur brashly with a flirtatious wink. Both brothers snorted into their mugs at my joke.

"Yes, with charm, you can easily get whoever you want," Amby said. I was about to tease him when he hesitated, looked from me to the floor, and said, "You know, actually... I think I'm done for tonight. I'm not feeling well. Sorry." He turned, handing me his last dart as he staggered away.

Worry hit me hard as I realized Amby thought I had charmed him in the barn. When I started after him, Arthur gripped my elbow to hold me back. Arthur was right, Amby wasn't my responsibility, but that didn't stop me from wanting to tell him I didn't consider him easily gotten. He was certainly hard to let go.

It was Todd who assisted Amby with retrieving his jacket, tugging it over his shoulders while Amby moved with jerky movements. He needed water, and a cold cloth to his head. I could—

"My brother's cabin isn't far from the Somerset estate," Arthur interrupted my stray thoughts. "He sometimes walks home with Amby when we drink, since Amby went missing for a whole night once. No one knew where he was till late the next day."

That made me worry more, but Arthur shrugged, his face softening. "I admit I worry about him. He's become too withdrawn lately, but he'll be fine tonight. Right as rain in the morning, I'm sure."

Nodding, I watched Amby stumble down the doorstep. I wished I felt so sure.

15

Ambrose

When a sliver of wood pierced my skin, I grimaced. I pulled it out quickly with a heavy sigh, then continued working a letter into the wooden sign with my chisel. I hadn't had a decent night's sleep in days. Every little thing reminded me of Zeth, even getting a damn splinter. I hoped to distract myself with woodworking, but now being in the barn was more troublesome than ever. I kept remembering laying in the hay with him, with his hand behind my neck, the warmth of his breath against me, the way he kissed me as if he'd lose me...

When I told him goodbye afterward, I thought we would keep our distance, but two days later, I was playing darts with him at the pub. That also ended in heartache. What a fool I was, letting myself become so comfortable as we played. I couldn't help myself around him as we reminisced about the good days with Arthur. Zeth always had a way of making me feel better when we were younger, and I'd felt that with him at the pub.

I recalled him laughing along with Arthur and Todd when they teased him for missing the dart board. The way his face lit up when he looked at me as if he were... having fun. I enjoyed Zeth's laughter. It did something to me, made me unravel.

I wondered if his mysterious eyes saw it the same way I did. He'd certainly been amused playing darts with me, but my mind had been so muddled with alcohol that I could have mistaken amusement for annoyance. Still, I imagined Zeth's hands in mine, holding me down as he pressed his lips against my neck. My mind went further, to waking up beside him and sitting at a table, talking as we ate breakfast together. Of walking outside through the field after a day of work.

I straightened my back atop my stool and set the draw knife on the workbench. Zeth hung on my mind too much for me to focus well. But I managed to complete the last 'T' in the word I was carving on the wooden nameplate. It was for my father, in hopes I could make him proud in some way. The plate would say 'Somerset & Sons'. It was my way of apologizing for speaking against his plans for me to own the bank one day. I would begin training tomorrow, as I had no choice in the matter. I needed to finally grow up and accept I had a duty to my inheritance, to my family. They were all I had.

Now for a wife...

Father had set me up with several women over the past year, and most of my relationships either ended as friendships or with them hating me. I'd even had several men come forward with interest in courting, but my father chased them away. Rumor spread that I wasn't serious about courting anyone, which made it harder to find potential prospects who aligned with my father's vision. I'd heard a few hushed whispers while strolling along the street and at events. 'Ambrose Somerset, you say? No, he's a sly one, quick to charm but unwilling to commit.'

The only family circle I could see myself in was the Washers, but losing Zeth after the barn had crushed my last hope for a happy future. Whoever I found next to charm, I would have to commit. Perhaps I could find a lady who was in a similar situation to mine. Otherwise, I didn't feel right continuing such deceit.

I rubbed a rough hand down my face, feeling flustered. I never thought this deeply when I'd been seeing Jamie Clark or Damien Cooligan. I had some sort of feelings for the drifter who'd come into Everdeen every once in a while for a lay before he would leave the next day. It took me too long to realize he wasn't a good man, and thankfully I hadn't seen him in a few years. I didn't even know his name, but none of them mattered anyhow.

Zeth was different from them all. He was never just a fling. He understood me. He cared for me. No one else had ever filled the gaping hole in my heart but Zeth. I could be myself around him, the real Amby, the one who did what he wanted regardless of others' expectations.

When a horse whinnied outside, I made my way to the door of the barn and looked out, willfully repressing the hope that it was Zeth riding up again. Instead, I saw only dark clouds hanging heavy over the fields, threatening rain. At the house, my father's carriage waited in the circular drive.

"Amby!"

Emiline's shout from the house could be heard for miles. She wasn't timid at all. Well, there went my Sunday afternoon sulking out here in the barn. I was needed for something else now, and I was willing to bet it had to do with Father.

I set the nameplate on the workbench and closed the barn doors with a heavy sigh. Then I stalked up the grassy hill to the house. It wasn't a long walk, but I took my time. Whatever they wanted required my focus, and I needed to think for a moment before facing Father. As I met Emiline on the porch, she clasped her hands before her and leaned against the railing.

I glanced from Father's black carriage to her. "What's going on?"

"Father wants you to ride with him to Anna's house."

I nodded slowly. Of course. Even though Annabelle had established our friendship, Father still expected me to court her. How was I going to tell him that she might be courting Zeth by now?

"Oh," was all I could get out.

"Hey," she started, her tone shifting from playful to serious. "You've been distant lately, even with me. I don't like you not talking to me."

"I've been working on something in the barn. You know how I get distracted."

"Yes, I do. So well, actually, that I know you stay in the barn longer when you're trying to distract yourself from something entirely. Fess up. Does it have to do with breakfast last Sunday, or Zeth?"

"Shh." I grabbed her hands and looked over at the door before I cut my eyes back at her. "Why are you bringing him up?"

"Because I like seeing my younger brother happy." She raised her chin, making me smile. She'd never let me forget she left the womb first, precisely eight minutes before I did. "He asked about you the other day."

"He did?" My heart picked up, but I shook my head. "Em, it doesn't matter. Zeth can't give me children."

"Oh, yes, carrying on our family bloodline. It's so important," she sang dramatically as she released my hands. "Amby, it's time for you to break free and fly, like Mother used to tell us."

"Okay, now you're just getting mushy on me." I chuckled and looked away to avoid the tears that threatened to form.

We had all been so close to Mother. She was a gentle, loving soul, grounded and steady. She encouraged us to be wild and free. It's why she let us run off on our own. She trusted us, and she wanted us to learn to trust ourselves. As long as we were home before supper. And we always were. We couldn't wait to share our adventures and discoveries with her, and she was always eager to hear them.

But Father? As soon as Mother passed, he took charge the only way he knew how, I suppose, filling our schedules with lessons and nannies. Much of his light and warmth died with Mother, and he became more strict. We fell into line.

"I just want you to know you have a choice, that's all," Emiline finally said.

"Well, Somerset sons don't get to make their own choices. That includes getting back together with old boyfriends." I sighed, pushing off the railing and making my way to the door.

"That's the lie you've told yourself, Amby."

Her words stopped me in my tracks. Reluctantly, I turned and waited for her to go on. Her face was earnest as she continued,

"Nothing is holding you back but yourself. This is your chance to break free from Father's hold. If you make the decision to shut Zeth out of your life and step up at the bank, I'm afraid you'll lock the key to your own cage... forever."

My fists clenched as my sister stared at me with that bold, matter-of-fact expression on her face. Emiline thought she was right, but she had no idea what I endured with Father. The pain I went through not to disappoint him. The loss I felt when his stern words echoed in my ears about his plans. The threat of losing something I loved so dearly, like the barn. She didn't know.

"It must be so easy for you to say that," I snapped. "I've seen the way you and Arthur look at each other lately. There's nothing holding either of you back. If you both wanted to court, Father would give you his blessing, because you're not a Somerset *son*."

The door opened then, making me jump. Father rushed out, looking like a fine, respectable banker of Everdeen as he took out his pocket watch from his vest and peered at it. "Ambrose, I have a day planned for us. Get dressed. I'll be in the carriage."

Without waiting for a reply, Father snapped the watch shut and sauntered down the porch steps. That meant I was on a time stamp. He was giving me no more than fifteen minutes to get dressed. I turned to my sister, who was fiddling with the hem of her dress. I deflated with regret, then turned on my heel for the door.

My body felt jittery as I hurried inside and upstairs. I sponged myself off in my room before quickly pulling on my clothes. Then I wetted my hair and brushed the top and sides, but it did nothing but curl anyway. Ready, I placed my cap on my head and grabbed my green wool jacket. As I went to leave, I hesitated. We were going into town, so I quickly dabbed a bit of perfume on my neck, in case I ran into a certain roguish jackass.

Leaving my room, I made my way downstairs, taking the steps one at a time as I tried to calm myself. Outside, Father was talking with our driver. That allowed me to stall and prepare to ride in the carriage with him. When I looked at Emiline, she regarded me softly, seeming to forget how I went off on her.

"I'm sorry," I told her, taking her hand. "You didn't deserve my anger."

She squeezed my fingers. "I understand, Amby. Just... think about it. About your own choices. Can you do that for your big sister?"

I moved to give her a tight hug before kissing her cheek. "Yes, just for you."

"Have a good time."

As I let her go and stepped away, my mind tumbled over the idea of choosing Zeth. Despite what she said, it felt impossible. I took in a deep breath as she left to go inside, and blew it out as I made my way to the carriage. When I found my father waiting inside, I hesitated. This was the first choice I had to make. I could tell him I had other plans here. I didn't have to go to town with him at all.

"Get in, Ambrose." Father gestured at the seat inside the carriage.

I tensed but obeyed, like the good son I was, and climbed into the carriage to sit opposite him. Once our driver closed the door, we were off to the Winters estate. And afterward? God only knew. I only hoped it wasn't a trip to the bank. That was the last place I wanted to be on my day off, and forcing Annabelle to sit through a tour of Father's banking empire would be miserable.

For a long while, we sat in silence. Father and I never had anything to talk about unless it was business or upcoming events he expected me to attend. It had been a week since the argument at the breakfast table, but Father either ignored it or forgot about it. He always did.

I sat stiff, my hands clasped tightly together between my knees, and stared out the window at the green fields. Then Father sighed that heavy sigh he gave before lectures, and I sat straighter, preparing.

"Ambrose..." he started.

I looked up at him, waiting, but he hesitated as he smoothed his fingers against his curled mustache.

"Yes?" I asked.

He avoided my eyes and crossed his legs as he gazed out the window. "I heard you and Miss Winters went shopping the other day."

Relieved that he chose not to lecture me, I nodded. "We did."

"It seems you're doing well in spending time with her," he finally said, smiling, and I desperately wished that smile didn't make me feel as good as it did.

"Thank you," I said, my lips twitching. Five minutes of approval from my father was better than none... until I realized it came with a wave of sickness, because I was lying to my father's face.

"I have brief business at the bank today. Miss Winters makes it a habit to go into town every Sunday. We will stop by her house on the way and see if she would like a ride. And you..." He stopped short, and I blinked at him, waiting for instructions. He cleared his throat, "I shouldn't be there more than an hour."

"Sure," I said, trying to sound chipper. If Annabelle even agreed to go with us, we'd only end up shopping as we did the other day. As friends.

Emiline's words about locking my own cage whirled in my head. It was clear she wanted me to choose Zeth, but after enduring his talk about courting Annabelle at the pub, there was no doubt where my choice lay.

Swallowing the bile rising in my throat, I said, "I'm ready... to begin training tomorrow. With Mr. Dawsey, correct?"

Father's brow raised high, and for a moment, he looked pleased. But then he frowned, as if I'd said something wrong, and nodded. "Yes. You will train in the mornings."

Nothing else was said on our awkward ride to Annabelle's house. My body slumped into a dark hole along with my mind. I wasn't sure what I expected from my father. Perhaps more recognition that I was back to being the obedient son again. But he only adjusted his tie and peered out the carriage window. The momentary joy of experiencing my father's approval evaporated.

The stretch to Annabelle's house was absolute torture, and when her big brick house finally came into view, my stomach knotted as it hit me. Annabelle might tell my father that we were only friends. She might excitedly tell us both of Zeth's courtship.

My face grew hot, the bile returning. When the carriage stopped, I got out first and stood still on the gravel drive, swallowing hard to keep down my breakfast. The wind blew the pink blooms of cherry trees our way, and with it came a few sprinkles of rain.

Good. That was calming and helped tremendously as I closed my eyes to settle my stomach. I listened to the carriage rattle as Father joined me.

Then the door of Annabelle's house opened, and she walked out in friendly greeting with one of her maids trailing behind.

"Mr. Somerset, Amby, what brings you out this way?"

"We were just on our way into town, Miss Winters," Father answered, before turning to me expectantly.

I nodded. "We wanted to see if you'd like a ride with us for the day. Unless you're busy, of course."

"Oh, that sounds lovely! I have some social calls to make, and as they say, the more, the merrier. I'll simply freshen up. Please, enjoy the porch chairs."

She made for the door, and I was left standing alone with my father once again. As I made my way up the steps to her porch, I realized how awful it would be for Annabelle if she honestly liked Zeth, only for it to be nothing more than a ruse. A lie. A con. With Annabelle and me becoming friends, would I be able to keep a straight face if I saw her on Zeth's arm in town? At Chapel? With kids?

A pang struck me so hard across my collarbone that I rubbed it. I leaned against the white column beneath the porch and frowned as I surveyed Annabelle's land. When the rain finally let out from the heavy clouds, I let out a sigh, welcoming it.

* * *

The rain drenched our carriage as Annabelle and Father chatted the *entire* way to town. There wasn't a topic uncovered, from the bank to both of our lands, to the salon coming up, and finally the

Founders Day Festival. She would be helping tie the colorful ribbons to the Everdeen Oak, the centerpiece of the festival.

I was hardly part of the conversation. Every time I tried to chime in with my own thoughts, my father would speak over me instead. Finally, I gave up and turned to look out the window. Annabelle and my father got along so well. Perhaps they should just marry instead. After all, he was still capable of producing more offspring. She could give him another son who might actually be interested in the bank.

The corner of my mouth twitched imagining the ridiculous pairing.

As we came into town, the rain finally subsided and the sun peeked out from the clouds. When I glimpsed the colorful chipped door of the laundry, my heart sped up. I peered out the window to try and see if Zeth was around. There was no movement in front of the shop, nor the window, but a flash of white on the roof caught my eye. There Zeth was, standing with Todd on the flat roof of the laundry in rugged trousers, a sleeveless undershirt, and suspenders.

Instant memories of us in the barn flooded back to me. Of his hand tightening in my hair, of his lips on mine, of his warm embrace...

"Oh, this is right where I need to be!" Annabelle exclaimed, and Father quickly tapped the roof of the carriage to stop it.

"Is there a shop you want to visit on Main?" I asked.

"I came here to see Millie and Zeth. They're my top priority today."

Father inclined his head to Annabelle, but his eyes narrowed on me. I couldn't help but wonder what he thought of Annabelle's behavior. Perhaps he remembered that Zeth was pursuing her as well, but he didn't comment as the carriage halted and our driver came around to open the door.

I followed Annabelle out and inspected the wet street, then tilted my head up at the roof. When Todd moved to examine the sheeting, Zeth followed, standing precariously close to the edge. My stomach flipped, and I took a nervous step forward. It had to be slick up there after the rain. Zeth could slip and fall easily. But the roof was flat, and he seemed confident. I couldn't help but admire him in a sodden white undershirt with suspenders. The defined muscles in his bare arms shimmered with rain, and his hair was damp and messy. I watched the hollow of his throat work as he spoke to Todd.

I groaned, low enough so my father couldn't hear. I couldn't help myself. The man was absolutely alluring. Even if I wanted to avoid him, I couldn't. And if I remained friends with Annabelle, it would make things much harder on me than I thought. I couldn't simply say goodbye to Zeth if he kept popping up in my life every other day.

Hopefully, whatever god was out there might grant me mercy as I stood on this damp street with my father while such a beautiful sight worked from above. As far as I was concerned, Zeth was the only god I could see.

"What are you all doing here?" I heard Millie call out. Lowering my gaze, I found her holding the shop's door open with a bright grin. Her unkempt curls flew away from her face in the breeze, and her brown riding skirt was just her style. Though grown and much prettier, Millie still reminded me of the girl who would stop what she was doing to chase frogs.

Annabelle appeared in good humor as she made her way up the walkway. "Amby and his father offered me a ride into town, and we thought we'd stop to say hello."

"Well, hello, then." Millie beamed at her. "I'm glad you're here, because you haven't seen the place yet. Zeth's been working hard to fix it up for sale. Wanna come in?"

Annabelle agreed and beckoned me to follow, but my eyes drifted up again to the roof. Hearing us, Zeth glanced down and granted me a gratifying grin, as if glad to see me. Then his gaze shifted over to Annabelle, and his face fell. He wiped his chin and looked away nervously.

Shit, what am I walking into here?

"Ambrose," Father's voice froze me from the carriage. I turned to where he stood in the doorway, having forgotten he was even there. "It seems you and Miss Winters have become reacquainted with the Washers. I'll head on to the bank and have the carriage brought back here soon."

Then he closed the door and was off, riding along the street and leaving me completely dumbfounded. What was I supposed to do at the laundry? Did Father expect me to claim Annabelle, ensuring that Zeth made no advances?

My stomach was in several knots now. I turned and splashed through a puddle as I made my way inside, where I found Millie showing Annabelle around. The place was cleaner than the last time I'd been here. The cozy storefront was just the right size for selling nearly anything. There was the counter where the Washers took care of customers, and the magnificent wide windows where the dresser still sat.

What an amazing storefront. So much potential.

I took off my cap to hang it on the hook in the wall, then ran my fingers over my hair to tame the curls. Sniffing, I walked over to the dresser I'd helped Zeth move and smoothed my hand over the wood. Such a fine piece of furniture. With a little sanding, wood stain, and love, it could stand beautiful again. The idea warmed me, and I couldn't resist the thought of claiming something that was Zeth's as my own.

"I'll take this dresser off your hands," I said before thinking twice.

Millie stopped chatting with Annabelle and glanced at me with surprise. "I think you're joking, Amby, but I'll say sold before you change your mind."

She strolled over to shake my hand but hesitated and pulled her hand back. "Wait, how much? Zeth will kill me if I don't haggle."

"Oh." I looked at the sign, realizing it was priced a little higher than I expected. Before I could ask for a lower price, Millie tried doubling the amount listed. My father would strangle me if he found out I'd spent my own money on such a thing. "I will admit that's a bit out of my range. I would love to fix it up, but I'll also need to buy the materials to do so."

Millie regarded me thoughtfully before replying, "Then you're in luck. It's half off today, since you're taking it to a good home."

"Well, that's generous of you. I'll have someone come and pick it up tomorrow."

"Nicely done," Annabelle chimed in as if she thought I'd haggled the price down. I enjoyed her admiration until she looked at Millie and asked, "Would you like to accompany me today? I'm visiting some acquaintances for tea."

Millie's face lit up, and she sputtered, "I... yes... that sounds fun. I can't wait to meet your friends. We can stop by the tailor shop too. I'd love to show you what I'm starting to sew. Would that be alright?"

Annabelle nodded primly with a twinkle in her gaze. "Whatever you wish. I don't mind detours."

If they were both leaving, I should probably accompany them. But before I could offer, the side door opened with a scrape of wood. The loud sound echoed through the empty shop, making me jump. Zeth stumbled in with his shoulder against the door.

He caught sight of us standing not far from him and instantly straightened before pushing the thing shut with a grumble, "Damn door."

My breath caught as I took him in, still looking wet and messy and using that dirty mouth of his to swear. When I glimpsed the week-old bruise yellowing on his neck from where I'd sucked his skin between my teeth, my body flushed.

I glanced at Annabelle and Millie to see if they noticed, but they were distracted chatting to themselves about the warped door, so I turned back to Zeth and rubbed my collar with my thumb to give him a hint.

Zeth seemed confused briefly before his hand flew to cover the bruise a second before Annabelle and Millie turned to him.

"Any luck with the roof?" Millie asked.

"Oh, aye," Zeth answered, pretending to massage the side of his neck. "Todd found the crack and helped me seal it with asphalt and sand. We just finished." He granted Annabelle an awkward nod.

"No more leak!" Millie cheered.

"Yeah, Arthur's big brother is heading home. He says I'm good at construction." Zeth looked at the floor where water dripped from his clothes and laughed. "And it comes with free baths. Do you think I should take up roofing?"

"No!" I blurted out, and everyone regarded me with surprise. I cleared my throat. "Uh, it's just... I've heard of a few roofers falling and being badly injured."

"Amby's right. And you're better at business, so that's where you should stay," Millie agreed, much to my relief. "Speaking of, I sold the dresser for the full price while you were up there."

"You did? To whom?"

I tensed, hoping she wouldn't rat me out. She eyed me curiously and answered, "Oh, just a passerby. Said they'll pick it up tomorrow."

"Good work, Mils." Zeth praised his sister so warmly that I felt some of the heat in my cheeks as well. I sent Millie a silent thank you for keeping it secret, and she winked around Zeth at me.

"Apologies for my attire," Zeth told us. "As you can see, we're cleaning things out to add this property to our portfolio. I enjoy being part of that process. If you give me the chance to change, we can visit properly."

"No need, since Millie and I already made plans. I did mean to tell you, I thoroughly enjoyed our outing yesterday."

My brow popped up as my eyes flitted from Annabelle to Zeth.

He was still massaging his neck awkwardly, but looked pleased as he replied to her, "I hope to go again soon." His gaze shifted to me. "You should join us next time too."

"Oh, do!" Millie agreed quickly. "It would be fun for us to all go together."

I raised my chin, trying to mask my confusion as I asked, "Oh? Where is that?"

"We met up with Anna for a walk in town," Millie explained. "But then Zeth saw a charming bookstore and got the clever idea to visit the orphanage to read to the kids. And Anna said 'wait here' and returned from the store a minute later with new books. The kids loved them."

When Zeth chuckled, I smiled tightly as my jealousy rose. They all seemed to be having a wonderful time together lately.

I rubbed a sore spot on my thumb as I said, "That was a very thoughtful thing to do. I'm sure the children were grateful to have those books."

"Speaking of books," Annabelle added. "The salon is coming up, and I still need a new hat."

Millie perked up. "There's a lovely straw hat with ribbons in the shop next door. It's a new style from the City, but I bet we can get a great deal from the Old Man. He likes me. Shall we stop there first?"

"Lovely plan," Annabelle nodded with a twist of her lips at Millie.

"Ah..." Zeth started, but when his eyes darted to me, my face flushed.

Annabelle snorted and grabbed Millie's hand. "It's already settled. Thank you Amby, for giving me a ride into town. Shall we rendezvous later?"

"Oh, yes. My father should be done in an hour or so, so I may stroll up to the garden square for a while."

Annabelle nodded and led Millie out of the shop. As silence filled the room, I turned to face Zeth. He lowered his arm with a grateful sigh and settled both of his hands on his hips. Water gleamed on his muscles even in the low light. With his tall frame, fine looks, and alluring presence, Zeth had a way of claiming the space.

When he nodded at me, a wet lock of hair fell charmingly to his forehead. An unshaved shadow roughened his delicate jawline, which I found tempting to touch. He clearly didn't expect company today, especially me.

The silence thickened. I couldn't tell what he was thinking about Annabelle leaving us behind. Perhaps he didn't want her to leave. Perhaps I was ruining his plans by being here.

"Um..." I squeezed my thumb hard. Seeing each other at the pub was one thing, but standing here alone with Zeth in his home was another. I shouldn't be with him at all. But I did want to know one thing. "Why... Why did you invite me to go along with you to the orphanage next time?"

Zeth scratched the bristle on his cheek before answering,

196

"Because I thought you might enjoy it too. The kids were a delight, and you used to love reading."

A pang tore through me. "Oh. Yes, I'm sure I would enjoy it." I searched Zeth's face, wondering if he could sense my despair as I asked, "Are you... courting Annabelle now?"

His gaze remained steady, observing me as he answered, "No. I should be, but haven't kissed her yet."

I blinked at him. Yet. Not *yet*. "Right. Um, I should probably go, then."

As I turned, Zeth pleaded, "Amby, wait."

Stopping at the desperation in his voice, I turned back to face him but avoided his eyes. Was he going to bring up what happened in the barn? Or how he was acting like nothing ever happened between us? Or invite me on another of his dates? Was he going to cover that damn bruise on his neck, or display my mark proudly? It confused me, and his calling me back wasn't helping.

"What is it?" I asked, waiting for him to go on.

"I just want to tell you that our time—"

A sudden crash shook the building, making us both flinch. Something heavy had fallen upstairs. Zeth turned and ran for the stairwell, and I rushed after him up the steps.

When we reached the top, I trailed him through the main room and into the kitchen, where I heard a squawking animal. Inside, a sizable bird flapped around the ceiling, trying to find a way out. Hunching low, I entered the room and found a nest on the floor, along with parts of a cabinet that had fallen from the wall.

Before me, Zeth looked around to see how to get the bird out as it flew from one side of the room to the other.

"How'd it get in here?" I asked.

Zeth turned to me in surprise, as if he hadn't expected me to follow. "There's a hole in the window. I'm sure it got in that way."

"It had a whole nest in the cabinet!"

"I know. Hold on, I'll go get the broom."

He made his way out, and I leaned out the door to call after him, "You're going to leave me up here with it?"

Zeth shook his head and disappeared down the stairwell. I

looked back up at the bird flying from cabinet to cabinet, no doubt startled by its nest falling. And now we were intruding on it. The poor thing. I had an idea of how it felt, trying to take up in someone's space but feeling forced to leave.

When Zeth came back into the room with the broom, I inched closer to him. He clapped my shoulder in encouragement and motioned the bristle end of his broom. "Help me get it."

"What are you going to do, whack it?" Surely he wouldn't.

He rolled his eyes. "No, I need you to raise the window while I shoo it out."

Nodding, I kept the animal in my sight and slowly made my way over to the window. The bird gave a distressed call as it watched me, making me jump, but I reached the window and swiftly unlocked it.

When I tried to open it, the wooden frame wouldn't budge. The thing was stuck, so I pulled on it forcefully until it moved with a sharp cracking noise that sent the animal flying off the cabinet. I flinched away from it and covered my head with my arms.

"Amby..." Zeth laughed from behind me. I turned to see him shaking his head, a soft smile on his stubbled face. "It's just a little bird."

"Well, I don't want it attacking me!" I stooped over and moved out of the way of the window, my eyes glued on the animal now perched on another cabinet.

"It's not going to attack you. Go over there and block the doorway."

Huffing, I made my way over to the door to close it. But the bird flew right at me, its wings flapping around my head. I spun and crashed into Zeth, and we both staggered against the wall.

His hand grabbed my waist and steadied me. Even in the chaos, his touch burned me wonderfully. Our eyes locked for a brief moment, both of us letting out a breath, before Zeth let me go and moved slowly around as the bird landed on the floor with an angry flap of wings. He used the broom carefully to encourage it away until it hopped up onto the windowsill.

We both paused with excitement while it perched on the ledge and peered outside for a moment before flying off.

Zeth looked delighted as he placed the broom aside and closed the window. I joined him there to see the bird soaring over the rooftops. Happiness glowed in me from knowing the little thing was where it belonged now. I met Zeth's eyes, and we both broke into laughter.

"Goodness," I said. "That was exciting. Reminds me of when the mouse got into Hattie's room, and she squealed so loud, we thought she was dying."

Zeth grinned from ear to ear and planted his hands on his hips. "Yeah, took us an hour to get the thing out. Hattie wanted us to kill it, but it had the cutest pink ears, so neither of us could. I'm still glad we took it to the field and released it instead."

I bit my lip as I leaned my back against the windowsill. "Those were the days."

When Zeth went quiet, I glanced up to find him staring at me. It was hard to look away from such perfect eyes. The way they observed me carefully, deeply...

"I should get a cat," he suddenly said, dropping his gaze to the mess on the floor. "A cat would keep birds and mice out."

"Fixing the hole in your window might solve that too," I teased.

"Hm, maybe fix the window *and* get a fluffy kitty? But first, thank you for bravely assisting me in defeating the intruder."

"Psh, more like cowering in the corner."

"You leaped into my arms, and I wasn't objecting," Zeth said with husky humor. He shifted closer until all I could see was him towering over me in that soaked shirt, and I couldn't help but notice the outline of his nipples through the cotton.

Ah, shit.

I crossed my arms but didn't move. No, I didn't dare move, because he had that tender expression on his face. If he inched any closer, I was in trouble. I needed a distraction, so I averted my gaze to refocus my thoughts.

"You've been working hard," I told him. "The downstairs looks wonderful."

"Aye, I've little else to do but think and clean. And I enjoy accomplishing things. Working hard, seeing the results. I'm sure you feel the same while making a chair."

My body tingled with good feelings. Just being around him did that. "You should be proud of yourself. You're doing a lot to help you and Millie."

Zeth shrugged. "That's what big brothers do."

"That's true," I eyed him, hoping he didn't take offense at my next words. "Have you... Have you considered that you don't need to marry into wealth to get by? You're remarkably smart, Zeth, you always have been. You could work doing nearly anything. Appraising, warehouse work, or even the bank. You have ambition. Drive. You work hard no matter what comes your way, and you don't complain about it."

He studied me curiously. I knew it sounded like I was trying to stop him from courting Annabelle—and perhaps a part of me was —but I spoke the truth. He always had more initiative and motivation than I did, more than most people I knew. If anyone deserved to be successful, it was Zeth.

"I started asking around for work, but no luck," he countered as he pulled my glasses off and held them up before trying them on. He blinked through them at me, looking so cute. "You know, Rosie, I think we may need to get your glasses checked. That's probably why you see me differently than everyone else."

I tilted my head at him. "Even with those off, I can still see an incredibly smart and handsome man."

Zeth's eyes lit up from behind my gold frames. "You think I'm handsome?"

I looked at him as if he was crazy for asking. "No doubt about it."

"Well..." He removed my glasses and gently secured them on my face again, letting his hands linger there. "I think you're adorable. Creative, kind, hardworking too."

My lips twitched, and I laughed softly. It was either hot in this room, or Zeth's sweet words were getting to me. God, we were being so sappy with one another. Was this how all adults spoke when they found someone they wanted?

"Amby," Zeth said softly. "About what happened in the barn, I want you to know I don't regret it."

"Neither do I," I whispered.

Zeth stepped closer. His fingers smoothed over both of my temples and around the backs of my ears until his palms cupped each side of my face. I held my breath, wondering what he was doing, what he wanted. I knew what I wanted, and I also knew it would lead me into more trouble with him. But the pain and loneliness I'd been carrying with me since our time in the barn suddenly disappeared. I didn't care one bit what heartache this may bring me later. I just wanted this moment.

I gazed fondly at Zeth, and he beheld me like I was the sun, moon, and stars. A fervent heat built up inside me. I could see Zeth felt the same way, yet he didn't move any closer. Unable to take this tension between us anymore, I grabbed his shirt and yanked him to me, tilting my head up so that my lips crushed against his.

His lips parted for me immediately, encouraging my daring nature. Kissing him came so naturally. He tasted of rain and salt, of freedom, and something wild that I craved since laying eyes on him again at the picnic.

My hand cupped his rough cheek, my thumb smoothing against the bristled hairs growing there. I had never seen him with hair on his face before. The rugged look fit him. His soft moans of approval impelled me to kiss him rougher. He returned my aggression by sucking my tongue, which was an excellent reminder of how good Zeth was with his mouth.

When I realized what we were doing, I pulled away. "Sorry... I shouldn't have kissed you."

"Shouldn't have, or didn't want to?"

I closed my eyes in hopes of curbing my desire. "I want to, so badly. But with us both trying to court other people, we certainly shouldn't."

His breath tickled my cheek before he whispered, "I thought you like it when I'm not a gentleman."

I bit my lip, unable to resist him. "You're right, I do."

Zeth groaned as he captured my chin with firm fingers and jerked my head back to face him. My eyes opened to lock onto his lovely golden browns, and I licked my lips in invitation for him to kiss me again. When his gaze dropped to my mouth with longing, I tugged on Zeth's shirt until he dove back in hungrily.

Our lips met even harder this time, and my hands roved up to his shoulders and arms so I could squeeze them. I twisted my fingers into his damp shirt to keep him close.

Now there was no turning back. It seemed I was intent on hurting myself despite knowing that at the end of the day, he would never be mine. But we weren't married men yet. There was nothing wrong in simply... indulging while we were both still free. Was there?

16

Zeth

I pushed Amby backward until he hit the kitchen wall with a needy groan that caressed my skin. When one of his hands twisted in my shirt, I welcomed it, and when his other hand slipped around to cup the back of my neck, I followed his unspoken command to kiss him.

But I wasn't in the mood for obeying yet. I wanted Amby to know how much I wanted him to stay in my life. I crushed his lips with a demand for his breath as I pressed against him. Then I easily claimed his wrists and guided his arms above his head to hold him still while I explored every inch of his daring mouth.

Just like before, capturing Amby like this sent a thrill through me that pushed me to grip him harder. His sharp gasp told me he wanted more, so I held him at my mercy to explore lower, pecking sweet kisses on his jawline.

When he leaned his head back to the wall and moaned in encouragement, I accepted his offering and focused on his exposed throat. Kissing a trail along his buttoned collar, I found his thumping pulse with my lips. His perfume tickled my nose, so I paused to inhale the musky-sweet scent of sandalwood mixed with vanilla. Manly and sweet, all Amby.

"You smell so good," I said, licking his neck.

Amby broke free from my grip on his wrists and found my hair.

He slid his fingers over my scalp while I cherished the scented spot. "I put perfume on for you," he whispered. "I wanted to run into you today, so you can do exactly what you're doing to me right now."

His husky admission sent need vibrating through me that Amby responded to with a shiver of his own. I wanted to pay attention to him, feel all of his responses and hear all of his moans.

I loosened his tie to reveal that patch of skin I saw at the pub. Only faded bruises remained where I sucked on him in the barn.

"I love seeing my marks on you, Rosie." I kissed one softly. "Shall I make more love bites?"

"Mm, yes, please bruise me with your mouth wherever you want," he whispered against my ear.

Fuck.

I sucked on Amby's exposed neck to claim him, savoring him. He tasted delicious, salty. I wanted to taste all of him. He said to bruise him wherever I wanted, and the thought of worshiping Amby from my knees made my mouth water. Half the fun was getting there.

I opened his jacket quickly, and Amby shrugged it off. He bit his lip playfully as he leaned back again, pressing his palms flat against the wall without me even needing to pin him there.

Oh, I liked that. I rewarded him with a husky, "You're such a good boy."

"I'm your good boy," Amby replied so confidently that my knees weakened. I got lost in his brown eyes until he boldly moved his hips out against me.

"Fuck yes, you're mine," I growled with approval, needing my words to be true, needing this moment to be more than an escape. How did I fool myself into thinking that I would ever be satisfied with only a fraction of Amby? Looking wasn't enough, not when I enjoyed everything about him, from the way his smile lit up the whole room, to how he was always so kind, no matter what happened between us. I thought I lost him completely when his goodbye broke me apart, yet here he was again, willing to be my lover.

He stayed perfectly still as I undid each of his shirt buttons and followed with rough, suctioning kisses. Red patches appeared on his toned chest and filled me with pride until I reached the waistband of his pants. There, a trail of dark-red hair begged for my attention.

I dropped to my knees and licked the skin of his lean stomach, using my tongue to dip into his pants. He gripped my hair to hold me still while he took in a sharp breath. I thought he might stop me, but he pressed me closer.

"Beg me to keep going," I commanded against his stomach. "I want to hear you beg for my mouth."

Amby spread his fingers against my head as he slowly raked his hand through my hair. Then his fist clenched in my tendrils, and he tugged my head back to make me meet his eyes. "Please... suck your boy dry."

"Yes..." I groaned, so happy my boy needed me. It felt right to please Amby like this, and I didn't lose any control by doing so either. I made him wait as I pressed my lips against the hardness in his pants and huffed hot air through the cotton.

Amby smoothed back my damp hair with a gentle touch. When his fingers drifted along my cheek, I closed my eyes and moved into his touch, treasuring it. Amby held me softly for a moment before making a featherlight trail to my mouth, where I parted my lips in invitation. I was desperate for him, but he rubbed his thumb against my bottom lip, teasing me with delay. I didn't mind because he touched me so... lovingly. I could only pant with longing while he explored my upturned face with his wonderful adoration. I didn't deserve his kindness, but I would take it for as long as he offered it to me.

When Amby pushed his thumb inside my mouth, I rewarded him with a deep groan as I immediately sucked him in, relishing the comfort in connecting so intimately. Having any part of him in my mouth again was perfect. Yet, Amby needed me elsewhere.

My hands fumbled at his waistband while still worshiping his thumb, and I unbuckled his belt with a rough tug of leather that had him grunting. I found his buttons to unfasten them swiftly.

"Zeth," Amby got out with a ragged breath that pleased me. I wanted to make him speechless. Gazing up to him, I caught his eyes half-lidded with desire for me. He was so handsome. That strong jaw, those tousled curls, that adoring look as I teased his thumb with my tongue.

When I leaned back to separate from his hand, Amby placed his palms back against the wall again. He tilted his head and willingly offered his whole body to me.

That trust was beautiful. He was the one to make me speechless. Amby was giving himself to me, body and soul. I felt that in the barn too, when Amby held me close, but I closed off my emotions and fled. This time, I was ready to appreciate the blessing Amby granted me. If he was daring enough to trust his heart in my care, then I wanted to keep it safe while I held it.

Fuck, I adored him. I kissed Amby's stomach and parted his pants, pulling them down to free him. Then I leaned in to lick the underside of his cock from base to tip with one long, slow stroke. Amby sucked air through his teeth before he let it out.

When I kissed the silky skin of his head, he shuddered and bucked against my lips, demanding me to go beyond gentle kisses. He was a grown man, he knew what he wanted. I slid my rough jaw along the side of his cock and licked the soft skin at his base before sucking him there. Amby's answering growl was low and approving, and damn me for loving it.

I nuzzled into his springy hair and appreciated his musk before sucking on his base again, leaving my mark. I made sure he whimpered at the edge of pleasure and pain before I let his skin go with a soft pop. "Aye, there's my naughty boy," I said against him, moving to span my hands around his hips. My grip wasn't gentle as I pushed his ass against the wall.

"You want my mouth quick and rough, don't you?"

"Yes, my body is yours. Do what you want with it."

I knew it was, but I was grateful to hear him say it. I grabbed his shaft to draw him into my hungry mouth to show him just how I planned on making my body his.

Amby let out a passionate sigh. I growled ever deeper against him, drawing him in as I fisted around his base. He tasted so heavenly, I thought I was dreaming. I sucked him this way for a long moment, tightening my fist often to hear him whimper. When I moved faster, his heavy breaths filled the air and his hands touched whatever they could of me, caressing my hair and roving over my ears and my spread jaw. Then he held my hand on his hip and stroked over my bare arms.

When his hands found my shoulders and stiffened, I knew he was close to spilling, so I opened my hand and slid my lips all the way down his firm shaft, welcoming the feel of his head against the top of my mouth.

Amby groaned roughly and tugged on my hair to remove my mouth. "You... are certainly no gentleman. Just how I like you."

I huffed up at him with a wicked grin, knowing full well he pulled me off to stop himself from losing control. He was right. I didn't want to be gentle, or polite. I wanted him to fall apart in my mouth, but I didn't mind prolonging his pleasure too. I leaned forward again to lick his sensitive head. Sucking in the tip, I caressed him with my tongue until his thighs shook and he bucked against me.

"Zeth, please touch yourself for me," he said, "I want you to come with me."

My moan of agreement came only seconds before my greedy hands found the buttons of my pants.

I released myself and promptly stole some of the wetness at my tip to make stroking easier. Pleasure washed through me, and I groaned from the dual sensations of sucking Amby and fisting myself. I needed him closer, so I reached around Amby's hip to grab his ass cheek, squeezing him until I heard his sweet groan. My grip tightened, and I pulled him toward me to take him so deep that his cock hit the back of my throat.

"You handle me so well," Amby moaned, his hand gripping my hair until tears stung my eyes, and I relished it. His words spurred me on to go faster, and I used my rough grip on his ass to control him. My peak was building fast. I tugged his cheeks apart and nudged my middle finger over to find his hole.

That did something magical to him, because as soon as my

finger circled his soft flesh, both of Amby's hands clenched in my hair. He let out a ragged breath as he leaned over me, unraveling. "Yes..." he got out. "Push it in, please..."

How could I deny such a request? My own cock twitched in my hand as I pushed my middle finger slightly into him, then out. Over and over, until Amby moaned so loudly, I was sure if someone was standing outside, they'd hear him.

"Fuck, Zeth, I'm gonna come. I'm gonna come." He tried to pull out again, but I clutched his hips to show that I wanted all of him. He spasmed against me with a loud, guttural cry, and then claimed my mouth with a heavy thrust that filled me with his release.

He pushed me right over the edge. My mouth became sloppy as I lost my own seed, feeling it wash over my palm while Amby whimpered from above. My mind drifted to a peaceful place, my muscles loosening in a way they hadn't for years. A moment later, Amby stilled and panted, leaning his hand on my shoulder to keep himself upright. I let him go and melted until my forehead leaned against Amby's stomach for support too. My body and soul glowed.

Amby panted heavily as he stayed on the wall, unable to move. Or at least, I hoped I did that to him, because that's how I felt. Empty and floating, yet so incredibly full. And when Amby smoothed my hair back from my face, I felt even better, if such a thing was possible.

"I see stars," Amby laughed. He tilted his head back against the wall and closed his eyes. His fingers lightly massaged my head, and I grinned like a fool.

My limbs were weak, so I stayed on the floor for a moment and took out my—or rather Amby's—handkerchief to wipe my hand before pocketing it. I kissed his stomach and purred, "I hope I satisfied you."

Amby took my chin in his hand and tilted my face up to caress my stubbly jaw. "I'm floating. Thank you."

"Me too." I met his affectionate gaze, and he smiled so widely that his dimple appeared. A sight more lovely never existed.

He lowered a hand, and I gratefully accepted the assistance to rise up on shaky legs. Once steady, I tucked myself back into order while Amby did the same, buttoning his shirt but leaving off his tie.

When Amby pouted, my heart constricted, because I realized he was holding in his next goodbye. I didn't want that pain again, at least not yet, so before he could say a damn thing, I grabbed his stubborn jaw and gripped him hard until he whined. Then I kissed him deeply, ensuring he tasted himself on me. I needed him to want more from me because fuck, I couldn't get enough of him.

When we parted for air, Amby wrapped his arms around me and pressed his face against my neck to draw in a shaky breath. My heart flipped. He was hurting too. He trusted me, and I was hurting him. I felt horrible, but there was nothing I could do about our situation except pull him in tighter to bury my nose into his curls, treasuring the soft tickle of his hair against my cheek. I would hold him all day, if that's what Amby needed.

Dammit, couldn't our situation change? If Amby gave up his dad's plan of continuing his family's bloodline, if I asked him for a courting kiss, he could be mine. It would be like a bonus, having him along with his family's security.

I opened my mouth to ask him, but Amby spoke first.

"You feel so different now," he said, as his hand pawed my upper arm. "Stronger, taller."

"Then why do I feel weaker?" I asked like a fool.

"Weak in what way?"

"Well, just that as kids, we were invincible. We flew off barn roofs and rolled in hay stacks, but now..." Now I was scared to risk my heart. And Amby didn't dare step off his path. We were both in danger of breaking. Our planned futures meant unhappy marriages and shared moments like this one. I imagined waiting for Amby's lovely eyes to meet mine across a party so we could sneak outside to be together. I never saw myself as the cheating kind, but if that was the only way to keep him close, then I would.

I finally got out, "It's just not the same. You know?"

"I know." Amby's fingers curled in my shirt around my waist. "Everything was easier when we were younger, wasn't it? When we didn't have... responsibilities."

And that was it. Amby defined our fate with one word: Responsibility. He wouldn't give up the Somerset legacy for me, and I needed to let him go in order to marry for wealth.

Swallowing, I shut my eyes tight against a wave of disappointment and nodded, glad to have him with me briefly. I ran a palm over Amby's hair and shifted to rub his back with strong strokes as we stayed together for a bit longer. I could almost hear the thoughts swirling around in his lovely head, while mine just stopped.

Once we both relaxed, Amby moved his head and gently kissed my neck before he looked up at me. "Do you want me to help you clean the kitchen? Or I could go out and ask someone I know about the window." He turned to the hole in the glass.

I glanced at the mess around me, then grabbed Amby's hand. "Stay, I would love your help."

17

Ambrose

"These are our current interest percentages on loans, and then the number the bank made last year in that interest. Calculate the number of last year's interest we accrued in loans, and we'll compare numbers."

I scanned the numbers on the paper that Henry Dawsey showed me. He was supervisor for loans at the bank, handling each account as if it was the easiest thing in the world. But it was hard to focus on what I was supposed to do as we both worked separately on our own pieces of paper. Nothing written in ink made sense. I was too foolish to understand. Too distracted...

This was my fifth day of training, and working with Henry all week had been nothing short of a headache. By the tired look on his face, he probably had a headache too from training me. There had certainly been many near eyerolls on his part. I knew I wouldn't be easy to train for this sort of work.

After a few minutes, Henry shifted in the chair from across the table. "Let me see what you have."

I hesitated and leaned back. I didn't even get halfway through the assignment.

When Henry saw I wasn't finished, he eyed me. "What's taking you so long?"

"I want to make sure they all add up correctly."

"Right." He sighed heavily. "Maybe you should take a break."

"I'm almost done." I gripped my pen and bit my tongue from saying any more, but it was hard to add the numbers in my head. I had to use the method I was taught in school, adding the numbers in small groups on the paper before finally getting the total. It took much longer than I knew it should, and by the time I handed the paper over, Henry had an annoyed expression on his face.

He looked them over, then sighed. "Well, Amby, you're off by a couple of hundred."

"What?" I took the paper back, and his own, to compare them. "No, I..." But I didn't have to look long to know I was wrong and he was right. Henry was a *supervisor*, and who was I? Just the Somerset son. My last name was the only reason Henry didn't tell me bluntly that I was an idiot.

I didn't want to learn about loans, but what choice did I have? God, how I wished to go back to my desk in the corner and fill out invoices before doing my afternoon courier work. I could do that forever and be fine. It was *easy* work. It didn't put me under immense pressure to succeed. But this new work... It was awful.

"I think that may be enough for today, Ambrose." Henry rose from his chair.

I got up too. "I know it's been a long week, but I'm trying."

"Are you? Currently, I don't see you stepping up into the loans department anytime soon."

"I have to train to do this work."

"Then *try* harder. Otherwise, Mr. Somerset will be here until he's on his last leg. Would you really put your father out like that?" When my jaw tightened, Henry shook his head. "Perhaps being a messenger boy has made you used to easy work."

My blood ran hot at that insult, and I blurted out the first thing that came to mind, "Well, it's a good thing someone is a messenger here, otherwise your consort wouldn't get her blessing from your bank account once a month. Don't worry, I won't tell your wife."

Henry stared sharply at me, looking as if he might throttle me if he could. But before he could do or say anything, I turned on my heel and left his office. I felt slightly better telling him off. But he was right about one thing, I wasn't ready. Even Henry could see that from only a few hours spent with me.

My wish had been granted to go back to my other work, and I happily made my way to the mailroom, where someone handed me a courier bag. I was so used to delivering or picking up mail that I knew what I had to do without much thought. Yes, being a messenger boy was easy work, though it required me to still work at a place where numbers were not my friend. But put a piece of wood in my hand and I could shape it into whatever Henry wanted. I doubt he could put together a table and six chairs to complete a dining set.

Eager to leave the bank, I made my way outside and inhaled the breezy air. Everdeen was bustling with the upcoming spring events. Everyone was out and about, purchasing or selling something, which was good for the town's prosperity.

As I walked along the sidewalk to my first stop, I pulled on my cap, nodding at familiar faces as they passed. The patio of the Rustic Rose Cafe was filled with people drinking tea and eating pastries. A young group of men in finery shared a cake topped with a small wooden horse, gossiping about the upcoming derby.

Across the street, Suzie Myers swept the doorstep of her jewelry shop, while Brody Swells cleaned the windows of the line of shops on Main Street. Birds chirped in the scattered trees, and the chapel bell in the distance rang up to twelve. A group of girls walked past me, chatting about the upcoming Founders Day Festival in a few weeks.

"I'm tying a yellow ribbon around my wrist," said a blonde-haired girl in pigtails. "So the rest of the year will bring me joy and happiness."

"Ella and I want to give each other purple for friendship." A girl with short brown hair grabbed her friend's hand.

I wondered what color ribbon I might choose this year. If I could tie one around someone's wrist, as many of the courting lovers did, I'd choose pink for Zeth, for his affections toward me.

Zeth...

When I raised my head, I saw the green ivy that covered the laundry in the distance, and my stomach fluttered. After our intimate encounter the other day, I wasn't sure where Zeth and I stood. We weren't acquaintances, and we weren't courting lovers. We were in between. Familiar friends, but also more than that...

I adjusted the strap of the courier bag on my shoulder and peered down at the sidewalk. Zeth never mentioned giving up his courtship of Annabelle. We didn't talk about *us* at all. I helped him clean the kitchen and stuffed the hole in the window with one of Zeth's undershirts. Then he gave me a quick kiss on the nose before Annabelle and Millie returned from their visits, leaving me confused.

I still felt confused.

I planted my hands in my pockets, watching as the sidewalk became rougher. There was a specific crack that reminded me of a wishbone, and I stopped, knowing right where I was. I looked over at the laundry's wide windows to see no one inside. That didn't stop me from walking over to the chipping door, where an array of blue, green, and yellow showed through from being repainted so many times. I hesitated before I pulled up my arm and knocked.

The rush of seeing Zeth made my mind swirl. Would he be happy to see me? Was he still planning to marry Annabelle? Zeth needed money and security, yet he could work for those things on his own. Millie had already gotten a job in town. He could do the same. Why, exactly, did he need to marry into money? Then again, I'd never been in his situation before, where one needs money so badly, their very survival depends on it.

I was being selfish. But...

We needed to talk about this. About us. The feeling of shrugging this whole thing off and not talking about it was bothering me. It made me hurt, and it was hard to eat or sleep. Zeth's words about things being different now hit me hard. Things *were* different. We couldn't control our futures, and it was drowning us. I needed to know if my choice to pursue the bank and a wife was the right one. I needed answers from Zeth. Perhaps a sign.

When Zeth didn't come to the door, I turned around. He and

Millie had to be gone somewhere. Or maybe he saw it was me and didn't want to open the door.

I looked across the street in time to see Damien Cooligan tip his cap at me with a wink. I gave him the finger, which made him frown, before he walked on. It was rude, but Damien wanted one thing, and that was sex. I didn't want him. I didn't want just sex. I wanted a connection, a companionship that made sense.

Zeth and I made sense. Every intimate encounter with him was magnetic. Each tender touch was like static. The things we did together, the topics we talked about, had always been full of meaning. We'd always had each other's backs as kids, and as teens, Zeth had helped me through the sadness when my mother died. He was always there for me whenever I needed him, in body and soul.

But I admit, both of us could have talked *more* to each other about the things that bothered us. Zeth often guarded himself and clammed up, and I used to get so frustrated with him. I should have been willing to listen and understand.

When he asked me to marry him, we were only sixteen. I knew of my father's expectations then. The fear of him rejecting me was more powerful than my fear of losing Zeth. I had refused his proposal to please my father. If I could talk to my younger self, I'd have to admit things never got any better for following Father's legacy. I still didn't want to be at the bank, I still couldn't attain Father's approval no matter what I did, and I still hadn't married a woman. And to top it all off...

I was still deeply in love with Zeth Washer.

This realization struck me powerfully as I stared at the laundry's chipping paint. For nine years, I had made no progress toward happiness, sinking ever further into the shadow of my father's disappointment. My heart fluttered like a hummingbird's wings against the bars of its cage. I had to get out of my own prison.

Why *couldn't* I have Zeth? And why couldn't he have me? Even if my father didn't approve of us, and I lost my inheritance, I would still strive to give Zeth what I could. My devotion, my love, what money I did make. Together, we could make enough to live. I just didn't know if he felt strongly enough about me to abandon his dreams of elite living for him and Millie, to risk it all by chancing a courtship with me.

Still, I had to know. I had to talk to him, because I was aching from imagining him married to Annabelle while glancing at me from afar at social events... I deserved to be happy too, like my sisters. So did he, if he wanted me. This was the choice that hung over my head, to talk to Zeth about being together, or lose him forever.

Emboldened, I dug in my carrier bag until I found my notepad. I pulled out the pen from my pocket and scribbled a note for Zeth, hesitating on how I should sign my name. My breath hitched as I chose my signature wisely. Then I folded the paper and slipped it in the crack of the door near the knob so he would easily see it.

Then I left the laundry in a rush, my stomach full of anxious butterflies.

18

Zeth

*Can we talk about us? Meet me after Chapel tomor-
row. - your Rosie*

Millie stomped around Mum's room as I waited at the foot of the
stairs, thumbing Amby's signature for the twenty-sixth time since
finding his note. What did he want to say? *About us.* That part gave
me hope, and made me nervous. All I knew for certain was that I
would go blind if I kept staring at Amby's pretty writing, so I folded
the note back up and tucked it into my inner jacket pocket for safekeeping. Having something of his felt nice, even if Amby wanted to
tell me we needed to be just friends.

Millie finally clopped her way down the stairs in her lovely,
white, lace dress with a matching bonnet. She looked pretty. I
hardly recognized her as my playful sister at all, if not for the
mischievous grin.

"There's my Mils. You took your sweet time."

She puckered her lips and led us to the front door. "Because I
don't want to go to Chapel. I think you gave me a piggyback ride
the last time we went."

That wasn't far off the mark. She might have been seven when we stopped attending. One of the wealthy girls made fun of Millie for wearing the brat's cast-off clothes. No need to remind Millie of that embarrassment as I locked the door.

"I barely remember what to do," she huffed. Then she hopped off the stoop. "Sit, stand, sing?"

"Those are the basics, and we should go because we're proper, upstanding citizens of Everdeen."

"Is that what we are?"

I chuckled at her dubious expression and joined her on the sidewalk. "Aye, at least we can pretend we're proper, eh?"

She nodded saucily and placed her arm around mine to pull me forward with a tilt of her bonnet. "Help me walk, before people think you're rude for forcing your injured sister to join you today."

"Your ankle is healed," I reminded her while holding her arm against my side, happy for the company. "But you could certainly use some prayers."

She clicked her tongue and muttered, "Pish posh."

That didn't sound like my sister. Maybe she learned the fancy saying from Anna or Emiline. She had been spending time with them both lately. I never thought my unconventional sister would enjoy the company of Everdeen's elite, but here we were. I shook my head at Millie as we strolled in the sunshine through the main thoroughfare behind other service goers. Arriving a little late meant we could slip into a back pew and bide our time unnoticed until I could meet Amby after the service.

I didn't want to see Anna there, though I was certain she attended Chapel weekly. She seemed the type who kept her family pew warm. All the elite families had reserved seats up front to show off their status. I thought about sitting as Anna's husband there, and my chest constricted with pain.

Marriage to Anna felt like a punishment after spending time with Amby again. He made me ache in a good way every time he glanced at me with those enticing brown eyes. He was the only one who saw the real me, even if his vision was a bit distorted.

What does he want to talk about? Hopefully, he didn't regret our intimate time together in the kitchen. I treasured that memory, so grateful for his trust while I worshipped him from my knees. Maybe he felt the same, and now he wanted us to be secret lovers. He did sign the note *Rosie*. I didn't know why else he would sign it so intimately.

I would accept a love affair. I decided that around the tenth time I read his note. Of course I would rather choose Amby as my spouse, but life was not that kind. He was not going to marry me. I didn't fit into his plan to marry a woman. Or rather, his father's plan. I was a variable in the Somerset equation. Having an affair with Amby meant I could wedge my way into his heart as a secret lover. If that was our only chance to be together, then I would take it. Anything, to keep my Rosie close. I missed him this past week.

Millie was busy chatting away on my arm, and I caught the tail end of her saying, "I want to make a good impression, is all."

"Who wouldn't like you?" I assured her, feeling bad for not listening. Not long ago, she hinted that she had her cap set for someone, and I wondered again who caught her eye in town. "Is there someone you wish to impress today?"

"Maybe..." she teased. "Shall we make a bet? The first to marry, wins."

"Heaven help me, you're incorrigible. If this is some ruse to push me into marrying Anna faster, it won't work. These things take time."

"Do you think she'll make you happy?"

"Well, that's a question," I hedged as I narrowed my gaze at her. Millie regarded me seriously, and my head filled with platitudes that belonged on Anna's embroidered pillows. I wasn't in the mood for that nonsense. "Marrying Anna is our quickest option for a comfortable life. For a house that doesn't leak and a respectable position in society. For a contented family. Those are the things that will make me happy."

Millie frowned. "What if Anna wants someone else?"

"That makes two of us," I grumbled so low that the surrounding chatter and traffic covered my confession. Then I added, louder, "She must want to marry me, though. She's been welcoming."

"It does seem so..." Millie trailed off.

But what if Millie was right, and Anna did pine for another? Someone she also couldn't have. Maybe she planned on having her own affairs, and marrying me would bring her that same benefit. That would be fine. I was conning Anna into marriage with lies about my finances while cheating on her with my old lover; it was only fair if she planned to cheat on me.

Fuck, when did I turn into a cad? Did I just hope my future wife *cheated* on me? What a horrid turn.

Millie pulled my hand from where it was pinching my nose. I didn't even realize I was holding myself in like that. My whole body felt tight as Millie's brow knitted. Then she asked, "Are you okay?"

No, I wasn't okay. I was holding myself up while I was fucking hurt and lost. No job to support us, no parents to tell me I could do better, and no right to be anything but fine. I was heading to Chapel as if my soul wasn't tearing in two from planning an affair. I was *not* okay.

I cringed inwardly but got out a weak, "I'm fine."

Thankfully, Millie glanced away without asking anything more of me. She looked glum. Was she upset that I hadn't given Anna a courting kiss yet? Maybe she was seeing how much I was dragging my feet and calling me out on it. She was probably doubting my devotion to provide for her. Maybe I should seek out Anna today and ask for that kiss...

No, I needed to speak with Amby first, to hear what he wanted to say *about us*. Then I would worry about Anna.

Needing to cross the street, Millie and I stepped out just as a peppy little motor vehicle in classy gray enamel and chrome honked its horn. A passing wagon didn't move fast enough to get out of the way, and the car swerved right for where Millie was about to step. I flung my arm out in front of her, barely stopping her from getting run over. Millie's white ribbon fluttered against me as the damn car barreled on by.

"Fucking maniac," I grumbled after the rich prick. We weren't important citizens, but we weren't trash either.

The car screeched to a halt not far up the road, too damn late, and the driver turned around in the seat. With the roof down, I could see clearly that it was Anna. She wore driving goggles and a crisp white hat with a big purple bow around the brim. When she lifted her goggles, I never wanted to see anyone less. That didn't stop her from waving to get our attention.

"Good day, Washers. Where are you headed? Perhaps I can give you a ride."

"It's Anna in her car!" Millie chirped and bounced, as if my eyes weren't working, then she shouted ahead, "We're headed to Chapel, are you?"

When Anna nodded, Millie left me to run over to the car and rounded to the passenger side. She quickly hopped into the second seat, next to Anna.

I took my sweet time strolling over and tried to look grateful for the ride as I reached the back of her sporty car to turn a latch in the curved back. I'd seen such things in the City and opened the car's rumble seat. It was nicely upholstered with plush, purple velvet, but it didn't welcome a man who grew to over six feet. I used the spotless chrome bumper to step up and wedge myself into place. When Anna restarted the motor and we leapt off, I had to slap my cap onto my head or lose it.

Millie squealed happier than a pig as she and Anna swerved around the slower traffic. They flung me this way and that, and I did my best to hold on tight. It took effort to avoid spilling right out onto the road. And although Anna's car was expensive, it wasn't meant for three. I would have preferred walking.

In moments, the tall steeples of the Chapel appeared over Main Street. Anna rounded a quick corner to park abruptly across the street.

When the engine quieted, I descended and tried to hide how my legs wobbled. Anna *was* a maniac. The girls both exited their comfortable compartment with more grace and joined me as I stashed the purple velvet seat neatly away. That's when I noticed Anna's ribbon and purple dress matched her car.

I swear to god, if this woman had a vehicle to match every outfit, I might expire from the extravagance. It wasn't necessary. In fact, it was distasteful. Distasteful when I could barely put food on the table for my little sister to eat. Who was I fooling? I didn't even own a table.

I bit the inside of my lip to keep from asking Anna how many cars she owned. She probably had one for each day of the week. I wasn't feeling very fond of her as she led us across the street.

"It's such a nice day," she said, wiping at the pink imprints left on her cheeks from her goggles. "I'd love to have you both over for tea and lunch after Chapel, if you'd like."

"That sounds delightful," Millie said for us both, before I could even get a word in. When she eyed me, I sent her a tight smile.

"Actually, I made plans with Amby after Chapel," I admitted in a conversational tone that didn't keep pace with my racing pulse. I didn't want to insult Anna, but there was no way I would join her for refreshments when Amby wished to speak with me. "May I join you another time?"

When we reached the sidewalk in front of the chapel, Anna gave my shoulder a friendly pat. "Of course, you should visit with Amby. As my mother used to say, sometimes you meet people you can't forget. Those are your friends."

Friends... and in this case, hopefully lovers. Heaven help me, I truly was a cad.

"I'll take Millie with me this afternoon, then." Annabelle continued. "My next event is at the Washington salon. I'd love for you both to attend as my guests."

"We would love that," I answered smoothly for Millie and me, but my head hurt just thinking about it. A salon would toss us even more into Everdeen's elite, with Anna at my side. Was Amby attending too? If I could spend time with him, maybe it wouldn't be so bad.

The Chapel bells chimed loudly from above, calling in the lingering parishioners. We arrived right on time. So much for my plan to arrive late and sneak in the back. I held my arm out to Millie, waiting for her to take it, while I searched for Amby's auburn curls among those entering. He wasn't there. Maybe he was sitting already. I anticipated seeing him dressed in his Chapel best.

Millie took my arm, and I turned to her with an encouraging smile, only to find Anna. She regarded me softly, her lacy gloved hand tucking tighter against me. I didn't even mean to offer my arm to her. Yet there she was, already tugging me up the steps. We looked like a courting couple in front of the whole congregation. If we walked in like this...

My mouth went dry while Millie hopped over to my other side. I don't know why she shot me an angry glare, but when she glanced over at Anna, they both shared a knowing glance. Perhaps they thought it was cute, both being on my arm. I didn't find it cute. I actually felt a bit sick.

The townsfolk at the entrance greeted Anna and turned curious eyes upon my sister and me. Anna replied to them all by name, introducing us quickly as we shuffled through the wide doors.

When I planned to come to Chapel today, I didn't envision entering with Anna. Yet here I was about to reach my goal of marriage and stability. A goal which promised an undetermined number of cars, an estimated sixteen tea sets, one plush chair, and a pretty vase. And Anna Winters, I shouldn't forget her.

So why did I want Amby's porch rocker instead? And Amby's teasing brown eyes through golden frames. And that dimpled smile that brightened the whole room. And that gentle hand trailing along my bare back that almost made me cry in his arms. I wanted to talk with him today, and afterward maybe kiss him, and walk with him.

"I like the music," Millie piped up.

Chapel, right. I snapped back to the present. Music? Only then did I notice an organ playing from a balcony above the entrance. Tall pipes lined the front of the long chamber, their metal tubes reaching for the high ceiling. I admired the beautiful instrument and architecture while Anna pulled me toward an open pew.

Anna went in first. Did she want us to follow? This was her family's pew. If we sat here, it was like accepting a marriage proposal...

Millie slipped in next, quick as a wink.

I reluctantly scooted into the Winters' pew and sat down,

enjoying the end of the aisle beside Millie because that gave me space to stretch out my legs. I did so slightly now and looked across the aisle to find a familiar auburn head facing me from the other side. Those same brown eyes I longed for were now widening behind his glasses. That adorable mouth dropped open slightly before tightening into a pout, and then those cheeks turned pink before he turned to face the front of the chapel. He was clearly upset.

Fuck.

This wasn't how I wished for today to go. I should have sat elsewhere, but I was also glad to have him so close. My whole body sang in response to seeing him. That wasn't good. Not good at all. How would we hide an affair if I couldn't control myself around him? I sat up and swallowed, tucking my leg back in. Then I faced the front where a few people were taking their places to start service.

Stealing a sideways glance, I was relieved to see Amby busy with Hattie. She held a book and showed him something while Amby nodded. His curls looked soft today, his back lean and straight under a well-fitted jacket in deep blue that paired well with his fair skin. The black ascot tucked into his high collar didn't fit Amby's style, but there was no denying how handsome it was on him as he sat with his fancy family.

When Hattie raised her head, I caught her eye by accident. She waved so violently that her blonde ringlets fluttered. It was too late to avoid her, so I waved back.

"Zeth! So good to see you here!" Hattie whisper-yelled over Amby's shoulder.

Amby shut his eyes and ignored us, keeping his face straight forward.

Then Amby's dad tapped Hattie on her arm and pointed to the front of the chapel. When she turned and sat straight again, he peered around her to look at me.

I stiffened, scared of Mr. Somerset's disapproval like the little kid I used to be, but the intimidating man actually smiled at me. His strictly trained mustache moved as he nodded in friendly greeting. That was encouraging. I thought for sure he would snub me, but then, he did often stop by the laundry to visit with Mum,

Uncle, and Memaw. Maybe he wasn't as strict and elitist as I remembered.

Hattie leaned forward once more with her hand cupped to whisper across, "We can talk after service."

I snorted at her foolery. Amby's little sister wasn't much different than mine. She further proved that by nudging Amby's ribs with her elbow, teasing him for ignoring me, and making his ears quickly redden. I felt his big brotherly pain. Millie was actually behaving, for once. She and Anna sat close so they could share a book.

The music swelled and the congregation stood. I followed, feeling awkward once everyone began to sing. I didn't know the song but Amby did. His lovely baritone crossed the aisle. He didn't even have a music book. He had the words memorized. And he was standing so stiffly, not enjoying the music at all. Did he like attending service? I couldn't recall, but he always seemed more interested in the folktales that surrounded Everdeen than any gods. None of it mattered to me.

We sat again, and I settled in next to Millie to listen to the various readings. One about vines, and another about money. I couldn't help but glance over the aisle to see if Amby was listening or staring off into the tall roof. It was hard to tell. He sometimes watched the readers, and sometimes fiddled with his thumbnail. What he didn't do was meet my eye, no matter how long I stared at him, and I knew he sensed me staring.

The Leader stood at the front to speak. I didn't pay much attention until she emphasized the word *infidelity*. Then she said *adultery*, and a couple behind me tittered some gossip. It wasn't about me. I wasn't married, yet, but I still inched lower in Anna's pew. Across the aisle, Amby didn't appear happy either. Red rose up his neck until it colored his ears yet again.

Then he tugged at his collar, trying to pull it up, and I spotted what he was trying to hide. My fresh marks on him. Only we knew he carried bruises in other places as well. Fuck me if I didn't want to claim him again with rough kisses right there in the middle of Chapel, infidelity be damned.

If I wasn't going to hell before, I was surely going now. My ears were suddenly on fire too, so I straightened and closed my eyes to focus on prayers. Millie wasn't the only one who needed them.

When a song started again, we all rose, and my eyes wandered. I couldn't help it. While everyone was looking in their books for the words, Amby sang with his head tilted high. I admired his calm dedication.

When Amby finally turned to face me, he met my gaze with a stone-like expression. I longed for our old camaraderie, so I sent him my most dashing smile, but he rejected me with an angry scowl and used his middle finger to adjust his glasses.

I laughed, because it was better than crying. Amby was over there fuming, and there was nothing I could do about it. My uselessness was as frustrating as when I couldn't help Amby walk home from the tavern. It was like I was married to Anna already. She had me tied to her pew while the man who needed me was so close yet out of reach, as if we still lived cities apart. I couldn't lose Amby, not again. I wanted him by my side. I needed him in my life, every day, every moment. Maybe if we—

"What are you doing?" Millie hissed from where she sat on the pew. Beside her, Anna appeared amused.

Millie poked my leg, and I looked around to see I was still standing while the rest of the chapel was now sitting and staring at me. When did the song end?

I sat swiftly.

It was too late; the service was over. Everyone stood again. The aisles filled with people while the organist played something fancy with dramatic leaps that matched my stomach trying to lodge in my throat. Yesterday, Amby sent me a note for us to talk. He gave me his trust, and I showed up at Chapel with Anna and gave him nothing but embarrassment and pain. I hoped to keep Amby in my life, but I chased him away. I had to make this right. We *really* needed to talk.

When Amby entered the middle aisle, I sprang up to join him. I didn't give him a chance to move away and grabbed his arm to tug him along with the exiting crowd until we reached an empty pew.

There, I claimed my chance to pull him behind me so we could flee through a side door.

As soon as we slipped outside, Amby pulled out of my grip and glared at me. "What are you doing?" he huffed.

"Hoping to apologize," I replied as heartfelt as I could manage. "I got your note. I'm here for you, Rosie."

His face contorted in pain as he took a step back. It was like a chasm opened between us as Amby questioned, "With Annabelle on your arm and sitting in her pew? Are you mocking me?" He choked on his words. "Am I just a cheap fuck for you to use?"

"No... It's not like that at all. I arrived with Anna because she tried to run me over with her car."

"What?"

"It's true, and then she took my arm, and Millie sat in her pew, and I felt like I had to follow along, even though I knew how it would look. I'm so sorry. I'd feel better if you called me an ass."

Amby straightened, his face souring as he said, "You're an ass."

"Thank you. Now can we pretend that I came in late and sat in the back as planned?" I laughed nervously and raked a hand through my hair. When he only raised an eyebrow in reply, I sent him a pleading glance. I wanted to embrace him, but he was holding himself out of reach. That didn't bode well. I asked anyway, "Please, will you tell me why you wrote your note?"

Amby's jaw drew taut. "Because... I need to tell you something, before it's too late." He paused for a long moment, his eyes intense, serious.

I took a step forward. "Rosie, what is it?"

"Annabelle doesn't have to be your only choice, you know," Amby shot out. "I'm perfectly capable of being someone to you."

I wasn't sure what he meant. *Being someone to me?* That sounded like he wanted to have an affair with me, just as I hoped. Strangely, I wasn't happy to hear it.

Maybe Amby wasn't happy either, because his face grew red. Then he reclaimed his step, drawing closer as he searched for his next words, "Annabelle doesn't have our inside jokes, she's never... dared you to do things. You don't have a whole *history* with her. She doesn't know how you relate real life to equations, or that you worked so hard as a boy to help your family get by. She hasn't laid with you and counted each star in the sky until you've fallen asleep, or kissed you until you're breathless... I hope."

He was right and saw me so clearly. I'd not done any of those things with Anna, so I shook my head in answer. Amby's lovely sentiments completely stole the air from my lungs.

He looked at me as if he might cry. "You asked me not long ago, the reason why I let you go if I was so heartbroken. The truth is, I let my father scare me. I just wanted him to be proud of me, so I chose him." He took a deep breath. "But I chose wrong, because each day without you has been nothing but empty. It doesn't matter to me if you don't have money, or if you're not one of the elite. Zeth, I've wanted to be with you since the moment I dared you to kiss me. I know I hurt you, and I'm so sorry for that." His voice cracked. "But I didn't realize how much you made my life whole until you came back into it, and now I know I can't live without you. And I'm afraid if I don't tell you how I feel now, I'll lose you again, forever."

"I..." My mind was adding up his sentences into neat columns for my brain to calculate. It sounded like... "Are you saying you're choosing me? You want to be with just me?"

"Yes," he got out. "All of you. You and me. Our whole hearts. Ahh, I sound so stupid." He rubbed the back of his neck. "If... you want me, that is. If you haven't already given a kiss to—"

"No, fuck no. That woman has too many fucking tea sets," I said with a crazy little laugh. "I never kissed Anna. I couldn't bring myself to, and I don't want to either."

Amby blinked at me with glossy eyes, and also with a visible look of relief. Letting out a breath, he stated, "You didn't..." His lips twitched as he let out a nervous breath. "Now it's my turn to tell you to call me an ass, for misunderstanding what happened today."

"You have a nice ass," I said to lighten the mood. "Oh wait, did I say that wrong?"

Amby laughed and looked away timidly. I felt the air shifting, no longer pushing us apart, so I closed the gap between us and used the back of my hand to caress his cheek. Then I tucked two fingers under his chin to bring his gaze up to mine. I was so grateful to see tenderness shining there once again.

There was so much to tell him about my past, and I had so many doubts and fears about the future, but there was one thing I knew for sure. "You're the one I want, Rosie. You're the only one I've ever wanted. Shall we take a walk and figure this out together?"

His dimple showed, and I let go of his chin to offer him my hand. Maybe we could find a spot away from the chapel to talk.

Amby appeared as tentatively hopeful as I felt as he slid his bruised and calloused fingers into mine. "I'd like that."

19

Ambrose

I was full of so many thoughts and feelings as I walked with Zeth along the dirt path that led away from the chapel. I admit it was my own fault for misunderstanding his intentions today. When he came into the chapel and sat in Annabelle's pew, I felt so sick, I thought I would need to rush outside and vomit. But he hadn't meant to come with her, and more importantly, he hadn't given her a courting kiss.

I stared at the path as we walked side by side, our hands clasped together. When I glanced over at Zeth, he gave me a reassuring smile that made me flush with affection. Regardless of our past relationship, of how shaky our reunion was, Zeth chose me over Annabelle. That made me so elated, yet I couldn't forget all the things I had done to try and prevent him and Annabelle from getting together.

"I'm sorry, Zeth. When you came back home with your own goals, I suppose I was... jealous. I said things I didn't mean, tried to distract you. I also ruined your suit at the lake."

"I deserved it," he pointed out with a shake of his head. "But I still can't believe you pushed me into that cold water."

I laughed and clutched his arm with my other hand. "Haven't you ever heard it said not to piss off a redhead, love?"

"Love?" Zeth's face lit up. "I like that. Say it to me again."

My face tingled at his husky command, and I immediately said, "Love. My love. Zeth Washer, man of my dreams."

Zeth stopped, making me falter a few steps ahead, then he tugged me around by my hand. I spun until I landed against his chest, right where I wanted to be.

I loved how his eyes watched me so intently, as if trying to figure me out. "What is it, Zeth?"

He captured one of my hands and raised it to kiss the back. "You just have me sort of lost for words."

"That's alright, you don't have to say anything."

The breeze stirred, swirling the blooms from the trees encircling us in colors of pink and white. We both glanced up, mesmerized by the beauty of it. Then Zeth reached up and plucked a petal from my hair, making me laugh. This moment, this *choice* I had made to be with Zeth, felt so right. I knew as we stood out here in the open air that it would be the best decision I ever made.

"What happened to the schoolhouse?" Zeth suddenly asked, squinting at something over my shoulder. "It looks run-down."

I followed his gaze to our old school set off the path. The building's blue paint was chipped in many places, and there was a broken window. A few dented balls sat in the grass, and two wooden swings creaked on their ropes attached to the sturdy sycamore tree we used to climb.

"Edward Cooligan invested in another schoolhouse closer to the square. A larger one, with multiple classrooms."

"That was kind of him, but I rather liked the old one. It was ours," Zeth replied with a hint of mischief in his eyes. "Shall we try to go inside? I wouldn't mind getting you alone so we can do some math equations."

"Hm, knowing you, we'll end up actually doing an assignment." I bit my lip and raked my eyes along his body. "But I'm sure I could distract the teacher."

Zeth chuckled low, "You're distracting me already. Better lead the way."

Laughing, I tugged on his hand to lead him to the school yard fence. It had once been whitewashed, but stood now mostly stripped of its paint. As we walked through its gate, memories flooded me. There were the swings Zeth and I would compete on to see who could jump the furthest off their seat to land in the dirt, and the ball reminded me of a time I'd kicked one so hard, it hit Janice Shears in the face. I felt so bad for giving her a bloody nose.

"That tree is a hazard," Zeth said from beside me.

I followed his gaze at the giant sycamore. Though much bigger now, the tree indeed had been the cause of many broken bones at the schoolhouse. "Remember when I dared you to climb to the very top and it took an hour to get you down?"

"It wasn't because I was afraid, I'll have you know. The branches were too thin and snapped each time I tried to descend. Now looking back..." He crossed his arms with a mock-accusing glare. "I suspect you tried to kill me, Ambrose Somerset."

"Never." I pinched his hip playfully. When he reacted to get me back, I swiftly stepped out of reach and laughed at him. Then I shuffled backward to the building, summoning him with my eyes to follow.

When we reached the school, I turned and pushed on the door. It opened easily, creaking on its hinges. Inside, the place held a few empty liquor bottles. As I stepped in, my shoes crunched over broken pieces of glass. There were desks pushed against the wall and filthy rags in the corner. On the far wall was the blackboard, full of chalked graffiti.

Though I once described school as my own personal hell, this place brought back memories of more than assignments. Laughter once graced these walls from jokes or pranks, and many friends were made. Some of them went on to become part of the snobby elites of Everdeen, while others, like Arthur, worked hard to pursue the things they loved. I wanted that too.

Zeth's firm hand plopped on my shoulder. He eyed the room too, no doubt as overrun with memories as I was. "Hm." He cocked his head. "With the place so empty, that ink stain really stands out now."

I knew exactly what he was talking about as my eyes found the massive black stain still marring the wood floor. I snickered and covered my mouth with my hand. "Mrs. Marsh was so mad at you."

Zeth slid his arm around my shoulders and pulled me against his side. "Well, if you hadn't been throwing rocks at me from behind to get my attention, I wouldn't have tipped my inkwell off the desk."

I looked at him and grabbed his jacket lapels playfully. "They were pebbles, Zeth. *Pebbles.*"

He huffed and rolled his eyes. "They felt like rocks. I still have scars."

"No, you don't. I would have noticed." I winked at him as I thought back to all the times I'd seen him naked. Besides the scar on his shoulder from the fence post, nothing else blemished that handsome body of his.

Zeth pecked my nose affectionately before he pulled away and made his way over to the desks. He hefted one up as if it weighed nothing and carried it to his old spot where the ink stain was.

It was odd seeing this taller Zeth next to the smaller furniture. There was no denying how much he'd changed. His shoulders were broader, his face was slimmer, and there was a shadow of hair on his jaw. The parts of him that had changed had my body aching with a new craving I desperately wanted to satisfy. To be under his control, to surrender to him. And more than that... I wanted to know this older, more complicated Zeth. What he now liked and disliked. How his mind worked, what he was feeling in the moment.

At the current moment, Zeth was preoccupied with rearranging furniture. He placed another desk chair at the spot where I used to sit, just opposite the main aisle, before he scooted back to the first desk. His long frame slid into the chair until his knees hit the underside of the desk with a thump.

"Fuck me," Zeth said with a chuckle while adjusting to his new height.

I tsked as I made my way to his desk and peered down at him. "Imagine Mrs. Marsh's response if she heard you say that."

"Who needs to imagine?" Zeth pressed his palm against the desk. "I think I still have lines on my knuckles from the ruler she smacked me with."

"Mm, you poor thing. Rulers weren't enough to get me to behave. I spent too much time in that corner over there."

Zeth nudged me with a pinch to my hip, as I'd done to him outside. "Go, sit, and be a good boy now. I'm trying to line the desks up properly."

"Fine, I'll go sit, and be a *good* boy." Zeth's eyes lit up while I sat in the other desk. "Like this?" I asked, drumming my fingertips on the wooden surface.

"Yes..." Zeth's face soured on me. "No."

He sprang to his feet to grab my desk. The legs of my chair scraped across the floor, and I gripped the edges to steady myself, until he moved me to the middle of the aisle next to his own desk.

"Want me close?" I asked.

"Aye. There shouldn't be an aisle separating us. Never again." He touched my cheek softly before he maneuvered into his own chair.

I propped my elbow up on the desk and rested my chin in my hand to stare at Zeth's amused expression. He remained quiet as I admired him, and he observed me too, as if trying to figure out my thoughts.

Feeling comfortable with him, I leaned back to look at the chalkboard, glad of the memories we shared but also happy I no longer had to attend class.

"I always loved school," Zeth said, glancing around. What he loved, I hated, and I could respect that. "It was a place away from the laundry, where I could hang out with a certain boy. You always won the art competitions. I was in awe of your creativity."

His compliments added more strings to my heart. I reached over and grabbed his hand, glad he pulled me closer. "Art is about the only thing I'm good at. But you have that sharp wit, a quick mind that knows how numbers work."

"I can't explain how it works. Calculating, adjusting, finding the right answer, it just makes sense. I should have studied to be an accountant, or an estate manager, or something boring like that. Something that puts food on the table. Instead, I'm no better than the thief everyone thinks of me."

His words wedged into me, deep and stinging, and I thought back to the day we met at the picnic, when he accused me of calling him a thief. I'd insinuated as much in Annabelle's parlor too. I took a deep breath, preparing my next words.

"That day I pushed you in the lake, I didn't mean what I said about you pawning your loot. I was hurt at the picnic when you mentioned me having all the power in our relationship. Then you told me to leave you alone, and I just... wanted you to hurt too. But I went too far."

"That shit I said about power was unfair, because I was the one who clammed up instead of speaking my mind. I was just so afraid of losing you and our friends."

My brow furrowed. "I'm so sorry for making you feel powerless. That was never my intention."

"I know. You were only being your adorable, adventurous self. I would never change that about you." Zeth's gaze roamed over me as he shifted in his chair to sit closer. "In fact, I long to see more of the old Amby. My feisty Rosie. I want a second chance with him, honestly sharing our fears and dreams this time. Do you think we can do that?"

I smiled at him, choking back tears. "You trying to make me cry over here? Yes, I want that for us. I want to show you how much I care about you."

"Good, because you already opened my book and now you're stuck reading my story."

"Oh, I like reading stories. Tell me more?"

Zeth's lips quirked. He opened his mouth before squinting at the blackboard, looking hesitant and a little worried. "I have a lot I've written from the past nine years of my life that I need to explain. I'm just not sure how to flip the page. I guess... I'm still a little afraid that if I let you in, I might lose you."

"Zeth..." I said, placing my other hand beneath his to capture it between both my own. "I just got you back. I'm willing to do anything to keep you. You don't have to be afraid to talk to me."

Leaning over, Zeth stole a kiss before whispering against my mouth, "Thank you."

I licked my lips as he stood from his desk and strolled over to the board before us to claim an eraser.

"I think this will help." Zeth cleaned off the graffiti with wide strokes of his long arms. He looked like a teacher, no doubt appearing the same as his father. I'd never met his father before, but the last I heard, he'd left Everdeen to instruct at an academy in Port Winchester and never returned to his family. It was something Zeth never opened up about as a kid, but I hoped he might feel comfortable enough to talk about it with me soon. I'd give him all the time in the world.

Once the board was clean, Zeth set the eraser back into its tray and glanced over at me briefly. Then he pulled up a broken piece of chalk to draw a small circle on the board. The circle was only as big as a fingerprint, and I tilted my head at it, wondering what he was drawing.

"Leaving Everdeen was hard for me," he started, tapping the spot he just drew. "I had a small circle of friends and family, and I did everything I could to keep that circle happy. Business at the laundry slowly failed until Mum had to take Millie and me to the City so she could find factory work."

Zeth stepped to his right and drew a massive circle this time. It was off-center, but I found it cute and smiled.

He made a dot within the massive shape. "And this was me, a little nobody in a huge new city. The capital is massive. I was so..." His shoulders tensed and raised under his jacket while he searched for words. "I was angry. I left my home and friends behind, and life wasn't any better for it. The factory refused to pay Mum an honest rate during her probationary period, so we lost our first apartment and had to move into a charity house. That dashed my hopes to finish school. I set out to help pay the bills, begging store to store for work until an auction house agreed to apprentice me. After that, we settled down."

I imagined him trying to get a grasp on his emotions while in a new place, stepping up and taking charge to help his family. He held courage and strength that I wished I possessed myself.

Zeth drew a slightly larger circle around his dot. "When the auctioneer went to estates, I tagged along and made new connections. Eventually, my circle grew to include business associates and wealthy elites. A few months ago, the Mayor's son even asked me to attend the opera with him in his private box." His face turned into a blank slate, and his voice steadied out to sound like a teacher. "I achieved success in my social life and in my field. I even started payments to lease a building across town to open my own auction house."

Impressed, I waited for Zeth to draw that business on the board, but he picked up the eraser instead and slowly wiped away the collection of city circles. "Then, during a big estate sale, boxes of items began to disappear, and my logs didn't match the inventory. No matter how hard I tried to make the numbers add up, they didn't. When I showed the client, she accused me of thievery, but..." Zeth looked out the classroom window. "It was the client's son. He stole the boxes because his greedy mother was going to auction it all off and leave the country. I meant nothing to them, just someone to take the blame. Their family squabble cost me my job and livelihood."

As Zeth stared at the board, I was left dumbfounded. "Wait, you mean you... built up a reputation and had a good job, but someone betrayed you and had you fired?"

"Yes, exactly." Zeth turned toward me. "That family spread vicious rumors around the City about me seducing and stealing. The mayor himself even snubbed me for ruining his son's name. Nothing I said, all my hard work... it didn't change a damn thing. I even lost the advance payments on the building because my contract had a morality clause. I was ruined. Then Mum got sick, and I couldn't even make her last days comfortable."

I gripped the sides of the desk hard. Zeth watched his mother suffer because he lost everything he had. He'd endured too much for one person to handle. Remorse hit me tenfold that I hadn't been there for him when she passed, just as he'd been for me.

"What about your father?" I asked in disbelief. "He was there in the City. He never..."

Zeth stared at the eraser as he rotated it in his fingers. "He didn't know we moved closer, and I didn't have the guts to find him. Not even when Mum needed help. I can't tell you how many times I walked past the academy gates in her last days. Maybe he was in there, or maybe he was dead. Either way, I was too scared to learn the truth."

I wasn't sure what to say to that. I knew what I was feeling, which was anger for Zeth's father never being around for him growing up. But the man wasn't even deserving of anger, or any other emotion, nor even a thought. So I grit my teeth and let Zeth finish.

He stayed quiet as he placed the eraser down to point at the tiny Everdeen circle that started his demonstration. "So here we are again. Only now, I'm a grown man who can't get work without employer references. I have no way to support myself... or you."

No wonder Zeth tried to win Annabelle's hand. He was desperate to survive, to protect Millie and himself. If I could, I'd give him everything he needed, and more. If only my father wasn't standing in my way. But...

I could give him comfort. I knew how to give that.

Rising from the desk, I made my way over to him. I grabbed his arms and pulled him against me into a tight embrace. Zeth's arms instantly wrapped around my waist, holding me tightly, and I raised my head so I could rest my chin on his shoulder.

"So many people wronged you, and you didn't deserve any of it. I hate that you and Millie had to go through all this alone. I wish I had been there for you when your mother..." I couldn't finish the words, as my voice cracked. Damn my emotions, but this time I let them out as I pulled away and looked at him. "You don't have to worry about being alone again. I'm here for you."

Zeth nodded and glanced away at the board, and I deflated, wondering if he was going to stop talking to me. But then he sniffed and wiped an eye with the back of his chalky hand, and I realized he was holding back tears.

"Well... I didn't mean to make you cry." I leaned up to kiss the wet spot right near his eye. Then I kissed him again, and again, pecking tender kisses along his cheek, until he clutched me against him and exhaled roughly into my hair.

His voice was shaky as he replied, "You're so mean. Now I believe what they say about redheads."

"That we're daring in bed?" I tilted my head up at him. "That's another common phrase."

Zeth cracked a smile before he broke into a deep laugh that filled the school room, and my heart. "You're a blessing, Amby. I've missed your adorable humor in the last nine years, two months, and twenty-six days since we parted."

His obsession with counting was humorous. To me, the numbers all blurred, but I did recognize one odd thing... "Wait a minute, that number was smaller before. Have you been counting our days apart this whole time, even since we met at the picnic?"

"Well, yes, and I hope you don't mind if I count today as our first day back together, officially."

"You mean, as in courting?"

"Aye, I want to go on walks in the park with you and kiss under the trees, and do whatever else adult men do on dates. Maybe drink tea."

Zeth sounded so innocent, he made me laugh. Something deep in my soul revived. An energy connecting us both. The very man I'd hurt so long ago still wanted me, so much that he was willing to give me—give *us*—a second chance. Feeling grateful, I took his hands in mine and squeezed them with the reassurance that I would never hurt him again. I was so happy.

But then a sense of dread passed over me at the thought of what my father would think of me and Zeth courting. The idea of telling him terrified me, and his possible rejection would hit me hard.

"What are you thinking so long about, Amby?" Zeth's forehead wrinkled in concern. "You've got me nervous."

"I'm sorry, I am thinking." Pulling away, I took off my cap and ran my hand over my hair as the burning anxiety climbed up my throat. "It's my father. I just..."

Looking over at the blackboard, I secured my cap back on and grabbed the piece of chalk to draw a stick figure. Pointing at it, I explained, "That's me."

Zeth's lips twitched slightly with amusement before he crossed his arms and met my gaze. "Alright."

"And this is you." I drew another stick figure with a line extended out to touch my stick figure's hand, and drew a heart between us.

This time, Zeth chuckled delightfully, and there was something in the way he looked at me that melted me. Especially as he leaned forward to say, "You're fucking adorable."

I wrinkled my nose at that comment, then made a bigger figure at a distance that represented my father. I wrote out the words 'LEGACY' and 'BANK' behind him, and childishly gave him an angry expression. Drawing a big line, I divided us and him.

I stepped back to glance over at Zeth. He appeared to be taking me seriously.

"That's my biggest obstacle, and if my father doesn't approve of our courtship, then he may cut me off. I'll have nothing to give you but myself and a low-paying job as a bank courier, maybe not even that. So..." I put the chalk down and faced him. "I need you to know there's not much I can promise you besides my devotion."

Zeth stared at me for a moment before asking, "Do *you* want to be with me?"

He was sensing my hesitation, so I clutched his hand, feeling the aura ring I gave him on his pinky. I rubbed the smooth stone as I looked at him desperately. "More than anything."

"Good," he sighed with relief before standing taller. "Then I need you to work with me. I don't think your dad hates me, so there's hope we can win him over. Help me find a way into your father's esteem. Then we can work on changing his mind about your role in his legacy. As my mum said, where there's a Washer, there's a way. We'll erase that line together."

I blinked at him in surprise. "You... want to try and gain his blessing?" When Zeth nodded, looking so certain, I filled with bliss at the idea of gaining my father's approval. "I'm willing to do what-ever it takes to keep you, though I admit I'm terrified."

"So am I, and I have no fucking idea what I'm doing. But I'm tired of holding my troubles in and letting fate choke me. This time, we're speaking our fears and seeking solutions. This is a new start for us."

Hearing how excited Zeth was had my stomach full of so many butterflies. If I did this with him, I would have to eventually confront my father. And I'd do it, but I needed time to prepare.

I met his eyes and nodded. "Just please promise you'll be patient with me."

"I can do that." Zeth agreed as he caressed the edge of my jaw. "You mean the world to me. I don't want to lose you again."

"You have me, and I'm never letting you go. That's my promise."

20

Zeth

Millie came home that afternoon smiling from ear to ear, teasing me endlessly about my Chapel blunders and rushed escape with Amby. We created quite a stir for the gossip mill. Most of the folks thought I succumbed to a fear of commitment, and according to my dear sister, Anna laughed them off with a simple "Boys will be boys" before gracefully leading her off to have tea. But not before Emiline invited them to go swimming the next day. Millie was making friends hand over fist.

She might have been in a good mood, but with each reminder of my public mistakes, my mood soured. I didn't want the townsfolk talking about me. It felt too much like losing my reputation all over again. And what were they saying about Amby?

By the next day, I wasn't good company. No wonder Millie seemed anxious to escape as she knelt on the floor in preparation for her swim, rolling up her blanket into a tight log.

I crossed my arms and grumbled, "It's far too cold to go swimming. It's still spring."

She ignored me, reaching for an old ribbon sitting on the bed. It sat too far away, so she used a toe to keep her roll from unraveling as she stood and stretched, wiggling her fingers just shy of the target. I watched her struggle, as a big brother does.

Eventually, she straightened, foot on the blanket, and shot me a glare. "A little help?"

"Of course." I squatted to replace her toe with my hand. "And why do you need a blanket to go swimming?"

My question was nagging, and Millie proved it with an eye roll.

"Because it's cold, as you kindly stated," she sassed back. "Besides, it gives me something to sit on."

Sitting around on blankets with only-she-knew-who sounded even worse than swimming, especially if young men were involved. Emiline invited her to what might be a river party, and I didn't like the idea at all.

Millie didn't care how hard I frowned at her. She tied the ribbon and moved to the bed to start putting on her shoes, completely ignoring me. Then she pulled on her white bonnet and stuffed her curls into it. Her split skirt, blouse, and long, brown coat completed the ensemble.

Still, something bothered me about her adventure. There was more going on than my grumpy mood. "Who else is going to be there?"

"Emiline. She invited me. Anna had prior plans she couldn't get out of. Emiline's so nice and responsible. Surely you don't mind if we become friends?"

My nose itched to call out her obvious ploy to get me to agree. "Who else will be there, Mils?"

"I don't know. How will I know until I get there?"

"And where's *there*, exactly?"

She stood with a huff and grabbed the blanket roll. "There's a public garden by the river. We'll be safe. Emiline says she goes once a month with Arthur and that it's fun, so I want to go. I'm an adult and I'm going."

Five years ago, that statement would have ended with a foot stomp. Now, she was twenty and ready to spread her wings. That didn't stop me from wanting to protect my little sister from harm. She was so innocent about so many things. What if there was an undercurrent in the river? Or she got frostbite? Or some man tried to lure her away from her friends?

Millie didn't care about any of that. She only gave me an exasperated stare from under her lashes and headed for the stairs, ignoring my disapproval and not asking me to join.

Ugh, maybe that last part was the problem. Millie never went anywhere without me until we returned to Everdeen. Now she was working, running errands around town, going swimming, and making new connections with people like Emiline and Anna, people who were not me.

I thought about that as I followed her down the stairs, feeling my spirits lower with each step. This must be how parents feel when their children leave them behind.

"When can I expect you to return?"

"You mean, when can you start a search party?" Millie saw right through me. We both reached the front door at the same time, and I claimed the knob first to stop her from leaving. She eyed it and patted my shoulder. "You don't have to protect me, you know. I have a mean upper punch."

Chuckling, I let go, and she opened the door. When did I age from twenty-five to fifty? Or maybe I always smothered Millie and she was only now gaining the strength to stand up to me. If that was the case, I felt bad for holding her back, but also proud of her new step forward.

Just then, Emiline and Hattie, and also Arthur and Amby, headed toward the laundry.

Was Amby going to the swim party too? Great, now I really did feel lonely. I know we agreed to take this new step in our relationship slowly, but I hoped we could spend some time together.

I rubbed my shirt sleeves while Millie waved to the group. When they returned her wave, Millie turned back to me, practically hopping on her heels.

"So, I think the swimming ends at sunset," Millie said in a rush. "But they have some sort of dinner too, and Arthur said he'd buy me a plate for my good work this week. I promise to return safely."

I narrowed my eyes at her, not sure if I should point out her earlier lie about not knowing who was attending. Deciding to prove my maturity, I refrained. Instead, I pushed her off the step. Like a bird from the nest.

She caught her footing just fine, and I grumbled, "Alright, have fun without me."

"I will!" she assured quickly with a playful expression that stopped me from taking offense. Still, I glared at her, which caused her to stick out her tongue.

The group reached us, and we all said our hellos. When Millie entered their midst, they left with their blanket rolls and good humor. Then Amby stepped free of everyone to stand with me in front of the laundry, and my mood lifted as he waved them goodbye. He was dressed much more casually than usual, with his shirt-sleeves rolled up to his elbows and his brown vest looking soft and cozy. His brown pants matched his cap, and his collar was unbuttoned to reveal his glowing skin.

I still couldn't believe Amby agreed to start courting. I was courting Ambrose Somerset of Everdeen.

When he turned to me, I beamed like a fool and asked, "Not going swimming, handsome?"

Amby gave a timid smile and shook his head. "No, I wanted to see if you'd like to go out somewhere else, just you and me. Unless you want to swim. Then we can join them."

"I don't see the appeal of freezing my ass off. Have you ever gone?"

"A few times." He shrugged and watched as our sisters walked arm in arm. "The Rios family opened the place a few years back. It's popular with younger folks on the weekends now. The Covenant Hall has tried to shut it down many times, with no success."

I raised an eyebrow as I opened the door for him to come inside. "Covenant Hall?"

Amby shrugged as he stepped over the threshold. "A newer church. They've been here for the past fifteen years, but their numbers are growing. Very... odd, always trying to spoil the fun. Same god, just much different beliefs from the Shepherd's Chapel where we attend."

"I'm good with attending neither," I muttered, closing the

door. When I caught Amby's dimpled cheek, I backpedaled. "Unless you want to attend your church. I'll sit in your family's pew every day for the rest of my life if you want me to."

"Mm, such devotion. I love it." Amby came close and caressed the back of my neck before kissing me on the lips. A quick peck, then another, before I finally grabbed him to keep him there.

He giggled against me. "We should probably get lost somewhere before we end up against the wall like last time."

"Where do you suggest, darling?"

"Perhaps... a walk through the garden?" he asked. I grabbed his hips and moved in to kiss his neck to distract him as he named other places, "Mm, maybe... an eatery? Or... out for drinks? God, you're good at kissing me... We could always follow the girls and Arthur to the distillery. We don't have to swim, just eat and talk."

My hands stiffened on him, and I moved away from his neck to look at him sharply, my trust in Millie quickly evaporating. "Distillery? As in hard liquor, and they'll be swimming too? I knew Millie was leaving something out."

"She didn't tell you there would be drinking?"

"No, she deviously left that part out. I was worried about her going off on her own, but if she's drinking too, I want to be there in case she needs me. She's never even had a sip. She's bound to get sloshed." I sighed. "Do you mind if we follow them?"

"Oh." Amby nodded in approval instead of pointing out my over-protectiveness. "Yes, we can go if it makes you feel better. Maybe watch from a distance?"

"Bless you, what an excellent plan. She won't even know we're there. I'll grab my blanket, so we can pretend we decided to swim. Be right back." I kissed him quickly on the lips and sprinted up the steps in a blur to swiftly roll up my blanket. Then I finished dressing in a worn-out jacket and cap to rejoin Amby downstairs. We locked up and headed for the river.

Our companionship felt nice in the silence of our steps as we made our way out of town. It didn't take us long to reach a spot in the woodsy treeline by the river where Amby pointed out a worn path for us to take next. Across the river, new houses lined the way with even more buildings in various stages of construction. My, how Everdeen had grown since I left.

"Hey," Amby started from my side as we walked. "You look good. How was your day?"

His sweet question was unexpected. No one ever asked me about my day. I liked that Amby did. We barely separated twenty-four hours ago, and here he was wondering about me. How was my day?

"Millie's pestering aside, my day was productive. I borrowed a ladder and some tools from Todd to chip off the kitchen's wet ceiling plaster. He said I have to do that to dry the beams before he can fix the inside."

"He's a saint. I'm glad you're getting some help. Did you decide if you want any of the furniture from the barn?"

"I'll not lie, I dream about your rocking chair, but it'll be a waste of effort and time to move it into the laundry. I'll just sit on it when I visit you in the barn. Until it sells, that is."

"It wouldn't be a waste. You're worth it. If you want it, it's yours."

I didn't know what to say in the face of such kindness, so I laughed off his offer and kept walking. "We'll see. If chairs went to people who deserve them, then a person as good as you should have five hundred and fifty-two."

"That's a very random number of chairs, but thank you." Amby chuckled and grabbed my hand. He really did deserve that many chairs and anything else he wanted out of life.

I squeezed his fingers and asked, "Are you still thinking about selling your furniture at the Founders Day Festival?"

"Yes. Do you want to help me? I'll split the profits with you."

"Split them? Evenly?" I eyed him sharply, but he looked earnest. "That's hardly right. Thirty-to-seventy is the usual ratio. If you agree to give me thirty percent of the sales, then I'm your man."

"You're already my man." Amby brought my hand up to kiss it. "Good thing you told me about the cuts. I think I might have over-paid someone for moving something the other day... But yes, if you don't mind, I'd appreciate your help. I have no idea what I'm doing."

"Don't doubt yourself, darling. You'll sell out."

Amby leaned against me, kissing my shoulder before he said, "You're too good to me."

I smiled at him. This connection between us tied so easily back together that it felt like we never parted. Walking side by side with the love of my life was such a blessing. Amby's promise to be with me still stole my breath every time I thought about it.

Just ahead, the river widened, and I could see people jumping in. I heard their mirth from here. They reminded me of how Amby and I used to play in a shallower part of the river as kids. It also reminded me of something that happened recently. "Hm, maybe I should push you in the water? A bit of retribution."

"If you do, you're going down with me."

"Oh, I have no doubt. You're a brat."

Amby came close to my ear to whisper, "You like it when I'm a brat."

"You know me well." I tugged him closer by his waist.

He lingered only a moment before slipping out of my embrace, and disappointment hit me. Then I realized how public we were being with our affection. I wanted to court him officially, but Amby asked for patience. That might be more difficult than I estimated. I also hated that there was a bit of doubt hovering around inside me.

"Soon, I promise," he said.

His reassurance helped. I winked at him and looked forward to the day we could walk as a couple. *Soon.*

The riverside gathering spread before us. There were at least twenty young people in the river and several others huddled in blankets on the sandy banks by a blazing fire pit. This drinking party was much larger than Millie led me to believe. I didn't see her sitting anywhere, so I scanned the water. Not there either.

The bend in the river formed a semicircle of land upon which sat the distillery. It was a large stone building with floor-to-ceiling glass doors that emptied out into a patio of flagstone and grass beneath a wooden pergola covered with wisteria vines. Just beyond, the second floor of a house was visible, made of the same beautiful stones. A low, iron fence lined the patio. Lush greenery, rose bushes, and wisteria vines grew along the spools, creating a secluded patio. Several tables and chairs held dozens of lively, imbibing patrons. This was the distillery garden Amby mentioned, and it looked lovely. I wondered why he didn't attend more often.

Amby and I walked under an arched arbor into the garden. Jovial conversation surrounded us while we hugged the edge of the crowd to search for my sister. Most people cuddled under a rainbow of quilted blankets, just like on the shore. Some sipped from small cups or ate from wooden bowls. The food and drinks came from a massive wooden bar top outside the glass doors.

That's where I found Millie, Emiline, Hattie, and Arthur. They were still dry and standing in line. Millie was bound to get toasted if she took more than a sip of liquor. Thankfully, Arthur was buying her a meal as well. Filling her belly would help.

The steaming bowls of boiled fish and potatoes made my mouth water. Just then, my own belly made its demand for food.

"I'm hungry," Amby said. "You want to get some food?"

I eyed him. "Are you only saying that for my sake? I think the next town over heard my stomach just now."

"I mean, yes, I am hungry. Obviously you are too."

Feeling conspicuous, I used the bottom edge of Amby's vest to lead him against the fence with me to an empty table nestled against a tall plant. The vines above were thicker here, and the sun speckled his face as his brown eyes questioned me. I straightened his shirt collar as I said, "Thank you for taking care of me, but wasn't our plan to stay hidden?"

"Good idea." Amby grabbed my arm with friendly affection. "You can sit at the table here behind this huge plant while I get our food." He left swiftly, and I chuckled at his way around my objections.

Since my pockets were as empty as my stomach, I appreciated his generosity. His insistence on feeding me was as familiar as his laughter. Both sustained me.

Tucking myself into a seat, I set my blanket roll against the fence and sat low to avoid attention. Amby got in line behind a well-endowed woman. Our sisters chatted to themselves just in front of her. Not a moment later, Emiline turned toward Amby, as if sensing her twin. Amby ducked comically behind the woman between them. When she shifted, he moved with the woman's skirts, and I laughed.

A few tables over, two men turned my way, and I quickly recognized them from my school days. Ben was a quiet rich kid a few years younger than us. I recalled his wealthy family coming over from the far west, and Ben having to learn our language. I didn't remember the other fellow's name, but I did remember how much he picked on me during lunchtime. His hair had grown out, the brown locks knotted on top of his head, and his sharp, blue eyes locked on me. His smile widened with recognition through a scruffy beard.

My stomach knotted. I scooted my chair until I hid behind the big plant, much to my shame. Suddenly feeling ten years old again, I stayed out of sight and watched through the leaves as the men stood and approached. The bully was named... Richard... That's right. *Dick* was what everyone called him. How did I forget such a fitting name? Maybe I pushed his name to the bottom of my paper pile with all the other unpleasantries of being a poor kid.

Dick stepped up to my empty table, appearing very tall as he peered down where I sat with no food. Fuck, this felt familiar. When Ben walked up behind him, I forced myself to offer them seats.

Dick reached his arm out, making me flinch, but he only slapped my shoulder in greeting as he barked, "I thought that was you! Zeth, right? Welcome back, friend, how've you been?"

Friend? I tipped a bit sideways in my seat, more from shock than anything else. This camaraderie certainly wasn't expected. "Um, good. You?"

"Wonderful. I'm working here at the distillery. You remember Ben? We started courting a few weeks ago." He wound an arm around Ben's waist, and the two of them beamed at each other. "He really helped me become less of an asshole."

"Rich doesn't give himself much credit," Ben said with a twitch of his lips as he offered me a hand to shake. I never would have paired these two from different social classes. They gave me more hope for Amby and myself.

"I wasn't nice, and we all know it." Dick shook his head. "Sorry for how I was back then, Zeth."

"That's... honorable of you to say."

Dick whistled at me, and my shoulders tensed in anticipation for his teasing. It didn't take long, "Listen to you, putting on fancy pants."

Before I could defend myself, Ben tapped his mate with a soft, "Manners," and Dick sent him a remorseful look.

"I mean that in the best way," Dick reiterated. Well, I'll be damned, he did change for the better.

Just then, Amby joined us balancing two bowls and drinks in his arms. I helped him by taking mine, and he slid into a chair beside me until our shoulders touched.

"Rich, Ben, good to see you." Amby nodded at them.

"Ah, the Daring Duo returns," Dick... or rather, Rich, chuckled. "I wondered who Zeth came here with. Boy, you two sure got into trouble when we were kids. Rekindling your friendship, are you?"

Amby put his arm around my shoulder. "We're like two peas in a pod. Distance and time aren't enough to snuff out our friendship."

I snorted. Two peas? He was so cute. I glanced at Amby's handsome face so close to mine and slipped a hand under the table to rub his thigh. "What if I don't like peas? They feel weird when I swallow."

I was being serious, but Rich and Ben were quick to laugh. It was only after Amby's eyes widened with humor and a quick blush lit his cheeks that I grasped the sexual suggestion. I winked at Amby in play, and he lightly punched my side in jest.

"Good to see you two together again," Ben said, and I believed he meant it. He looped his arm through Rich's. "We'll have to catch up later, perhaps at the bonfire?"

"Or around town," I answered and waved them off, almost sad

to see them leave. I was still getting used to social visits that didn't have hidden agendas. No one wanted a business deal or increased social status like they did in the City. These were just acquaintances chatting and enjoying a river party. I turned to Amby, "That was nice."

"Mm," Amby hummed. He was already eating, bent over his bowl. He *had* been hungry. Finishing his bite, he said, "Rich's much nicer than he used to be."

"Yeah, I thought he was going to beat me up when he first walked over." I pulled my bowl over to start eating. With a mouthful of potato, I mumbled, "Not many fond memories. Most of the kids at school weren't kind. Just you, Arthur, and a few others because of you."

"One thing I've learned, my love, is that you only need a few friends in life to be happy."

Trying not to choke on my food, I got out, "Are you quoting Anna?"

His eyes widened. "What?"

"In case you didn't notice, she's a walking anthology of wise sayings."

Amby covered his mouth to stifle a laugh that scrunched his face. Then he pushed me playfully with his arm.

I chuckled and went back to eating until my bowl only had an oily mix of water and butter on the bottom. I pushed it aside to pick up my cup. I swirled the clear liquid slowly, as the auctioneer taught me, to evaluate how it clung to the sides of the pottery. Quite well, so it was either high proof or sugary. Taking a stinging sniff convinced me it was the former. I shook my head from the fumes and debated drinking. That's when I remembered Millie.

A quick look around confirmed she wasn't drunk yet. She sat closer to the shore at a table with Amby's sisters, Arthur, and two others. She was fine at the moment, so I turned to Amby.

He was just lowering his cup, and it appeared empty as he set it down with a sharp snap, like he was having an enjoyable time.

Maybe the drink wasn't as strong as I imagined. Taking courage from Amby, I raised mine and tipped the liquid over my lips, letting it fall to the back of my throat. The burn was instant. I coughed and sputtered until tears stung my eyes. I couldn't even manage a *fuck*. How had Amby drunk that with no problem?

"Zeth?" Amby's hand patted my back. "You alright? You're supposed to swallow, remember?"

Laughing didn't help me breathe through the fire that was my throat. It certainly didn't stop the tears, especially once I started laughing at myself in earnest. Suddenly, two more cups appeared on the table in front of us. I glanced up to find a man with darker skin and black hair curling to his shoulders standing before us. He watched us curiously with bold eyes that looked like they'd seen many regions of the Commonwealth.

"Oh, why thank you," Amby said, smiling up at him. "Good to see you again, Nathaniel."

"Always a pleasure to see you, Amby," Nathaniel replied, his Leoneas accent smooth as butter. He gripped the edge of the table and leaned over it to get closer, jutting his ass out. I didn't like him, even if he was eyeing me sensually with approval. "Who's your handsome friend?"

"This is Zeth Washer. Zeth, this is Nathaniel Rios. He and his mothers run the distillery here." Amby nodded at the man, seemingly unworried about Nathaniel's obvious flirting.

I tried to speak, but it only came out as a rough cough. Damn Nathaniel's strong liquor.

"Looks like you're enjoying the fruits of my labor, Zeth Washer. Here's another drab on me." He pushed the cups closer with ringed fingers. "Drink up, boys. I like my parties to go late, and my guests to be loose."

Nathaniel stood with a deep chuckle and wandered off to another table, kissing the cheeks of everyone there. He was quite the character. And here I thought my pea comment sounded inappropriate for mixed company.

"Good friend of yours?" I asked Amby as soon as I could mumble out the words.

"Everyone knows Nathaniel. He's an acquaintance." He leaned his elbow on the table so he could stare right at me. "You don't have to worry about him. Or anyone else. I see what I want right now."

I moved closer, glad to hear Amby's reassurances. The soft glow of love in his eyes drugged me far quicker than liquor, and I found myself admitting, "I see what I want too."

"Oh, good, because when we get alone, I..." Amby's gaze shot over my shoulder, his brow creasing. "I see our sisters walking this way."

"Shit," I swore softly. I shielded the side of my face with a hand to hide, but Amby took it a step further by kneeling under the table. I blinked at his half-ass actions, but when he pulled the edge of my sleeve, I joined him, grunting as I sat on the flagstone tile.

"What are we doing?" I whispered.

"Hiding. Isn't that what we're supposed to do?"

I snorted and tried to get more comfortable with my head sideways. "We look ridiculous—"

"Shh!" Amby pressed his finger against my lips to shush me.

Growling playfully, I grabbed his wrist and opened my mouth to lightly bite the pad of his finger.

Amby gasped and eyed me sharply, but by the way his lips tugged up in the corners, I could tell he enjoyed the rough play. I leaned forward to—

"Ambrose Heath Somerset, what on earth are you doing down there with Zeth Washer?" came a familiar voice, and we both snapped our heads around the table with guilt. Emiline stared at us with her hands on her hips and a smirk on her face. Beside her, Arthur laughed loudly at us, while Millie stood on her other side, raising a curious eyebrow.

"Oh, um," Amby started, moving to sit on his knees. "We just..." He turned to me, as if needing my help. "I was looking..."

"For his glasses," I finished, and straightened the frames on Amby's face. "See, good as new. You should sneeze a little more carefully next time, Amby."

Millie wasn't the only Washer who could bend the truth. I bent it so far, I broke it. Millie narrowed her eyes at me, so I sent her a charming grin while I helped Amby get to his feet with me. "You're right, Mils, this is a fun place. Are you all going swimming now?"

Arthur motioned over the distillery. "We're all heading that way to watch the tomfoolery. They just got the rope swing back up. It broke last year."

Rope swing? That sounded like a horrid idea.

"I'll jump off it," Amby said, his face glowing with excitement. "It's been some time since I swam in the river."

I was about to object when Emiline beat me to it, "Amby, it's *freezing*."

He waved her off before turning to me. "Join me?"

My first thought was the cost of my medical bill when the rope broke again. My second thought was fear for Amby's safety. And the third... he was so damn cute when he gazed at me with those expressive brown eyes. That's why I said to Amby, "Aye, let's go freeze our asses off."

21

Ambrose

The rope swing hung from a sturdy branch overlooking the river. One glance at someone swinging forward off the high bank and into the water had my blood rushing with excitement. When I peered over at Zeth, he didn't seem as enthused. His forehead creased while he eyed the rope, then the water. This was just like the old Zeth I grew up with, who calculated risks before taking them. I bit back a smile. Some things never change.

A young woman with a lively colored headwrap was next to use the swing. She hung onto the wooden dowel tied to the end of the rope before running forward and lifting her feet up in the air. Her body swung out, and when she let go, she screamed as she fell and splashed into the water. Laughter and whistles followed from the crowd along the bank.

If someone swung the wrong way, they would certainly get hurt. From the thrilling sensation in my bones, I knew I wouldn't be leaving this party without taking a turn. I put my hand on Zeth's shoulder to steady myself and pulled off my shoes and socks. I ended up losing my balance and fell into him until we both landed against one of the many surrounding trees. Zeth hummed with delight as his comforting hands grabbed me and set me upright.

"Good God, Amby, you're acting like a child over that swing," Emiline chuckled.

Hattie gave her cute giggle that always brightened my day and said, "I'm going to sit with the girls and watch how this all plays out. Millie, care to join us? There's someone who wants to see you from our school days."

Millie's brow raised as she peered over at the shore, where several of Hattie's friends were, most of them wearing swimsuits. "Sure," she said with a nod, and followed my sister.

Emiline waited to take our clothes, so I pulled off my jacket and trousers and passed them over, along with my glasses. As I unbuttoned my shirt, I eyed Zeth briefly while he stripped to his white cotton underpants. They were old-fashioned and baggy, covering everything between his trim waist and knees.

My lips curved up playfully before I cut my gaze over to Emiline, and she raised her eyebrows in amusement. I hadn't told her yet that Zeth and I were secretly courting, but from the knowing look she threw at me, I didn't have to. She gave my bare arm an affectionate squeeze. At least one person was happy for us.

This whole day was lifting my spirits. After going to boring elite events for so long, it was invigorating to be doing something so casual. I was part of the informal crowd once again by indulging in riverside shenanigans, a feeling I'd forgotten about in the past couple of years. No matter how much older I got, I still craved adventure in some way.

Moving to stand on the hill in only my undershorts, I grabbed the rope and held it out to Zeth. "Want to go first?"

He joined me and peered over the edge to the river. "Are you planning to land on my head?"

"Of course not. I'll wait until you swim out of the way." I grabbed Zeth's hand and placed the dowel in his palms, wrapping his fingers around it.

He walked backwards with the rope, poised to run, but paused and walked back to lean into me. "I'm going to be honest, I'm a bit nervous."

"Oh?" I gave him a reassuring smile. "You don't have to jump, you know."

Zeth blinked at me with surprise. "You're right, I don't."

"Do you want to sit with the others? You can have the blanket warm and ready for me." I tried to take the rope but Zeth held it tight.

"No, I want to have fun with you. I miss doing stupid stuff," he admitted, and walked backward to draw the rope taut again. I felt his excitement as he inhaled and said, "I dare you to swing higher than this."

Before I could reply, Zeth sprinted past me and swung out. I hooted as he flew out over the water before letting go. He splashed in with a joyful shout. When he resurfaced and swam out of the way, looking happy, something delightful and fiery surrounded me.

As the rope swung back, I grabbed it and ran as fast as I could along the sloping bank before soaring out over the water. I twisted as I fell through the air, feeling free, and then hit the icy water. The shock to my body revived me, releasing a part of me I'd kept locked away for so long.

When I emerged at the surface, I wiped my eyes and searched for Zeth. When I didn't see him, panic rose in my chest.

"Zeth?" I called out, but I couldn't find him anywhere.

Shit, where did he go?

Then something grabbed my hips to tug at me. I gasped as my chin dipped into the water, but before I went under, Zeth popped up in front of me with a smirk.

I grabbed onto his arms and spit some water out at him. "Jackass," I laughed.

"Prick," he teased back. He made a small wave toward me as he confidently stated, "My jump was higher."

"Oh, was it?"

"At least twenty-six feet higher."

"Alright, now you're just full of shit."

"Shit doesn't float." Zeth's chuckle was rich as he tried to float on his back to look peacefully at the sky.

I looked around as well, marveling at the full trees as late spring took over. On the river bank, Arthur and Emiline walked together and chatted while Hattie and Millie waved to us from their small party.

When I felt a splash on my face, I splashed Zeth back. He flinched dramatically and I swam closer to capture his hand under the water. That earned me a wide grin as Zeth opened his eyes again. It was pleasantly familiar to spend time with him like this, an echo of our youth. But I had to admit I was freezing, and my teeth were starting to chatter. Perhaps if we were alone, and it was a hot summer day, I'd stay here all day long.

"God, it's cold in here." I shivered. "How did we do this when we were kids?"

"I recall a lot of touching to keep warm," Zeth answered with a heated glance as he used our joined hands to pull me through the water until our legs bumped. "Maybe we can find a spot to cuddle under my blanket?"

"Yes, I could use your body to warm me up now."

"In that case, I'm all yours," Zeth assured me and started pulling me toward the shore.

"Zeth," I laughed, letting go of his hand so I could swim quicker. As I passed him, I dunked his head under.

I felt his hand around my ankle a moment later, pulling me under. By the time I popped back up, Zeth had already reached the shore. He ran out of the river, raising his fists in victory. I licked my bottom lip free of water as I trudged through the rocky shallows, my eyes tracing the outline of his muscled arms and bare chest. My gaze lowered to where his white undergarments clung to his thighs and...

God, I had to look away. Zeth's body was so appealing, he had Hattie's friends eyeing him too, and now I was flustered as well in front of them all. I found my sister and focused on her. But my eyes drifted to a girl gawking at Zeth while twisting her hair around her finger with a smile.

He smiled back at her as he bent to pick up his blanket from our pile of clothes Emiline brought over. I walked a little faster, and when I reached him, I let out a heavy breath. I wanted to take his hand and show everyone there he was mine, but I was too nervous.

"Millie, aren't you going to introduce us to your brother?" Hattie's friend asked.

"Don't bother," Millie replied. The gathering turned to her with curiosity. "You're too late, because Zeth already set his cap for someone."

I wasn't sure if she meant me or Anna, but the girl gave up with a pout.

When Zeth turned to me with a rakish grin that told me he was enjoying the attention, I glanced away, my teeth chattering.

"Goodness, Amby, you look miserable," Edgar Shears pointed out to everyone. He eyed me with a gleam in his eye. "You can share my blanket and stand by the bonfire if you'd like."

"Actually, we need to get into dry clothes," Zeth said with a hint of assertiveness. He unfurled his blanket and shook it out before throwing it around my shoulders in a protective way. The old, blue-patterned quilt brought instant comfort, and I had to keep myself from acting like a silly fool as I wrapped the fabric tighter around me. It smelled like Zeth's fresh, earthy fragrance that always intoxicated me. As much as I wanted to take things slow with him, this was too much for me to brush aside. His affection had me beaming with pride. Here was my friend and lover taking care of me, for all to see.

"Thank you," I said, turning back to Zeth to see him smiling adoringly at me. I was sure by now that the surrounding group knew there was much more between us than simple friendship.

Zeth grabbed up our clothes from the ground, and we slipped on our shoes as Hattie and her friends scattered away. After seeing that Millie was safe with my sisters, Zeth and I waved them off.

We walked past the crowd of people to a back trail that wound through the trees along the river. Once we were well out of range of others, I looked over at Zeth and said, "You cold?"

"I'll be fine," Zeth responded and moved his arm around my back to grab my hip.

I leaned up against him as we walked and grabbed around his

waist too. "We should find a place to lay on the blanket and cuddle. I can think of about five hundred and fifty-two things we could do to warm up."

Zeth shot me a glance. "You remember that number, do you? It's the amount of places on your body I wish to kiss. It might take me a while."

"Then I guess it's a good thing I get to keep you forever, so we can take our time. Come on."

I led us to a secluded area beside the river, where draping willows grew on the bank. Walking through the swaying branches, I took my dry clothes from Zeth and set them and my glasses on a nearby rock. We removed our shoes before I spread the blanket out beneath the tree. Beside us, the river gurgled over rocks and pebbles, and above us, the orange haze of sun rays filtered through the leaves. This was perfect for a peaceful evening.

"I missed this," Zeth said as he turned toward me and began to untie my undershorts. "The City was so dingy and fast-moving. I much prefer a lazy day out in nature."

His fingers grazed my bare stomach, making me gasp. It took me a moment to focus on what he'd said as he tugged at the fabric around my waist. "Yes, it's beautiful..."

"You're beautiful." He gazed fondly at me, and I bit my lip against a smile. "And cold. Let's get these wet things off, shall we? I don't want you getting sick. Then we can get dressed and lay on the blanket for a while. Sound good?"

"That sounds wonderful."

When Zeth moved in close to me, I thought he might kiss me, so I closed my eyes.

Instead, I felt his lips gently kiss one of my eyelids, and then the other. As his mouth pressed against my forehead, goosebumps spilled from my neck and along my arms. I savored his sweet kisses all over my face as my waistband loosened. The wet fabric fell from my hips to my feet. When his lips reached the skin beneath my earlobe, I sighed with pleasure.

"I-I thought you were just changing my clothes," I stuttered.

"You're right, I am. Never said I can't indulge in you while I do. Can't help myself."

My eyes popped open to see him staring intently at me. That stare reminded me of our time in the Ivory Room. He'd undressed me there too, just as he was doing now.

I waited patiently while Zeth turned for the rock to sort through my dry clothes. He found my trousers first and took a knee to hold them out for me to step into.

I placed my hands on his solid shoulders and followed his lead. Sliding the dry fabric up my cold calves, Zeth stopped to kiss each thigh before covering up the spots and tugging the waistband onto my hips.

His mouth pressed beneath my belly button, and the hot steam against my skin made me suck the air through my teeth. As Zeth stood up, he fastened my buttons while he pecked soft kisses all the way to my neck. He was certainly indulging, and it was getting me aroused. But knowing we shouldn't go further out in the open, I was perfectly content to just receive his teasing kisses and gentle caresses while we got dressed. This slower pace allowed me to value Zeth's care.

Wanting to indulge in him too, I combed my fingers through his damp hair, admiring his dark strands. "Mm, you're so handsome, Zeth. Those girls at the river seemed to think so too. I saw how they were all swooning over you, especially that one you smiled at." I pouted a bit, hoping he noticed.

He gave me a funny look and caught my hand to kiss the tip of my pinky. "I was just being nice to Hattie's friends. I wanted to feel welcome, so I smiled."

I furrowed my brow as Zeth shook out my shirt, letting his words sink in. From what I'd seen from him lately, and even as kids, Zeth seemed to worry about others liking him. He sometimes put on a facade around people, then he'd fall back into being himself when he was with me. And yet there were times he tried too hard to please me, as he'd told me recently. Going along because he didn't want to lose me. I never realized...

Was he doing that now?

"Here, I can see you shivering already," Zeth said, holding my shirt out for me.

I suddenly drew my arms in. "Do you... really enjoy this?" I asked. "You're not just doing it because you think you have to?"

Zeth smoothed his knuckles against my cheek. "I want to be here with you. Ensuring you're safe gives me pleasure, and today turned out to be an adventure I didn't expect. There's nothing I'd rather be doing right now."

His response reassured my unease. Sighing softly, I moved my arms to slip them into the sleeves. "You're such a good lover, Zeth. I'm sure you had many admirers in the City who were smitten."

"Admirers?" Instead of explaining further, Zeth grabbed my arm to kiss the inside of my wrist before fastening the cuffs. His silence had me wondering as he made quick work of my shirt buttons.

When he was done, he moved back and paused to count on his fingers, deep in thought, and my forehead creased in surprise. That many lovers?

When he counted all ten fingers, Zeth caught my eye with a playful half smile while he tucked in my shirt. "The answer is zero."

I let out a laugh. "You don't have to say that just for me. I imagine you must have had other lovers before."

He shrugged his scarred shoulder. "Nah, I was too busy working, and no one else struck my fancy the way you do. Though..." he trailed off, looking away into the trees, "There was the mayor's son... he did try grabbing my *program* during the opera."

"Oh, really? Do tell me m—"

Zeth cut me off with a claiming kiss to my lips. I clasped the back of his neck and pulled him against me, but he broke away too soon. As our eyes met, we both panted softly.

"And what about you?" he asked, embracing me so tightly, there was no way for me to get away. "How many lovers have you had?"

I hesitated as I focused on his mouth, all red now from where I'd kissed him so roughly. I didn't want to talk about this, but he deserved to know since he asked. "Besides you? Three..."

Zeth stilled, and I froze, awaiting his answer.

"Only three men to beat up? That's not bad," he finally said. "So that means you're the more experienced one between us. You better start telling me if I'm doing things wrong."

"With that mouth of yours? You can do no wrong." I winked. "Thank you for dressing me. And you?"

"I've got it. You lay on the blanket. I'm not done with you yet."

My stomach fluttered from his demand, and I complied without question. Moving onto the blanket, I laid on my side and watched Zeth get dressed. There was something incredibly alluring about watching him pull dry clothes over his gleaming skin, even more so than watching him take them off. It was the way he moved, how he tugged the fabric on and buttoned his shirt, all in my presence.

When Zeth was done, he joined me on the blanket. I grabbed his arm to pull him against me, and he returned the embrace, supporting my head with one arm and wrapping his other around my middle. Content, I turned my face to watch the swaying branches from above, and Zeth pressed his forehead against my ear with a soft sigh.

I closed my eyes, listening to the rustle of the leaves and the sounds of crickets chirping in the grass. The gurgling river before us soothed my mind. The tranquil air was ripe with something magical I couldn't explain, as if I was connecting with Zeth and the nature surrounding us. I wanted to stay here forever with him, exposed and free in these woods without any obligations tying us down. For this quiet moment, it was just us.

I drew in close to Zeth as we basked in the solitude. I had this urge to take care of him as he did for me. By choosing me, he took a risk of losing financial security. I wanted to help him in some way, and a thought occurred to me about what he could do to earn money.

"Zeth," I started, and he turned his head, waiting. "Have you considered... going to the hiring agency? They can find you jobs, not only in Everdeen but a few surrounding towns as well. Nothing too far." The last thing I wanted was to be separated from him again.

"Hm," he grunted, glancing up at the leaves with me, seemingly at peace, but I felt his heart pick up beneath my hand. If not for being so close to him, I might have believed his confidence as he said, "I'll go tomorrow and knock their socks off."

"I'll go with you if you'd like, during my break. But I suggest leaving *your* socks on. First impressions and all that, you wouldn't want to stink up the room." I poked his ribs playfully.

Zeth's grin eased my worries about him as he shifted on his side to brush his nose against mine. "Thank you, for supporting me, for challenging me. You push me to experience life, and I find myself wanting to do new things with you. Like swinging on ropes. I want to bite you in all the same places as my kisses, and..." He slid his strong hands down my back and cupped a cheek. "And slap your ass to make you mine. Is that alright?"

My body lit with excitement. "I like the sound of that. You can fuck me if you'd like, too."

"Mm, you have excellent ideas. Never stop telling me what to do, you hear?"

"Deal."

We both grinned, and then Zeth regarded me for a long moment, his golden-hued eyes searching my face as if I was the most valuable thing in his world. There was sincerity in his gaze as he said, "I adore you, Amby."

I grabbed Zeth's collar and tugged him to my lips. "I'm so glad you're mine," I murmured, before giving him a passionate kiss. Then I curled against Zeth's side so he could wrap his arms around me as I laid against him. He ran his nails lightly over the fabric of my shirt while I held him close.

I closed my eyes against the setting sun and cherished his warmth as if it was something I might lose. But my heart was steadfast, and I knew I would never lose Zeth Washer again.

22

Zeth

"Name?"

"Zeth Washer."

"Occupation?"

"Auctioneer."

The young lady interviewing me raised a thin eyebrow in perfect imitation of Mrs. Marsh's glare when I used to misbehave in class. She even spoke like a schoolmarm. "I'm afraid to inform you that we don't have an auction house in Everdeen, Mr. Washer. What other occupations might I list?"

Mr. Washer? I waited for a ruler to hit me next.

Glancing sideways, I made sure Amby was still there with me. It really did feel like a school day again. He sat on a matching chair, and we both faced the employment agent's desk. The way Amby was sitting ramrod straight at the edge of his seat made it clear he thought her strict too.

He looked so damn cute like that, paying attention and being a good boy. I'd never tell him, but his offer to spend his lunch hour at the employment agency to support me might have been the sweetest thing he ever gave me. Even better than the notebook with graph lines in fourth grade.

"Occupation?" the agent asked again.

The devil in me suggested ruining this already. I should just cross my legs and act nonchalant. Getting kicked out for being an ass certainly sounded better than the alternative. I knew how badly this would end the moment Amby suggested an agency, but I needed to give this a try. I followed Amby's example and sat up straighter.

Feeling the lady's gaze bore into me, I quickly searched for additional answers. This was a word game, and I was clever. "You can list me as an appraiser... purchaser, counter clerk, accountant, bookkeeper, and sales associate."

Amby's brow raised as if impressed, and I basked in his appreciation.

The employment agent didn't praise me at all. She only jotted all those words with her fountain pen. I swear, I could hear the nib scratching the paper. Why was it so damn quiet?

Maybe I should have alphabetized my answer.

It didn't matter, as she read the next line. "Last place of employment?"

Ah, here was the first of many questions that I dreaded. Hopefully, the agency wouldn't check my answers before hiring me out. If I could prove myself before they got a reply... or lie. I could lie. *Just say the truth*, "Winfield's Estate Sales and Auction."

Her pen notated the proof of my failures to paper with neat, little strokes. Then she asked, "City?"

"Everdeen."

The lady frowned. "Where is Winfield's located, Mr. Washer? In which city were you working?"

"Oh, uh, Port—" I swallowed, hating how I'd grown this physical reaction to dredging up the past. I was smart enough before, but now I couldn't name the city I lived in for almost ten years.

"Port Winchester, Ms."

My gaze shot to Amby for answering, and he gave a quick pat to my knee, an excellent reminder I wasn't alone. Not any more. He pledged himself to me and offered to do more with me than I ever hoped for. He called me his. Amby was amazing.

"Schooling?"

"Yes," I hedged. "But, I moved before graduating."

"College?" she asked with interest. When I shook my head, her eyes dimmed. Apparently, my partial schooling wasn't going to cut it. Not for the skilled trades I enjoyed. No matter how well I spoke, or how much I taught myself, studying a fucking encyclopedia didn't count as an education. Or maybe it did? I could say that—

"Alright, Mr. Washer, we'll skip the rest of this form for now. Hand me your references so I can see what others say about you."

She was holding her hand out over the desk. I had nothing with me, so I wanted to shake her hand, as a joke. Something told me she wouldn't like my humor. That was made abundantly clear by her tight bun of black hair and bland work dress, if not by her no-nonsense attitude. At least her dress was well-made with a double row of buttons along the front that mimicked the uniforms I saw on the high guard in the City. Maybe she wanted to be in the military and got stuck here instead.

I would have to lie about my references. Without them, I was clearly hiding my past.

But as I said nothing, Amby leaned forward to speak instead, "He's a hard worker, and wonderful with numbers."

"That's high praise, Mr. Somerset, especially considering your line of work. I'm sure you're a fine mathematician yourself."

Amby's cheeks reddened a bit. I felt bad for putting him in this position with me. I wanted to list off all of Amby's skills, but that would make it worse.

"Well, gentlemen, if that's everything..." *we can't find you work.* At least she was being polite. I had to give her praise for that.

But I wasn't done. I didn't mind groveling a bit. My cals were limited, and I needed to make another payment on the property bill soon. Millie was working, but she couldn't provide a dry roof and bed. Amby would need me to provide in the future too, when we got the chance to be together. I didn't know where that would be, or how it would look, but I never wanted him hungry or worried. That meant taking control of my fate.

"No, it's not everything," I spoke up, sitting forward to give the employment agent my most serious I-am-worthy-of-your-damn-time stare. "I know how to put my head down and work hard until my job is done, and I don't mind starting from the bottom. Give me manual labor, I'll do it. Find me a hire, and your client will tell everyone about the superb employee you found for them."

"Yes, well, you may be persuasive, Mr. Washer, but we can't stand behind a ghost. Maybe your connections"—she glanced at Amby and back at me—"can employ you, and then provide a written reference. Until then, good day, gentlemen."

That was it.

I was back to begging for work door to door like I did as a sixteen-year-old kid with no experience. All my useless knowledge of scrollwork, trade marks, and pottery glaze was just that, useless.

Amby squeezed my hand before letting it go and getting up. I let him lead the way outside until the sun hit my face, and I inhaled the tang of horses and smoking chimneys. Still, the air was far better here than in the City... in *Port Winchester*.

"Don't listen to her," Amby kindly assured me.

"No, she's right," I sighed. "Without references for the last decade, I am a ghost, but thank you for suffering through that with me. It meant a lot to have you there."

"You'll find something. I can ask a few others I know if they're hiring. There's also an opening at the pub."

I liked his positivity. I brushed my knuckles against his but didn't take his hand. I didn't want to pressure him in town. Instead, I started along the sidewalk to walk him back to the bank. "Maybe your distillery friend has a job for me? I could work for him. Surely there's something he may want me to do."

"No, you don't want to work for him," he muttered. "He's a nice man, but his friends are... questionable."

"I was teasing. I didn't like him anyway. Your idea of the pub is better, so I'll stop there after dropping you off at work. I'm just sorry you missed eating lunch."

"Don't be. I can eat later. I wanted to be with you." Amby grabbed my arm in a friendly, but affectionate, manner, and I didn't realize how much I wanted his touch until I had it back. I pressed my elbow against my side, trapping him in close as we walked on, arm and arm like we used to when we were kids. Before we became lovers, our friendship was so platonic, people often said we were tied at the waist.

Amby nudged me with his shoulder. "Hey, remember when we used to skip along the sidewalk making fun of the girls in class?"

"Heaven, we looked like idiots," I chuckled. "I think Anna was one of those girls. She was always so prim and proper, it made us horrible to her."

"That's true... We haven't been very good to her lately either, squabbling over her hand." His eyes darted to the sidewalk, as if pondering, then continued, "Did you... let Annabelle know you're no longer interested in her?"

My face scrunched up in distaste. "Not yet. I'm nervous about her reaction. I don't want her to ruin me before I can win over your dad. But to be honest, I'm not sure why she's encouraging me."

"Well... she did tell me she felt a spark." He put a finger to his lips. "I only assumed it was with you. Perhaps you were too forward with her, and she likes that. You should definitely not be forward with her anymore."

"Forward how?"

Amby suddenly clutched my hand. "'Oh, Anna, I must seek your assistance. My sister is in the woods, being attacked by a deer! We must find her.'"

I laughed at his melodrama. "Was I that bad?"

"No. Maybe more like... aggressively charming." He winked at me as he let me go.

"Aggressively charming," I mused with a cluck of my tongue. "Not sure I'm fond of that description, but it's probably accurate. Sometimes I do come across as phony, don't I?"

"What do you mean?"

"I mean, I struggle to make friends. You might be right, I try too hard. Maybe people realize that I'm putting on, so that's why they end up hating me."

"I think we all do that to a certain extent. I have noticed you want to be accepted by everyone so you try to please them. But it's not your job to make others happy. Be yourself first. If you do that, people will accept you. And perhaps some won't, but that's alright. They won't be your sort of people anyway."

His advice knotted my stomach a bit, which said there was truth to his words. "Thank you. Feel free to punch me with more advice. I need to be better, especially at the upcoming salon. Millie and I are invited."

"Hattie told me. She visited the tailor shop to pick out a suit for me to wear to the salon, and said Millie was talking about going too. If you decide to attend, just be the dashing Zeth I know you are. Handsome, strong, funny, intelligent, resilient..." He cut his eyes to me. "Want me to go on?"

"Keep complimenting me like that, and it's your fault if I kiss you right here," I answered with my best *dashing* smile.

Amby poked my ribs. "I'll save it for a rainy day, then. Oh, and before I forget to warn you, my father will be at the salon."

"Good. I can slip into his circle to suggest your bank may want to buy my laundry. Maybe I can impress your dad through fine bargaining and trade talk. He should like that, right?"

Amby's face fell. "You really are selling the laundry?"

My steps faltered to a stop. "Of course I'm selling it, the laundry failed. Too many elites have staff now, and everyone else has washboards and basins."

Amby stopped walking as well. Just behind him, the large pillars of his family's business towered over us as I took in Amby's confused expression.

"But... where will you live?"

"I honestly don't know," I sighed, pulling off my cap to rake a hand through my hair. "My plans to marry Anna were shitty, so I'm glad they changed, but now everything's up in the air. I could look for a small apartment once the sale happens." As I gazed at Amby's gathered brow, it occurred to me that maybe I didn't need all the answers. "What do you want to do?"

Amby blinked in confusion. "You're asking me? I mean... I'd be happy to help you with anything you need in order to stay warm and fed."

"No, darling, I mean, where do you want to live? When we're together?"

Amby's expression cleared, and he put his hands on his hips, thinking. "Well, ideally, in a beachside cottage with cats." He laughed, but I liked the idea. Mostly the part about cats. Amby continued, "The Somerset estate goes to me when I marry, but I don't know if it applies if I marry outside of what my father has planned for me. But you know, if I need to move... you *do* have a spacey place of your own. The laundry may not be in operation anymore, but it's a nice building since you've cleaned and done repairs. If you don't sell, we could live there. It's your home, after all."

"My home?"

I could see Amby moving in with me, filling the old upper floor with his lovely furniture and loving smiles. Maybe two new height marks on the doorway. But that felt like a dream. If I didn't sell my inheritance, I lost that profit. And with no money or job, I'd default even more on the property taxes until the bank took the laundry. It was much easier to have money in my pocket than a giant bill hanging over my head.

Sighing, I tugged my cap back on. "You know, I've not called the laundry my home in a while, so I'll think about it. We should focus on winning over your dad first. If he gives us his blessing, then we won't need to worry about anything."

That sounded harshly like I was gold digging again, but it was a possibility that Amby could keep his wealth. No matter what happened, I was happy to be talking it all out with him.

Amby's face softened. "Of course... One day at a time. No matter what happens, I'll be with you through it. I'm going to take care of you, just like you take care of me."

"You're delightful," I said with relief, enjoying the reassurance. Amby scrunched up his nose at the compliment, and I wished he could see how adorable he was.

The bells chimed the one o'clock hour. Our lunch break was well spent, but time was up. My boy had to return to his job, so I nudged him onward, "Now off to work."

Amby raised an eyebrow and nodded toward me. "Yes, sir."

Damn, I enjoyed his sass. I longed to call him a good boy right here, but that could wait. For now, I watched his fine ass as he walked away and enjoyed the view until he entered one of the double doors. Then I stared up at the marble carving above the entrance that read *Somerset & Sons Bank*.

There was some irony to Amby having a job he hated when I would gladly take his place. Unfortunately, Mr. Somerset would never hire me, not even if Amby made a good argument. My past was too shady. Yet, maybe there was a chance I could win him over personally. Maybe *dashing Zeth* had a chance to convince the grand Mr. Somerset to invest in his own son.

23

Ambrose

The next day, Zeth and I met for a late lunch at the Rustic Rose Cafe. It was warm, and the birds chirped happily as they flew to the ground of the cafe to peck at leftover food. Several iron tables stood outside under the bakery's pavilion. At this time of day, there weren't many others eating. I was glad, as it meant I could spend time with Zeth in solitude as we sat together.

I looked over at him as I pushed my plate aside, finishing my sandwich and fruit after him. He was fiddling with the cover of my mother's favorite poetry book. I'd brought it in hopes we could both find a poem we liked enough to read at the salon.

However, Zeth seemed a little off today, distracted, and I wondered at his mood. "Did you get the job at the pub?" I asked.

"No, they said the job is already taken." Zeth's eyes left the book to focus on me. "I even asked about being a busboy, but they didn't need me."

"I'll ask my sisters if they know of anyone who needs a hire. They know every piece of gossip in town."

That cheered him up briefly before a painful expression passed over his features. "Fuck, I forgot to ask, how is your day going?"

My cheeks heated, and I circled the rim of my teacup with my finger before picking it up to drink. Zeth ordered coffee, drinking it black, while I loaded my tea with sugar. "It's been fine. What about you? Did you get the ceiling dried out?"

"It's still drying. Nothing I can do to help that, so I started chipping the paint off the front door. It's been painted over so many times that I can't get it all off. It looks horrible, like someone vomited a rainbow at the laundry."

I choked on my tea, and a bit dribbled out of my mouth and onto my trousers as I glanced over at him and laughed.

Zeth handed me his napkin with a sheepish quirk to his lips. "Sorry, maybe that was acting too much like myself? I can be more gentlemanly."

"Don't you dare." I grinned as I set my cup on the table. "I love when you make me laugh."

He smiled, but only for a moment before he looked at the table, his eyes downcast.

I cleaned the spill with the napkin and asked, "Is something bothering you?"

"Yes, sorry, I couldn't get to sleep last night." Zeth picked up the poetry book and set it back with a sigh. "I was thinking about you and your dad, and the laundry, and Millie. And how I should act at the fancy salon party. But mostly about you."

"Oh?" I scooted my chair closer to him, until his arm touched mine. "You really shouldn't lose sleep over me, love."

His lips twitched, and he moved even closer to whisper, "There have been plenty of nights when I lost sleep over you. Sometimes I even need to slip out of bed for some privacy."

"Ah, so you have a very... vivid imagination. That makes two of us." I grabbed his thigh and squeezed it.

"Your pastry, sirs."

My heart slammed against my ribs as I let go of Zeth and turned around. I blinked up at a man a little older than us with short dark hair. He wore a tan apron, and I instantly recognized him as the cafe owner's son, Tobe. He stood by our table with an amused expression, serving the plate of dessert I'd ordered for us to share.

"Thank you," I said, nodding at him, and he smiled before leaving.

Zeth was biting his lip to keep from laughing as I pulled on my collar to release the flush from my neck. Smiling, I pushed the pastry shell filled with whipped cream and drizzled with chocolate between us.

"Want some?" I asked.

"No thank you, I'm not fond of sugar," Zeth answered as he poured me another cup of tea before sipping the last of his coffee.

"Really? Why haven't I ever known that?" I took a bite and savored the crisp shell and soft cream, trying to recall the times Zeth might have eaten sweets growing up, but couldn't. I ticked that off as learning something new about him. I did notice, however, how Zeth had lined up all his fruit as if they were something special before he'd eaten them.

"We should order more fruit next time," I finally said.

Zeth looked pleased, as if I'd just told him we'd kiss by the river again. Yes, I would give him all the fruit he wanted if it meant he was content and fed.

But all too quickly, Zeth's face darkened again as he set his cup down. He turned it slowly around on its saucer. His mood had me entirely too worried to keep carrying on without a care.

"Zeth," I started, getting his attention. "We agreed to talk out our troubles. So please tell me what's bothering you."

He nodded and straightened in his seat. "It's... When I said I was thinking about you last night, I should have said, I thought about how rude I was to you. I've been incredibly selfish. I don't want to be like that anymore."

I turned to face him with surprise. "What do you mean?"

"Just that I focus on my goals and don't give a damn who stands in my way. That was you, until recently. I didn't realize how afraid you were of your dad." Zeth met my gaze with sincerity. "I'm sorry for being so awful when I returned to Everdeen. I should've treated you better. You didn't deserve it."

"Oh." Relieved it wasn't something detrimental, I smiled and said, "It's forgiven, Zeth. I know you care about me. We were both... rather confused, I think. Thank you all the same for telling me."

Tickled by his worry, I gently pinched his cheek. "You're sweet, you know that?"

He chuckled, appearing more relaxed now. "I'm not sure about that, but perhaps I could use some tutoring in decorum and gentlemanly behavior. Would you be so kind as to assist?"

"Of course." I patted the poetry book on the table. "We can start here, with lessons in reciting poetry for the salon meet."

Zeth blinked at me, his lips pulling up in the corner as if he hadn't been serious about such tutoring, but I was going to milk this for all it was worth. Hearing Zeth deliver a poem would light me up inside.

"I concede to your expertise. Do you think participating in the salon will impress your dad?"

"Yes. He loves poetry. He and my mother went to the meets all the time. When my sisters and I were able to go, it made him happy. I usually recite, but I haven't in a while." I took another bite of my dessert as Zeth picked up the book and flipped through the pages. "Maybe I will this time, though."

"Why haven't you joined in lately?"

"I was just... feeling a little low in spirits for a while this past year." I used my fork to scrape up the last of the whipped cream.

"Is that something you want to talk about?"

My fork froze in my mouth. All of Zeth's caring attention was on me now, and I felt vulnerable as I set the utensil on my empty plate. My problems were nothing in comparison to what he'd faced, what he was still facing with needing money and security. Honestly, what did I truly have to complain about? Zeth seemed interested in hearing me out, though.

"I was feeling a little lost for a while," I admitted. "Lonely, maybe. I suppose ever since my mother passed, I did what my father wanted because I felt I didn't have a choice. But I hated it. I lost my voice, and myself."

Zeth narrowed his eyes, staring intently at me. "Let me ask you something, Amby. What has being the perfect son gained you?"

I tapped my thumb on my plate as I recalled how my father gave me no choice but to work at the bank after Zeth left. How he'd tried setting me up with several women, only for each attempt at courting to fail. But I did it without question, because as the only man of my siblings, I had to keep our family name going, and I knew my sisters looked up to me as their reliable brother. But what they saw on the surface was a sham. I'd been breaking inside for a long time with the strain of familial traditions always on my shoulders.

Complying with my father's wishes gained his approval, but it was a temporary elation that never actually deepened our relationship. Despite compliance, my father and I were still as distant now as we were ten years ago. What had I gained by following the path of his legacy?

Finally, I shook my head and said, "Nothing."

Zeth nodded. "You got lost following the wrong path and no one is happy, not even your dad." He rubbed the back of my hand on the table. "I got lost too, for Millie. I stuffed all my desires inside because of my responsibilities to her. Now she calls me a grumpy bear."

"Look at us," I laughed. "Two idiots who felt sacrificing our happiness was better than embracing it. We both wanted each other but made choices based on what we thought our families needed... And if we'd kept going with our plans, our responsibilities, I hate to think what kind of men we'd become." I glanced at Zeth, seeing how he watched me as I rattled on. "Am I talking too much?"

"Rosie, darling, your cleverness is one of the things I admire most about you."

I met his eyes. "I've realized how... liberating it is to pave your own path, make your own choices. Some of us aren't meant to be bankers, or go on to continue family bloodlines." I smiled crookedly. "Or marry rich women with fancy tea sets."

"You're fucking right. We would have been horrid husbands, grumpy and dull. Thank God we're escaping that fate, though I wouldn't mind a few kids running around. One day, maybe. If you wish."

"Oh. You want... to adopt? You'd do that with me?"

"Yeah. Thinking about a family didn't feel right until I thought about starting one with you. You can let the little brats run free, and I'll bandage them up. How does that sound?"

"I'd say it sounds like you've been thinking hard about our future, and I like it."

Zeth pulled up my hand to kiss it. It was such a quick act, but it made me blush nonetheless. The best part was that I wasn't even worried if anyone saw us. I was too full of bliss to care at the moment.

Clearing my throat, I gestured at the poetry book. "Perhaps you can find a poem in there about finding oneself in this difficult journey called life?"

"Good idea." Zeth gave me an appreciative nod before he flipped through the pages again. "Are those the sort of poems your mom liked?"

Leaning my arms on the table, I peered up at the tree nearby where the birds flew about. "Yes, but she loved nature poems the most. About birds, trees, flowers. Anything like that. Those tend to be my favorites as well." I turned to him, moving closer, and flipped to a page with a short poem about summer that I enjoyed. "Short and sweet. I like those."

Zeth's eyes gleamed as he looked me up and down, and I waited for him to say something coy, but he only asked, "What poems does your dad like?"

"He likes those that speak deeper meanings about the soul, and love. Connection, I suppose. Romance." I'd invested a great deal of time getting to know my father. I was sure he knew little about my poetry preferences.

"Huh, I expected you to say he enjoys balance sheets. There's nothing quite like liabilities and expenditures to get the heart racing."

My laughter attracted a few stares from people walking past on the sidewalk. I'm not sure why the idea of my father reciting numbers at a poetry reading tickled me so, but they did. I laughed until tears formed.

After a moment, I looked up to see an amused smile on Zeth's lips and a handkerchief in his hand. He held the white cloth out, so

I took it to dab my eyes, enjoying the simple lye scent. When I went to give it back, my gaze narrowed as I recognized the gold initials of my name embroidered into the fabric, AHS.

"This is my handkerchief," I said with surprise.

"Aye," Zeth agreed, but gently yanked the cloth from me. I stared as he tucked it deeply into his sleeve and crossed his strong arms with a daring grin. "It was yours, but finders keepers. You'll need to fight me to get it back."

"Mm, you keeping it shows me how much you valued our intimate time in the hay." I winked before flipping another page of the poetry book. "Speaking of intimacy, I do think a love poem would be ideal to recite. My father loved my mother dearly. I'm convinced it's why he won't marry again. I suppose sometimes love is so deep... it's painful to be parted."

Zeth's face softened, and something bright glowed between us. "I think I'll write a romantic poem for your dad," he declared.

"Which Somerset are you trying to woo here?"

He chuckled. "I mean, I'll write something to impress your dad. If a man as serious as him appreciates poetry, then I'm suddenly inspired to be romantic. And maybe my cleverness and witty turn of phrases will please you too. How many days do I have to craft this masterpiece before the salon?"

"Two days."

"Fuck me, that's not much time. What can you teach me about love in two days?"

Zeth leaned toward me with a daring grin. There were several things I could teach him, and I was eager for him to teach me too, especially after he mentioned slapping my ass at the river. That intrigued me. I thought about it every day. I opened my mouth to tell him we could leave and find someplace more private, but the sound of a chair scraping pulled me away from him. I turned to find Damien Cooligan sitting at our table.

The unwelcome man flashed me a knowing smirk and flipped his light-blond braid over his shoulder before turning to Zeth. "Is Amby giving out lessons in love again?"

"They're private lessons, so move on," Zeth practically growled in threat to Damien, reminding me of how they didn't get along in school. God, this wasn't good...

My hand curled into a fist in my lap. "Mr. Cooligan, I believe you order food inside."

"I know what I want, and I don't have to go far to get it." He eyed me as he waved a hand up. When Tobe walked over, Damien asked him for a pastry before leaning back and crossing his arms, making himself comfortable.

Zeth crossed his legs with a slow grace that reminded me of how he acted as man of the house in Annabelle's parlor. He looked Damien over carefully and asked, "Still picking on people to feel better about yourself?"

It was a low blow to Damien, and by the way he sat up with an ugly scowl, the insult hit. "Don't act like you're above me, Washer. It seems Amby really is desperate for whoever's available."

When Zeth's glare narrowed at him, I grabbed the poetry book, tucked it beneath my arm, and stood from my chair. We needed to leave, or a fight would ensue with the way these two were staring at each other.

Clearing my throat, I looked over at Zeth as if he was the only person sitting there and asked, "Ready to head back to the laundry?"

Zeth exhaled and gave an encouraging nod before standing up beside me. I was ready to teach him two days' worth of love. I wouldn't let Damien ruin this moment, or anything between us.

Damien reached for the pot of tea in the middle of the table. "You shouldn't hang around tramps, Amby. You're better than this."

"Hey," I said, my voice stern. "You're unbelievable. And you wonder why I'm so cold to you. The next time you see me out, kindly leave me alone."

Before Damien could say more, I tugged Zeth away from the table and out onto the sidewalk. Once we were walking, I let go of him and stared at the ground. My whole body shook from the encounter. What would Zeth think of me after hearing all that?

When Zeth wrapped an arm around my back to guide me into a

narrow alleyway between a few buildings, I wondered what he was doing. But the shade instantly cooled me off, and I followed along with him until we moved far enough away from the bustle of the street.

When we stopped, Zeth took the book from me and set it on the ground. Then he faced me and asked, "Is everything alright?"

"I'm sorry for that back there."

"The way you stood up to that prick was commendable. I never liked Damien in school, and he's worse now. I take it he's one of the three I need to beat up?"

I leaned back against the brick siding with a sigh. "Yes, but he was a mistake."

Zeth set one of his hands against the wall by my head, then used his other to tilt my chin up to meet his golden-brown eyes. "Thank you for choosing me, Rosie."

"I will always choose you, Zeth."

He moved in to kiss me, his tender touch evaporating my stress. So much, that I was ready to have him all to myself.

Breaking away from his lips, I straightened his collar and asked, "Ready to head to the laundry so I can teach you a few things about love?"

Zeth gave a husky laugh before he nodded. He swiftly bent to grab the book before taking my hand to lead us along the alley.

As we neared the street, I felt his hold slipping from mine, but I gripped him tight, not wanting to let go. Zeth blinked at me in surprise. When I squeezed his hand, letting him know I wanted to keep him there, he smiled. Then he pulled me out of the shadows of the alley and into the sunshine of Everdeen.

24

Zeth

Two days proved to be enough time for Amby to teach me a thing or two about love. We found a few occasions to meet in the laundry when it was just us, without responsibilities, or sisters, or cares. Amby recited some poetry examples for me, and I worshiped twelve more spots on his beautiful body. I never guessed that kissing the inside of his wrist while he held his book would be so sensual. I even dared him to keep reading while I disrobed us and knelt to distract him with my mouth. Feeling his soft skin under my lips as he watched me with pink cheeks and a hot stare... bliss. I rather enjoyed poetry.

When Amby wasn't around, I pondered phrases and scribbled romantic words onto the backside of can labels until I wrote something to read at the salon. And then, the morning of the salon, Millie received a gift from Anna; the top hat Millie must have shown her while shopping.

Anna shouldn't be buying my sister incredibly expensive things to woo herself into our family. It reminded me that I'd yet to clear up our courtship status. Reciting personal poetry for Amby in front of Anna would be wrong. She had treated me kindly. I wasn't a cad. It was past time to end my con for her hand.

So, I walked over to Anna's estate that afternoon to dissolve our courtship. I was let in quickly to wait in her front hall while the butler went off to find her. To occupy myself, I read through the lines of my poem for the salon tonight. I was glad for the distraction, as the rude butler hadn't invited me into the parlor or offered me snacks. He should've at least taken my cap.

The grandfather clock nearby ticked. And ticked...

I refolded the sheet of paper that held my heart and tucked it safely into the breast pocket of my brown jacket, then peered down the hall for some sign of life. None. The large estate felt hollow today. In that unease, the weight of my decision to court Amby pressed forcibly against my chest. So much so that I had to close my eyes and remind myself to breathe.

I didn't fear falling for Amby. I was confident in his love for me. It was all the other consequences that made my knees weak. I chose him over a comfortable life in the Winters estate. I didn't know where I would work, or if I could work. I worried that Amby's dad would hate me and disown Amby. I was terrified that dear, old Somerset and Sons Bank would suddenly demand my taxes in full to claim the laundry, tossing us into the streets. And my decisions could ruin Millie, right when she was starting her own life. It would be so easy for the town to sabotage her too.

I still couldn't believe that I tried to con Anna into marriage, going so far as telling her I wanted to arrange one between us. She never refused. Instead, she continued meeting with me while telling Amby she just wanted to be friends. Now, I was tossing her over with no explanation except for a simple, we do not pair well together.

There was a risk in telling her I chose Amby. Anna could become upset and gossip about me to the whole town, spoiling my chance to win over Amby's dad. It only took one person to ruin your life. I needed her understanding, especially since she and Millie were close. Best-case scenario, I hoped to befriend Anna. She was nice to be around, when she wasn't spouting annoying quotes that belonged on embroidered pillows or running me over with her peppy little car.

Where was that *fucking* butler?

The man went to tell Anna of my arrival and was making me wait on purpose.

Inhaling deeply of the lightly perfumed front entrance, I calmly hung up my cap to make myself welcome. I tugged on my vest and nodded with a confidence that I sure as hell didn't feel and strolled down the hall on my own. It wasn't the first time I let myself in. I could find Anna and talk to her before the butler returned with reinforcements to kick me out, or whatever he was up to currently. I just knew he wasn't baking me fresh cookies.

Each door I came to opened easily, and I peeked inside to find fancy front parlors and sitting rooms all in different colors. In the hallway, I encountered that nice little table and Chince vase which caught my attention a few weeks ago. Today, it was overfilled with pink roses that reminded me of my Rosie. My interest at the picnic had only been for money, but I still couldn't believe Amby thought I returned to Everdeen to steal Anna's vase. He was close, though. I did plan on selling it after marrying Anna. I had calculated a number of items that day and tallied quite a substantial amount before Amby interrupted me with his adorably flustered presence.

I would always pick Amby over that vase.

I opened another door, this time to a beautiful library filled with wall-to-wall bookcases and wide windows with the curtains drawn. I was about to close the door when Anna's blonde head popped up from a massive desk. She blinked her blue eyes at me to rid them of slumber. I held onto the doorknob and tried not to smile at the red crease in her cheek from sleeping face-first on a book.

"Oh! So sorry, Zeth. Were you waiting long?"

"Not at all," I fibbed politely. When she sat back in her chair to wave me in, I joined her, keeping the door slightly ajar to avoid rumors.

Reaching her desk, I felt very tall. "Forgive me for interrupting your work, but do you have a moment so we may talk before this evening's social?"

"Yes, I was actually hoping to visit you. Then I became distracted with the estate finances." Anna gestured at the column of blurry ink entries. Before I could read any of them, she closed the thick book and rose to join me by the two leather chairs facing the desk. When she motioned for us to sit together, I found mine had a decorative pillow propped on the seat.

Flowery, yellow and orange fabric formed a rectangle, and over that, delicate stitchwork... 'Pick up the lemons that Fate sends and start a lemonade stand.'

You have to be fucking kidding me. I knew I'd conjured up the idea of quotes on pillows, but I didn't expect Miss Annabelle Winters to actually *own* embroidered pillows. She probably jotted out sayings and sewed each thread herself. Sipping tea in her matching tea set room while stitching out nonsense in her spare time. And that quote, what *lemons* did Fate give her?

I moved the atrocity to rest against the chair's foot before taking the seat for myself.

"Do you like these armchairs?" Anna asked, stealing into my annoyance. When I glanced over, she continued, "They belonged to my father. He and Mother passed away last year in a carriage accident. Very sudden... but they left me so many fond memories."

"Oh, I'm sorry."

"For what?" She blinked, and I felt like an absolute ass for not seeing her struggles. Yes, she had money, but that didn't make her life perfect. While my mum's illness drained me over months, I couldn't imagine how painful it must have been for Anna to lose both parents at once, in one day. Like me, she was probably over-whelmed and angry at her inheritance.

I bent over to retrieve the pillow and tucked it behind me, understanding a little better. "I'm so sorry for your loss, Anna. You've done well holding up on your own."

She blinked again, only this time it was to clear away moisture as she smoothed her hand along the desk, probably also her father's.

Giving her a moment, I eased back to appreciate the leather chair. It was lush, smooth, and firm, but not as nice as Amby's rocking chair. Crossing my legs, I examined the shelving around us too. Leather spines lined the walls. Around... two hundred books, give or take twenty-five.

Old and expensive volumes that would make any collector proud. There was also a gold-framed map of all the Commonwealths, with Caldor being the smallest one on the Northeastern coast. In the corner of the room sat a mahogany side-bar filled with cut crystal. Anna's father was a man of fine tastes. No wonder she liked this room enough to nap.

Anna wasn't asleep now. She sat on the edge of her armchair like a prim miss. She even folded her hands together on her knees as she watched me. When I turned to her, she deliberately opened her mouth to say, "Zeth, I'm so glad—"

"Anna, allow me to say something first, please."

"Oh," she replied softly, and I could tell she wasn't used to people interrupting her. "Alright, you have the floor."

That phrasing sounded like she dabbled in politics. She was such a stickler for rules in school, I could just imagine her leading a town hall. I wondered what *did* interest her and realized I never bothered to learn. She deserved better than a selfish prick like me. Now, to part with her kindly...

"Anna, I made my intentions t—" Anna's face pinched. "—toward you clear—" Now her fingers twisted together. "—from the beginning, but—" My worries cranked a notch higher with each reaction. "I'm fairly certain you'll agree that I..."

I... was messing this up. I should stop speaking as aggressively charming Zeth, as Amby said I acted. He told me to be myself. It was worth a try... "Fuck, I'm sorry, Anna. Turns out that un-arranging a courtship is difficult."

Her brow shot up as I uncrossed my legs to lean my elbows on my knees and met her confused gaze head-on. It was scary to open up, but that's what I needed to do with her, finally. "What I should be saying is that I treated you poorly. I returned to Everdeen with a plan to trick you into an arrangement with me. You're rich, and I'm poor, and I remembered us getting along, when I wasn't playing stupid pranks on you."

"I liked you too. You and Millie both," Anna assured me. "Life here in this big house was getting incredibly boring until you two returned to town. I didn't know what I was missing."

That wasn't what I expected from Anna after my confession. Did she not just hear me admit that I tried to con her?

I took in her tilted head and knew she was listening. Maybe she needed to hear more. "I sold everything I owned to put on the con that I was wealthy, with plans to sell the laundry before you found out I was actually broke." When she nodded for me to go on, I swallowed. "Not once did I think about our... *your*... happiness. I was wrong to push myself on you. Neither of us wants to marry—"

"Actually, I do want to marry," Anna corrected matter-of-factly, and I frowned. Oh shit, I was wrong. I— "Just not you."

"Just not..." I shook my head, doubting my ears. "Excuse me?"

A gentle smile creased her face. "I was going to say, I wish to officially court your sister. We've bonded over similar interests in the past few weeks, and I think she's open to courting me. I knew about your con because Millie already confessed. I hope this doesn't come as a shock. We weren't completely open with our activities or attractions either."

"Millie?"

"Yes, your handsome and devilish sister."

"That's certainly my Mildred Louise Washer."

Anna laughed, a light and charming sound. "There's a soiree next week, and I plan to ask Millie if she will attend with me. After our first dance, I'll request a courting kiss. As long as I'm granted her brother's permission..."

"Of course. Of course!" I quickly agreed while my tension eased. Not only was Anna not mad at me for breaking off our arrangement, she was relieved, letting out a grateful sigh. We both laughed over clearing the air. Anna wanted to marry Millie, not me. "Were you chasing after my sister this whole time?"

"I wouldn't say it like that, but... yes. She had me the moment I saw her woe-is-me act with twigs in her hair. Millie's just my sort of handful."

My eyebrows must have hit the ceiling as I tried not to think too much about my sister in Anna's hands. And here I was worried about hurting her feelings. With all Anna's mixed messages of welcoming us into her house, yet not wanting to flirt with me, I thought she just didn't care about love. The whole time, she didn't care about men. Anna had been chasing my sister, and Millie enjoyed Anna's suit. No wonder Millie hounded me endlessly about us visiting Anna.

"And you," she said. "I believe you have an eye for someone else as well?"

"I do, and he fills my heart," I answered her honestly, now that I knew she wasn't upset over breaking this off. "Amby always had my heart, but please don't tell anyone about us yet. We're still paving our way to be together, and I don't want it to be a rocky road."

"I can keep a secret. Will you keep my plan a surprise too?"

"Gladly. I can't wait to see Millie's face at the dance when you ask to court her."

I stood and observed the library collection that was easily equal to my inheritance, not giving a flying shit about walking away from it all. I was wrong to think Anna's money was a solution. I just hoped Amby and I might find some stability and acceptance from his dad. Amby was lucky to still have him around.

Speaking of... I felt fatherly as I offered my hand to Anna, and she stood quickly to shake an agreement. When her face lit up, I brought her in for a quick hug. "Anna, as long as you love our bratty Mils and keep her out of trouble, you'll be welcome in our family."

She pulled away and rolled her eyes. "No promises on behaving." Her teasing sounded stiff, as if she just learned how to tell a joke, a sign of Millie's influence. Apparently, I was destined to have two strong-willed sisters in my life now. Anna would fit right in with us Washers.

* * *

Later that evening, Millie and I reached the Washington house for the poetry salon. The town was bustling with evening travel as I slowed my steps on the front walk and stared at the impressive columns on the enormous house. Looking over at Millie, I decided to mess with her before telling her Anna and I called things off.

"I need to tell you something before we enter the party," I started. "Something important."

Millie didn't say anything, so I glanced over to find her big round eyes blinking in surprise beneath the brim of her lovely top hat that Anna gifted her. Millie was sure to impress Anna tonight.

Feigning deep sorrow with drama equal to Millie's, I took her hands and squeezed. "I visited Anna earlier today while you were working and confessed about our con. Now she doesn't want to marry me. She seemed to be interested in someone else. Someone smart and attractive, with a hell of a mouth on her."

"Oh?" Millie said softly. I could almost see my half-truths filtering through her smart head until her face cleared. When she squealed and pulled out of my grasp to dance a little jig up and down the Washingtons' front steps, I chuckled at her excitement.

"So then, I take it you like her?" I asked as I reached out to straighten her tipping hat.

But Millie straightened it herself with a grin. "Oh aye, and she's fond of me too. We're the ones who set you and Amby up."

"Excuse me?" I asked for the second time that day. These girls were determined to surprise me.

"Anna saw right through our con at the picnic. She's sharp, and wanted to turn the tables on us by inviting you to fish with Amby. After you both fought so much that you fell into the lake, she told me about it, and we had a good laugh. That's when Anna and I came up with our plan to leave you and Amby alone as much as possible."

"So the idea to ride horses around the Winters estate?" I asked, never questioning that Millie had suggested that scheme as a way for me to woo Anna, but Anna was the one who had the same idea to invite us over.

"Our idea. We wanted you to visit Amby in his barn."

"Uh-huh." I frowned at her, slightly annoyed since that day ended poorly for Amby and me.

At least Millie had the good grace to dip her head slightly. I guess I couldn't be too mad that she played matchmaker, since she helped push me past all the grief that had lodged in my throat, keeping my emotions trapped.

That didn't excuse coy tricks, though, so I used my fatherly voice to make sure she understood, "We were wrong to start this con in the first place. Let's pledge that the plotting is over."

"Aye," Millie agreed. I was about to thank her when she added, "Then I probably should confess, I'm plotting a surprise for you that's happening next week."

"Heaven help me."

"And I want to court Anna. I hope you approve."

She should have said that last part easily, but the uncertainty in her voice made me ache. Did she doubt me? Of course I would always support her. I wanted her to experience true love, no matter who it might be with. She was my sister.

I turned to face Millie and took her smaller hands in mine again. Then I caught her moist eyes full of worry. "Mils, Anna's a better match for you than me, and I couldn't be happier for you both."

"Thank you. Home is where the heart is, after all."

"Oh no, not you too!"

"What?" She blinked up at me, and I tugged the brim of her hat down to blind her.

"You and Anna can keep your silly sayings to yourself. I'm a logical man," I teased.

Millie snorted into her hat before tipping it back. "So logically, does that mean you'll give someone quite handsome a courting kiss soon?"

I grinned widely. "I hope to hell it does."

Her chuckle was joyous, and I felt grateful she approved of me and Amby as we ascended the steps to the Washingtons' front door, where she nudged my arm with hers.

She looked damn cute in her newly tailored attire. I never would have chosen a men's suit for Millie, yet the sleek black jacket added a commanding presence that caught the eye. The matching split skirt and white blouse showed off her curves, and Anna's top hat was the cherry on top of my handsome sister.

"You should know, I'm proud of how hard you worked at the

tailor shop to buy those clothes. They look good on you. You're dressed to impress the elite of Everdeen."

"Damn right I am." Millie snorted and reached up to grab the golden pineapple knocker, slamming it far harder than necessary.

I was still flinching when she turned back to me. "I just wish you had a fancy new suit too. That cravat isn't enough."

"It's an ascot," I corrected with dramatic offense and caressed the smooth amber and black paisley. Amby liked how it matched my eyes. Hopefully, it also distracted everyone from my plain, brown jacket. His ring on my pinky flashed a nervous deep gray, and I couldn't wait for it to shift colors once I saw Amby again.

The door swung open to a butler in livery who looked at us with a shadow of disdain in his wrinkled face. He thankfully gave Millie a kind nod and waved us both into a massive entrance with two staircases lining the sides. They curved up to join at the top, and piano music floated down as I marveled. I didn't even know Everdeen had houses like this downtown. The facade was stately with columns around the doorway, but the inside extravagance was unexpected. Now, I fully expected a ballroom. Similar houses in the City had them when I entered as an appraiser. Entering this one as a guest made my stomach go queasy.

The butler shut the door behind us and took our hats and gloves with a sniff before handing them off to a second servant who waited behind him. I didn't understand why the Washingtons needed two men to take hats, except to show off. When a third man descended the stairs to lead us up them, I did my best to hide my contempt at their display of wealth. Millie's eyeroll didn't help.

After ascending the right side stairs, the third man walked us to a set of giant double doors and pushed them open for us to enter. As we walked through, a warm, smoky haze surrounded me while chinking piano music and spirited chatter filled my ears.

Millie appeared as overwhelmed as I was. I should have anticipated this. She spent her time in the City fairly secluded, so I took her hand and pulled her to the closest inner wall right away to ask, "You okay?"

"Of course, it's fantastic." Her brown eyes weren't sparkling with tears, she was excited. I followed them as she admired the fifty or so people in lavish attire all lingering in small groups around the room. Women filled the left side where velvet chairs and settees lined up in rows for the reading. On the right side, men claimed armchairs in small social circles. They puffed cigars while holding short liquor glasses as they talked. A long table separated the room, packed with fancy hors d'oeuvres, tall gelatin molds, fat cakes, and a huge punch bowl.

It didn't take long for our entrance to cause a stir. The pianist to our right eyed us suspiciously, and the music paused briefly as several guests giggled behind their hands or snubbed their noses at our grand entrance. We were definitely being noticed, and the reception wasn't well met. I felt like an outsider with all their eyes upon me, no doubt calculating why the Washer siblings were here.

I looked around for Amby, or even Anna, but when a familiar man approached from the left, my stomach dropped. Of course Damien was here, and he was strolling over as if he couldn't wait to make a fool of *the washer boy*. I needed a plan to stay composed. Instead, my eyes flew to Damien's clothes. He was actually wearing that flower-embroidered atrocity—the very jacket I thought Amby would pick out for me in the tailor shop as the worst item there.

I snorted as he reached me. "Nice suit."

Damien's haughty green eyes narrowed on me. "We have similar tastes, but not in attire, I see. So..." He raked an unpleasant glance over Millie. "Who invited you two? We didn't order a laundry pickup."

God damn fucker—

If he didn't leave me and mine alone, I was going to punch the flamboyant asshole right in his smart mouth. This party could use a few of Damien's teeth rolling around the polished floor.

"Zeth, Millie, you made it," came a familiar voice as Amby's comforting hand slipped into mine to still my fist. I couldn't be happier to see his beautiful head of curls and reassuring smile. "Don't mind Cooligan. His sense of fashion matches his inflated ego."

I laughed at Amby's dig at Damien. So did Damien, in that

polite way one does to avoid making a scene. When his eyes dropped to where Amby and I held hands, his gaze narrowed, and I savored his annoyance. He shot me one last look that said I wouldn't be seeing the last of him before wandering off to the drinks.

That's when Anna strolled over in an ivory evening dress with layered skirts that dripped wealth in her wake. There was a whole entourage behind her too.

She stepped up to Millie to give her a big hug. "I'm so pleased you could attend. You're absolutely ravishing, Millie, dear."

"And you look beautiful." Millie beamed at Anna, and their eyes met with a warm glow before Anna took her hand with a blush. They both stared at each other for a long moment, seemingly unaware of everyone else around them watching, and also whispering. But the wealthiest woman here didn't seem to care one bit about the growing interest happening around her.

When Amby's face contorted in confusion, I cleared my throat, and Anna broke her gaze to us.

Smiling, she pulled on Millie's hand and said, "Shall we seek refreshments before the reading starts?"

"Actually," Millie started, "I was hoping for a moment like this. Annabelle Winters... Will you give me the honor of a courting kiss?"

The gasp that rose from Anna's entourage was louder than the piano music. When Amby's hand squeezed mine, I looked over to see his eyes widen. I understood how surprised he felt, and he clearly wasn't the only one. Anna was blushing as the growing crowd surrounded us with a fair share of whispered gossip.

Several eyes darted my way as well. After all, they thought I was practically engaged to Anna just last week in the Chapel. Thankfully, a handful of people applauded Anna and Millie, encouraging them to kiss.

I released Amby's hand to touch the small of his back and leaned into his shoulder. "The girls grew close while we were distracted. I just learned that myself today, when I told Anna the truth. All of it. Well, not all of it. Enough."

"The truth?" Amby whispered. "You mean about... not wanting to court her?"

"Yes, and about us. She promised to keep our secret."

"Oh!" He looked at me excitedly. "Now it's feeling official for us, Zeth. It means a lot to me that you went to her about it. That must have been a nerve-wracking thing to do. Thank you."

"You're welcome, my darling." I'd been so scared of ruining things for us, so it was nice to have at least one thing work out.

The girl's courting kiss was sweet, just a peck on the lips, until Anna wrapped a hand around the back of Millie's neck to pull them together for an additional kiss. The whole thing was impromptu, but that was exactly how Millie would want it. Plus, her black ensemble and Anna's ivory dress made them quite the dapper couple.

So much for Anna's surprise dance with Millie. At least they glowed with happiness as they bowed to the cheering crowd. Then the piano started back up into an uppity tune that eased any leftover tension. Anna Winters had just declared herself taken by someone of much lower status than herself, but the way she looked at my sister showed me status meant nothing to her.

"It's been ages since I saw her so animated." A woman dressed in a sky blue dress regarded Amby with a friendly smile. Her silver hair shone amid the dim light.

"Miss Winters," Amby greeted her with a polite nod, then he turned to me and held out his hand. "I'd like you to meet Zeth Washer. Zeth, this is Anna's aunt, Sloane Winters."

I took her hand and bowed over it politely. "It's a pleasure."

"Anna told me about you and your adorable sister, but she didn't tell me how *charming* you are. Will you be reading tonight?"

I patted my jacket pocket to rattle the paper. "Yes, I prepare—"

"Ah, this must be Zeth Washer."

We all turned at the loud interruption of a woman in a burgundy gown that paired well with her glass of dark wine. She raked me up and down with prurient eyes that made me stand up straighter while she grinned into her glass. "I must say, you clean up well."

I wasn't sure whether to be flattered or insulted, so humor split the difference, "Thank you. I had a proper bath last night."

Sloane and the wine drinker laughed.

Amby gestured at her. "Zeth, this is Estella Washington, our host tonight."

"Excuse my brazenness," Estella said. "I've heard you've come into a prized inheritance. You must tell me more."

"Oh, I, um..."

"My apologies, Mrs. Washington," Amby cut in, rescuing me. "But I believe I see my sister waving us over at the food table. Perhaps we can talk more about it later?"

"Of course, darlings. Do indulge in some of our wonderful refreshments." Estella patted my arm before leaving with Sloane to mingle with others.

I blew out a breath and turned to Amby as we stepped toward the wall near the food table. "Thanks for that."

"Most of these folks are only interested in money talk. They can be intimidating."

Nodding, I entangled my fingers back between Amby's as we sandwiched our hands between our sides like we used to do when we stood together in school. The old thrill of keeping my relationship secret with the best boy in town surged through me.

He was so handsome tonight, but his suit was an odd mix of pale blue colors that didn't flatter his auburn hair. I was about to ask about it when I remembered he told me the other day that he let his little sister dress him. Just when he seemed too cute, he got cuter.

I wanted to kiss his upturned nose, but I resisted the temptation. I even released his hand. Like it or not, it was time to face the opposition head-on. "Well, shall we join your dad?"

"Yes," Amby started. "He's having cigars over there. So, you're going to try and sell the laundry to him?"

"Well, it's still the best option I see. The tax on it is hefty, and I shouldn't rely on Millie marrying Anna. Selling the laundry will give us what we need for a fresh start. I want you and me to have a secure future. A nice place to rest our heads together at the end of a hard day."

Amby's cheeks flushed a pretty pink. "You would... use the money to make sure we have a home?"

"With fluffy, white cats, preferably," I teased, making him chuckle. "Honestly, I'd be happy anywhere with you. A cabin, a house, or a large estate. Here in Everdeen, or in some far-off place. Maybe selling the laundry can be the foundation to fund our new dreams?"

"That's probably more than I deserve, but I would love to find a place for us to settle, wherever you want." His face glowed as he said, "You should get over to my father before he has his second cigar. After that, he usually excuses himself. If it's alright, I'll sit this one out. I don't want to distract you. Meet me on the balcony in a bit? I'll need a kiss to calm my nerves before I read."

When I inhaled deeply, liking his suggestion, Amby's cheek dimpled. He laughed before walking off to join Emiline, Hattie, and a few other women standing near the windows drinking wine. They welcomed him with arm squeezes, and it was delightful to witness Amby content with family and friends.

I walked to the opposite side of the parlor where Mr. Somerset was holding court, speaking to four men and a woman. As I approached the group, Amby's dad finished, "Frankly, it's out of hand."

"I agree," an older fellow said with animation to his busy brow. "Those hooligans drink and do nothing but cause trouble. Hopefully, someone stops them."

"They're nobodies," the woman clarified. "They're nothing but derivative gangsters who think they'll turn Everdeen's streets into theirs. If you pay them no mind, they'll fizzle out."

Cigar smoke hazed the air around them as the woman casually posed on the arm of the extravagant burgundy chair—how devastating for that piece of furniture. She looked familiar. Her short bob of blonde hair was a similar hue to Hattie's, and her intelligent, blue eyes reminded me of Amby's dad. That must be Marigold Somerset, Amby's eldest sister, all grown up. She used to roll her eyes at us as boys. Now she appeared to be a sophisticated woman with sharp angles to her face.

The man in the seat where she perched hooked an arm around her waist. His black hair was combed over nicely. He was about as tall as me and much better dressed, but with a mustache so similar to Amby's dad that it made me instantly suspicious of his goals.

As I stepped within their circle, all of their heads turned my way. For a long moment, the air stilled, and my nerves cranked up a notch. There was always danger and excitement when exploring new business opportunities. I felt that thrill now... and I wanted to run for my life. There was more at stake here than just making new contacts.

The man sitting with Marigold got to his feet and nodded at me. "Name's Jack, I'm Marigold's husband," he said, holding out his hand. "And you're Zeth Washer? My family used to visit your laundry once a week."

I thought he was being condescending until he broke into a friendly smile. Maybe this Jack fellow wasn't so bad.

I leaned forward quickly to shake his hand. "Sorry, I don't remember, but it's nice to meet you, Jack. Were you talking business? And mind if I join?"

"The more, the merrier. We could use some outside input for the new branch of Somerset and Sons Bank."

"The bank is expanding?"

"Yes, to Port Winchester," he answered happily, and I cringed at the mention of the City. "We're looking at a few potential areas and will be recruiting for employees not long after."

"Let the man sit, Jack," Mr. Somerset chuckled and set his cigar on a side table to stand. He offered me a firm handshake. "Good to see you again, Zeth. You're much taller than I remember."

My neck tensed at the reminder, and he saw it, giving me a deep chuckle and a friendly arm pat. I straightened. "Mr. Somerset, it's wonderful to see you again, sir. You're shorter than *I* remember."

I tossed that back at him just to see where Amby's dad sat with his humor. When his chortle grew heartier, and he placed a friendly arm around my back, I knew I was in. Some tension eased from my shoulders.

He pulled me toward the others and introduced them all, bankers themselves or shareholders with other companies. When he got to his daughter, he said, "And you remember Marigold. She and Jack work at the bank with me."

Marigold gave me a tight smile. Maybe she never forgave me for putting jelly in her shoes, at Amby's dare. If that was the case, her distaste was worth it because I'd made Amby laugh for days. She certainly wasn't laughing as she greeted me, "Good to see you again, Zeth."

"It's always a pleasure to see a Somerset," I told her, glancing over her head to find Amby's auburn curls leaning over the dessert table. He placed a slice of cake on a plate with his fingers and stopped to lick his thumb clean.

I'd be lying if I said that didn't distract me.

Marigold caught my eye, so I sent her a charming nod. Then I greeted the men with nods as I claimed an empty chair. Once everyone was seated, I leaned back, crossed my legs, and said, "So the new branch will be in the City? I just returned from... Port Winchester myself. Please tell me you're not investing in the City center. A bank there would be a risky investment."

One of the younger men glanced around the circle. He struck me as nervous as he pushed up his oversized glasses. "That's nonsense. The heart of the City is always booming with business," he said emphatically. "I am one of the bank's managers and visited last month to confirm."

Walter nodded once in agreement to Mr. Glasses before he looked my way, awaiting my reply.

Did his manager visit the wrong city? "I lived near the City center for over nine years and watched the area decline. It's a breeding ground for underground criminals. Speakeasies, guns, and rum. Is your goal to spoil the good name of Somerset and Sons?"

Maybe I spoke brazenly. As the men grumbled back and forth, Amby's dad leaned forward and took up another cigar from the table. He lit it and rubbed his mustache before looking at his daughter.

Marigold appeared to be silently turning my words over as well. She kept her cards close, and I could respect that. Her serious gaze was growing on me.

As the discussion grew, the man in the glasses gave a slight huff and turned to Mr. Somerset. "Walter, why would we go on his word? What are his credentials?"

"He's a family friend," Mr. Somerset said matter-of-factly. "I knew his parents for a long time. I trust his word."

Mr. Glasses drew in a sharp breath and got to his feet. "If you'll excuse me." He nodded and left our group, giving me an odd feeling. I didn't have time to ponder it as Amby's dad puffed on his cigar and regarded me.

"Is there anything else you've got up that sleeve of yours, Mr. Washer?"

I nodded, relieved to have passed some sort of test. Now was the time to press my advantage. "Actually, yes. I've recently acquired a nice retail space with rent potential, and I'm ready to sell. I'll give the bank first dibs."

Marigold gave a shrug I respected as mock disinterest. "Do you mean the laundry?"

I templed my hands across my chest. "Yes, quite a prime property on Main Street, seeing how the town is revitalizing. The cafe is a few fashionable shops away. My property will sell quickly once I put it on the market, but if you're interested..."

Marigold smoothed something off her dress. Jack cut his eyes to her, and when she met them, she straightened. "I pass it many times during the week. The outside needs repair."

She probably saw my chipped rainbow door. "A fair point. I've already begun investing in improvements. When I'm done, the building can be turned into something everyone needs." I lowered my leg and leaned my elbows on my knees, fixing Marigold with my eyes as I said, "Shall we schedule a visit for you to look at the property?"

"I'm sure we could work out a deal without having to do all of that," Mr. Somerset said, and he named a price that almost made me laugh.

Then I decided to go ahead and laugh.

Mr. Somerset joined in with a nod, clearly seeing I wouldn't bite. Yet, as we both silenced, he didn't up his offer.

"We won't be able to go higher than that," Marigold seconded. "Besides, why buy it, when we can wait for it to default to the bank?"

"Marigold," Jack snapped, but she only sighed.

"Listen, I know that's harsh, but it's the truth." She fixed me with her hard stare, and I tried not to sneer. "I mean this in the nicest way possible, Zeth, but the bank won't buy your property for any higher price knowing there are dues. My father is being generous by offering to take it off your hands for the price he gave. That way, when the bank invests and cleans it up, it'll go for a much higher price when it goes on the market. You asked to talk business, and this is how we conduct."

She was good at negotiating, I had to give her that. But the deal still sat sour in my stomach, so I tapped my fingers together to stall for time. The party went on around me—such bigwigs—chatting and schmoozing. And here I sat in cigar smoke, making decisions that would change my life. I would need a higher offer to afford a home for Amby and me if his dad didn't give us his blessing.

I glanced up at Marigold, ready to face the facts just as she did to me, "You're offering me scraps from the trough, but we both know my building's worth more. I'm a hard worker. I won't default. So when you decide to offer me the prized pig, you know where to find me. Until then, it's been a pleasure."

Mr. Somerset's approving "Ha" certainly affirmed my choice to stand strong.

Standing, I offered them all courteous farewells, because we did have a solid negotiation. Sometimes business meant waiting for the second party to change their minds.

When I held my hand out to Marigold for a respectful handshake, she accepted it with a nonchalant nod of her head.

Having gained some good ground with the Somerset family, it was now time to move on to more important business, kissing Amby.

25

Ambrose

The night was cool, with wispy clouds straying across the sky. I gazed up at the stars twinkling as the crickets chirped in the bushes below, taking comfort in their song. It was quiet out here on the Washingtons' balcony, a good place for me to clear my mind before preparing to recite my poem.

I had a book of my own to read from with a short haiku that struck me as perfect, so I tried to memorize the words over the course of the week. After spending so much time in a low state of mind over the past few years, I was ready to join the merriment again. Zeth was helping pull me from the wreckage of my own worries about my future, and I was so grateful that I wanted to sing about it.

I wondered what Zeth planned to recite. I looked so forward to hearing it, I was thrumming with excitement.

When footsteps clicked from behind, I turned, hoping Zeth had finally found me, but Damien Cooligan stood before me instead. His tall frame blocked all the light from inside.

I let out a sigh. "What do you want?"

Damien raised his chin. "Always so rude to me, aren't you? Especially lately. Is it Washer?" He pointed his thumb in the direction of the door. "Are you two fucking?"

"Now who's being rude?" I muttered, shaking my head.

"I'm just wondering if he knows..." Damien took in a deep breath before continuing, "Well, how much you'll break his heart after you're done with him, like you did to me."

My face soured. "Don't even try to pretend that there was anything between us. After you got too drunk and handsy with me that one time, that was it. And to top it off?" I dug my fists into my pockets to keep myself grounded and leaned forward, hating that devilish smile he gave me. "You're the most uninspiring person I've ever been around."

That wiped the grin clean off his face. Damien moved forward, causing me to step back, and glared down his nose at me. But I didn't yield. Instead, I stared right back at him.

"The problem with you, Amby, is you run your mouth too much. It could get you into trouble if you don't learn to tame it. Or perhaps you need *someone* to tame it for you." He reached up to snag my jaw, but I knocked his arm away and took another step back.

"Don't you dare touch me. You're out of line."

"No, *you* were out of line earlier when you insulted me in front of everyone. You and your trash boyfriend both need to understand that."

"The only thing I understand is that you're standing in my light. Kindly fuck off."

"You are such a cocky little bastard." Damien managed to grab my chin this time and pushed me against the railing. My back hit the stone roughly, and my book fell to the ground with a thump.

I tried to push him away, but Damien grabbed me harder and pressed me against the rail until I grunted in pain.

He leaned in close. "I'm not done talking to you, Somerset. I want you to know your place, and I want that washer boy to stay in his lane. He doesn't belong here with the rest of us."

"Damien Cooligan, remove your fucking fingers from Amby, or I'll break them one by one," came Zeth's calm but stern voice, cutting clear across the balcony.

When Damien released his grip on my chin, I was able to push him away. In the doorway, Zeth stood with a callous expression that told me he'd witnessed enough.

"Piece of shit," I muttered as I rubbed my sore jaw as Zeth strolled toward us, calm and reserved. He stopped next to me and leaned back against the railing, so close I felt his arm cross behind me for support.

"Well, Cooligan, are you going to kindly fuck off?" Zeth kept his eyes locked on Damien. "Looks like you're outnumbered, and no one gives a shit to back you up."

Damien scowled at Zeth as he straightened his jacket, then he nodded at me. "I see your guard dog follows wherever you go. Some things never change."

When Zeth growled, Damien glowered at him before stepping away and leaving the balcony.

As soon as we were alone, Zeth deflated and turned to me. "Holy shit, I almost tossed him over the fucking railing."

The idea of Zeth doing such a thing was entertaining, but this was my fight. "I should have just punched him."

"I don't know why you didn't. When I was rude, you smacked me upside my head and knocked my cap right off."

My lips twitched as I recalled Zeth's furious expression the day of the picnic, when he'd used his cap to smack me right back. He appeared worried about me now, so I took his hand and unfurled his stiff fingers to kiss them, longing for his protective touch.

"I'll take any punishment you deem necessary to show me how awful of a boy I've been." I bit my lip, hoping my teasing riled him in all the right ways.

"Mm," he inhaled deeply, his eyes twinkling. "If we weren't at this damn party, I'd smack your ass for saying that."

"But that's not a punishment if I want it, now is it?" I smiled crookedly, unable to help myself from imagining how Zeth's hard hand would feel on my ass right now, taking me as his.

He reached up as if he would grab my chin, but he only traced his fingers along my jaw. "Careful, Rosie, you're tempting fate."

Laughing, I leaned into his touch and hummed my pleasure against him, enjoying how his hand made me relax. I closed my eyes against his caress. Zeth gently kissed the side of my jaw where Damien had gripped me.

Opening my eyes, I found him smiling adoringly at me. "Thank you for having my back, for making me feel better."

"You don't have to thank me. I enjoy taking care of you. And when you get all worked up inside, I'll always do my best to make you feel better."

My arms wound around his waist. "Mm, such a good lover."

Zeth grinned from ear to ear. God, he was gorgeous.

Enamored, I moved in to kiss him, but I stepped on something. I looked down to find my book on the ground and bent to pick it up. "Oh... I brought this to recite a haiku tonight."

"What's a haiku?"

I handed him the book so he could flip through it. "It's a short poem, made up of only three lines and seventeen syllables."

His face puckered in confusion as he turned a page. "What are syllables?"

I tilted his chin up from the book until his eyes met mine. When I had his attention, I held up my hands, ready to put up a finger for every syllable I was about to say. "You. Are. One. Hand-some. Man."

"Oh, I like syllables," he teased, opening my jacket to tuck the little book into my inner pocket and wrapping his arms around my waist.

"I'm sure the reading is about to start," I whispered, but I pulled Zeth's arms tighter around me anyway.

"But Rosie," Zeth pouted, "I believe you asked for a kiss earlier to calm your nerves."

My hands found his, and I made his fingers dig into my hips. "You're right. You should kiss me. Right now." I tilted my head, waiting for him. I didn't need to ask twice. Zeth moved in close to run his tongue along my lower lip before he bit down gently, and I groaned my approval.

My hands found the lapels of his jacket to pull him against me until we both stumbled back, and my shoulders hit the side of the house, out of sight of the party. Zeth groaned against me. My hand clasped around the back of his neck while the other pulled against his jacket, showing him I wanted more as our lips crushed together.

Then something came over me, a desire that went beyond kissing or messing around. Something bright and hot burned deep within me, stinging me. I grabbed Zeth's arms and broke away from his lips to hold him closer. I wanted to feel his beating heart against mine, wanted the assurance that I was his and that he would never let me go.

When his strong arms surrounded me, the stress of Zeth trying to gain my father's approval hit me so hard, my stomach knotted. What if reciting love poems and talking business were all in vain? What if Father spouted off to Zeth that he wasn't able to give me children, and ran Zeth off?

I couldn't help but choke back tears. Shit, how I hated crying. Luckily, Zeth couldn't see me, and I held him tighter as I blinked away the moisture. I needed to focus on the moment.

Zeth was here with me right now. He was really here, in my arms, making me feel wanted. Someone who could *see* me, who was holding me. I was afraid of what our future held, but at least he would be with me through it, and that's all I needed.

"Hey now," Zeth whispered into my hair. His deep voice rumbled under my ear, sounding so calm and mature that I got goosebumps. "My kiss wasn't that bad, was it?"

I pulled away enough to look up at him. "Your kiss was perfect. So perfect, you have me torn up. I'm a mess, Zeth."

He frowned and reached up to straighten my glasses, and then my hair. "Alright, you can cry, but just try to spare my new ascot. I don't want it ruined." He smiled crookedly.

I laughed, thankful my stress hadn't fully surfaced. I didn't want to break down here. When I looked away, Zeth tilted my chin up, looking more serious now.

"Hey, you okay?"

Sniffing, I nodded. "Yes. Just thinking too much about my father."

"No need. I dazzled him with charm, as you advised."

"You did?" That gave me some hope. "Good. But... now I have jitters about reading."

Kissing my nose with a small peck, Zeth tapped the book in my pocket. "You'll do great, but are you prepared to hear my horrible poetry?"

"It'll be absolutely wonderful." I smoothed a wrinkle from his ascot. Smiling, I nodded at the door and slipped out of his hold to go back inside.

The room was loud with applause as we entered. Emiline and Hattie had just finished reading a poem together in the cleared area near the far wall and were leaving to sit among the others. Everyone else faced forward, so Zeth and I walked in without drawing any attention. We made a beeline to a few empty chairs in the last row, beside the dessert table.

"Ambrose Somerset," someone called out.

I glanced up as Damien pointed us out as we balanced awkwardly between sitting and standing. "Where have you been? And with Zeth Washer, no less. Hoping to get out of reading?"

Everyone swiveled in their seats, and my eyes darted around the room. We certainly appeared guilty arriving so late. I mostly felt bad for Zeth, but he didn't look bothered in the least.

I stood tall and smoothed my hand down my jacket. "Of course not. I was practicing my haiku." I stepped out from my seat to make my way to the front.

"That's a poem with seventeen syllables," Zeth explained to Damien, very boldly, and Damien's face soured.

Several chuckles rose from the crowd, including my father. Zeth remembered what I told him about being himself, and my father was amused. I just hoped I could get through this brief reading.

God, it was *hot* up here with everyone facing me. Most people said I was good at being social, and perhaps I was, but I was terrified of getting up in front of crowds like this. I didn't like all the attention. I didn't like looking at the sea of faces as they stared back. It made me nervous.

"Tonight, my reading will be a haiku," I told everyone. A

woman in the audience snorted with amusement, and I was glad the room was dim to hide my burning face.

I peered into Zeth's encouraging gaze before focusing on the dessert table. A white-frosted cake held my attention as I placed my hands behind my back. Then my eyes drifted back to Zeth's encouraging expression. I relaxed, and the words came to me, "A caged bird won't sing. He's meant to fly with spirit. The golden sky calls."

When I finished, glad I remembered it all, I bowed and took my seat beside Zeth as everyone clapped. The adoration in his golden eyes had my body warming. To calm myself, I whispered, "You should go next."

"I would be honored to follow you," he said much louder. "Especially after your last-minute *poetry* lesson eased my nerves."

I'd been the one wanting Zeth to calm me, but I'd unknowingly helped him too. "Anytime."

Zeth moved to the front of the room, where he pulled a sheet of folded paper out from his jacket pocket. He smoothed it out while nodding at my father, my sisters, Millie and Annabelle, and our host. The paper shook slightly, the only sign that Zeth was nervous, but he still managed to send a quick grin my way that promised surprises.

Clearing his throat, Zeth announced, "I wrote this poem, titled 'Half a Page of Happiness.'"

My cheeks glowed with pride already.

"I'll not pretend to be a poet," Zeth started adorably. Everyone leaned closer to catch his rich baritone. "I'd rather formulate love into a simple equation. In fact, words escape me while gazing into your daring eyes. And when we touch? I am lost."

A woman sighed, and I didn't blame her. Zeth put passion into his words. He swept his gaze over the audience and continued even softer, "Yet here I stand to open my heart through sentences and syllables scribbled onto imaginary paper. Stupid risks, held hands, and precious nights spent admiring the stars from your arms. Eventually, I couldn't read those reminders without ripping myself in two, so I crumpled it all into a tight ball and swallowed my pain until your light faded away. I was blind before sparks flew between us one last time. You unfolded my small scrap of happiness. You smoothed out the wrinkles in my soul with kind words and bold kisses. Now my page is ragged and worn, yet still I cling to it, because I never want to forget again how you light up my life. How you push me to be better than I am, and..."

Zeth met a few adoring gazes, including my own, as he confidently finished, "And how much I cherish what's always been mine."

I held my breath, my face so hot I was sure everyone was looking at me. But they weren't. Many of them eyed the others Zeth had looked at during the end of his poem. He did that to protect me. But Nathaniel Rios turned from a few chairs down and sent me a rakish grin, as if he suspected the truth. Part of me was thrilled to be Zeth's secret lover. The other part of me broke, because I wanted *all* of them to know I was his, and he was mine. *Always*, he'd said. I'd always been his.

Everyone clapped, including my father, and Sloane stood to applaud him. Zeth bowed to her before leaving the front to sit with me. I could hardly sit through the rest of the readings, as my mind constantly wandered to Zeth, and how his meaningful words were more than a poem. They were a declaration.

I lit up his life. That thought made my soul sing.

It was hard not to take his hand over the course of the next hour, but I sat close to him, and Zeth sent me plenty of small, playful glances. He even inconspicuously stretched his arm over the back of my chair so he could trace little circles onto the back of my shoulder. When the last person finished, I was honestly disappointed the night was ending.

Mrs. Washington got up to thank everyone for coming before they left. My father was in a hurry, as he grabbed his jacket and tried to gather Emiline and Hattie, but they were busy talking with others now. It would take him a few minutes to get my sisters out the door.

I moved around the crowd with Zeth to join Millie and Annabelle. A few others gathered around them as well.

"It was a lovely poem, Zeth, and Amby." Annabelle smiled. "Shall we all walk out together?"

I nodded, but the thought of going home to my cold bed made me ache. After bidding a few people goodbye, and flipping Damien off behind everyone's backs, we made our way to the foyer to gather our caps and outerwear before stepping outside.

"Oh, Millie-Bug, that hat completes your outfit," Annabelle said.

"Why thank you, Annabells."

I looked over swiftly to see them both walking arm in arm to her car, parked behind my father's carriage. They already had nicknames for one another? How long *had* they liked each other?

Zeth and I walked the line of vehicles along the street, and I inhaled the night air, glad it was dark. A few people lingered to talk, as they always did. When we reached our black carriage, my father and Emiline spoke with Annabelle and Millie for a moment while I moved closer to Zeth.

"Do you and Millie need a ride home?" I asked.

Zeth peered inside the little window on the door. "I'm not sure there's room for all of us."

"We could strap Hattie to the top of the carriage." I shrugged. "Or I could sit in your lap."

"Oh," Zeth chuckled low. "I like the second option, but what would your dad say?"

"Just talk business with him. He probably won't even notice I'm there." I meant it as a jest, but Zeth frowned.

"Zeth," came my father's bold voice as he turned to us. "It was good to see you. I enjoyed talking with you tonight."

"You too, sir, and I wanted to tell you..." Zeth leaned closer to my Father to share, "Watch out for your manager, Mr. Glasses. I've known enough betrayal to spot it when I see it."

"You mean Robert Wilson?" I asked Zeth with surprise. Quite the accusation. The prudish man hardly looked at me when I talked to him, but I never would have thought he'd betray the bank.

"Hmm," Father hummed as he rubbed his mustache. "I wouldn't mind hearing what else you have to say about my bank and Port Winchester. Perhaps we can speak over supper Sunday night at my home?"

My eyes widened, and I made a weird noise in my throat. When they looked curiously at me, I pretended to scratch something off my neck. My father was asking Zeth to dinner?

Father shook his head and turned back to Zeth. I rubbed my thumb and waited for his reply. Things were moving much faster than I thought they would, and now that anxious knot from earlier returned in my stomach, because it meant I was closer to telling my father the truth. About everything.

When Zeth eyed me, he seemed to sense my nervousness. His smile faltered briefly, but he turned to my father and answered assuredly, "I'd love to join your family for dinner."

26

Zeth

Millie took the longest time to fall asleep that night. She spent hours chatting about the reading and all the new people she met. And Anna. She definitely mentioned Anna a few too many times. I was glad those two made their relationship public. I just didn't need to hear the monologue. But overall, I was pleased by the turn of events. If all went well with her courtship, my sister was going to be one of the wealthiest people in Everdeen. Millie, the socialite. A trendsetter. Hopefully, she continued with her new passion for clothes and pursued her own career. Success looked good on Millie.

Once we said our good nights, I pretended to sleep while listening for her to snore. That's when I knew I could slip out of Mum's old bed without waking her. I did so carefully, sliding my bare feet to touch the cool wood of the floor. Millie sniffed, so I froze, but when she settled in again, I stood quietly in my nightshirt for a moment to watch her in the moonlight from the windows.

I made sure Millie was warm and cozy by tucking my own blankets against her back. I hoped it fooled her sleeping brain into thinking I slept beside her.

Grabbing my pants from the foot of the bed, I quickly slipped them on and tucked my night shirt into them, not bothering to change. My brown jacket went on top of that. I picked up my shoes to put on downstairs and left the laundry to start walking to the Somerset estate.

After watching Amby leave the reading, I couldn't stop thinking about him. So much happened at the party. Seeing Damien's hand on my boy's jaw tore me up inside. Jealousy played a small role in my feelings at first, but now I only worried over Amby's quick dismissal of the whole encounter. Not to mention that nervous tell of rubbing his thumb after his dad invited me to dinner. There was a darkness behind Amby's adorable glasses that shadowed his eyes from time to time, and that shadow covered him a few times tonight. I didn't like it. Not at all. I couldn't shake the feeling that we needed to talk.

A breeze chilled me, and I briskly rubbed my arms before burying my hands in my jacket pockets to hurry down Main Street. The shops were all closed, and I was the only one out besides a few peace officers patrolling the streets. I used to do this walk so often that I didn't even pay attention.

Quickly enough, I was passing the barn where Amby worked at his craft. I was in awe of the lovely furniture he made, although I should have guessed he would develop such skills. I always liked that artistic side of him. It warmed me that he was using the old barn where we had fun together. Did he think of me over the years while crafting his chairs? I certainly thought of him as I worked at the auction house and saw artwork and sculptures that he might appreciate.

Just beyond the wood siding of the barn, the Somerset house came into sight next, appearing asleep with dark windows all around. Such memories this place brought back. And not once did I step in through the front door. I either followed Amby directly into the kitchen to steal snacks or climbed the side of his house to sneak through his bedroom window.

If all went well at dinner, maybe that would mean no more sneaking in. Amby's dad was always the line that kept Amby and I from being together, and that line also kept me from dreaming as kids. Even when I proposed to Amby at sixteen, I never allowed myself to plan beyond his *yes*. And then he said *no*. Only recently did I see myself with kids, a family, and maybe one day a house and land. A legacy of our own. Maybe one day Amby and I would live here together.

Bypassing the front door for the last time, I followed the bushes to find the old wooden trellis against the side of the house. Far more ivy clung to the trellis now. I eyed my path upward with doubt, hands on my hips, and found Amby's room flickering with light.

Framed in the window, Amby sat on his window seat. He was still up. I knew he needed me. His wayward curls glowed, turning him into an angel, if heavenly creatures had naughty thoughts.

Cracking my knuckles in the quiet night, I nodded at the trellis and decided to try it out. What was the worst that could happen? I already impaled myself once and lived. I could climb a wall without doing anything worse. A broken bone, *pah*, that was nothing.

Using the diamond-shaped gaps as hand and foot holds, I started climbing. The first few feet went well. The next diamond brace I wedged my shoe into snapped. My foot slipped out with a crunch of wood, and my heart tried to leap out of my throat. Maybe a broken bone wasn't the best idea. When did I stop worrying about doctor bills?

Glancing up, I focused on the light from the window and told myself to keep going. Funny how these silly things were so much easier as a kid without cares. I kept climbing, not listening to the wood creaking under my heavier weight. Thankfully, the window ledge appeared, and I latched on to pull myself high enough to look through.

I tapped the glass softly, trying not to scare Amby out of his wits.

Try as I might, Amby still whipped around with surprise. When he saw me, he jumped back and fell out of the seat and onto the floor with a thump. I felt awful for scaring him like a ghost. But it was also kinda funny, especially when he popped back up with a hand placed over his heart. He stood for a good moment before he rushed to the window and swung the left side open.

I tried to look like I wasn't hanging on for dear life and gave him a dashing smile.

"Zeth, what the hell are you doing?" he asked. "Are you trying to make my heart stop?" I began to open my mouth, but he grabbed me by my jacket. "No, just get in here first, before you fucking fall."

Hearing my boy swear pleased me, like I taught him something. I grinned stupidly as he helped me stumble in. When my larger legs struggled to navigate through the frame, I chuckled at myself. Then Amby started laughing too. It was so nice to hear him laugh.

Even better was seeing him in only his skivvies. I ate up the sight of him. The definition in his upper arms was no doubt from his woodworking. His deliciously pale skin gleamed in the soft light as I followed the trail of crisp, dark-red hair along his firm stomach until it disappeared into the thin cotton waistline.

"Damn, Amby, you trying to kill me now?" I teased him as I straightened my jacket over my growing interest.

"I wasn't expecting company." Amby tilted his head and eyed me invitingly. "Or an incredibly charming man at my window."

I tugged off my cap, tossed it onto the window seat, and raked a hand through my hair to steady myself. Once I felt half-decent again, I faced Amby with a pretend pout, ignoring his undress. "Then why rush me in? I was going to recite a poem to you through the window in hopes of seducing you. You ruined my romantic moment."

"I think you put it perfectly tonight at the reading. Now, tell me, do I have *daring eyes*, as you said?" Amby looked me over with a good dose of sass. "You certainly are daring by coming here in the middle of the night."

"Seeing those gorgeous eyes of yours makes it worth the risk."

"Mm, you know how to make me swoon, don't you? Come here." Amby grabbed my jacket to pull me against him until his lips crushed against mine. I gladly leaned into him, but he was already breaking away from my mouth, ending our kiss far too quickly. He gave me one last peck at the corner of my mouth before tugging me by my hands toward his bed.

I chuckled at his excitement, taking in the rest of the furniture as we passed. A dresser next to his bed caught my eye. It was my mum's dresser, the old one Millie sold while I repaired the roof.

Stopping in my tracks, I tugged my hand free and crossed my arms with disappointment that everyone hid this from me. "You're the guy who bought it?"

"Please don't be upset..." Amby glanced over at it. "I enjoy restoring old pieces and felt the urge to buy it."

I didn't know what to make of this. My mum's furniture in Amby's room felt wrong, and right, and everything kinda jumbled. He knew I was selling it for money to eat on, so I mostly resented the pity move, but when I walked over, I could see that he really had sanded and restained it. It looked like a new piece of furniture, and when I pulled on the first drawer, it slid open smoothly.

Awe fell over me. Amby had put care into something I once owned, and that alone made me feel special. "You did a lovely job, Amby. I'm glad it was you who took it in and treated it with love. Mum would be pleased." I closed the drawer and rubbed the top as my eyes blurred.

He strolled up next to me and rubbed my back. "Thank you. I planned to regift it to you, so you have something that belonged to your mother. You deserve that. It can be ours one day, hopefully soon."

Ours, fuck if I didn't adore hearing him say that. I blinked away moisture and went to inspect the second drawer.

"Oh, wait—"

The drawer slid open to show a stack of envelopes inside, neatly tied with a pink ribbon. The top one was stamped in bold, red letters, *Return to Sender*. Hattie's statement about Amby writing to me suddenly felt true.

Shocked, my gaze flew to him. "Are these my letters?"

"No." Amby pulled the drawer right out of my hand and quickly shut it. "Wait, what do you mean *your* letters?"

"So, you wrote love letters to someone else, then?"

Amby looked almost offended at the question, then he shook his head as he opened the drawer again. Sighing, he took the stack of letters out and held them between us. "How did you know I wrote these?"

"Hattie told me at the tailor shop, after I tried on the jackets."

He blinked at me before looking at the top letter. I followed Amby's gaze to where his swirly print spelled out my name and an address in the City I didn't recognize. For a moment, I imagined what joy I would have felt receiving such a thing.

Taking the precious package from him, I thumbed *Port Winchester* and inhaled deeply. "Maybe this address was where we moved, but we bounced around four times in the first year, so these never reached me. I hope you didn't think I refused your letters."

"Oh... well, that makes sense."

I eyed him to judge his answer as he failed to hide a mix of emotions behind a faint smile. With the way his mind flew, Amby probably thought of every scenario under the sun.

Handing him the stack, I cupped his cheeks and kissed him with all the passion and care I would have poured into my correspondence to him for nine years, three months, and one day.

His soft moan hinted that he received my message, so I gave him a last peck before telling him, "Thank you, for trying to find me."

He nodded. "I regretted letting you go, so there are... a lot of confessions in these letters. Perhaps some... pining." His lips tugged up in the corner. "I wasn't sure if you received them. When Hattie's letter to Millie was sent back, I figured I got the address wrong."

He kept me in his heart for far longer than I deserved. "I didn't even write. I should have. I should have understood what you were going through." That gave me an idea. "How many letters are there?"

He smoothed his thumb along each one quickly. "Ten."

I tucked the letters back in the drawer and closed it. "Then I'll write you ten letters, and when I'm done spilling out all my regrets and secrets from those years, we can exchange. Deal?"

What a ridiculous idea, but I hoped he liked it.

"Hm." Amby put his hand to his mouth, thinking, then he cut his eyes up to me and said, "Fine. But remember, you'll be reading from the mind of a seventeen-year-old. He was very stupid."

I chuckled, relieved he wanted to trade letters. "That stupid kid was the best person I knew. He was caring, lively, and audacious. I can't imagine your letters are anything different."

Amby came close to my ear and whispered. "I wrote some rather sensual things too, things I knew I'd never send to you."

"Damn, can we read them now?" I joked, reaching for the drawer handle.

"No, I need your attention instead." He grabbed my wrists and pushed me back. His hands tucked into my jacket to slip it over my shoulders. Then he folded it over the back of a chair and looped his fingers into my belt with a grin. When he walked backwards to lead me to the bed, my mind raced. As much as I enjoyed our recent encounters, my main desire was to hold him tonight.

"I'm tired," Amby said, his eyes on my night shirt still tucked into my pants. "I just want you in my bed, by my side. Is that alright?"

"That's perfect." I chuckled in relief, glad we were both on the same page.

While Amby sat on the side of the bed, I scooted around him to the right side, claiming my old spot. He picked up his book and set it on the end table, along with his glasses. I tugged off my shoes and placed them neatly on the floor, enjoying how comfortable this moment felt. Then I shimmied out of my pants and folded them to sit on top of my shoes.

Lying on my side, I asked, "Were you doing some reading?"

His eyes shone as he settled on his side, facing me. "I couldn't sleep. But this is much better."

I agreed, but being this close, the faint bruise on Amby's jaw from Damien's abuse became visible. I intertwined Amby's fingers with mine and brought them up to hold between us. "I really did have a poem to recite through your window, but more importantly, I'm here to talk about the evening, if you want to."

"You mean, about Damien?"

"Yes, you told him to leave, and he forcibly didn't. I guess I'm still bothered by that."

He moved to lay on his back, still holding my hand as he stared at the ceiling. "Damien just thinks he and his family are above everyone else, so he has a bad habit of thinking no means yes."

My gut knotted, and I leaned up on my elbow, imagining far too much. "Has he ever hurt you?"

"No, but he's damn pushy, and he seems to have a particular disdain for you. When the distillery first opened, I went there every weekend and started talking to him there. He was interested in me, but only in messing around. One night, he got drunk, and I had to shove him off to get him to stop. When he passed out, I left. Haven't liked him since."

"We should have fucking punched him when we had the chance, then. No one touches my Rosie."

Amby gently jabbed my ribs with a grin, and I grabbed his hand to kiss it.

"And what about these other two men you've been with before? Did they treat you better?"

"One of them liked me enough to want to court me, but I declined."

"Because of your dad?"

He nodded. "Yes, but... It would have never worked out. He's married now, to a man *and* a woman."

"Hm, and number three?"

"Another jerk," Amby said. He stared at the ceiling, maybe picking his words carefully, so I shifted closer to lend him my support. He tilted his head against my shoulder and shrugged. "Some drifter I met at the pub. He came to town every few months, only interested in sex. The last time he was here, I turned him down, and he gave me a black eye. He'd even offered to *pay* me. Kind of pathetic, isn't it?" he teased.

"Oh, darling, no." Pained by his words, I moved to lay half over him. I wanted to block out whatever he saw as he spoke of that absolute prick who hurt him. When his eyes flew to me, they were filled with approval as they searched my face. Maybe he needed to know that I didn't take this personally, or that I still wanted to be with him, so I told him, "Nothing you've said changes a damn thing about how I feel about you." I grabbed his chin to hold his gaze. "You're mine."

His eyes lit up, and a tear escaped the corner to roll down the side of his face. I thumbed the wetness away as Amby reached up to smooth my hair behind my ear. I leaned into his touch, and he said, "I felt like a ghost wandering through Everdeen for so long, trying to find my heart with all these other men, even though I knew I couldn't be with any of them. Just like I thought I couldn't be with you."

His hand slid down to touch my chest. "But my heart was hundreds of miles away from me for so long. You're the only man who's visited me in my dreams, and I dreamed of your visits so often that I never stopped longing for you. I beat myself up for letting you go, for not reaching you with letters to fix *us*." Amby leaned up on his elbow and brushed his lips against mine. "You know me inside and out, Zeth. My fears, my strengths. That day I saw you at the picnic, it felt as if we'd never been apart. I'm safe with you. I'm wanted. Needed."

His words melted me inside and out, but it was the way he looked at me that held me captive. I pressed my lips against his to kiss him deeply, marveling at how beautifully he responded to my touch, as if our souls were connected.

When Amby shifted under me, asking for more, I moved to peck his nose, and Amby sighed with pleasure. His need for attention called to me. I gave his lovely freckles my adoration before worshiping the sharp edges of his jaw, a testament of his strength. I didn't know why he had trouble believing in himself. Maybe if I kissed him enough, he would see how wonderful he was. I would kiss him all night, if that's what he needed.

Amby's arms surrounded me, pulling me in tighter, his hand in my hair once again. "Zeth," he breathed, "Is this how you plan to kiss me goodnight all the time?"

"Yes," I muttered against him, content to spoil him. His angelic voice was like a smooth melody in my ears. After showing Amby some affection, we settled into the bed, and warmth surrounded me as he pulled the covers over us. He laid his head on my arm and curled against my side as I held him. My fingers skimmed the bare skin of his back under the blanket while his arm wrapped around my middle.

"Mm, I'm glad you came to see me tonight," he said, snuggling his face against my cotton shirt. "I've waited so long for you to come through my window again."

"So have I," I admitted. "Are you okay with your dad inviting me to dinner? You seemed anxious about that when we were leaving."

Amby was quiet for a moment. "I'm happy my father invited you. I just didn't know it would be so soon. Only a few days. I'm having a hard time grasping it all, because I'm terrified that no matter what, my father will reject our plan. He truly thinks our family is special enough that it must continue on through blood."

"I hate the idea of getting between you and your dad, but if he can't accept our courtship because of the illusion he's built in his own mind, then that's his fucking problem. We'll find a way to move on."

Amby squeezed me affectionately.

His silence tugged at my heart because we both had shit to work through, but we were doing that now, together. I wrapped my hand into his curls, stroking his soft hair to tell him without words that I had faith we could figure this all out.

"Unfortunately, we can't count on selling the laundry yet. Your dad's offer was too low."

"Maybe it's a sign for us to stay there," Amby said sweetly.

I liked his point of view, seeing the positive. Maybe the low offer wasn't bad luck, or life trying to ruin me. Maybe it was a nudge toward a new direction, one I failed to see without Amby's help. "What a nice thought."

Amby's reply was a soft snore. I leaned away carefully until I could see his lashes already fluttering in slumber. He'd fallen asleep so fast. Damn, if he wasn't the most precious thing I'd ever seen in my life. I couldn't help but give him one last gentle kiss, this time against his forehead, before settling down myself.

27

Ambrose

Thunder boomed outside, interrupting me from my work. I stared at the bank's white ceiling while rain pounded on the roof. This storm moved in overnight, and it had been raining since early this morning. I felt bad that Zeth left my room right as the bottom fell out. He was no doubt soaked when he got home.

I'd rather think about Zeth in wet clothes, but I glanced back at my invoice instead. It was the thirtieth one I'd written so far today, and the headache pounding in my head wasn't helping the work go by faster. I wished I were in my bed with a good book and Zeth curled up beside me.

I was still training for a higher position in the mornings, but in the afternoons, I continued my quiet desk work before delivering mail. Soon, I would have to face my father and tell him Zeth and I were courting. I also would have to tell him I didn't want to own the bank. My uncertainty about how he would respond to either of those terrified me.

One step at a time, Amby.

As I began another invoice, I lifted my head to see Selena Peters in front of me doing the same thing I was, but more efficiently. If only Zeth could work here too. He'd be good at handling loans and estate sales. I could ask my father if there was an opening for Zeth, but I didn't want to push my luck with him.

"You're adding too many zeros."

I nearly jumped out of my skin as I turned in my seat. Marigold stood there in a brown dress with a raised eyebrow. Looking back at the invoice, I realized I had written out one thousand and fifty instead of one hundred and fifty. I crumpled it up and started over.

"Ambrose Heath Somerset," Marigold huffed and crossed her arms. "What is it with you lately? Mistakes happen, but you've made many of them this week."

I glanced at Selena. She paused at her desk and looked slightly to the side, as if curious about our conversation, before turning back to her desk again.

Gritting my teeth, I made sure my numbers were accurate as I answered Marigold, "I've been distracted with all the events we've had lately."

She leaned down to whisper, "Distracted with events, or with Zeth?"

My eyes darted around the small area, but no one nearby reacted, so I got to my feet to stand beside Marigold. She stood slightly taller than me in her heels. "I'm done with these, but I will go over them in your office before sending them to the mailroom."

"You didn't answer my question."

"*Not* here." My voice was firm, and she regarded me with surprise. I didn't want details of my life filtering out to whoever was within earshot. Zeth, Annabelle, Millie, and I all happened to be the subject of gossip lately. First with what happened at Chapel and now with the salon. I'd already endured enough stares this morning. It would only be a matter of time before my father found out about us.

Marigold gave me a stern look before she nodded to follow her. As soon as I stepped inside her small office and the door closed, she didn't spare a moment to rip into me, "Father is putting faith in *you* to run this bank one day, and you've proved you can't handle anything beyond simple tasks and delivering mail. And Henry told me you're putting little effort into training."

I placed my hands in my pockets. "I'm not cut out for managing the bank. You know it, I know it."

"You *will* inherit this bank one day, whether you like it or not, and you need to show everyone here that you will carry on the Somerset and Sons legacy. The way things are going, you're more likely to sell it to the first person who offers to buy it."

"And you're right!"

Marigold blinked at me, clearly not expecting such an outburst. But I was tired. Of her unrealistic expectations. Of Father's plans for me. I always did as they said and tried to do better. I would never be better. It was time to tell her how I really felt about this whole thing.

Taking in a deep breath, I fixed my gaze on her and admitted, "I don't want Somerset and Sons. I never have. You're right, if I acquire it, I would sell it. I'm not a banker. I can't own something this big." I took her hands in mine. "But I know *you* can."

"Me?" Marigold gave a little laugh, her face faltering slightly. "You forget I'm not the son, Amby."

"You deserve this bank more than I do."

This struck her speechless for a moment. She pulled her hands away to straighten her skirt. "As much as I want to inherit this bank one day, I don't think it will happen. Father is very bent on carrying on Somerset... and *Sons*."

She was in a similar predicament as mine. She *wanted* this bank, yet she couldn't have it because it wasn't in our father's plans. How did I never see her side?

"Marigold, Father knows you're the finest, hardest worker he has. You should tell him you want to be the manager."

"And what makes you think he'd listen to me?" She crossed her arms. "I've tried. Father ignores whatever he doesn't want to deal with. That's as far as I've gotten with him."

"If you could just—"

"I can't do this right now. Go." Marigold opened the door and gestured with her hand for me to leave.

But I wasn't done yet.

My sister was closing her office door when I spun on my heel and flung my hand out to stop it. "Wait. I know we haven't always gotten along, but I mean it when I say you deserve this bank. More than I ever could. Despite being an awful brother to you in the past... I do look up to you. I want you to know that."

Marigold raised her chin, trying to stay reserved, and I swear her eyes watered. "Thank you, Amby. Now, excuse me..."

It was best to let her be, so I removed my hand to let her gently close the door.

I wasn't sure if Marigold considered my words or not. Regardless, at least I had said them, and that made me feel a little better. Leaving her door, I collected the invoices on my desk to take to the mailroom. Once I dropped them off, I came back to the main room and stopped in my tracks when a familiar, handsome man who woke up in my bed just this morning walked into the bank.

Zeth and Millie approached a desk with Charles, who handled requests to sell land or homes. Were they here to sell the laundry? Zeth did say my father gave a low offer. Was he going to take it anyway?

Fuck, this headache was getting worse. I put a hand to my head and shuffled away to my desk, not wanting to disturb Zeth and Millie. I'd wait until they were done doing whatever it was they came here for.

My hands began shaking for some reason, and I was so distracted that I ran right into Selena's desk. She gasped at me in surprise.

"Sorry," I said, picking up a few papers that had fallen before moving to my chair. By now, I was garnering attention from a few of my colleagues. Their amused faces glanced from me to Zeth and Millie. I heard Robert Wilson mutter low to someone about Annabelle Winters courting the youngest Washer sibling with a laugh. Then he looked in my direction and narrowed his eyes.

Shit.

I propped my elbow up on the desk and covered my eyes so I couldn't see anyone else staring at me as I started working on... There was nothing else on my desk to work on. Instead, I took an envelope and scribbled out a random name and address with my pen, looking as if I was working.

I did this for several minutes, until I finally chanced a look up.

Marigold stood next to Zeth now, who had gotten up from his seat. He looked pissed, and from the disgruntled expression on Charles' face, something was happening. I wondered for a moment if I should go over, but then my father stepped up to lead Zeth and Millie to his office.

I exhaled slowly. Whatever had happened, my father would fix it, I hoped. But that didn't stop my head from pounding, this time with questions.

Zeth told me he wanted to sell the laundry for us to have a place to settle, but how much money would the laundry bring? It wasn't Zeth that needed to try and find us a home. If anything, *I* should be the one supporting us. If Zeth sold the laundry, where would he live until he found a new home? And if no one hired him for work, would he leave Everdeen to find work elsewhere? He told me he'd think about living at the laundry, but he seemed to have made up his mind about selling. Who was I to stop that?

"Hello, dear brother."

I jolted in my seat and looked up to see Emiline standing before me, holding a basket. How many sisters were going to show up unannounced today?

"Em." I nodded at her. My eyes cut over to see my father's office door close, right as a low rumble of thunder vibrated my desk. "Did you walk over in this storm?"

"Anna gave me a ride over in her car. She was at the shop for a Founders Day dress. Have you eaten yet?"

The last thing I wanted right now was food as so many thoughts swirled around me.

"No, I'm... just finishing up here." I set aside the envelope with ten addresses on it and did my best to smile at her. "Did you bring lunch for me?"

"I did. Arthur made a chicken and rice casserole. We had enough left over, I thought I'd bring you some."

"So, he's making casseroles for you now?"

A blush tinted Emiline's cheeks. "He's been doing a lot of

things for me lately. He actually... asked me to attend the theatre with him on Sunday. There's a play we both like."

"Really?"

Emiline nudged me and teased, "Only as friends."

"I know that's not true. Arthur's liked you for a long time, so when he kisses you at the end of your night out together, do let me know how it went." Well, there went my oath to Arthur, but in this case, it felt right to let it be known. No need to let Emiline go the whole night thinking Arthur is just being friendly.

Maybe I made the right choice, because Emiline's dreamy eyes lit up. Arthur was a good man and a good friend. If Emiline wanted to officially court him, I'd add my blessing on top of our father's, as I knew he adored Arthur and his business.

"How are you and Zeth doing?" Emiline asked. "You both made quite the spectacle last night. A few people are suspicious of you courting him."

"A correct assumption..." I stood up to lean into her side and whispered, "Father invited him to supper on Sunday, and I'm anxious about it. No doubt I should tell him about what's going on then."

"Oh, the same night as the theatre... Is that why you hardly talked on the ride home last night?" When I nodded, she continued, "This is good for you both, Amby. I just hate that I can't be there. Do you want me to stay instead? I don't mind."

I laughed, seeing how she was willing to do it but also aware of her disappointment in skipping a night out with Arthur. "No, I want you and Arthur to go out. Your little brother can handle himself, I promise. Besides, I'll have Zeth. And... Hattie." When Emiline giggled, I nodded at the basket. "Thank you for bringing this over. Tell Arthur thank you as well."

"Of course. I have to get back to the shop. Have a good day, Amby, and don't let the talk around town get to you." Emiline kissed my cheek before she whisked away to speak with Marigold.

I looked at the basket and pulled back the cloth to see a dish, along with some wrapped bread and grapes. Suddenly, I knew who I wanted to share the meal with.

* * *

Not long after Zeth and Millie left the bank, I did too, carrying the basket of food in the rain. When I arrived at the laundry, my back and hair were wet. Damn me for forgetting my cap and umbrella in my rush. I tried protecting the basket of food by hunching over it and knocked on the door. I stared at the colorful chipped paint as I waited. It really did look like a mess of rainbows. I loved it.

When Zeth opened the door, his face glowed as he waved me quickly in. He closed the door behind me and instructed, "Wait here," before leaving me in the middle of the empty floor while I listened to his quick steps up the side stairwell. He spoke to someone, and a moment later, his footsteps descended.

"Sorry about that. Todd just arrived as well. I told him I'm taking a break already," Zeth chuckled as he rounded the long counter with a faded towel. "Here, let's get you dry."

"Thank you." I took off my jacket to hang it on the hooks next to the door. Water dripped from my hair along my neck, making me shiver, so I placed the towel around my shoulders. I ran my eyes over Zeth, noticing the bits of white in his messy hair and on his worn-out clothes. When the sound of a hammer echoed from upstairs, I said, "Todd's been helping you out a lot. That's good."

"Aye, the man has some odd notion that I helped his little brother growing up, so he's paying me back now. Maybe Arthur needed friends as much as I did at that age, or he needed someone to take him down a peg. Either way, I'm glad they're both my friends now. I'm lucky too, because Todd had free time due to the storm. He and his crew are building the roofs for those houses across the river, and..." Zeth paused mid-sentence and smiled sheepishly. "Enough about me. What brings you and your handsome face to my doorstep?"

"I'm glad you're making friends." I laughed softly and held up the basket. "Em brought this casserole. I wanted to share it with you, unless you've already eaten supper."

"I'm hungry for something, and it's not in that basket," Zeth assured me with roaming eyes and a deep chuckle. "But since we're not alone, food will do."

"Don't you hate when that happens?" I teased, and searched for a place to eat, finding nothing but the long counter that once held a register. "Should we eat here?"

"Sure." Zeth followed me over and sniffed the basket with exaggerated sounds while I set it down. "Smells good. Roast beef with lobster?"

"I think you need your nose checked." I grabbed his nose and tugged it gently. "It's chicken and rice casserole. Arthur made it." I nudged him. "For my sister."

"Oh, is it like that? Arthur and Emiline?"

"He's liked her since our early school days, but she's just now noticing him in that way."

Zeth nodded as he reached into the basket and brought up the vine of grapes. He popped one into his mouth before muttering, "My thanks to Arthur. I hope you don't mind skipping the fancy setup. We don't have plates. Or utensils. Or chairs."

"That's alright, I can improvise." I hopped up onto the counter to sit and looked into the basket. "Oh, lucky us." I pulled out a fork and held it out, but Zeth shook his head and ate another grape, so I tore off a chunk of bread to start on myself.

As we ate, my thoughts drifted to earlier. "I saw you at the bank today. I would have said hello, but I didn't want to interrupt."

"Hmm," Zeth grumbled around his mouthful of fruit. He turned to lean his back against the counter edge, and his mood shifted as if a dark cloud hung over his head.

"Did something happen?"

"Well, there's something I tried not to worry about, but you should know.... A large property tax is hanging over this building, and the bank can claim the laundry if I stop making payments."

"Oh..." My stomach dropped.

"So, when Mils and I went to open an account today, as people do when they move to a town, we were instantly denied. The clerk said we need to pay off our bill first. Fucking insult. My family goes back generations too."

I paused, chewing my bread slowly. "So, what happened?"

"I told the clerk that I was a good investment. That he was missing out, and then your big sis came over. And your dad. It was ridiculous, but we eventually opened a fucking account with Somerset and Sons."

"You did?"

"Of course, who wouldn't want me as a customer?" Zeth winked, but there was still frustration behind his smirk as he leaned closer. "Now I just need something to deposit. Maybe you can give me a donation. Do banks accept kisses?"

I clicked my tongue. "Sorry, they don't, but I'm sure we can set up a private meeting to arrange such a thing." I kissed his cheek anyway, and he grinned before eating another grape.

He easily let go of his worries, but what he said about the large bill was troubling.

"I can help you pay the tax bill," I said. "I wouldn't mind. Just say the word, and I'm there for you."

Zeth's brow popped up, then creased in thought. The air stilled between us for a moment until he looked at me. "I appreciate that, but your dad may suspect we're courting if you help me so generously. That does make me wonder, though... How rich are you, without your dad? If I may ask."

The question caught me off guard, but I answered truthfully, "I have some money saved up. Just not enough to buy us a home. I'm sorry to say I've been dependent on my father. He makes me work for my money and earn what he wants to be mine one day."

"I know you're a hard worker, darling."

I felt the sincerity in Zeth's words, but I felt no better about this unpaid bill sitting on his shoulders. Water trickled down my neck, so I set the rest of the bread back in the basket to smooth a hand over my wet hair, shaking a few water droplets out. My father and Marigold had helped Zeth open an account, which at least made me hopeful for Sunday's dinner. Gaining my father's blessing would guarantee us a place to live after we marry, and maybe my father would give him more time to pay the property tax. Perhaps Zeth could get some kind of use out of the laundry if it didn't sell. Being on Main Street, he could turn it into anything.

I only hoped everything went well with my father. Since people were beginning to gossip, it would be good for me to tell him on Sunday that Zeth and I were courting. If only I didn't have such anxiety over it...

When I looked over to see Zeth watching me, as if trying to figure out my thoughts, I smiled at him. His lips spread into a devious grin before he snagged the towel from my shoulders. He flipped it up to cover my hair, and the room disappeared as he rubbed my head vigorously, as my mother used to do when she helped me bathe.

"Zeth!" I grabbed his arms to stop him, and he let the towel go to rest on my head like a shepherd. "This rain, plus doing that, makes my hair do very odd things."

"I like those things. I like your hair a lot, especially when it's a fiery riot, like you," Zeth chuckled, his golden-brown eyes lighting up with delight as they roamed over my messy curls poking out from the towel. He took a deep breath to ask, "So where's this casserole you mentioned?"

"Oh, right." I brought the dish out from the basket and set it in front of him. Then I pulled off the top to reveal plenty of chicken and rice.

But he handed me the dish right back. "Eat, you're the one sharing this."

"Perhaps we can take turns?" I said, as I took up the one fork and dug into the casserole for a bite. It tasted amazing; the rice was buttery, and the chicken had some sort of robust seasoning in it that made it incredibly flavorful. I took another big bite and chewed before scooping up one for Zeth. His gaze dropped to the forkful of food before he leaned forward and took the bite into his mouth.

Several more bites from him were enough to satisfy me. I was glad to see him eating. "How are you feeling about Sunday?" I asked.

Zeth chewed and wiped his mouth with the back of his sleeve before answering, "I'm nervous to eat dinner with your family, but also looking forward to being a part of it too. And I'm really excited to use your front door. This morning, I thought I might die as I slipped on your trellis in the rain. But I'm not complaining, if a window means holding you in the morning."

"Mm, I slept so well last night. I think you spoiled me. Especially playing with my hair."

"Spoiling you brings me pleasure too. I can barely keep myself from touching you now."

"Well, what's stopping you?"

Zeth straightened and gave me a fervent stare. He pushed the basket and dish aside to hop up onto the counter to sit next to me, and patted his lap. "Come here, darling, and rest your head a moment."

I bit my lip as I shifted on the counter and moved my legs up. Lying back, I rested my head in Zeth's lap, over the towel to keep him dry. My face heated as I realized how we would look if anyone peered into the laundry's window, but I didn't care as I stared up at him. "My head has been aching all day. You can massage it if you want. I like that."

Zeth gazed at me softly and ran his hand through my hair, his fingers lightly massaging my scalp. He had such a caring touch. It made my skin tingle with good sensations that trailed down my neck and into my back. It was so calming, my body relaxed, and I closed my eyes.

"I'm also nervous about dinner with my father," I muttered.

"Don't worry, I won't use the soup spoon for my pudding," Zeth teased.

I tried to smile, but I let out a ragged sigh instead. "I'm afraid of confronting him. But I want to tell him on Sunday about us. I want him to know—I want everyone to officially know—that we're courting. I don't want to wait any longer. The thought of waiting makes me feel sick."

Opening my eyes, I found Zeth watching me carefully, his fingers soothing as they smoothed back my hair.

"You're strong, Rosie." Zeth traced my jaw with his thumb. "You have the strength right here. Honoring your father's wishes all these years took more strength than you give yourself credit for. I have faith in you. And now, you have me. I'm honored to stand by your side as we tell him we want to start courting, officially."

I clutched his hand against my face. Zeth made me feel worlds better, but I was still terrified of things going wrong. "And if he doesn't bless us?"

"If the worst happens, we'll figure it out. I just..." Zeth shrugged. "I think your dad loves you enough to approve."

"What...?" I sat up and stared hard at the floor. "My father hasn't ever told me he loves me. Come to think of it, I'm not sure he's told my sisters either."

"And he dotes on them, you can't deny that. They get whatever they want. He doesn't stop them from working or roaming around town at their own whims. He even lets Marigold negotiate for him. He loves them. So why do you think he doesn't love you too? He allows you the same freedom, in that sense."

I nodded, but I still couldn't shake my nerves. My father never talked to me about my troubles, or even his own. Then again, I never went to him to talk about those things either. There was no telling how he would react.

Jumping off the counter, I sighed. "I just... wish I had some sort of reassurance, that no matter what happens, things will work out for you and me."

Zeth stared at me for the longest moment, which made me feel hopeless, until his face brightened. "Ah, I know just the thing to show you. Come with me." He hopped down to take my hand and pulled me swiftly around the counter to the back workroom.

As I stepped inside, my eyes roamed the room, taking in the water pump and copper laundry tub with some socks and a shirt draped over its rim to dry. A sloping tin roof above us extended out to create a long workspace. Steady rain fell on the roof, the constant pitter-patter of drops on metal echoing wonderfully. I could imagine myself going to sleep here listening to it, especially if Zeth massaged my head again.

Zeth led me toward a far corner of the room, and I followed him to the back wall of windows. I wondered what could possibly be back here, especially as he pointed into a far corner.

I walked around him to see what he was trying to show me and faced a large corner beam that had darkened with age. There were several marks in the wood, carvings with Zeth's name or tallys or symbols.

Zeth came up behind me and placed his gentle hand on my shoulder. "This is where I was sent to cool off when my emotions got out of hand as a kid. I needed to cool off a lot. But that's not why we're here. Do you see it?"

"Hm," I hummed as I looked back at the carvings. "I see a lot of equations. I know how much you love those. You were an artist in your own way."

"You're the artist, darling. But no, look closer to the floor."

I licked my lips and squatted. From the light of the window, I was able to make out two big letters with a plus symbol between them.

"A plus Z?" Deciding to tease him, I playfully asked, "Annabelle plus Zeth?"

When he didn't say anything, I glanced over my shoulder to find him glaring at me with mock annoyance. Laughing, I got to my feet and grabbed his waist.

"Who's the lucky boy, my love?" I asked softly.

Zeth shook his head with a grin. "*Amby* plus Zeth. You and me. We add up." He tugged me close. "We make sense, like one of these math equations. I was around fourteen when I carved that, a year before you dared me to kiss you, and even then, I knew the truth. We belong together."

My heart swelled, enamored by his words and enchanted by the engraved letters. I imagined a young Zeth sitting here stewing in his anger while carving the 'A' of the one boy in his life who made him feel better.

Our bond was deeper than friendship, and even love. From the moment I'd met Zeth at the schoolhouse, an imaginary ribbon of fate had tied us both together, and with each passing year, more ribbons joined the main one to make up our memories and experiences. And while this primary ribbon had thinned somewhat from the years we were apart, it could never be severed.

"We're kindred spirits," I finally said, moving closer to him. "That's... how I feel when I'm with you. It hurts to be apart from you. Even when we were just friends, I hated us being separated."

"That's how I've always felt too. Our bond is strong, Amby," Zeth replied with a soft sigh. His eyes sparked with desire as he reached up to thumb my bottom lip. "It's why, no matter how bitter I was at you when I came back, I couldn't deny how much I cared about you." His fingers caressed my jaw and slid to the back of my head to my hair. When his fingers curled gently in my tendrils, I took in a sharp breath, the sensation jolting me in all the right ways.

Zeth pressed his lips under my chin and whispered, "My sweet darling, if you ever need assurance, I'll give it to you, be it by words or touch or silent companionship. I'll give you anything you need."

I smiled warmly at him, believing every word. And Zeth pulled me in for a rough but reassuring kiss that promised his acceptance. This sign that we were meant to be together made me feel much better. It reassured me that, no matter what happened, I would have Zeth.

We could marry, become parents someday, have cats and a tree swing. I could see myself working on furniture for our home, perhaps even trying to cook with Zeth for the first time in my life. Truly experience things with him, things I never thought I'd do before.

I was suddenly looking forward to Sunday dinner.

28

Zeth

When the Somerset estate came into sight Sunday night, I took in the clean white siding and spotless windows all glowing orange with the setting sun. Everything hinged on tonight. We needed to secure Amby's relations with his family. My handsome, artistic, smart boy was being held down by his dad and all of the man's expectations. Despite Amby's wealth and privilege, he lived in the same cage as a poor boy like me.

I would do anything to free us and make our dreams come true. Anything. And where there's a Washer, there's a way. *Thanks Mum.*

Instinct had me walking off to the garden path, but I veered back to leap up the front porch steps, taking them two at a time with excitement. It was hard to believe that tonight was the night I would finally tell Mr. Somerset that I wanted a future with his son.

"Zeth, hey," came from the shadows of the porch, and I jumped out of my skin. How was I so lost in dreams that I didn't see the very object of my obsessions standing against a pillar?

Amby's relaxed, long-sleeved shirt, cotton vest, and casual pants were unexpected for dinner, but the outfit fit him. It was something he'd wear to work in the barn, which was probably exactly what he wanted to do. I preferred this casual look on him to his usual fancy suits for the bank.

I made my way over to quickly peck his cheek. "Hey there handsome, you been waiting for me long?"

"Not too long. Only about an hour or so." Amby poked my ribs lightly in jest, making me step back. I didn't like how Amby put space between us, but I understood. His dad might be watching, and we needed to wait.

I clasped my hands behind my back and asked, "What did you do yesterday? Go to Chapel?"

"No, I worked in the barn most of the morning. And what about you? Did you get some more things done around the laundry?"

"Yes, I chipped paint off the door. It's almost respectable looking again."

"Oh, I loved the colorful door," Amby sulked.

I refrained from kissing those pouty lips. "Then you can help me repaint it. Any color you wish."

"Yeah? Maybe pink, then."

"That will certainly attract attention to the building," I chuckled, rather liking Amby's idea. "Speaking of doors, will you acquaint me with yours?"

"With pleasure. Have you truly never been through it?" Amby made for the door and opened it, then put his hand out for me to go first.

When I walked in, Hattie descended the main stairs in a lilac evening gown that appeared far fancier than dinner at home deserved. It certainly outdid my brown jacket and old cap.

"Zeth!" she cried, coming right toward me and hugging me. I felt like an honored guest and family all at the same time. I hugged her back as I would my own sister, but without the tight squeeze.

"Hattie, let the man get his jacket off first," Amby chided.

"Oh, I'm sure he doesn't mind." She pulled away. "I'm happy to see you back in our home. I've missed you being here with us."

"You just miss me pushing you in the swing until your toes hit the clouds. Do you ever sit in that now?"

She rolled her eyes. "Well, I would if Father hadn't taken it down for being *unsafe*."

"It was rickety," I admitted. "I found that rope in a muddy back alley, and the seat came from an old carriage that got junked. Your dad was right to remove it."

"Oh, pish posh." Hattie waved me off, giggling as she made her way into the parlor.

When I offered my arm to Amby, he hesitated. "Let's take this first part slow, is that alright?"

"Of course. I'm sorry."

"It's me, Zeth. I just need to relax. Here, give me your jacket and I'll hang it up. And your cap."

I did as he asked, trying to fight off a rising nervousness before it got the better of me. Standing in the foyer of Amby's house in my shirt, vest, and ascot seemed so informal. Suddenly, dinner with the Somersets felt real.

And why was it so quiet? I expected twenty servants, as Anna had in her place, but the main entrance was empty. It displayed less wealth too. The decor was traditional and simple. The rug under my shoes was of quality, but not new. Maybe the Somersets put their money into investments and property instead of vases and matching tea sets.

When Amby returned, I quipped, "What, no butler to take my jacket?"

"Our housemaid usually does that, but you're a special guest tonight. I wanted to serve you myself." When he bowed gracefully, an urge came over me to push him against the wall and have my way with him. Seeing my wanton stare, Amby stifled a laugh as he said, "Besides, Father is somewhat frugal."

"The best businessmen and women usually are," I agreed, eyeing him with a sultry gaze before clearing my throat. "It's better to put something to good use and make it grow than ignore it for safekeeping."

"A fine statement," came Mr. Somerset's voice from the doorway of the parlor. He regarded me with a nod of his head. "I'd love to hear more. Shall we have an aperitif?"

I barely knew the man meant a drink. Shaking his offered hand, I pushed back a million polite replies and decided on the truth. "No, thank you, Mr. Somerset. As Amby can tell you, I don't hold my liquor very well. Dinner will be over before we start."

"Oh, I know too well," Amby said. "I believe Arthur was responsible for getting you drunk once."

Smiling, I said, "I remember. He stole a jug of moonshine from his dad and met us behind the Everdeen Oak. And he got so drunk, we couldn't walk him home."

"Yes, and we didn't know what to do being drunk ourselves, so we just covered him with leaves and left." Amby's cheeks dimpled adorably as we indulged in a laugh, and he put a hand on my shoulder. "I can't believe we left him there all night. He was like a walking corpse the next day."

I snorted at how wrong that was, now that I looked back. We teased Arthur for weeks, and he loved it. Maybe he did need some friends back then. Probably better ones, but we were only teens.

When I caught Amby's dad's raised brow, I straightened and said seriously, "But I've certainly moved on from such shenanigans, Mr. Somerset. I'm sure Amby has too."

Mr. Somerset chuckled and waved us off. "You two got into plenty of trouble, some of which I did not know of, clearly. But I recall doing the same things when I was younger. And Zeth, call me Walter."

"Walter," I repeated, rather stunned. When I shot a sideways look at Amby, he lifted his eyebrows in surprise. I didn't expect to be on a first-name basis with his dad already. We didn't even leave the front hall yet. Amby's advice to me about being myself was clearly working.

My spirit was soaring as Walter turned and led us into the dining room. Amby joined me, moving to the right side of the table with two settings, so I quickly followed, glad we could sit next to each other. Hattie stood against a window and claimed the chair facing us, while Walter moved to the head of the table, as was proper.

In the City, it was traditional for a first son to sit next to the head of the house, so I left the chair next to Walter for Amby. As I claimed the other, Amby floundered, and Walter gave me the oddest look. Did he want me closer to chat business at the table? I would never try to replace the man's son. That seemed oddly rude to me.

Yet, Walter didn't say anything. He quietly settled in and then nodded at us all. I was unsure what was happening when Amby and Walter bowed their heads. When Amby nudged my knee with his, I looked up to see him smiling and silently mouthing for me to bow my head too.

I did so, feeling awkward, and cut my eyes over at Walter as he said a short prayer over the food. Then everyone began passing dishes of lamb with assortments of veggies. The food was well-made and nicely plated on large platters. It was just the atmosphere that was lacking. No one talked as Amby passed me each item. I scooped out a sampling before handing them over to Hattie. At least they both smiled at me each time.

Once the food went around, Hattie started chatting about the upcoming Founders Day Festival while Amby quietly nibbled his greens. When Walter asked me about Port Winchester, I answered his questions as best I could until he appeared satisfied and the room relaxed.

"How do you like the food?" Amby asked me as Hattie talked about school.

I blinked at him, realizing I only had a few bites left of mashed potatoes and green beans, and that made me wonder when I stopped tasting my food and considered it sustenance. Maybe when sustenance became nothing more than beans, bread, cheese, and jerky. Amby's question had me curious now, so I took my time to stab a few green beans with my fork and plowed them through the creamy potatoes. That bite was juicy and fresh with some salt and buttery goodness. Maybe I liked vegetables too, in addition to fruit.

Making sure to chew and swallow before speaking, I answered Amby honestly, "It's delicious."

He flashed me a dazzling grin, and I didn't realize how perfect his teeth were until that moment. Wanting to please him even more, I shifted the conversation to the City's art museum and watched as Amby lit up with questions. When Hattie joined in too, I told her about the science museum and the massive medical school.

At the head of the table, Walter listened and watched his children with sharp attention, but I didn't understand why he wasn't engaging with Amby. It was like something wedged between those two so long ago that no one knew how to remove the obstacle.

So, I started pushing, "Walter, do you enjoy art?"

"Yes, I have several paintings," he replied, wiping his mouth with a cloth napkin. "Most of them were acquired by Eleanor."

"Your wife, I remember her beauty and kindness. I also remember how she fussed when we trampled mud into the kitchen."

"It was mostly you," Amby lied, nudging my shoe playfully with his. "But it's alright, I proudly took the blame for you."

My indignant scoff at Amby raised Walter's brow, and I kicked Amby back under the table. He flinched in mock offense. Smiling, I waved to a nice landscape painting behind Hattie. "Eleanor had fine taste in art."

"It was a painting she adored but never had a chance to see in here," Amby said, gesturing at the landscape of a lonely lighthouse against a bright blue sea. "Father and I bought it together, right after she passed."

Walter nodded, looking as if he appreciated Amby's words. "We did. At the local antique shop in Westshire, while visiting your aunt."

Amby shared a moment with his dad, one that was ripe with some sort of understanding, as if they both connected. It was nice to see, but then they both glanced away and the moment was over.

"I remember that trip," Hattie added. "I cried for Mother the whole time, and Amby let me hang on his arm the entire ride home." When she looked at Amby, he smiled softly at her.

"I miss sitting next to her at the table." Amby eyed the empty chair beside me, and it struck me that I was wrong about the seating arrangements. Walter didn't push Amby away; he granted him freedom, and Amby chose to sweetly honor his mother's presence by continuing to sit next to her chair. No doubt a silent agreement between them...

Maybe one day I could honor my Mum in the same ways.

Dinner time like this made me miss her the most, because gathering around a table wasn't only about food, it was about company. She believed in talking as a family. It hurt to continue her traditions without her. That's probably why I stopped talking with Millie after Mum's passing. She was right to call me Grumpy Bear, and I was lucky she didn't call me more names. I shouldn't have shut her out like that.

But I was opening up again, thanks to Amby. He reminded me of Mum. They both found ways to show love through everyday things like a meal. Even now, while Walter and Hattie conversed about the painting, Amby slid his hand under the table to squeeze my thigh. I quickly tangled my fingers with his, in awe of my perfect boy for knowing when I needed him.

Clearing my throat of emotion, I addressed Walter, "That's a lovely landscape. I see why you have it in a place of honor."

Hattie propped her arm on the back of her chair to get a better view. "I never noticed how colorful it is in the evening light."

Walter turned too, remarking on the brush strokes. When Amby tried to remove his hand, I held on. Dinner was going so well, I didn't think Walter would care if Amby chose me as his spouse. Maybe Amby misunderstood his father. Maybe we could talk to him right now. As Walter grinned at his painting that he bought with Amby, I realized there were no more maybes about it. There was love in this family. They just needed to speak their feelings out loud.

Feeling determined and confident, I pulled our joined hands to the top of the table. My pinky ring glowed an excited bluish-purple, matching my racing heart at being open about my relationship with the wonderful man at my side. This step felt so right.

Amby stiffened, his face going red before he suddenly jumped up from the table, right as Walter and Hattie looked back. He knocked his chair down, and his water glass fell and shattered on the floor.

Instantly, the mood of the room darkened. Amby, Hattie, and I stilled in silence while Walter turned to the kitchen with a hint of annoyance and called for a maid to assist.

As she came into the room, my excitement sank to the floor with the shattered glass. The maid acknowledged the spill and nodded. "I'll get the broom right away, sir."

While she scurried off, Amby dropped to the floor and fumbled to grab up the rest of the glass. Horrified at the scene I caused, I pushed my chair back and knelt to help. I didn't want him to get a cut on my behalf. I tried nudging Amby's hands away from the shards, but he nudged me right back.

"I've got it," he muttered.

There was a fire in his eyes that only came out when Amby was passionate. I just wish I hadn't sparked it through anger.

Walter stood from his chair and drew closer, until the polish of his shoes filled my view. They were as polite as his words, "By the time Mary returns with the broom, she'll have nothing to clean. Let's move to the porch. We can talk business."

I stumbled up, embarrassed by my bad behavior, made even worse as everyone else was being nice.

Hattie stood from her chair and interjected with, "I'll leave you to that and retire. I have some anatomical diagrams to memorize. The spelling is challenging, so I want a head start." She turned to me and smiled. "Goodnight, Zeth. Come back soon, okay?"

"If I'm not forbidden from returning," I said as a joke to ease the mood. Hattie thankfully laughed, a bright sound that matched her spirit. I was glad she still liked me. There was also time to fix things with Walter, since he wished to continue with business talk.

"Goodnight, dear." Walter kissed her on the cheek before turning to Amby. "Ambrose, you should take care of that. Leave the glass for Esther to clean." He nodded at Amby's hand before making his way to the hall.

Amby watched his dad leave as blood ran to his wrist. I quickly took the shards from his hands and placed them in the bottom of the glass that was still intact. I set it aside and then pulled out my handkerchief to wrap around Amby's hand, tucking his gold initials in against his wrist. He grimaced as I pressed against the large gash.

"Do you want help?" I asked, holding the cloth firmly to stop the bleeding.

Amby met my eyes, his face softening. "It's fine. I'll bandage this up. You should go talk to my father. I'm sorry for panicking."

"I'm sorry for pushing."

"If you want to grab my hand on the porch, I'll be ready then, and we can tell him. Just let me go... clean this up."

"Are you certain? I don't want to push you. I can wait."

Amby fixed me with his gentle eyes. "I've never been more certain about anything else in my life."

He was trying to be brave, and that made me so proud of him. I gave him a confident nod to confirm his plan. Then I forced myself to separate from him for now, and he hurried to the washroom while I made my way to the hall.

Impressing Walter was the whole reason I attended this dinner, and I couldn't do that if I was kissing Amby's hand to make it all better. When I walked through the open front door, I found Walter relaxing in a large rocking chair, tipping it back and forth.

As soon as he sensed me, he motioned to a glass decanter on a table along the wall. He wanted me to pour drinks for us both. I turned one glass over to fill it with one finger's worth of the dark liquor, and I tried not to gag from the strong fumes. How did he drink this stuff? Strolling over to him, I gladly handed the vile thing over before claiming a chair.

By the stiff back, I could tell instantly that the chair wasn't Amby's design. I frowned, wondering why Amby's dad didn't use his son's superior furniture.

Beside me, Walter took a sip of his drink and sighed, as smooth a drinker as his son. "That's local, and very good. I'm investing in the current batch and will triple my money when it's done."

"The Mayor of Port Winchester enjoys a good drink too. You should send him a bottle once your new branch opens. If you want an intro—" and that's when my chest seized. I made it through the fucking city's name, but forgot that the mayor would never wish to see me again, not after I tainted his son's reputation. Good politicians don't want to associate with thieves. So much for offering Amby's dad my old connections. I would have to impress him in other ways. "Sorry, is it rye whiskey?"

Thankfully, he took the bait and went on to talk about the liquor while I eased into my chair. What little I knew of drinks came from listening to the auctioneer only. The man had trained me into manhood with lessons on customs and social graces, all needed to hobnob with high levels of clientele. Our time together just made his quick betrayal all the harder to swallow. I didn't have positive experiences with father figures. I hoped things might be different with Walter.

After a few minutes, Walter asked about my family, and I was surprised by how much he remembered about them. I explained how my mum passed, and he expressed his condolences, looking as if he was truly pained by her passing. Then he inquired after Millie, telling me how much he enjoyed speaking with her at the salon. He seemed enamored by her quirky personality, so I bragged about how well she was doing in the tailor shop, courting Anna, and making new friends, including Emiline.

"Hm, it was a surprise to me when Miss Winters and your sister shared a kiss at the salon. I was sure she was a good match for Ambrose." Walter glanced briefly at me before turning back. "I thought you might win her over as well. But Miss Washer clearly has a charm of her own."

"Aye, Millie's a diamond. Excellent cut and no flaws. Maybe just needs some polish."

Walter pointed at me with his glass. "Your quick wit reminds me of Issac. He was the smartest kid in our class." *Issac.* My dad's name sounded hollow to my ears since I hadn't heard it in years. I didn't want to hear it now, but Walter went on, "I wasn't surprised when the Denburg Academy offered Issac a tenured position. Did you get a chance to become better acquainted with him while together in the City?"

"No," I answered stiffly, running my thumb along a knot in the wooden armrest. Maybe I did get my intelligence from my dad, Mum said that too, but he stupidly left us. Some larger theoretical problem was more important to him than Millie and me, or our problems. Mum had always accepted his choice with a smile, so who was I to ruin that illusion?

"No," I repeated. "The City proved too big a place."

"Hm, that sounds like it's been a lot to deal with," Walter hummed as if he cared about the *washer boy,* and actually wanted to hear more than the gossip that went around town.

That must have been why my lips opened to convince him, "I'm not like my dad, not in the ways that really matter. I helped raise Millie, and always put my family's needs above my own desires. And I will continue to do so." *Especially now, with Amby in my life.*

"Thinking of others before yourself is an admirable trait." Walter looked away, seeming to think before he went on, "One we could all strive to do better on..."

He didn't give me a chance to ponder that praise when he shifted the conversation to Somerset and Sons Bank, and their new branch goals. I shared some marketing techniques that worked for the auction. By the way Walter leaned toward me as he listened, he was impressed. My nervousness settled into mild inconvenience.

However, I was starting to wonder why Amby hadn't joined us yet. Was the cut worse than it appeared? Did he change his mind about holding hands? "Zeth," Walter started, waiting for me. Only then did I realize that I was staring over my shoulder at the empty front door.

I turned to him with a grin, "You were saying?"

"I was asking if you'd be interested in working for me."

"Excuse me?" I blinked at him, thinking the liquor made me hear things, and I hadn't even drunk it. "Did you just invite me to work for you?"

He appeared pleased as he said, "You were right about Robert Wilson."

"Robert who?"

"Mr. Glasses, I believe you called him," Walter chuckled. "Just as you warned at the salon, he was dishonest. He made a deal behind my back with a competing bank, which I only discovered due to you. You would be an excellent choice to replace him. Heaven knows, Ambrose will need guidance when the day comes that I pass on."

Although I didn't like how he spoke about Amby, Walter was

offering me my dream job in finance. Here was my easy way to make money and work side by side with my boy. I already saw us breaking for lunch every day. What a grand opportunity.

"I would love to work at the bank. Anything, I'll take it."

"Excellent, I'm willing to train you and pay you well. Our new branch in Port Winchester will need you."

"Port Win—fuck no," I said before I could catch my words, "There's no way I'm moving back to the City."

When Walter's eyes widened, he reminded me of Amby, and shame blew through me for being so rude.

"I'm sorry, Mr. Somerset, but I have to decline your offer because my future is here in Everdeen. As I said, I put my family first. Please do not hold that against me."

Walter waved me off with a smile. "I did always appreciate your blunt honesty, Zeth."

"Too honest, perhaps," I said, hoping I sounded half as calm as he did. I eased back in my chair. "When Amby told me to be myself tonight, I don't think he meant swearing." I paused for a moment before saying gently, "You have a smart son."

"Agreed." Walter eyed me curiously, like he saw right through me. This time, he sounded like he loved his son as much as I did. If only Amby were here for his dad's praise. But he wasn't here, and this was a chance to help them.

"You know, speaking of your son," I started, weighing my words as I brushed lint off my pants. "He's given up a lot to follow your path, and proven how much he loves you." I turned to him, looking at him straight. "Now's a good time to make sure he sees how much you love him."

Walter propped his elbow on the arm of his rocker and pinned me with his eyes. "Lecturing me on how to be a father, Zeth?"

"No, well, yes, I guess," I huffed. "It's just that all your kids have good heads on their shoulders. Your Somerset values carry on through them. All of them. A legacy is more than a name."

When Walter's mustache twitched with annoyance, I didn't know what else to say. Thankfully, Amby cleared his throat and walked outside to join us, breaking the tense silence.

He'd removed his vest while gone. In only his casual shirt and pants, Amby was distracting, especially with his collar unbuttoned to expose his lovely neck. He cut quite the handsome figure of lean sophistication as he strolled over to us with a fresh glass of water in his bandaged hand.

When he reached his arm out, I thought he might take my hand now, as he said he would, but he only tucked something into my fingers before moving away.

It was the handkerchief he used, damp and still slightly stained, but washed enough. I was glad to have it back. I was glad to have Amby close again.

"Well, my offer still stands should you change your mind about the position," Walter said.

"A position at the bank?" Amby took a sip from his glass before placing it on the rail. I suspected he heard more than he was letting on. Hopefully, he wasn't mad at me for talking about his worries without him.

Sitting forward, I answered, "I refused your dad's offer because it would be in the new branch, and I don't want to move."

"Oh." Amby leaned his back against the rail, one hand in his pocket. "That's good, I'd miss you too much if you left again. You push me to be better than I am."

My heart stirred. Amby had just repeated the words I'd recited in my poem at the salon for him. It could be something simply said between friends, but not with how Amby's gaze held mine. Walter would have to be blind to miss the love shining for me in Amby's big, brown eyes.

And judging from Walter's sharp stare at me, something *had* clicked in his mind. I could see it from here. He grunted as he rose from his seat. "Well, it's certainly been an interesting evening, but I've had a feeling this was more than a visit to talk business. So, since you're good at being honest, young man, answer me this." He fixed me with a stern glare, and I sat rigid, waiting. "Are you trying to court my son?"

My eyes flew back to Amby, who froze against the rail. His widening eyes told me he was as surprised as I was at the direct question. But his words earlier gave me a clue, so I rose to stand next to Amby. As if connected, he pulled his hand out of his pocket, and we entangled our fingers while I answered proudly, "Yes, sir, I am. We hoped for your blessing before making it official."

Walter stiffened where he stood, and I feared he would say *no*. When he turned on Amby, I felt like I fucked everything up again, but that was just my own fear of yet another older man in my life turning his back on me. This wasn't about me. I needed to be strong for Amby as he faced his fears.

I squeezed Amby's hand as Walter's face soured. Sighing, the man turned to look out over his fields. "I'd be lying if I said this surprises me, especially with the rumors I've been hearing in town."

"I hoped you'd be happy for me," Amby started, "I found someone who wants me, all of me, someone who makes me happy."

Walter shook his head with a sigh. "What happened to our plan to continue the Somerset bloodline? It can't go on if you marry Zeth."

"Marigold and Jack can carry on the bloodline. Besides, any woman I marry could be barren. Or me." Amby waved his bandaged hand at himself. "What if *I* can't have children? What if I never have a son? Have you thought about that?"

Walter blinked at him, as if such a thing had never even crossed his mind. Amby had valid points.

"You care so much about a bloodline that you're willing to throw away my happiness for your own." Amby shook his head, trying to keep his voice steady. "But that's not what I feel is the right thing. Not for anyone. If standing up now means losing the estate, my job, and my own name... so be it. I'm willing to give it all up for Zeth Washer."

My heart raced hearing my name on Amby's lips with such a declaration. I knew he would choose me. He already said that, but to powerfully state it to the one man he both feared and loved made this whole crazy situation real. He chose me, and he didn't fucking care what happened.

There was no doubt how I felt about him now. I made sure my gaze at Amby expressed my admiration. He returned my glance with

349

such nervous excitement that I wanted to kiss him right then and there.

"Ambrose." Walter's stern voice cut sharply through my thoughts. Like Amby beside me, I felt the command to lower my head and listen to his lecture, but I didn't. Instead, I straightened to my full height and stared down at Walter with my best don't-you-dare-hurt-my-boy glare. Height had some damn fine advantages.

I was glad to make Walter take a breath before he calmly said, "It's probably best if we all retire for the night. This is all... overwhelming. I am going to bed. Zeth—" He only stared at me before moving around to the door without bothering to wait for our replies.

That was it. Dinner was done, and Walter left us without expressing clearly how he felt about our courtship. He preferred to lecture Amby about legacies, or ignore him completely. No wonder Amby struggled all these years.

It was so fucking unfair how many men took on a fatherly role and didn't take it seriously. They walked away, like my dad, or ignored the truth, like Amby's. I saw it enough in my own life, and it hurt all the worse to see it happen to the man I loved. My anger rose as Walter left us on the porch.

When the door clicked closed, Amby turned to the rail and started to shake. It was that jumbled anxiety that usually made him lash out. I saw this a few times now in the past weeks, and I knew Amby needed some kind of release.

I moved to his side, and he instantly leaned against me, pressing his face into my neck as he clutched me close to him. He shivered against me, making my heart crack.

"What do you need me to do?" I asked, stroking his hair. "Anything, just tell me."

"I don't know, I just... Please don't go yet."

"I'll stay here with you all night. I'm not leaving you."

He nodded and grabbed my hand. "Will you come with me to the barn?"

29

Ambrose

I couldn't recall a time in my life where my blood rushed so quickly, where my whole body shook with dread as it did now. I stumbled through the field to get to the barn, the one place I felt at home. Zeth walked alongside me, holding my hand as I led us forward. I needed him so much right now, and I was glad he agreed to come here with me so I could calm down before returning home.

As soon as we reached the barn doors, Zeth helped me pull them open. Once inside, I made my way to my workbench to light the lamp there and placed it on the dining table I'd made. When I faced him, he was looking at me with concern and a whole lot of care.

Taking a breath, I took Zeth's hand and held it. I was still shaking, so incredibly hurt from my father's rejection. His defeated expression reminded me of my place in the family, and it tore a piece of me away. And then when he walked away and refused to give us his blessing, my spirit broke completely. That moment was burned in my mind.

Now, I stared at a button on Zeth's shirt as I tried to hold it together, but I couldn't. The button blurred and my nose itched. I was about to embarrass myself. I wouldn't blame Zeth if he changed his mind about me once he saw how pathetic this rich boy truly was.

JORDAN LEE & SPARA SOLACE

Sniffling, I took off my glasses and pocketed them to pinch the bridge of my nose, just as the hot tears spilled down my fingers. Instead of fleeing, Zeth's hands found my shoulders, and he pulled me to him, so I leaned my head against his shoulder and let out a sob, twisting my fingers in his vest. My body shook from the fury and shame burning through me.

"If I were one of my sisters announcing I loved a man, it would have been a happy moment," I muttered against him. "I've failed you."

"Failed me?" Zeth asked incredulously, stroking my back. "You didn't fail me. Never."

"I didn't gain my father's blessing. Now I can't give you a home. I can't promise you the shelter and comfort you need. I'm so sorry, Zeth."

"You haven't failed me," he insisted, but that was hard to believe, and I cried harder, my shoulders shaking as I let my worries out through tears.

He tugged me even tighter to him, allowing me to use him as my support while I soaked his shirt with guilt and shame. Despite my failure, Zeth coddled me anyway. He stroked my hair and cooed comforting words in my ear.

"Amby, it's alright. You've been so brave. You did more for me tonight than anyone else has ever done. You welcomed me into your family and made me feel like I belonged in your circle, that we belonged there side-by-side." Zeth kissed my temple. "That's why I tried to grab your hand at dinner. You already changed my life for the better. I just wanted to shout it to the rooftops that I'm in love with Ambrose Somerset."

I lifted my head to look at him as tears ran along my cheeks, feeling too stunned by his words to even speak.

Zeth released a breath, and his chin trembled. "Look at me, spilling my truths all over the place tonight." He raised his hands to thumb my cheeks dry while his gaze roamed over my messy face. "I love you, Rosie. I never stopped, but the feelings are so much stronger now. I can't hold them in any longer. Is that okay?"

I'd ended the Somerset legacy... and yet the world hadn't

stopped. The sky hadn't crashed down, Zeth didn't leave me. My lips twitched as I realized it no longer mattered what my father thought about the whole thing. Someone loved me, accepted me, and that overtook any other emotion I felt.

I wrapped my arms around Zeth and nuzzled my face against his neck. "I love you too, Zeth. Every bit of you."

Zeth shivered in my arms and chuckled against my hair, "You just gave me goosebumps, darling."

I laughed through my tears and hugged him tighter. This man who was so bitter at me for so long, loved me. He loved me enough to give me a second chance to be his again. Sniffling, I kissed Zeth's neck gently, then kissed him again, and again, making a path up to the underside of his jaw until Zeth tilted his head back with a soft gasp. I needed him, his touch, to focus solely on us. I'd just chosen him for life, and that made me so full of happiness, I wanted to show him I'd never leave his side.

I wanted all of him.

"Show me how much you love me," I said against him, before I pushed him back playfully.

Caught off guard, Zeth stumbled but raised an eyebrow and swiftly grabbed my belt loops to pull me hard against his chest. My hands flew to his shoulders to steady myself, and when Zeth made a low, possessive growl in his throat, I looked up at him to see his hungry stare.

My body flushed as Zeth nudged us toward the horse stalls, our feet shuffling together. When he pushed me against the wall, a thrilling sensation enraptured my body. I wanted his hard hands and rough kisses.

As he leaned in to kiss me, our lips barely touching, I said, "Since we're being honest... I don't want you to play nice tonight."

"Since when do I play nice?" Zeth replied huskily against my lips.

Smiling, I caressed the nape of his neck and spread my fingers out to feel the soft prickle of his hair. "I want your hand on my ass, hard. I've wanted it since you brought it up at the river. Make me forget everything but you. Make me *yours*."

"Yeah?" Zeth smiled crookedly as he crowded me against the stall. My face warmed under his covetous gaze. "I'll spank you so hard, you'll forget your name. You're going to be my good boy tonight. You deserve my attention and praise."

My heart thrummed wildly with excitement as Zeth reached between us and undid his vest to slide it off his broad shoulders with ease.

"I'm so proud of you for choosing your path." He locked his eyes on me as he popped a few buttons from his collar, exposing his thick neck before moving to roll the sleeves of his white dress shirt up those lean arms. "You faced your fears, love, and good boys deserve rewards."

I was flushing all over, my stomach fluttering so much I could hardly stand it. Zeth was going to give me what I wanted, and he'd called me his good boy. This side of him that took control had me so spellbound, I couldn't think straight.

Finally, I nodded, finding my voice, "I-I want it. Please."

"You're so pretty when you beg."

When Zeth grabbed my chin with firm fingers, I groaned. He stroked his thumb along my mouth, parting my lips to capture me in a heavy kiss as he held me tight against his warm body. I grabbed Zeth's arm and traced over the raised veins there, memorizing them by touch.

He pulled away too quickly to tilt my face to the side, until my cheek pressed against the rough wood of the stall. With a deep groan, Zeth licked my neck with a wet, claiming stroke of his tongue. He was giving me exactly what I needed, and I shivered from the flutter in my stomach, humming my pleasure in my throat.

"There's my good boy. You like it when I take control, don't you?"

I did, and tried to nod in agreement, but the way he held me against the wood prevented me. Yes, I wanted to surrender completely to him. I wanted to play along with whatever he had up his sleeve.

Zeth planted kisses from my tear-stained cheeks and up to my ear. "My Rosie, I want to make your ass so red that you feel my claim for days. You'll remember who wants you, who loves you. Tell me you want that too."

"Yes, I want that," I breathed, needing his praise.

"Yes... *Sir*," Zeth commanded, tugging me back to look at him.

My mouth twitched. Oh, I liked this. "Yes, Sir."

"Good boy, so obliging," he complimented. His amber eyes darkened with desire as he gazed into mine. He reached between us to pull at the buckle on my trousers, undoing it. The rough scrape of his knuckles against my stomach made me thrust my hips against him.

When Zeth grabbed my waistband and yanked my trousers and undershorts down, I gasped. As I sprang free, he refastened the buckle of my trousers below my cheeks, binding me, keeping me still. I bit my lip as I realized I was granting him much more than my body. I was giving him my trust, and accepting his too. His hand bumped against my cock as he straightened, and I sucked in a sharp breath.

"So tempting," Zeth purred. "But first, I want to hear how much you need me. Don't hold back."

I swallowed hard and voiced my approval through a whimper, "Yes, sir."

"Oh, how I love hearing you say that," Zeth replied passionately, and swiftly grabbed my left wrist to flip me around.

I stumbled to face the stall, with my trousers still fastened around my thighs. Zeth twisted my arm behind me and lifted my wrist to my shoulder blades. He didn't hurt me, only used my helpless position to push me forward until my chest hit the wood. His rough hands were so big and loving in hard ways that I craved. Zeth balanced along the knife edge between discomfort and pleasure.

He closed in to trap me in place with his firm body. Soft lips grazed the skin behind my ear, and I marveled at his gentleness. When he shifted to the side, keeping my arm held tight, he tugged my hip against him crudely, until I felt how aroused he was through his trousers. His touch trailed my shirt until his warm fingers caressed my right cheek with such loving care that I shivered.

"Rosie, when you want me to *stop*, just say the word."

I nodded. "I trust you."

"I know you do."

Zeth's husky reply made my skin tingle. As he moved his hand away, I braced for his first slap, but nothing prepared me for the sharp sting that landed. It traveled through my body with a wonderful jolt of joy, pulling a gasp from my throat. When he withdrew, I held my breath. His palm came down again in the same place, smacking me so hard, I groaned. Oh, how delicious this was.

When I felt his palm strike again, I continued to voice my pleasure. Zeth's attention loosened something deep within me, a desire to see how much I could take from him. With the next slap, my gasp echoed from the rafters.

Zeth's fingers traced a circle over the hot spot he was creating. Rough and gentle. His tenderness hit me as strongly as his hand, and I inhaled sharply as I pressed my face against the stall. Just when I eased into his stroke, he smacked me so hard, I gave a laugh that was half moan.

"Oh, sir... You're treating me so well."

"I'm giving you what you deserve, lots of love," Zeth said against my ear, making me quiver with pleasure. His next strong smack had my eyelids fluttering closed as I exhaled with mirth, relishing the prickly vibration Zeth's hand left behind. Then his hand slapped again, even harder this time.

My heart slammed against my ribs, but he didn't relent. He slapped me once, twice, and three times more, making me cry out, each smack in succession feeling sharper than the last. By the fourth, a delightful pain spiraled through more than my ass cheek. It went deep into my groin, making my cock twitch as I let out a pathetic, whimpering moan. I shuddered, my legs feeling weak. A dizzying, blissful sensation passed through my mind. Every trouble I held deep within me was melting away.

Zeth panted as he kissed my ear. He bit my lobe lightly before growling, "You're such a good boy."

"Yes... Sir..." I groaned, moved by how incredibly *good* it felt to be called that by him, to be worthy of being his once again. By the way he handled me, the way he gave me what I wanted and took care of me while in his arms, I knew he loved me.

While I was still reeling from his words, he released my trapped arm to slide his hand up the back of my neck and through my curls until he gripped my hair. The light tug to my scalp drew all of my attention until Zeth delivered another smack to my ass, making me flinch and groan even louder than before. I was rewarded with a gentle kiss against my temple.

His rhythmic smacks started up again, and this time I knew what to expect. Each of his touches had me moaning louder in rapture as my cheek turned hot and raw. His hand burned me up so much, I moaned and cursed with each hit as if I were some depraved madman. And perhaps I was. I was mad for Zeth Washer, for how well he knew my body, my mind and soul.

Another hard slap stole my breath. It was getting painful, deep, but God, how I treasured the bite. I loved whatever this was between us. "Zeth—Sir..." I bit my trembling lip against the mishap.

"Do you want me to stop?"

"I can take a few more..." I panted, as tears gathered in my eyes.

"Yes, you've been so strong, for so long, darling. But you're not alone anymore. Tell me who you belong to."

When Zeth's palm met my stinging ass with hot, solid conviction, I let out a guttural moan, "You."

"Louder." He drew back his hand again, but I no longer needed it.

"You," my voice cracked. "I'm yours, only yours. I'm your good boy."

My knees buckled, and Zeth's arms found me, pulling me close by my waist. We were both panting, our bodies hot against each other. I bit my lip as my mind wavered. I was so dazed that I feared falling, but Zeth kept me upright until I found my footing.

"Are you okay?" he asked against the side of my mussed hair.

"Yes," I got out, keeping my eyes closed with a smile on my face. "I'm just floating is all." I felt safe enough with him to let myself go. No one had ever been able to do such a thing for me before.

"You were perfect. I loved hearing you let go so beautifully."

I let him hold me and leaned my head back to rest on his shoulder. "Will you... kiss me?"

"Always," Zeth answered like a pledge as he turned me around. I clung to his shoulders, letting my head hang, feeling strangely relaxed as if all the tension had left my body. Zeth hummed pleasantly as he pulled up my trousers—always so considerate—and I sucked air through my teeth as the fabric slid over my sore cheek. He pecked several gentle kisses along my temple before moving to my mouth with the same care. I embraced him, craving his calm affection.

Seeing how flushed and damp his skin was around his open collar aroused me more, and I nuzzled my face against his neck. "Mm, I want you."

"I want you too," Zeth breathed. "If only we had what we need..."

"What do you mean? A bed? I'm sure we can just use the hay like last time," I murmured against him.

Zeth laughed and pulled back to kiss my nose. "Rosie, love, I mean I want to fuck your red ass right now, but we don't have any oil."

"Oh..." I got out, my lips twitching, as I knew we were both in luck. I slipped my hand into his and stepped backward to my workbench, pulling Zeth along with me. I rummaged through the drawers to find my vial of Linseed oil and held it up in the orange glow of the flame before facing him again.

Tonight, I wanted to surrender to him completely.

30

Zeth

I couldn't believe how lucky I was to have Amby—he was my air, my heart, and my support—as we embraced in the dim light of the barn. His hands were all over me, undressing me and burning my bare skin, while I couldn't get enough of touching him either. Removing the rest of his clothes, I adored his smooth body and demanding mouth.

I kissed him harder, forcing my tongue into his wet mouth and roaming around the sharp edges of his bite. For such an adorable man, Amby sure knew how to give as good as he took.

Looping my arms around his waist, I hefted Amby against my chest, and he wrapped his legs around my hips without needing a command. I growled my approval into his mouth and started walking. I knew exactly how I wanted him, bent over that beautiful dining table he built.

He was ready for me, all blissed out and waiting to spill at my command. He set his feet down and I helped him stand against the edge of the table. His cock looked so needy, so tempting, but I kissed his tender lips instead. I craved that connection, and by the way he melted into me, he did too.

When I pecked along his jaw, Amby leaned his arm back on the table and let out a sigh. He tilted his head to the side so I could access his neck as I planted wet pecks against him. His hand smoothed up my arm, squeezing me gently as he ran his fingers over my scar.

He tasted so delicious, I was content to just keep him here like this and devour him until we could no longer stand. But the way he pulled on me and continued making those delightful noises told me he demanded to be claimed further.

I pulled away, and Amby pressed his vial of oil into my palm. With it came some unspoken strength. He stood courageous earlier, granting me control over what he needed, but now he didn't want to be strong. He wanted to let go. I understood how vulnerable he must feel. It shivered through him, so I held him tighter, guiding him to turn around in my arms until I bent him onto the polished surface of the table.

He eased down, and I ran a strong caress up his spine and back until I roamed his unblemished ass cheek, savoring how fair it looked. The other appeared bright red and sore from my hand. I would be lying if I said that didn't fill me with pride. He was mine. "So beautiful."

I dropped to my knees and kissed him there, cherishing him for taking my strength and giving it back. When he sighed softly, I flicked out my tongue and licked the tender imprint, tasting heat.

Amby gasped and rose up on his elbows, arching his back gracefully to ask, "See something you like?"

"I see something I own," I purred from the floor.

"Oh, this ass is undeniably yours." Amby answered, and fever spiked through me to still hear that sassy mouth of his. How I adored that about him.

He challenged me to meet him at his level, and go further. He wanted me inside of him, and holy shit... I never wanted anyone the way I wanted this man before me.

"I hope you don't plan on walking anywhere tomorrow," I chuckled. Raising to my feet, I uncorked the vial and spread the oil over my fingers as I traced my gaze along Amby's wide hips and strong back. I enjoyed looking down on him like this, while he watched me over his shoulder.

"Mm," he hummed, and folded his arms on the table, relaxing. "You sound so sure of yourself back there."

"I'm sure that you want me."

"I do, every inch." He laughed softly.

Groaning, I roamed my dry hand over his back, loving the give and play of his muscles moving under my touch. When I moved my other hand toward his ass, Amby spread his feet wider in invitation.

"You're so goddamn beautiful, Rosie, and I mean every fucking syllable."

Amby's lashes fluttered closed against his flushed face, and he bit that bottom lip like he always did when he liked what I said. He reacted like a giddy mess when I praised him. I loved watching him melt with pleasure. He was a good person, and undeniably good for me.

Eager to please Amby, I reached between his cheeks to prepare him. My slick finger circled his entrance before prodding him. He tensed against me, his breath catching. I stopped there and teased him with small strokes, waiting for his response before exploring deeper.

"Keep going," Amby groaned.

His mix of command and need had me following without thought. I dove in deeper, using one finger to find my way and start a nice, slow rhythm. Amby moaned softly and eased off his elbows to lie flat, shifting his hips to take more of my finger. I was happy he relaxed into my attention. I imagined myself there. That alone could have made me spill.

"That's good. Zeth, please..."

"I'm making you ready for me, love," I assured him, and myself.

"Mm, I've been ready for you for years. Please don't make me wait anymore."

"Yes," I agreed, trusting him as I removed my finger and lined myself up. One slick stroke down my cock had me ready to enter, yet I rubbed his entrance with my tip and inhaled with awe. I couldn't begin to count all the times I imagined Amby wanting me, and here he was, bent over and begging. This amazing moment needed to last. I wanted to make our joining pleasurable for him too.

Determined, I grabbed his hip and tilted myself forward to push through his first ring. Slipping in proved easier than I imagined, and he felt so spectacular that I longed to slam myself home and fuck him into next week. It took everything in me to pause before I did just that. Even my hand shook on him with the strength of my selfish desires.

"Are you trying to take it easy on me?" Amby asked.

"I don't want to hurt you."

"The only thing you're going to do is make me lose my mind," he whined, and I squeezed him in agreement. When he reached back to intertwine our fingers, I treasured our connection and thrust deeper to give him what he wanted, what I wanted. We explored this new bond until Amby slowly took me whole with a delightful gasp.

"Yes... You feel so good," he sighed, easing back to settle his round cheeks against my groin. I roamed over the smooth curves and angles of his wider hips. We fit so snug together. I watched where we joined as I slid myself out and back in with a measured stroke that had Amby groaning with each thrust.

"You like taking my ass, don't you?" he asked with a raspy voice. "Tell me how it feels."

"Amazing," I offered out, hardly a poet as that one word filled my mind. He felt amazing. I blinked a bit to see him clearer, and found him leaning up on an elbow, twisting back to gaze at me with such love that I was moved to search for words that did him justice, "You're... marvelous, phenomenal, sensational." I buried myself in his spectacular ass as I said each word, "Breath-taking"—he was— "awe-inspiring"—so—"magnificent"—this felt so—"Fuck, Amby, I can't..."

I couldn't think. My thrusting took over. Amby might have replied, but it sounded like moans as I bent over him and picked up my pace. Once I found a rhythm, I bent to kiss my way up his gorgeous back. When I reached his neck, my body pressed flush against his fiery skin, and I grabbed a handful of his hair. I pulled his head back slightly, tilting it enough so that I could press my mouth against his jaw. He was mine, this beautiful man, so I claimed his neck with a bruising kiss as I claimed his plump ass.

Amby's perfect lips opened and closed with each push inside him. His flushed face pressed against the polished mahogany, and in the lamp light, his auburn curls shone like copper.

"So gorgeous, all mine." I pulled him off the table, and we both stood so I could hold him against me, inhaling his soft strands.

"All yours..." Amby let out the huskiest groan, such a sweet sound.

I was close, but I needed to pleasure him first. With my oiled fingers, I reached around and found Amby's cock jutting over the table. He shuddered in my grip, so ready for attention. "Such a good boy, waiting for me."

Amby's voice broke, and he pushed himself back on me hard, his cock sliding through my hand and his wonderful ass taking me whole. White hot pleasure streaked up my spine, and I grunted, "Fuck..."

"Yes," Amby laughed delightfully. "You love fucking your boy, don't you?"

"Mm," I hummed in agreement, enjoying his uncouth mouth as much as his ass. That tongue of his was going to break me.

Bracing my stance, I stood still to hold my dominance and secured my other arm around his chest, trapping him to me. I fisted Amby harder from head to base. He arched and tightened around my cock, pulling a groan from us both. Then he moved on me in time with my heavy strokes.

"So good..." I sighed in approval, but I slowed my hand on him, afraid I would come before him. God, I was hungry, and so was he. My composure was chipping away more and more with every pant.

When my hips moved again, Amby leaned his head back on my shoulder, yielding. My hand trailed up his body and lightly caressed his throat.

"Yes, like that. Don't stop," he rasped.

"Come on, baby," I cooed against his hair, feeling his pulse thrum under my fingers.

Amby trembled and whimpered, his quick, ragged breaths

breaking. So beautiful. He was both heaven and hell, his sweetness touching my soul and that fiery spirit scorching my heart.

"Rosie, my love, I'm going to fill you until you're dripping with my seed," I growled, pumping him harder.

"Zeth..." Amby's voice cracked as it rose an octave, his body tensing beneath me, and I understood his plea.

I pulled his head close to my face to rasp against his ear, "Let go for me."

Amby reared back into my hips, grabbing my arm with his hand as he cried out in pleasure, his sweet voice going hoarse as it echoed around us. His body quivered as he released into my hand.

"Shit," I muttered, my vision blurring. His enjoyment thrilled me to heights I didn't expect, and I found myself falling for him all over again. I slammed into him, losing myself inside my Rosie. My entire body shook, and my face grew hot as I gave him what felt like a lifetime of my love... he was my other half, my first and only love, reunited.

Completely spent, I guided us to lean over the table again and buried my face in the crook of his neck. We both panted, basking in the afterglow of what we just shared. My lips brushed his skin, feeling a vibrant energy there against his racing pulse. With a heavy exhale, I eased up to claim a spot at his side. Opening my eyes, I found my boy slumped against the table, looking absolutely wrecked, and I kissed his shoulder gently.

He twisted to regard me with a drowsy smile.

"You..." Amby started, raising up and wobbling slightly as he turned to face me, "are incredible." He gave a shaky laugh and closed his eyes.

"Yes, I am," I teased, tugging him into my arms to hold him close. He snuggled against me. Then I glanced up to the rafters to find the old hayloft we used when we were younger. "Tell me, do you still have blankets up there? I'd love another go at it, but sleep is needed first."

Amby's head tilted back to stare up at me, feeling like jelly in my arms. "I have a hay bed with lots of blankets, and some water. You can take care of me up there."

"That sounds superb," I agreed, and I meant it. I looked forward to caring for Amby for the rest of our lives, starting with this blessed night. No matter what came after this, we had each other.

* * *

I woke up the next day wondering if Anna would embroider me a pillow with one of her quotes, because home truly was where the heart is. There was no other way to explain how a bed of spare blankets, old straw, flat pillows, and a cold barn felt so wonderful, if not for Amby by my side.

Lazily, I stretched my bare body against his—so warm—and nudged my chin into his rambunctious auburn curls. When I opened my eyes, I blinked against the sunlight streaming through the loft door. Last night, we opened them to watch the stars until slumber found us, but now the air sparkled with specks of dust in the morning rays. The barn looked as blessed as I felt after our night together. I was so proud of my boy for accepting me fully into his life. I wanted to always care for him and keep him safe.

Amby stirred, but was still trying to sleep, so I nibbled his ear. Keeping him safe didn't mean I couldn't tease him. How did I never notice his cute ears? This one was pink from being squished. I licked underneath his lobe, and when Amby didn't stir, I sucked him into my mouth with a groan that expressed the best sort of *good morning*.

Amby jerked away with a gasp, slipping free from my mouth. His arm flung out so fast that I didn't see him hit me until the pain stung my nose.

Scrambled, I sat up and swore, rubbing my abused face.

Sitting up too, Amby got out, "Shit, Zeth. I'm sorry." He took my jaw in his hands and leaned close to search for injury. My pain disappeared the moment Amby's freckled face glowed with an adorable grin. I wanted to kiss those playful lips, but he sat back and asked, "Is anything broken? Can you wiggle your toes?"

"Let me check," I answered in all seriousness. Then I flipped the blankets off us both. The big swish of my arm caused a gust of cold air, and Amby's delightful cry of protest filled my ears. When he tried to curl up in a ball, I reached for his toes, tickling the arch of his foot until his laughter joined mine.

He tried to playfully kick me, but I clung to him. "Yup, they're wiggling."

Amby grumbled, and I let him go to peck his pouty lips. Then he groaned and twisted to look at his backside. "Oh..."

"Something wrong?" I asked.

He showed me his rosy cheek. "This is all delightfully sore. I need you to kiss it and make it better."

He enjoyed the soreness, and that made me growl, even more so feeling needed. Leaning down, I planted a wet kiss right on the sore spot, making him hiss delightfully. Raising, I asked, "Better?"

"Much." Sighing contentedly, he unraveled and sprawled out on his back, looking gorgeous. I just had time to take in the miles of pale skin and springy hair before Amby pulled the blanket back over us. I kissed the curve of his lean bicep before I rested my head on his outstretched arm. He rewarded me with artistic fingers threading through my hair until my scalp tingled.

Now I understood why he liked this attention. I moaned into his touch as he lightly traced my arm from elbow to shoulder to outline my muscles. I wasn't built as strongly as other men, but I had some definition that Amby seemed to adore, so I made sure to flex my arm under his touch.

"I never thought I'd wake up with you in this hayloft again," he said with awe. "It's a good thing. The best thing, really."

"I was thinking something similar. Can you believe how much has changed since the last time we laid here? I recall we had a quick blow and then lounged while we plotted revenge on Dick for pouring ink in Emiline's hair."

"Yes..." Amby went quiet for a long moment before he regarded me seriously. "I love you," he whispered.

Moved by his words, I wrapped my arms around him. "I love you too," I returned sincerely. Those words were so new to my lips, but I'd felt this way for years. Resting my palm over his racing heart, I said, "You're my home."

He smiled. "One day we'll have more than this hayloft bed to share, I promise."

"I'd be happy here forever, as long as I can warm you through the winters. And maybe use that table again."

Amby laughed and pushed me up to move me onto my back. He fluffed the pillows behind my head and then settled his chest across mine. Placing his hand over my heart, he rested his chin there to look at me. I enjoyed viewing him from this angle while he gazed at me, his face glowing.

"What are you thinking?" I asked, smoothing back his soft curls.

"About the table." He smirked. "Well, really, about all the furniture in general. It's all just collecting dust in this old barn. I hope I'll be able to sell most of it at the festival."

"I'm positive you will. I've seen craftsmanship like yours in the City, and it's carried in the best shops, often selling out. With all the new construction across the river, I bet demand is even higher here."

"Perhaps? I wish I had a shop of my own."

"Aye, I can see you there, making rocking chairs to display in the big shop windows. If you need someone to wash them, let me know."

Amby's cheek dimpled. "I think I'd rather you help me sell."

"Hm, wouldn't that be a dream?"

"To sell things?" When I nodded, his big brown eyes gleamed curiously as he swirled a finger through the hair on my chest. "Hm, that gives me an idea. You need to pay off your property bill. If you don't mind, we can use the laundry to sell some of my pieces. Your share of the profits could help pay off the tax. We could partner until you find a buyer for the laundry."

With every word Amby said, my excitement grew. My mind lit up, like someone turning on a lightbulb. Wasn't my dream to own my own business? Well, here it was. I already owned it. Mum left me a solid building that could be repurposed into a shop right on Main Street, and the town was already booming with business. With some investment capital from Amby's furniture at the festival, we could finish renovations. Amby saw the perfect way for me to support my family and feel accomplished. And the best part, Amby also wanted to own a shop. We could work together.

Amby had to be feeling my heart pounding with excitement under his palm. I sat up with him, the blankets falling around us as I pecked his nose. "Let's do it. You and me, partners. I can buy antiques, maybe run-down items that you can repair, like you did with Mum's dresser. I can even go to other towns to seek out cheap finds in their auctions, using all my training and bargain—"

"Wait, wait." Amby grabbed my arms and met my eyes with a serious gaze. "Traveling to other towns? Zeth, that's a lot for a temporary partnership."

"Who says it needs to be temporary? You suggested I keep the laundry, this is how. You can have a place to display your furniture, and I can sell it. We can turn the laundry into a home again, and a shop for us both."

Amby's features warmed. "You... want us to own a shop together?" When I nodded, he looked at me excitedly, as if pondering the idea.

"Rosie's Furniture," I tossed out, and his eyebrows perked up. "Washer Wares. Somerset Finds... Washer and Somerset Antiques. Cl—"

Amby covered my mouth with his hand, stopping me, and something twinkled in his eyes. "That last one. Yes." He nodded.

I grinned against his palm. I liked it too, *Washer and Somerset Antiques*. I already imagined us painting our names together above the storefront and the soon-to-be pink door. Mum would be so proud of us.

Amby removed his hand from my lips and kissed me there before he said, "I'd be honored to partner with you."

31

Ambrose

After Zeth and I left the barn, I returned home to dress, and we both walked into town. Along the way, I prepared myself to talk to Father, thinking through all the things I wanted to say to him. I only hoped I didn't forget them all. It helped that my relationship with Zeth was out in the open now. It motivated me for what I was about to do.

Now, I stood before my father's massive oak door. In my hand, I held the nameplate I made for my father's desk, freshly stained in dark wood with raised letters painted in gold.

Okay, Amby, you can do this.

I let out a breath and knocked on the solid door. When my father's voice called me in, I turned the knob and went inside. His expression immediately fell, but he recovered quickly and nodded my way.

"Ambrose," he said in greeting, before returning to his work scribbling something out on a paper.

I shut the door and stepped up to his desk. For a moment, we were both quiet. My mouth felt dry as I started, "I wanted to speak with you. About last night."

My father remained quiet and continued writing as if I weren't there. I ran my thumbnail over a piece of the nameplate, waiting for my heart to stop pounding. As long as I stood in this office, it never would. But I had to be strong, as Zeth always told me I was. He believed in me, in us.

"Zeth and I... we want to turn the laundry into a furniture and antiques store. I will continue living at home and keep working here at the bank to help invest in our plan."

I waited for him to respond, but he never looked up or said a word. The only sound between us was the rough scrawling of ink along the paper.

"I've been in love with Zeth for a long time," I continued, my face flushing. "I have a feeling you knew. He's always had my back growing up, he's always been there for me, especially after Mother passed..." This dented my father slightly, as a visible wince appeared on his features, but it was gone as quickly as it came. "And Mother used to say that when you love someone so much it aches when you're parted, that it's true. I became someone I didn't want to be when Zeth left Everdeen. When he came back, I found myself again. We found each other."

My father wasn't responding to anything I was saying, and I still had so many things I needed to say. My hands began to shake, and the sweat built on my brow. I had set out to tell him the truth, to show him I was no longer under his wing. That it was time to let me fly free from his cage of obligations. I had to do it for him, but also for myself.

"I suppose what I'm getting at is... I'm sorry that I couldn't take over this bank one day, as you hoped I would. I know how much it means to you. All I've ever wanted was to please you, to make you proud." I tried not to choke on my words, but I did anyway. Thankfully, I recovered enough to calmly say, "But if I want to be true to myself, then I have to do what I set out to do. And that's to be with Zeth, to make my own way in life with the things I enjoy."

This roused my father's attention, as he paused his writing, but only for a moment. He was set on ignoring me until I fell into line. There was no talking *with* him, it seemed, but I had tried, and that was the best I could do. He would have to see that I wasn't going to wait for his permission or acceptance anymore.

"I'm available to talk more, father and son, whenever you feel it's best for you." When he gave no response, I gripped the piece of stained wood in my hand and set it on top of his desk.

My father looked up at it, and then his eyes darted to me for the first time since I'd started talking, and I smiled softly at him. "There's a particular person in our family who would benefit from taking over your legacy. You should consider her."

I backed away, leaving the nameplate engraved with "Somerset Heritage Bank" on his desk before turning for the door. I left swiftly, my sweaty palms slipping on the knob as I hurried out of the room. When I shut the door, I exhaled and closed my eyes.

I had done it. I had faced my father and told him what *I* wanted, and also what I was going to do from now on. It surprised me how good I felt, despite not hearing him utter a word to me. It invigorated me. Made me feel as if I was in control of my life for once.

Smiling, I straightened my jacket and raised my chin before I made my way to my desk.

* * *

I left the bank early to walk to the laundry with a bag of supplies. Zeth's kitchen window still needed fixing if he was going to continue living there. I wondered how it might be to live with him. Waking up next to him in bed, no matter where it was—even in a hayloft—was enough to keep me happy. Then to work together, making both our dreams come true, was a bliss I'd always hoped for. He'd taken my toolbox and two pieces of wood already this morning to work on some repairs, so I hoped the extra things would be a nice surprise for him.

My thoughts were so far up in the clouds as I made my way along the sidewalk that I didn't even notice Damien Cooligan standing against the general goods shop until he laughed and said, "Well, well, look who it is."

When I glanced over, Damien threw me a sheepish smile and tipped his hat.

I walked past him without even sparing a nod.

He came up beside me anyway, keeping up with my pace. "You still sore at me?"

"There's nothing for me to be sore at. The fact is, you're an asshole, and you won't leave me alone. Until Zeth came home, you acted as if I didn't exist."

Damien straightened his jacket as he walked. "Well, you were trying to court all those women, so I let you be. But then you actually started noticing that prick."

My jaw clenched as it hit me. Damien didn't take my search for a wife seriously, so now he was jealous. Apparently, everyone but my own father knew I was full of shit for the past couple of years by trying to court women. Or perhaps Father *had* known and was just in denial the whole time. I knew I was. It was honestly laughable now.

"What's with all the stuff? Giving gifts to that tramp?"

I opened my mouth to curse him again, but Damien wasn't worth my anger. Instead, I said, "Zeth is a much better man than you'll ever be, so calling him something he isn't only makes you look like a fool."

"He's a nobody," Damien spat. "A poor boy with nothing to his name but the dirty shoes on his feet. He's trying to fool everyone into thinking he and his homely sister came into some money so he can marry into money instead. I don't like hypocrites."

"Like the pot calling the kettle black," I snapped, shaking my head.

"Don't you realize he's just using you?"

For a moment, I let his words get to me before I walked faster. He was ridiculous, and I was determined to get away from him. Unfortunately, the devil wouldn't leave me alone and continued to follow me.

"I know a conniving man when I see one, and Washer is it," he went on. "He lost his chance with Miss Winters, so he's moved on to you. You're just too naive to see it. He'll ruin your family name."

"Good. It's time we Somersets made some changes."

Damien's words were toxic, but I was grounded in my love for Zeth. I knew he loved me indefinitely.

"Aren't you hearing me, Amby?" Damien grabbed my arm to turn me around, and I pushed him off me. He sneered, "Washer doesn't belong here. I'll just have to see to it that he knows that."

My fists curled instinctively around my bag at the threat. "You leave Zeth alone, or I'll deal with you myself."

Damien's eyes flashed with fire. Rather than say anymore, he turned and walked away. A part of me wanted to follow him and punch him right in the face, while the other part hated to cause a scene on Main Street. Grown men didn't get into fights; they fought with words. Unfortunately, Damien stopped listening long ago, and he was becoming an incredibly big thorn in my side.

I tried to remove him from my thoughts as I approached Zeth's home. When his freshly chipped door came into sight, a layer of purple was now featured in the rainbow. Smiling at it, I knocked, and he opened it with a welcoming grin. I placed the bag of supplies in his arms, making him grunt, and kissed his stubbled chin.

"I brought a few things to replace in here," I said, taking off my cap and jacket to hang on the hook, feeling so comfortable in this place already. "Mostly cabinet knobs for the kitchen upstairs, and extra supplies to clean."

"That's really great of you." Zeth unloaded the items onto the counter. "I've been thinking about you all morning. How did it go with your dad? Did you two get a chance to talk?"

His question was so simple, yet full of so much care.

"I did," I said, looking down. "I told him the truth, that I've always loved you and that we want to open our own shop."

"I'm proud of you," Zeth replied affectionately. "And what did he say?"

I leaned my back against the counter and stared at the ground with a shrug. "Nothing."

"What do you mean?"

"He scribbled on a paper at his desk, looked at me once, and said absolutely nothing to me..."

"That's fucking rude." His jaw clenched tightly, and his fists curled. "Do you want me to go back with you?" Zeth's frustration was mounting, but I was already past any anger.

"No, I told my father what I wanted to say and that's that." I raised my chin and pushed off the counter to face him. "It could have gone worse. He could have told me to leave, or fired me. He didn't do either."

Zeth's glare darkened, so I uncurled his fist to kiss each of his fingers until I came to his ring. Its black color further exposed his unease.

I smiled sheepishly. "You're cute when you're protective."

He snorted and rolled his eyes. "I'm glad you believe so, since I plan on watching over you for the rest of our lives. But are you really okay with how it went?"

"I already decided to make my own way, whether he agrees or not."

"I guess that's true. Maybe you just need to be like water wearing away a path, eh?"

"I certainly hope so. I'm feeling good right now. And I've been thinking all day about us working together." Zeth's hands squeezed mine, the worry clearing from his face. I picked up the wood and toolbox. "Want to head upstairs to board the window? Just until we can get it properly fixed."

Zeth nodded, grabbing the remaining bag, and made his way upstairs. I followed his heels and came into the kitchen. The room was much cleaner than the last time I'd helped him. All the cabinets hung straight, the floor was swept free of debris, and the ceiling was in good shape.

I whistled as I stepped inside and set down the supplies. "It looks amazing in here."

"Thank you. Todd helped me hang the fallen cabinet while Arthur sang tavern songs to entertain us."

I made a disgruntled noise. "I'm sorry I missed that."

"Trust me, you wouldn't say that if you heard Arthur's singing."

I chuckled as I made my way to the window. Zeth's wadded-up shirt still plugged the hole in the glass. "This window will forever be a cherished place, the spot where you decided you couldn't keep your hands off me."

"I was going out of my mind trying to keep you in my life." He set the tool bag at our feet and took both boards from me. "I also needed someone handy with a tool."

I leaned in close to brush my lips against his stubbly jaw. "Oh, is that what it is? You needed someone to fix things for you? Or you needed someone to handle your *tools*?" I asked before grabbing a piece of wood from his arms.

"Both, if you don't mind."

"I suppose that means I could try and pleasure you while you work on repairs." I chuckled as I placed one of the boards across the window to see how to angle it. At my side, Zeth set the other board aside, then leaned against the wall and crossed his arms.

"I dare you to try."

I eyed him invitingly before aligning the wooden piece to fit precisely between the window's frame and up against the glass. "A dare," I finally said. "You know neither of us can turn down one of those."

"I know," he said with such heated certainty that he made my knees go weak.

"Right." I nodded as I wedged the other piece of wood in. "Work. Renovations. Pleasing you. Wonderful visions..."

Zeth chuckled softly, and I didn't have to look over to know he was staring at me, those gorgeous eyes of his burning me up. But I glanced over anyway, and when I did, he threw me a crooked smile.

Damn.

I stepped away from the window, evaluating it, and realized the top piece of wood wasn't cut as well as the one beneath it. It made me remember the chair I'd broken with a hammer only last month. "Hm, do you think my skills alone are good enough for us to get by on selling furniture?"

Zeth's hand found my shoulder, and he nudged me to turn as he stepped in close. "You just closed off my window when all I could do was stuff a shirt into it. I didn't even see you take any measurements. And your dining table was certainly sturdy." He winked. "So, you tell me. What do you think of yourself?"

I raised my chin and thought of all the things I'd made in the past couple of years, starting with a simple birdhouse. And now I had a barn full of pieces ready to be sold. I thought of the back room where Zeth's family once washed clothes and imagined myself woodworking there under the tin roof. Bringing this shop back to life with a new business would feel as if we were carrying on in their memory.

"I can do this," I whispered. "You and me. Two peas in a pod. The Daring Duo. Us."

"Us," Zeth agreed adoringly. "You'll make beautiful furniture, and I'll go antique shopping in other towns."

I crossed my arms. "And would you be bringing me with you?"

Zeth looped his arms around my waist and pulled me against him. "You have all the best ideas, darling. Let's spend the weekends on small trips, and dig through piles of junk for treasures to sell in our shop. I can't wait."

I moved in to kiss his neck. "Mm, that sounds wonderful. Let's go to the shore first. My aunt has a cabin there."

"Will we have the place to ourselves?" When I nodded with a lick of my lips, he hummed with a wicked gleam.

"I'd also like to put money into renovations," I added, before we became too distracted. Looking around the kitchen, I put my hand up, palm out, to mentally sketch out ideas. "Fresh wallpaper in here and downstairs in the shop to liven it up, and some lamps. Perhaps polish all the floors too. I can build shelves to use for displays too. We can add the dining table to the list of things to sell at the Founders Day Fest next week. Hopefully, it'll sell for a pretty cal. What do you think, my love?"

"Wait, sell the dining table? I was hoping to eat there next," Zeth said with a husky breath.

I blushed, knowing well what he meant.

He ruffled my curls with a teasing, "Is that a yes?" When I tried to smack his hand, he captured mine instead and moved us around slowly, as if we were dancing. I moved in close, enjoying his rumbling voice as he said, "You really did build a delightful table. It could be a nice addition to our kitchen, don't you think?"

"Zeth..." My stomach fluttered as I thought about what we'd

done on that table just last night. "It's much too large for this room, and it's the one thing that'll bring us the most money. But once we get this place going, I'll make us a smaller table, and you can do all the naughty things you want to me on it. Promise."

The way Zeth inhaled roughly, I knew he liked my idea.

32

Zeth

With Amby's artistic eye and craftsmanship, combined with my tenacity and business acumen, our partnership was off to a solid start. We boarded the window, discussed merchandise, and agreed to wallpaper the main shop walls to liven them up. We even snuck in a few heated kisses before I escorted him out of the shop that evening.

That affection would have to hold me over until I saw him again. We left off with plans to meet for dinner tomorrow, and I couldn't wait. Even more so since he gave me some money and detailed instructions for the wallpaper he wished me to shop for while he worked.

Doing as he asked gave me a thrill. Relationships were about give and take, and once Amby and I started being honest with our feelings, we got along so well. Even better than old times. When I saw his sparkle of excitement, I was willing to do anything for him. Now I was actually looking forward to the next week of preparation for the festival. It was bound to go quickly, and I wanted to make Amby proud of me for completing his tasks while he earned us funds to do more.

I just wished there wasn't a shadow over Amby whenever he mentioned his dad. That cloud would hang over him and our relationship until something was resolved between those two. Hopefully, it would resolve soon. I hated seeing Amby hurt by that silent rejection.

The sun was setting in gorgeous pinks and golds as I entered the tailor shop. Inside, the circular dais with the half circle of mirrors stood empty, and the blue-cushioned chair where Amby once lounged with his book was bereft of his flashing annoyance.

I strolled over to the chair and trailed a finger over the cool, wood trim, wishing Amby were sitting there and leaning back to glance at me with daring eyes. We just parted. How was I missing him this much already?

Glancing around, I found the dressing curtains all open and empty, so I called out, "Sassy Cat, where are you?"

I was rewarded with a deep sigh through the slightly ajar work-room door. Some rattling came next, and then Millie popped her curly head out of the gap with a squint that said she didn't appreciate my interruption.

"What are you doing here?" she asked with less kindness than her wonderful big brother deserved.

I shrugged. "I thought you might enjoy my company for the walk home, and I also wanted to see what you're making. I'm sure it's magnificent."

Millie stood up straighter in the doorway and gave me an odd look before opening the door wide enough for me to see through. A well-lit room housed tables, sewing machines, and barrels with bolts standing tall like pencils in a cup.

"See enough?" Millie teased. I didn't know why she was acting so nervous, but she also appeared dashing in new pants that hugged her curves and paired well with her yellow blouse with rolled up sleeves.

"You didn't leave the house in those," I noted as I joined her at the door and pecked her cheek. "Are you trying to make the old biddies in town blush from your boldness?"

"No," she grumbled. "But, is it a problem if I do?"

When we entered Everdeen, it would have been. Now... "Not at all. I want you to be yourself."

I didn't blame Millie for squinting at me like I had lost my mind. I spent the last month harping about ladylike behavior. It was surprising that she put up with me at all. I needed to turn those habits around, or I didn't deserve her in my life. "Seriously, Mils, I like the pants on you. Your design is flattering."

"Why are you being so nice?"

"Me? Nice?" I gasped with mock affront. "How dare you make such a dastardly accusation." I grabbed her shoulders to spin her around and nudged her to walk as I followed. "Now, show me what else you're making."

"But it's not ready."

"Pish posh," I replied, using her own words against her. No matter how poorly her sewing looked, I would make sure to praise it. "Ready or not, you're trying a new skill, and that's worth showing me. You can't get better without trying."

I thought my fancy saying was worthy of a pillow, but Millie grumbled and led me over to a smaller table by a back window. There, a pile of black fabric puddled on the surface, and a basket of sewing notions sat at the foot of a chair. When Millie lifted the black fabric, it unfolded to resemble a suit jacket.

It was... inside out. I was looking at the inner seams without lining. The basting work was neat and orderly, and brought back memories of when Memaw used to hem and alter clothes for customers.

Surely Millie didn't have those skills. She always made me do the sewing at home. I took the jacket, holding it closer to see the rows of straight lines. "Are you tailoring?"

"Heavens no, Arthur does that. I'm learning how to design and pattern like Emiline. But do you see this?" she asked with growing excitement as she pointed to some neat stitches that attached reinforcement to the pockets. "I did that."

"Oh... well done," I enthusiastically praised, like I did over her ugly school projects when we were young. Maybe one day I could do the same for the little rascals Amby and I hoped to raise. If they were lucky, they'd learn from Amby's excellent craftsmanship. *Aunt* Millie could teach them too. What a thought.

"Try it on," Emiline's voice intruded.

I turned to see her and Arthur entering the workroom. Arthur made the space less spacious but all the more welcoming. They must have stepped out and just returned, and it struck me as nice that these two trusted Millie with their shop already. They even trusted her to sew on pockets.

I was going to ask Amby's sister what she meant by trying something on when Millie turned her black jacket right-side out and handed it to me.

The cut and color reminded me strongly of the suit Amby picked out for me, the one he said looked swoon-worthy. I had decided to forego that one, and the loss to my wardrobe had been noticeable.

"Is this for me?" I asked Millie. It was probably a stupid question, but I wasn't used to receiving gifts.

When she nodded, my heart swelled at her kindness. At all of their kindness. Feeling grateful, I pulled out my handkerchief to dab at my eyes. Then I let Millie help me into the new jacket. Emiline watched with an approving grin while Arthur inclined his head and folded his thick arms over his apron. It was only after I turned to find Millie staring at me with pride that I knew we both found a new place in our lives. I couldn't be happier that we returned to Everdeen.

Once dressed, they encouraged me to model it in the mirror. I didn't give a shit how the jacket looked. They made it for me, and I loved the damn thing for that reason alone. Regardless, I modeled the jacket on the dais. As I rubbed a hand down my fabric, my pinky ring glimmered blue, and I swelled with importance. I couldn't wait to see Amby's reaction when I showed up at the Founders Day Festival wearing my new jacket with the ascot and ring he'd chosen for me.

Those thoughts made me happy as Emiline pinned a few adjustments. Arthur hung the closed sign and made his way to the back room while Millie began cleaning her station.

"By the way, Zeth," Emiline said as she placed another pin, "I'm glad you decided to come home. Amby's glad most of all. I haven't seen him this happy in a long time. Seeing the two of you together again really stirs up good memories." She stepped back and smiled. "He chose the right person."

Her words made me glow with happiness, because the last time I spoke to Emiline in the shop, she'd told me of Amby's sad mood, back when I foolishly believed we could just remain friends. No one had been happy then. I nodded in agreement to her now. "Maybe I can call you sister one day?"

"I'd be delighted." Emiline's eyes lit up, and I let go of a breath, grateful to gain her approval. She squeezed my arm before helping me out of the jacket.

Even if Mr. Somerset disapproved of Amby, at least his daughters would still call Amby family. Call *us* family. I liked the idea of adding three spirited and intelligent siblings to my life, and that included Marigold. She had some promise. Maybe after Amby and I fixed up the laundry, we could invite Marigold and her husband, Jack, over for dinner and casual conversation. I had a feeling we could win them both over too.

As Emiline, Arthur, and Millie finished closing, I redressed and waited in the chair. It was dark through the shop windows by the time Millie and I said our farewells.

Not two steps down Main Street, Millie turned to me. "You're in a good mood."

I crossed my arms and strolled a little faster. "I am not."

She gave a lighthearted laugh and smacked my elbow to make me slow my gait, so I did.

"You're right, I'm feeling blessed. Amby and I started planning our future."

"About time. You should've picked him in the first place."

I sent her a glare for her bratty reply. Then I offered her my arm so we could walk together. She made me think, though... "If we tried to con Amby into marriage, things wouldn't have worked out as well as they did."

"You're probably right."

"I'm always right."

She snorted, and I pretended she agreed with me.

"More seriously, Mils, would it be alright with you if we kept the laundry? I know we need the money, but Amby wants to help with renovations, and I'm going to sell his craftwork at the festival to raise funds. We've been talking about turning it into a shop."

She puckered her face long enough to make me worry before she smiled deviously, "Of course, you idiot. I never wanted to sell our home."

Our home. She'd called the laundry a home from the start. Perhaps I was the idiot. "Yes, well, I assume you plan on moving in with Anna?"

"Are you trying to kick me out already?" She snickered and tilted her head in thought. "Anna says her place is too big, so she's been thinking about selling, maybe to Amby's dad. She'd like to find a smaller house, perhaps a country cottage."

I could imagine the decorations already, busy and cozy.

"And then?" I asked.

"*And then,* I'm hoping she might marry me. How does a *winter* wedding sound?"

"Appropriate," was my teasing answer.

Winter was half a year away. Perfect. My excitement for her plan was three-quarters about her, and one-fourth about Amby moving in with me by the Winter Feast. Part of me knew he would be traditional and want marriage first, just like the girls. We had some talking to do, and some planning too, if I was to warm him up in my bed on Feast morning.

"Maybe we can plan a double wedding?"

"No way, get your own," Millie teased and hugged my arm.

"You're right, maybe spring. I'd rather see him surrounded by flowers as he becomes mine, officially."

Millie's mouth opened to bully me, so I nudged her to the edge of the sidewalk, enjoying her curses as she clung to her loving brother's arm. Once she agreed to be nice, we settled into an even pace that felt companionable. The sidewalk was empty except for a bakery shop girl putting their chairs upside down on the table tops and a townsperson walking in the opposite direction.

The townsperson passed us in a lovely gown, and I tipped my cap to her. I would need to be friendly if I wanted to make sure our shop succeeded. Unfortunately, the woman ignored me and went so far as sneering at Millie's pants, so I flipped her off.

The woman huffed off and Millie smirked from my side. At least I made Millie smile. "I guess Anna was correct, we don't need everyone's approval."

"Anna's very smart," Millie cooed from my side.

"How long have you liked her?"

"I think I liked Anna even before we left Everdeen. She used to stay after school every day to tutor me. I remember thinking she had the prettiest blue eyes I've ever seen as she lectured me."

"A teacher crush? So, that's why you never did your homework."

Millie turned her head to hide her blush, and I laughed even harder. My life was full of adorable brats, and I loved them. In only a month, our lives had changed so much. From leaving the City in mourning to facing the challenges of being on our own. Now, Millie and I had found new careers and reunited with old loves. I had a feeling Mum would be proud of us.

But the biggest change might have been my own. I was such a grumpy bear when we first walked into Everdeen. Now I was reciting poetry and learning how to wear my heart on my sleeve. I was learning trust. Amby and my new friends were teaching me so much. My life's equation changed, and I couldn't be more pleased that Amby was the solution.

33

Ambrose

I blew out a breath as I glanced over myself in the mirror. I was wearing my favorite dark sage suit today, perfect for the Founders Day Festival. I hadn't been to the barber for a shave in a few days and liked how the prickly hair looked on my jaw. Perhaps I was reverting to my old carefree self.

If only I felt carefree. Every once in a while, I'd think of Father and feel a little glum. Not because he was ignoring me, but because I still loved him and wanted his blessing for Zeth and me. His rejection hurt, and I would always carry some guilt that I had abandoned the Somerset legacy. I wondered if Father would ever speak to me again.

But today, I wasn't going to let anything get in my way, not even thoughts of my father. So, I straightened my back and raised my chin before opening the door of my room and stepping out.

I made my way downstairs to meet Emiline and Hattie for breakfast. To my surprise, Marigold was there too, sitting in her usual spot. Father was the only one missing, no doubt gone to the bank for the morning before attending the festival.

As I reached the table, Emiline said, "You're chipper today, dear brother."

I leaned down to kiss her cheek. "I suppose I am."

Hattie beamed at me as I moved around to do the same to her.

When I looked over at Marigold, she raised a delicate eyebrow. I smiled as I moved forward and bent to kiss her cheek too, which Hattie giggled at. I had never done such a thing to my oldest sister before, but seeing Marigold here raised my spirits for some reason.

"Marigold, you look well today. Are you going to the festival?"

"Yes, yes," Marigold replied nonchalantly, picking up her spoon to stir a sugar cube into her teacup. "I received good news this week that has me in a mood for socializing. Emiline said you're selling some furniture."

"I am." I took my seat across from her and glanced at my plate of eggs, sausage, mushrooms, toast, and oranges. "I rented a cart to take some end tables and chairs to sell."

"We all agreed to help you load your pieces from the barn." Emiline said. "Mari insisted."

I blinked in surprise as Marigold inclined her head. My heart glowed from my sisters' generosity. "Thank you. I could certainly use the help. Especially with the dining set."

"Oh, Amby, not the dining table!" Emiline groaned. "You put your all into it. Don't let just anyone have it."

"I'm working on something with Zeth, so we'll need the money."

"You mean turning the laundry into a store?" came Marigold's deadpan voice.

I stilled, my fork frozen midair, wondering how she'd found out. When I gave Hattie an accusing stare, she straightened to say, "Don't look at me, I didn't even know!"

I'd told Emiline yesterday of my plans, so I eyed her next. She only shook her head.

"Father told me," Marigold clarified. I expected to see her peeved expression, but I was surprised when she smiled crookedly.

Something clutched my stomach. "He did?"

"Well, when Zeth tried to sell his property during the salon, Father expected to negotiate further at the bank," she continued, and I picked up my glass of juice. "Then he told me yesterday that you and Zeth plan to do something with it. And to be honest, I'm glad. That old laundry has sat cold and unused on Main Street for years. It's about time someone put it to use. What better person than my brother and his clingy childhood boyfriend?"

I spit my drink out, luckily only getting it on my own plate. As I dabbed my chin with my napkin, Emiline and Hattie started laughing. Clearing my throat, I said, "How did you—"

"Amby, you were the worst at pretending as if you didn't have feelings for him. You moped around for a whole year after Zeth left! And those poems at the salon were obviously for each other." Marigold rolled her eyes, and I sat back in my chair, defeated.

When Hattie and Emiline snorted, I turned to them with a sour expression, but then I chuckled along with them. I suppose it was true that I didn't hide my love for Zeth very well.

"Well, it's all true," I boldly proclaimed. "We plan to fix up the old storefront and turn it into a proper furniture and antiques shop. I'll continue working at the bank and help Zeth when I can. He's a good businessman. He has years of experience at an auction house, in Port Winchester, at that. He's wonderful with numbers, and I do fairly well making furniture myself. We'll make a great team." I took another gulp of juice, getting it down this time, and then took a bite from my plate.

"You don't have to explain," Marigold assured, hesitating before she said, "I know I'm a hard person sometimes, but that doesn't mean I haven't seen your strengths. I've seen your furniture, and I'm impressed. You have a gift, and as Mother used to tell us, once we find that gift, we should embrace it." When my eldest sister met my eyes, I saw nothing but honesty and respect in hers.

This was truly a dream. I had to pinch my palm to make sure I *wasn't* dreaming and felt a sting. Yes, it was most certainly real.

"Goodness, Mari, what good things do you have to say about me?" Hattie broke in.

Marigold gave that annoyed look—lips tightening, eyelids lowering—before she glanced at our youngest sister. "You're blessed with getting your way."

When Emiline and I broke out in laughter yet again, Hattie huffed.

"I am not!" she cried.

"You are," I said, relaxing enough to prop my elbow up on the table to watch how she pouted. "But you're the last of the Somerset siblings. Little sisters get their way more than anyone."

Hattie rolled her eyes. "That is true, I suppose."

"We wouldn't have it any other way." Emiline took Hattie's hand from across the table.

As they broke into happy chatter, I picked up a piece of buttered toast to nibble on, far too excited about the day to eat much.

Just then, a firm kiss planted on my cheek. I twisted in my chair to find Zeth standing behind me, smiling handsomely. My eyes widened as I drank in a new black jacket and the paisley ascot I'd picked out for him. His brown hair was combed back, and his face freshly shaved. I swear I even smelled perfume.

"Wow," I said. "You look phenomenal."

"Thank you. I like that suit on you too," Zeth complimented. We weren't alone, but that didn't stop him from tracing a finger quickly over the scruff on my jaw. Then he gave me an appreciative wink before continuing, "I hope you don't mind that I let myself in through your front door. I wanted to surprise you."

"You're always welcome here, Zeth," Emiline said before I could.

I nodded in agreement, unable to take my eyes off Zeth as he stood there grinning at us all, with one hand on the post of my chair and the other behind his back. Then he leaned forward in front of me and stole a big bite from the toast in my hand.

Zeth stood straight again with a playful half-smile as he chewed. How did he appear so handsome while eating? I laughed, distracted, when he pulled out a full bouquet of pink roses from behind his back and said, "For you, my darling Rosie."

Emiline and Hattie shared a unified "Aww" that made me blush as I regarded Zeth tenderly. I'd never been given flowers by anyone before. I took the bouquet with gratitude. "Thank you, Zeth. I adore them."

"I'm glad you do," Zeth replied as he pulled out an empty chair to slide into the seat. "I liked the pink since it made me think of you."

"Oh? Is it because I'm so sweet?" I teased as I inhaled them.

He chuckled and leaned closer to smell them too. "Yes, and they also match your cheeks right now."

"Oh goodness, you two are made for each other," Marigold commented, and I was certain I would find an eye roll with that comment, but her face softened, "They are beautiful, Zeth. So good to see you again."

"You as well. I hope you and Jack are joining us at the festival. Just come early, before all of Amby's wonderful woodwork sells. He's sure to be a hit."

I gave Zeth a smirk as I booped his nose. "You mean *we'll* be a hit."

Zeth grinned and reached over to snatch an orange slice from my plate, eating it as Marigold confirmed her plans to visit. I pushed the plate between us so we could share, just as we did as kids eating snacks in the kitchen.

"I'll be sure to come to the tent as well," Hattie piped up. "Today is my last event before Father takes me to visit the nursing institute. I can't wait to start school in the fall."

"I'm sure you'll love the campus there," Marigold said. "But are you sure you want to attend an all-girls school?"

Hattie scrunched her face. "Of course. It's one of the best in the area for nursing. Don't worry, I'll find the boys in town."

"I'm sure you will," Emiline agreed with a twitch of her lips behind her teacup. "Arthur and I will make sure you have the prettiest dresses for your adventures."

I smiled at my twin, always the one most concerned with our happiness. She'd found her own as well, with Arthur, just as I thought might happen. My sisters were all doing the things they wanted. I knew we were all on the right paths for our lives.

Once we both had our fill of breakfast, I grabbed the roses and stood up from my seat. "The cart will be here any minute, but I want to find a vase for the flowers."

"We'll meet you at the barn," Emiline said, standing. Hattie and Marigold followed.

Zeth and I made our way outside to the garden behind the house. I stepped over the bricks inlaid into the ground, where grass and moss grew between them, and skimmed my eyes over the many flower pots and old vases my mother had collected when she was alive. Most of them had flowers or ivy growing out of them. It made this little area look green and lush.

Zeth strolled slowly behind me, as if he were appreciating the view, while I picked out a faded, yellow, porcelain vase with green ivy designs around the rim. There was a large chip in the side from when my mother dropped it, only to tell me she loved it more with its flaw. "Here's just the thing to put the roses in. I know it's a battered vase, but it'll do, don't you think?"

"I like it," Zeth agreed with a nod and moved in to hug my hips around the flowers. "Besides, didn't you hear? I don't need fancy vases in my life, or twenty tea sets, or purple upholstered cars. Just you."

"Look at you." I nudged him playfully. "Making me melt with your swoony words. I'll put the roses in the barn. We can look at them while you make my *cheeks* pink next time."

"Fuck me," Zeth exhaled, and I laughed at him. His eyes sparkled with longing as he thumbed the stubble on my cheek.

Smiling, I said, "I'm sure the cart for the furniture is here. You ready to get started?"

34

Zeth

Tapping the side of my pants, I enjoyed the spring of wadded paper. A pocket full of money and another pleased customer; the festival was going well. We set up our tent in the crafters' row and quickly sold one of Amby's side tables in the first hour. Next went two chairs. By noon, the festival became busy with families, and most of Amby's decorative knick-knacks went out to good homes.

Now, we just sold his second side table. I waved the nice man off as he made his way into the bustling festival foot traffic.

Other festival goers peeked into our tent, and none of them mattered as much as the clever man standing on the other side of the dining set he'd crafted. I couldn't stop staring at Amby. His green suit tried for casual, yet gave off an upper-crust impression, especially paired with those gold-rimmed glasses and shiny, auburn curls. There was no mistaking Amby's elite past, but here he was with me, the poor washer boy, selling his handicrafts to the towns-folk of Everdeen. With the hint of a beard on his strong jawline, he'd never appeared more handsome.

I just wished he didn't look so nervous. Even now, he rubbed a thumbnail as the crowds passed. He fumbled here and there today while answering questions about the types of wood he used and how he joined them. Yet, I had faith he would get better at talking about his work. And if he wanted to just build after this, then that was fine, because I memorized all his answers. Once our shop opened, he could freely enjoy the solitude of his workshop while I tended to the customers. I already enjoyed bragging about him to the shoppers. Haggling prices was second nature, and boy did I miss it. I never felt so useful as I did now, helping Amby.

When the crowd disappeared briefly, most of them shifting to other booths selling candles, soap, honey, and trinkets, I turned to Amby and leaned my arms over a chair back. "No need to worry, darling. They love your craft. You're a great success."

"This is a nice start," Amby replied, facing me across the table. "Thank you for having such faith in me. I wouldn't have been able to do this at all without you. You have a knack for talking with people."

"It's all about listening to what people want. For example, I can read you and…" I squinted at him in play, and he bit his lip adorably. "Ah, there, you're telling me you want a kiss."

Amby tapped the side of his face. "Right here, on my pretty cheek."

I growled at Amby's boldness and stalked around the table until I could tug him against me for a light peck to his cheek. Lingering there, I inhaled his vanilla musk scent before whispering into his ear, "Now I get to pick the next spot."

Despite the warmth of the tent, Amby shivered delightfully in my arms, and I was tempted to kiss his lips right there. But now wasn't the time, or place. Amby's dad had us too nervous to attempt a public courting kiss. Even after a week, his rejection still bothered us. I could wait for that to heal, but I chafed to claim my boy.

"Well, looks like you two are doing well," came a new voice, and I jumped slightly at Emiline standing with Arthur in our tent. "Did you already sell the end tables and rocking chairs?"

Amby slipped out of my arms to face his sister. He answered her while pushing up his glasses, but he couldn't hide that lovely pink tint on his cheek, right where I had just enjoyed kissing him. He glanced back at me to ask, "Right, Zeth?"

"Yes," I answered sweetly without a single clue as to what Amby just said.

He chuckled, seeing right through me, and I basked in the soft sound.

I fisted his shoulder in play and turned to tell Emiline, "See anything you wish to buy before it's gone?"

"Yes, isn't this dining set marvelous, Arthur?"

"It's a beauty," Arthur agreed with her enthusiastically. "I love the designs at the corners."

Arthur looked genuinely impressed as he moved his large frame closer to examine the smooth surface we used last week for our delicious lovemaking. Seeing how Amby glowed, I couldn't help but have some fun.

I leaned over the table to push on it with both hands. "Amby outdid himself on this one. It's well made. Nice and sturdy."

Arthur nodded, but it was Amby's widening eyes that had me amused. I winked at him as I slapped the mahogany hard to make sure Amby felt that delightful sound.

"It holds up well," I explained to Arthur. "No matter how much weight you put on it."

Arthur gazed longingly at the table, oblivious to our sexual banter. Then Amby coughed politely, and when his lips tugged up, I grinned at him. I wrapped my arm around his shoulder while his sparkling eyes found mine. It was satisfying to be connected again like this, like old times, but better. So much better.

"Yes, uh, great presentation. That set turned out to be very solid," Amby said, his voice cracking slightly. "Would you... like it for your house, Arthur?"

I snorted with humor because Amby actually dared to sell our table to our friend while I had just been playing around. What if Arthur and Emiline married and invited us over to dinner, and we exchanged pleasantries while I sat there remembering how much I enjoyed filling Amby up against it? Dear heaven... How would I survive such a family dinner? Amby's daring was going to kill me.

I had to be blushing now too as I stepped aside while Amby gripped the top of a chair to pull it out for Arthur to try. I rested my hand right next to Amby's. He sent me a smile before turning to Arthur with a price for the full dining set.

Arthur sat with a heavy sigh and wiggled in the chair. He seemed satisfied with how well it held up and asked, "Well, since I know you and your family, perhaps you could throw in a discount?"

"Arthur!" Emiline slapped his arm. "Amby and Zeth are trying to make profits. I'm sure they'd sell it to someone else at full price."

Amby interjected, "No, it's alright. The table's been sitting a while."

I nudged Amby's hand with a gentle cough. "You're supposed to haggle up, darling, not down."

"Hey, don't talk Amby out of the discount," Arthur groaned. "I thought we were friends? I'll take the set before the price changes."

"Sounds like a deal." Amby nodded at him. "Five percent off. Family and friends discount."

"What, only five?" Arthur said in mock offense.

"What he means is, he'd be *delighted* to take it," Emiline said. When Arthur went to protest, she raised her brow.

Arthur chuckled and held out his hand to Amby. "Well, can't say no to that. I'll take it."

Amby practically shook with excitement over selling his major piece. Arthur stood to join Emiline and wrapped his large arm around her waist, and Amby regarded them sweetly, clearly glad his sister found someone so good.

My stomach decided to make itself known at that moment, gurgling a protest louder than the bustling festival sounds. I rolled my eyes, and Arthur nodded at me.

"Sounds like you need to eat. Have you had lunch?"

"No, only breakfast," I answered.

"We could both use a bite," Amby agreed, no doubt feeling just as hungry.

Emiline waved out past the tent. "Then you two go wander off. Arthur and I can handle your booth."

Before Amby could object, I grabbed his hand and tugged him to follow me. He sputtered prices for the few items and thanked his sister and Arthur before exiting with a swing of our hands.

"So... food?" he asked.

"Yes, please," I answered quickly and followed the delectable aroma of meat cooking over stone pits. I remembered past festivals as a kid, watching townsfolk enjoying their charred beef on wooden sticks while I had nothing. It wasn't a sad memory, just the truth, and it made me all the more appreciative of my blessings as Amby paid for two sticks and handed one over to me.

Thanking him, I devoured mine while Amby also dug right in. The grilled meat was savory and tender to chew. I enjoyed it immensely as we watched the festival goers moving from tent to tent.

"I'd like some sweets," Amby said, nearly finished. "Maybe we can find you some fruit."

His thoughtfulness made me smile around my last bite. I nodded, and we walked through the food stalls. I wanted to find him the cake he used to talk about wanting for his birthdays, with whipped cream and strawberries.

When we found the cake stall, Amby pointed out all his favorite desserts in the painted picture menu while we waited in line. I couldn't care less about the food, but I was excited to please and feed him. I wanted him happy and well taken care of, even pampered. It wasn't about money; it was about the joy of sharing a moment. Amby's excitement over the free roses I'd plucked from Anna's garden had felt just as wonderful as buying him cake.

His wide, brown eyes encouraged me now as I paid for the dessert and took the wooden bowl from the vendor. It had a huge dollop of frothy cream and a single spoon, exactly what we both wanted. I led Amby to a private spot between two tents and scooped some cream to hold out for him to eat.

His gaze snagged on my daring grin first before dropping to the spoon, and fuck me for loving the blush that filled his beautiful cheeks. He was so handsome as he leaned forward and opened that sassy mouth of his to eat the cream from my spoon. Goosebumps raced along my arms. I couldn't get enough of watching his lips close and tilt with happiness. Then he groaned with delight.

Oh hell... I could feed my good boy all day.

"It's wonderful," Amby said, licking the cream off his lips. He stole my spoon to dig into the cake properly. "Do you want some of the strawberries?"

I was about to manage a reply when he found a piece of the red fruit covered in whipped cream and put the whole thing in his mouth to lick it off. Then he captured it between his thumb and finger to offer it to me.

I felt outright carnal as I opened my mouth to take the strawberry, licking it free from his grasp. His eyes raked over me as I took my time enjoying the taste of the fresh fruit.

When Amby laughed, I wanted to cherish his mouth. He held so many wonderful ideas and clever quips behind those lips. I was lucky to be the one he felt comfortable enough to open up around, who had him sharing his whole body, heart, and mind.

I reclaimed the spoon and fed us both from the bowl while we watched the crowds pass our little hiding spot. A few people spotted us, some of them catching on that we were both together.

Once done, we discarded the bowl and pushed out into the open. I offered my arm, and Amby looped it through his and leaned his head on the side of my shoulder. It encouraged me that he wanted to walk through the festival like this. I enjoyed our casual chatting over the vendors and games as we passed their booths and tents.

"Oh, Zeth, let's try ring toss," Amby said, tugging on my arm.

"Nuh-uh, your aim with darts was just as bad as mine."

"You know I was drunk that night."

"If only I had such an excuse," I chuckled and let him pull me over to the game.

Twenty-four glass bottles stood in three rows, daring us to win. We paid to play, and the vendor handed out four rings each to toss. Between my far-flung throws that hit the back of the tent, and Amby's ringing glass, we managed to score enough points to win a prize. Amby picked out a necklace of colorful wooden beads, and I placed it around his neck.

"Look at you, so pretty," I hummed, imagining him in nothing but the long strand.

He blushed and took my hand to intertwine our fingers.

After that, we made our way toward the Everdeen Oak in the distance. The giant tree sat at the far edge of the festival with colorful ribbons that fluttered in the breeze from its low branches. Many of the ribbons were already gone. In the distance, dark clouds were rolling in. As much fun as we were having, an approaching storm was going to dampen my mood, not to mention the whole festival.

Hopefully, we could exchange our ribbons peacefully, because I always wanted to give Amby red, for love. It meant more to me now than ever. He had my heart, no matter what his dad said or did, even if he disowned Amby.

35

Ambrose

When Zeth and I came to the ribbon tree, we saw Annabelle and Millie walking in the distance, hand in hand. They noticed us too and waved, so we waved back. They both looked much different now. Annabelle's golden hair flowed to her waist, a rare sight, and Millie wore trousers instead of her usual split skirt. Together, they made a delightful couple. The red ribbons around their wrists fluttered as they swung their hands between each other. It was reviving knowing Annabelle had found someone she truly wanted to be with, and that Millie found her happiness as well.

Who would have thought? Millie Washer and Annabelle Winters.

I glanced up at the clouds, noticing how dark they were, and when I inhaled, I smelled fresh rain in the air. A breeze picked up, ruffling the leaves and colorful ribbons surrounding us. I closed my eyes for a moment to enjoy the cool sensation on my face.

This was perfect.

When I opened my eyes to see Zeth admiring me, I blushed and placed one of my hands upon the tree's enormous trunk. "The legend of the Everdeen Oak says that the woman who founded Everdeen saw the strength of the tree and knew there must be value in the land. The roots of the tree are said to spread so far, it carries blessings to the crops and all the people who live here." I eyed Zeth, wondering if he thought it was silly, but he only watched me with a gleam in his eye. He knew this legend as well as I did.

I gazed at the ribbons as they swayed in the breeze on the low, sturdy limbs, then continued. "The spirit of the tree is said to bless the ribbons, and is humbled by those who share them beneath its canopy. In this way, the tree flourishes more each year, and Everdeen continues to grow." I touched a ribbon. "I think... it's all a metaphor for love, really."

When Zeth smiled crookedly at me, I tilted my head. "What? Was all that silly?"

He shook his head as he pulled me close. "No. I was enjoying your adorable enthusiasm. Feel free to say more."

I laughed softly. "Well, you know how this legend continues on. You have to give a ribbon to someone you care deeply about. Different colors for what you wish them to have most in the coming year."

"Mm, then I know just the one I want to give you," Zeth answered with fondness. He turned to the tree and reached up to pluck a red ribbon from one of the branches. As he smoothed his long, graceful fingers along the length of it, his purple pinky ring shone with passion. "I can't believe I'm saying this, Rosie, but I'm glad my life fell apart in Port Winchester. I was never happy in the City, not really. No matter how much I achieved, my life was empty. I was meant to return to you."

I looked at him in awe, surprised by his confession, but also happy to hear it. He'd gone through so much since leaving Everdeen. Really, he'd gone through so much when we were younger too. We'd lent our shoulders to each other then. Now, we were exchanging our hearts. The feeling of tying all the loose ends together enraptured me so deeply, a lump rose in my throat. Zeth was a different man now, one I cherished even more for how much he'd changed.

As Zeth moved closer to me to tie the red ribbon around my wrist, I held my breath. He tied it off into a lopsided bow, then held my hands. "My dearest Rosie," he began. "Here's my promise to make you the happiest person in Everdeen from this day forward, and I ask you to promise me the same. Your strength makes me strong, and your adorable cuteness makes me weak in all the right ways. Your ideas inspire me to challenge us both to achieve our dreams." He shrugged bashfully. "It's not a haiku, but I hope you like it."

A delightful shiver ran through me as I said, "I do."

His eyes widened upon my confession of accepting his promise, and I bit my lip from the hidden meaning of my words. I hoped we would talk about marriage soon, but for now, a red ribbon was all I needed. "Thank you, Zeth, this means so much to me."

I held his hand and took in all the surrounding colors around us. There were so many meanings to each of them, from the loyalty of blue to the growth of green, to the friendship of purple, and so on. I eyed the pink one and pulled it off. Then I took one of the red ones and twirled the colors together before tying it around Zeth's wrist.

"Pink for your caring affection, and red for your love." My heart pounded nervously as I glanced up at him. "I know it's been difficult for us both, but I..." It was hard keeping my emotions in check, and I turned my face to the side to keep those stubborn tears in. Zeth's firm hand captured my chin and tilted my head up just as a tear rolled down my cheek. His eyes gleamed with moisture too, shining so magnificently gold and brown. Those eyes held such tenderness for me. Love, acceptance. A *kindred spirit*.

"I'm so glad you came back," I said, choking on my simple words, but they said everything as my passion for him surrounded me. Zeth's strong arms found me, and I embraced him fully, wrapping myself tightly around his middle and laying my head against his shoulder as fresh tears of happiness flowed. I inhaled deeply, realizing how lost I would be without him.

The sounds of people taking ribbons from the tree faded into the distance as we stood under the branches. I closed my eyes as I listened to the leaves rustle against the wind.

After a long while, a chill made me shiver against Zeth, and I finally pulled away to look at him, sniffing as I wiped one of my cheeks with the back of my hand.

"Amby, you're beautiful, inside and out," he whispered as he pulled a handkerchief out of his jacket and wiped the rest of my tears away. "Thank you for making my ribbon uniquely you."

"You're welcome," I said with mirth, my heart and soul so full.

Zeth handed me his damp cloth to blow my nose with, and I saw it was my handkerchief. The crisp, white fabric smelled of lye, and my threaded, gold initials gleamed even in the cloudy light. He'd taken such care of it, just as he took care of me. It tickled me that Zeth adored such a thing.

When the wind ruffled Zeth's hair, I looked up at the sky beyond him to see darker clouds moving in. A storm was just the thing to top off this lovely day. But I was worried about our tent. "We should return to close up the tent before it rains."

Zeth nodded and took my hand, but we didn't get five steps away before two familiar men stepped into our path, blocking us. One of them draped an arm around Zeth's shoulders like a drinking buddy would, and the other man wound his arm around Zeth's back before pulling him away from me.

Jonathan and Ezekiel were part of Damien's little gang. Them touching my man bothered me, so I hurried forward, but a firm hand fell on my shoulder and pulled me back roughly. When I turned around to see who it was, Damien Cooligan stared down at me. My stomach dropped.

"What are you doing?" I started, tearing myself away from him, but Damien grabbed my wrist.

"Wait," he said sharply. His eyes cut over to his partners in crime and nodded. The two men pushed Zeth roughly away from us. When I tried to break away, Damien held me in place with a forceful grip on my wrist that made me hiss from the sharp pain. "They're just taking him for a walk. To talk over some business, since he enjoys doing that."

"You piece of shit," I seethed.

"Look, I need your little boyfriend away for one minute so I can talk to you. Is that too much to ask?" Damien shook his head as he reached up to yank a red ribbon from the tree.

I narrowed my eyes on him. As soon as Damien tried to tie the ribbon around my arm, I jerked away and stepped back. I shook my head, stunned by the nerve he had to do such a thing.

"Are you deluded?" I half-laughed at him, sure he'd gone mad. "I don't want anything to do with you." I turned to get Zeth, but Damien snatched the edge of my jacket and turned me around.

"Washer doesn't belong here." His face flashed with anger. "Let the boys *chat* about him leaving town for good. We're willing to pay good money to keep him out. I saw him talking with your father at the salon. I'm willing to bet he'll ditch you as soon as he worms his way into your father's bank."

"You're even more deluded than I thought. So fuck off."

Damien frowned and cracked his neck. "Alright, suppose I'll use threats, then." He nodded at his goons. "See who's outnumbered now."

Behind me, the ruffians were already leading Zeth away to beat him. Zeth struggled with each step to break out of their grasp.

My fists curled with fury. "You try so hard to be Everdeen's group of thugs, acting as if you own this town and its people. Well, not me, and certainly not *him*. Now back off."

Damien chuckled. "Maybe I will, if you let me tie a pretty ribbon around that gorgeous neck of yours. Let me show you who wishes to own you."

"Fucking asshole," Zeth growled, only steps behind me. Ezekiel and Jonathan followed behind him, making sure Zeth didn't get away.

Damien's fiery eyes widened as he stared Zeth down. They were both tall and lean but Zeth had more muscle on him. That didn't stop Damien from pushing me out of the way and stepping closer to him. "Want to say that to me again, you piece of shit?"

"I think my fist has some choice words for you," Zeth replied smoothly, unbuttoning his jacket with a furious glare.

"No." I rushed between them and put up my hands before either of them could move toward the other. The last thing I wanted was Zeth getting hurt. His cap was already missing, and one of his cheeks looked scuffed. This was my fight. I would have to end it.

"Consider this your final warning," I told him, my nostrils flaring, "Leave, or I won't hold back."

"Ah, Amby, you're gonna make me hit your pretty face." Damien struck me so hard across my cheek that I stumbled into the tree.

"Bastard," I heard Zeth swear, followed by a swift hit, and Damien's grunt of pain. When I glanced up, the man was still standing with his hand to his jaw while Zeth shook out his fist with a hiss. Damien's friends came at Zeth and kicked the backs of his legs. His knees gave out, and Zeth grunted as they shoved him to the ground and held him there. Then Damien approached him with his fist curled.

White-hot rage flowed through me. I set my sight on Damien and steadied myself. Then I barreled forward and tackled him. Damien landed in the dirt with a wheeze, and I bent over him with my fists flying. Just like my school fighting days, my blood rushed, making me full of fire and brimstone. I dealt two blows to his face before he struck his fist into my ribs.

The air tensed in my lungs and pain radiated through me, but I was determined to keep him down, so I dealt another punch to his nose.

Damien gasped and put up his hands in surrender. I staggered back while my fists clenched and unclenched. Panting, I glared at Damien as he slowly got to his knees. His blond braid was falling apart, and his fancy tan jacket was stained from our scuffle in the grass. He wiped his nose with the back of his hand, smearing blood, as he stared at me in disbelief.

I seethed, pointing at him. "Stay *away* from Zeth Washer."

Damien narrowed his eyes before he searched for his friends nearby, no doubt ready to crack skulls for him if need be. Thunder rumbled in the distance as I braced my feet, ready to take them all on.

Then several hoots and claps went up, and I looked over to see that a crowd had formed nearby. I eyed Zeth, glad to see him okay as he nodded up at me from the dirt.

"Ambrose."

Glancing over, I found my father standing a few feet away, and all the fire in me drained.

"Mr. Somerset," Damien started, spitting blood to the ground. That hardened expression he usually wore reappeared. "I do say, your son has some problems that need addressing."

My father took in a sharp breath before narrowing his eyes on Damien. "The only problem I see here, Mr. Cooligan, is you. It would be best if you left now."

Someone shouted for Damien to take his punishment and leave, while others laughed. Damien inclined his head, shooting me one last glare before he and his friends pushed their way through the small crowd. As soon as he was gone, the gathering dispersed, some of them thanking us as they left. This fight would be the latest gossip in town. The Daring Duo took on Damien and his thuggish friends.

Zeth joined my side with concern etched on his face as he looked me over. He straightened my hair and clothes, and once he was satisfied I wouldn't die, he asked, "You alright, hero?"

I made a face at that. I was no hero, but the rush of adrenaline still flowed through me. I nodded as I put a hand over my ribs. "I don't think I broke anything. What about you? You got kicked."

"My knuckles are worse off. I haven't fought since the school yard." Zeth chuckled and flexed his abused fingers.

I took his hand in mine and gently rubbed over the sore spots. When I realized my father still stood near us with an indiscernible expression on his face, I frowned. I wasn't sure what to say to him, as I had expected him to leave without a word.

Zeth retrieved my cap and handed it over. I placed it on my head and nodded for us to leave.

But my father put up his hand, stopping us. "Ambrose, I'd like to talk with you."

Tensing, I glanced at Zeth, wondering what he was thinking. His handsome face was serious, his piercing eyes aimed at my father as if ready to defend me if need be. But my father wanted to speak with me, and I was eager to hear what he had to say. Daring to look him in the eye, I nodded.

My father smoothed his mustache with his fingers. "I took time to think about what you told me. About your future. Sometimes... it takes me a while to understand that I was in the wrong. And after seeing you both fight for one another, I realize just how wrong I've been." He fixed me with his eyes as I blinked at him, baffled by his words.

"I haven't exactly been the best father to you lately," he tried to explain. "I let my own dreams carry me away, but I should have never put such dreams on your shoulders." He paused for a moment and beheld me fondly, as if he were seeing me for the first time. "My silence isn't rejection, Ambrose. I've heard you, and I want you to know that whatever you choose for your future, I will support it."

The tension I'd carried for years eased from me as I suddenly saw my father in a new light. My vision blurred as I choked out, "Thank you."

When Father's mouth tightened with emotion and he held his arm out, I moved into his embrace. It was quick, his hand patting my back briefly before he pulled away and turned his head. But I swore I heard him sniffle.

"I visited your tent," Father went on. "And just acquired my first piece from your collection. Consider it the first of many investments."

"What—you mean... you bought something from our booth?" I asked in surprise.

"I did. A nice rocking chair for the porch."

"About fucking time," Zeth muttered under his breath, and I nudged his arm with a smirk.

Father only chuckled and nodded at Zeth. "I'll need two more for when you both come to visit and talk about your business."

My eyes widened. "Does that mean..."

"Yes, Ambrose, you both have my blessing to court. I decided that upon waking and stopped at the bank before the festival to take care of the Washer property's remaining dues. This way, you two can have a fresh start."

Zeth perked up in surprise. "You paid off my property tax?"

When Father nodded, Zeth wrapped an arm over my shoulder to tug me closer, and I embraced him with a joyful laugh.

Zeth pulled away but still held my hand. "Thank you, sir. Walter. Your support means a lot to us. Family means a lot to us too."

A big boom of thunder suddenly rumbled, making us flinch. Then a sprinkle of rain landed on my nose, and I observed the remaining, colorful ribbons waving wildly in the wind.

"Amby, Zeth!" Emiline yelled from nearby. She and Hattie rushed up to us with excitement, as if they'd just witnessed mine and Father's reconciliation. "All your furniture sold, Arthur is holding the tent down. We should get going before this storm starts."

Father nodded, but Hattie stepped forward. "Oh, wait, I haven't given a ribbon yet! I know just the man I want to tie one to."

When she gazed up at Father, he held out his arm for her. "I'd be delighted, my dear."

Zeth and I watched as my sisters walked around the enormous tree with my father. Several others ran to snag off last-minute ribbons to give to each other as well, including Richard and Ben, and other familiar faces. A storm wouldn't stop any of them from proclaiming their truths to one another.

"Our booth isn't far," Zeth pointed out. "Let's join Arthur and hide from this awful weather."

"Actually..." I smiled at him as the rain picked up. "I enjoy the rain. It's calming after what happened today."

Zeth chuckled and tugged me against him by my belt loops and nuzzled my cheek. "You know I hate storms."

I beheld Zeth's handsome face as the rain dampened his dark hair, messing it up just how I liked it. Moving my hands beneath his warm jacket, I said, "But you love me."

"That I do," he exhaled, his focus shifting from the storm to me.

I felt like Zeth's everything as his golden, sunset eyes melted me from the inside. His lips tilted in a wicked little grin. Even his voice sounded sultry as he tapped his lips and said, "I dare you to kiss me, Rosie."

My fingers curled in his shirt, and I leaned up to capture those sweet lips. When Zeth wrapped his arms around my waist to hold me closer, I cupped his face.

The rain pelted us harder as we indulged in our public courting kiss, and my mind filled with bliss. I caught words of encouragement from my sisters, and the hoots and claps from some of our friends as they witnessed our love. This man smiling against me was who I wanted more than anything else in the world. Someone who set my heart racing like a river in spring, someone who dared me to follow my own dreams.

And finally, I felt free.

The End

Acknowledgments

We want to thank you, our wonderful reader, for joining us on this journey into Everdeen. We hope you enjoyed the ride more than Zeth did in Annabelle's car! Special thanks go out to our Alpha & Beta readers: Lynda, Sara @larksliterarynest, and Sara T. To Matt, Spara's daily example of love, and John P., her cheerleader and the first person to preorder. To Cory, supporting Jordan's constant flow of questions, and Amy, who kept getting autocorrected to Amby, for giving Jordan sisterly advice. To our ARC readers, and last but not least, we thank our family and friends who have been supportive beyond measure. We couldn't have made this beautiful story without all of you!

About Jordan

Jordan's first love is fantasy. Throw in a love story and it's the perfect mix. Writing primarily MM Romantasy, Jordan loves tackling the emotions and hardships within characters and delving into those deep parts of the mind that make us all who we are.

Hailing from west of Atlanta, GA, Jordan enjoys spending time with family, playing penny rummy, writing, reading, playing videogames, and walking on trails through nature.

Check out Jordan's socials for info on upcoming books:

Instagram: @jordanleeauthor
Website: https://jordanleewrites.com/
Co-author website: https://everdeenbooks.com/

About Spara

Spara accidentally read her first historical romance in middle school and was hooked. After that, dashing dukes, pirate captains, and willing captives filled her fantasies. Her favorite books featured male perspectives and women dressed as men, so once MM Romance hit the market, she never looked back.

Living in Milwaukee, WI, Spara puts her therapy degree to good use by writing complicated rogues in search of love. She also enjoys tabletop and board games with family and friends, when not binging anime.

Check out Spara's socials for info on upcoming books:

Instagram: @sparasolace
Website: https://sparasolace.my.canva.site/
Co-author website: https://everdeenbooks.com/